STAN LEE'S THE DEVIL'S QUINTET: THE SHADOW SOCIETY

STAN LEE'S
THE DEVIL'S QUINTET

THE SHADOW SOCIETY

STAN LEE AND JAY BONANSINGA

TOR

TOR PUBLISHING GROUP

NEW YORK

STAN LEE'S THE DEVIL'S QUINTET: THE SHADOW SOCIETY

Copyright © 2023 by POW Entertainment, LLC.

A Tor Book
Published by Tom Doherty Associates / Tor Publishing Group
120 Broadway
New York, NY 10271

www.tor-forge.com

Tor® is a registered trademark of Macmillan Publishing Group, LLC.

The Library of Congress Cataloging-in-Publication Data
is available upon request.

ISBN 978-1-250-77685-3 (hardcover)
ISBN 978-1-250-77686-0 (ebook)

Our books may be purchased in bulk for promotional, educational, or business use. Please contact your local bookseller or the Macmillan Corporate and Premium Sales Department at 1-800-221-7945, extension 5442, or by email at MacmillanSpecialMarkets@macmillan.com.

First Edition: 2023

Printed in the United States of America

0   9   8   7   6   5   4   3   2   1

Dedicated to

ALFRED PETER MILLER III
1948–2021

friend and mentor

PART I

INHUMAN RESOURCES

The evil that men do lives after them;
The good is oft interred with their bones.

—William Shakespeare

CHAPTER ONE

The Anointing of the Sick

1.

London sits atop a dark labyrinth. The true nature and extent of the tunnels, tube stations, nineteenth-century sewers, and connective conduits between key points of egress are closely guarded secrets known only to the supervisory staff at the Greater London Authority, Scotland Yard, and MI5. In fact, to call London's subterranean architecture otherworldly is to traffic in major understatement. The atmosphere of the tunnels is that of a fever dream. Dark, dank, desolate, rat infested, airless, and fairly close to impassable, the lower tunnels that link the catacombs beneath the Palace Gardens and the streets of Greater Kensington have seen very few humans traverse the fetid passageways in their three centuries of existence.

All of which is why the five operatives who materialize at the west end of Tunnel PG1—striding purposefully, two abreast, down the claustrophobic channel of corroded stone toward Palace Green—are hyperalert, each feeling like a stranger in a strange land. They wear matching black body armor, Kevlar, and bulletproof helmets. Each cradles a lightweight assault rifle across their chest. They navigate the gloom courtesy of night-vision goggles, and communicate via closed-circuit radio mikes attached to their collars. There are three men and two women.

At the present moment, only one of the men speaks—in a low, dour voice, a faint Texas twang marinating his words: "According to satellite imagery and on-the-ground intel, the Israeli embassy was breached at precisely 4:37 P.M. BST, on the afternoon of 10 August 2022. That's yesterday for those of you checking your calendars. So far, the bloodhounds at *The Sunday Times* and Channel Four have not smelled anything. Looks like we're getting in just under the wire. Captors haven't squawked any demands yet."

The others listen as they march along, their green-tinted visual fields latching on to the far end of the tunnel, their destination the landing beneath the service entrance of 4 Palace Green.

The one called Spur continues his rundown: "Benefiting from a week of surveillance, the hijacking of a delivery van, a series of forged documents, and a few phony workmen's uniforms, the intruders gained entry to the Israeli embassy via the loading dock on the north side of the property." Spur cocks his helmet toward the darkness twenty meters ahead of them. "That's about ten meters up yonder there, above the tunnel intersect."

Spur stops, and the rest of them halt behind him. He clicks his halogen light and points it up at the tunnel ceiling. They all see the underside of an ancient manhole cover.

"We'll join the party through here," he says. "Through the boiler room."

A bowlegged, muscle-bound former athlete moving into middle age, Spur serves as the de facto leader of this very special unit. He has the command position not because he is the most gifted, or the smartest, or the strongest, or the most skilled—far from it. All five operatives carry the burden of being endowed with special powers that are both preternatural and highly classified. But Spur is the natural-born leader, with a knack for psychological warfare.

"Okay, let's switch over," he says, shrugging off his Kevlar vest, revealing a medieval military coat, chain mail, and broadsword under the innocuous SWAT team attire. The imposing costume underneath the black Kevlar is the "psy-ops" element of the operation, the regalia designed not only to disguise their identities but also to intimidate—to frighten and rattle their adversaries. Spur and his supervisor at the U.S. Defense Intelligence Agency have been carefully crafting the five personas over the last year.

The helmets and vests come off one by one. The smallest of the group, the petite Asian assassin, code name Boo, now sheds her black military garb and reveals the formfitting robe of a Shaolin monk. The other woman in the group, a dark, exotic-looking Latina code-named Pin-Up, peels off her SWAT gear to reveal the gilded breastplate and black widow corset of a warrior priestess. She grips her machete and slices the air with it. "Come on, slowpokes," she taunts the two other men as they hurriedly transform into dreamlike ronin.

The tall, rangy African American sheds his Kevlar and reveals a multicolored shamanic robe of feathers draping his lean body, complete with beaded gauntlets and a bejeweled scabbard, an hourglass engraving across the gilded breastplate. His code name is Ticker, and he does not appreciate Pin-Up's wisecracks. "Hardy-har-har," he says as he takes the safety off his Glock and holsters it. "Pin-Up, I'll be done with the mission before you get your skinny ass up to the first floor."

"That's enough tongue waggin', now cork your goddamn pistols," Spur says in his Texas drawl. "I want safeties off, and silencers on, all mikes live now." He glances at a small index card taped to his gauntlet. "According to CENTCOM we got three hostiles currently in the building, a half dozen friendlies, mostly staff, and one member of the Israeli diplomatic corps. Hack? Can you tap into the line from here? Give us the geography?"

The fifth member of the unit—a younger man, his dark hair and handsome face shaded by the hood of a leather duster— climbs a series of steps embedded in the tunnel wall. Known for his acumen with all things digital, Hack yanks a cable loose from decades of congealed calcium deposits and grit in the ceiling.

He pinches the end of the cable, and the others watch his body begin to glitter with the blue-metal phosphorus of live current. "Two of the hostiles are on the second floor," he says in a strange droning voice, his eyes swimming with flickering signal from the building's security system. "Looks like they got all the friendlies up there, holding them at gunpoint. Third hostile on the ground floor checking windows and door locks. Each hostile has what looks like a MAC-10 machine pistol, extended clip, .45 ACP rounds, one in each chamber. At least that's what it looks like to me, but what do I know?"

"All right, y'all," Spur says, climbing the steps, drawing his sword, and prying open the manhole cover with its tip. He pauses and looks over his shoulder at the others. "We'll take down the yahoo on the ground floor first. I want this quick and decisive, in and out."

They all nod as Pin-Up mutters to herself, "That's what she said."

2.

According to official government records, Spur and his operatives no longer exist. They are deceased, killed in the line of duty, each of them buried at Arlington Cemetery. Their mere existence is known only to a handful of people in the global intelligence community. In fact, only one human being on earth knows the full extent of their uncanny powers: Colonel Sean McDermott—code name Silverback—a section chief at the DIA.

It took quite a bit of convincing for a military mind like McDermott's to grasp and process what had happened to the five members of the Quintet back in Karakistan a little over a year ago. The cover story that they all had subsequently agreed upon was pure comic book: Supposedly, while hunting down the warlord Abu Osamir, the five were exposed to radiation, which somehow, through some genetic mash-up, had enhanced their natural skills. But what had *really* happened to them was far more Théâtre du Grand-Guignol. After being ambushed and thrown into a dungeon straight out of *The Texas Chain Saw Massacre,* they were about to be tortured and killed when an unlikely savior came to the rescue, a gruesome revenant with a changing face, dripping with ancient evil.

"A transaction is what I propose . . . a proposition, if you prefer," the Devil had said to them in the fetid shadows of that torture chamber. And the deal was as simple as it was sinister: Satan would grant them incredible powers beyond their wildest dreams, powers that would enable them to easily escape the dungeon. And all he asked in return was for them to occasionally, on a freelance basis, hunt down and kill individuals who are in breach of contract. These individuals have, to put it coarsely, *skipped town* on the Devil.

Once they are terminated, Satan explained with a wink of his yellow reptilian eye, "I will take it from there, and damn them for eternity."

"Why don't you just hunt down these rascals yourself?" Spur had asked the Beast.

"Alas," the Devil explained, "the laws of the universe prevent me from directly killing a soul."

But the Quintet would soon be in breach itself, the members choosing to double-cross the creature with the horns and the tail by using these powers in service of mankind. And Colonel Sean McDermott was prescient enough to realize that the five could be transformed into urban folktales through a few well-placed leaks in the intelligence community, ghost stories that would live on in the hearts and imaginations of the bad guys.

Which is, as far as the upper echelon back in the States has been led to believe, the reason Spur chose the moniker the Devil's Quintet for his special unit. The idea is to scare enemy combatants, to put the fear of God in them. This is the single aspect of the five and their unearthly skills about which everyone other than McDermott has been misled.

"All right, hush up now, everybody," Spur whispers into his neck mike as they approach the door to the ground-floor lobby. "I want to go in quiet as a tumbleweed in a tornado. Hack, you get the door lock. Boo, you got the point position. Go in first, disarm, and then, Hack, follow up with the wipe. Let's boogie, chillun. Three, two, one . . . go."

Hack brushes his fingertips across the biometric lock, and the door latch disengages with a faint spark like a match tip striking flint. Hack carefully pulls the door back far enough for Boo to slip through the gap.

On the other side of the door she silently scales the wall.

Out of the corner of her eye she can see the trespasser strolling back and forth behind the front entrance a hundred feet away, a wiry-thin zealot with his back turned, a machine pistol clutched like a metal baby against his skinny solar plexus. Boo uses the ceiling joists as handholds, lifting herself up, and then crawls spiderlike, faceup, twelve feet above the floor toward the target.

The gunman looks down at the floor as she approaches. He notices her shadow passing between him and the recessed lighting, and with a start he looks up just as Boo pounces on him.

She lands on the man's shoulders before he has a chance to pull the trigger, her slender legs vise-gripping down on his neck and carotid artery and windpipe as they both fall to the floor with a muffled thump. The trespasser can't breathe, can't yell for help, cannot even move. His tendons seize up, his hands freezing on the gun. Boo squeezes and squeezes until the man passes out, sagging beneath her, going still and silent.

The sound of footsteps softly pads toward her. She looks up and sees Hack approaching with a shit-eating grin and a wink, offering her a hand. He helps her up and she backs off.

Hack kneels by the unconscious gunman. As though anointing the sick with the laying on of hands, he lightly touches the temple on each side of the gunman's cranium.

The electrical waves from the man's brain spark a connection, flowing into Hack, shooting up his tendons into his brain. Emotions of anger and vengefulness and homicidal righteousness flicker across Hack's mind's eye, the luminescent proteins tracing through Hack's visual field like comet tails. Hack's neuropeptides wash away the invading flames, putting out the fire, erasing, obliterating the man's memory and hatred. The streaks of light fade out and vanish, leaving behind no trace of themselves. On the floor the man's head lolls, empty now, episodic amnesia setting in.

"He won't remember a thing," Hack murmurs, lifting his hands from the man's temples. Hack rises and steps back. "Like a newborn baby terrorist."

Boo moves in with zip ties and shackles the man's wrists behind his back.

Looking on, Hack says with a nod, "Next stop, second floor, ladies' lingerie."

3.

The code name Hack was bestowed upon Aaron Boorstein early in his career. Born in Flatbush, New York, and raised in Crown Heights, New York, he grew up a smart-ass street kid who ultimately rebelled against joining his father's button-down accounting firm and instead enlisted in the Navy. He rose up the ranks quickly as a genius-level tech sergeant on nuclear submarines and eventually became a Navy SEAL. All of which was how he ultimately caught the eye of Paul "Spur" Candell. But who would have ever guessed that Hack would see his natural propensities for hacking into the most complex virtual ecosystems turned into a superpower by the Devil himself?

Maybe it was fate. Hack had always felt more at home in cyberspace, slipping through back doors and accessing fortresses of protected data. "Sometimes I think you'd rather have a girlfriend made out of ones and zeroes instead of flesh and blood," one of his many disgruntled exes once told him, and there was truth in it. Hack had left more than his share of disastrous breakups along the side of the road over the years. It had left a hole in his heart, a longing for love that he couldn't quite seem to fulfill. Maybe that's why, for the last twelve months, he has immersed himself in the mastery of his superpower, which is something he innately understands: altering himself on a cellular level, becoming pure digital signal, moving through circuitry as fluidly as water moves through an aqueduct.

That day, Hack and his fellow members of the Quintet gain access to the embassy through the service-elevator shaft on the far east side of the building, one by one, climbing up through the trapdoor at the top of the enclosure, then silently scaling the twenty feet or so of cables to the second-floor landing. They perch themselves on the ledge inside the shaft in a neat little row, shoulder to shoulder, capes and scabbards dangling off the edge—vultures waiting patiently for the roadkill.

Hack taps into the wiring, and gets an eyeball on the situation through the security cam. "Looking at all six friendlies scrunched against the wall, west end of the main corridor." He announces this in a low, soft whisper into his mike. "One hostile patrolling the hallway, the other one, big guy, looks like the muscle, keeping his short barrel trained on the hostages."

"That it?" Spur's query crackles in Hack's earbud.

Hack shakes his head. "What else do you want, their shoe sizes?"

"Weak links, soft spots."

"Believe it or not, the big gorilla looks shaky, sweaty, not too sure of himself."

"Pin-Up, can you lock on to this yahoo from this distance? Draw his attention away from the friendlies? Avoid any collateral mishap?"

Pin-Up's voice: "Ticker. You're closest to the door. Can you give me a clear shot?"

"Why don't I just hit the pause button, then go in nice and calm?"

"Negative," Spur says. "I don't want to drain you right away, might need you at full power at some point."

With a nod Ticker silently draws his cutlass and carefully wedges the business end into the seam between the elevator doors. He levers them open about a centimeter. Pin-Up leans over and peers through the crack at the people on the other side of the floor. The six captives bunch together, stone-still with fear.

Pin-Up can see the big guy—broad shoulders, beard, wild mop of dark hair, eyes shifting nervously across the group of hostages—reeking of nervous tension. "Got him," Pin-Up mutters, locking on to him. She sniffs him with her mind. She absorbs his deepest fear and feels the cellular structure of her skin changing as she whispers, almost to herself, "The Jinn."

It's a process not unlike a chameleon instinctively triggering a color shift. The layers of her skin begin to transform, pigmentation changing, the inner strata reshaping, her dark complexion becoming matted black fur, her bones elongating into monstrous, malformed limbs, her skull swelling and growing into the massive incarnation of the gunman's worst nightmare from his earliest childhood memories. Pin-Up's new eyes now burn like embers, her fangs dripping blood, the illusion complete.

She pushes the double doors apart and steps into the corridor.

Like a school of fish reacting violently and suddenly to the advent of a bigger, stronger species entering their habitat, the hostages press backward against the wall, some of them letting out gasps, others turning away, the big gunman standing paralyzed, gaping, bug-eyed, rapt with terror as he encounters the embodiment of his primal fears, the Jinn, the ghoul that has haunted many a society down through the ages.

The other trespasser starts bellowing loudly in a foreign language that Pin-Up can't decipher.

She does not hesitate. Does not blink. She knows she's about to be shot. With one quick and fluid movement she reaches behind her back, feeling for her pistol, which is wedged under a belt. She draws it and fires—four blasts, two and two—three of the rounds going into the big guy's upper chest and neck, sending blood mist across the wall, spattering half the hostages.

Pin-Up turns and sees the second gunman raising the machine pistol at her and firing a burst, and that's all she registers—a flicker in her eyes and a series of enormous pops in her eardrums.

4.

From inside the elevator shaft, Ticker performs the miracle that he's come to think of as the Caesura. Slamming his eyes shut the moment the second gunman's machine pistol is raised and discharged, Ticker sees in his mind's eye, over the course of a single instant, a distant memory of a piano lesson from his childhood. He sees his own hands, his long, tawny-brown fingers abruptly lifting off the keyboard, the sound of a dissonant C-sharp-minor chord halting instantly.

Over the last few months Ticker has learned many things about the gift—not the least of which is its impact on his stamina and strength. The process is draining, and requires a period of recovery. But he's always ready to use it in tight situations, when a conflict seems hopeless, and especially when innocent people or his own fellow operatives are in mortal danger, such as this very moment, as the second gunman unleashes a salvo of brilliant light-blasts directly at Pin-Up.

From his perch in the elevator shaft, Ticker blinks at the sudden silence. It crashes down on him like an invisible yoke.

He glances over his shoulder and sees the still life of his fellow warriors frozen in the Pause, each of them clinging to the ledge, shadowy figurines in a wax museum. He turns and climbs out of the shaft and into the corridor. Even the harsh fluorescent lights seem to have lost several degrees of intensity, as though a filter has been drawn down over the movement of molecules.

Tucker sees the hostages huddled together against the far wall, as still and wide-eyed as mannequins in a chaotic storefront window. Outside the building, the street traffic, two stories down, has halted, pedestrians motionless in midstride. Ticker feels the customary twinge of loneliness that the Caesura evokes in him.

Then he sees Pin-Up. Her back facing him, her shape-shifting body is caught in mid-reconstitution—half woman, half monstrous creature from the id—as she shields her face from the encroaching gunfire, one side of her head still the misshapen visage of an old-world demon.

Ticker approaches, moving through the Pause with a certain heaviness to his strides as though he were a visitor on a distant planet with a greater gravitational field than earth's. He notices directly in front of Pin-Up, only inches away from her midsection, a volley of high-powered bullets frozen in midair, eight rounds in a chevron-shaped pattern like a tiny flock of silver wasps on a kill vector toward Pin-Up's major organs.

Without hesitation, Ticker draws his cutlass and angrily slaps the frozen projectiles from the air as though swatting flies. The bullets bounce off the adjacent wall and clatter to the floor, the noise muffled and corrupted by the Caesura like a film soundtrack slipping off the playback spindles.

He turns and completes the last task before he lifts the Pause. The surviving gunman gets his gun taken away and his wrists shackled behind his back. His body—as stiff as if rigor mortis has set in—is lowered to the floor.

Ticker closes his eyes.

In his imagination his fingers come back down on the keys.

5.

Pin-Up gasps, jerking backward, blinking as though slapped in the face. The topography of the room has changed with the abruptness of a jump cut spliced into a film: One moment the gunman is aiming his machine pistol at her—the flash and roar of the muzzle spelling doom—and the next moment the man is on the floor. Shackled. Struggling against the pressure of the zip ties.

A new figure has joined the fray, popping into existence with the same suddenness. Ticker in his shamanic robe of crow feathers and beads stands three feet away from Pin-Up. He proffers a smile, shoving his cutlass back into the sheath on his hip. "Another day, another dollar, huh, Pin?"

Pin-Up feels her flesh reconstituting, returning to its normal complexion, the disguise receding back into the deeper cells of her skin, the sensation like ants crawling across her. She feels dizzy, nauseous. "Let me guess . . . you were doing your voodoo with the passage of time?"

"Just a little sleight of hand, the minute hand to be exact."

"Cute. Anyway . . . *muchas gracias.*" Pin-Up still has a lump of adrenaline in her throat, the odors of the sewer still lingering in her nostrils. She feels sick to her stomach, and that starts to worry her. She taps her mike. "Spur, let's wrap this up."

All during this exchange, across the corridor, the man on the floor writhes and struggles to figure out what the hell just happened, while the hostages remain paralyzed with shock and confusion, some of them probably wondering whether they're dreaming or hallucinating. The eldest of the group, a balding man in shirtsleeves, his face damp with fear sweat, steps forward cautiously.

Spur joins Pin-Up and Ticker, and addresses the hostages. "Everybody okay? Anybody hurt or needing a doctor?"

The balding man approaches. "We're all fine, I guess, maybe in need of therapy for a while." He speaks with a faint Israeli accent, burnished by a British lilt. His temples are greying, and the worry lines around his eyes reflect the stress of lifelong government work. Spur recognizes him from briefings—the deputy consul, the man in charge of the staff.

"Sir, you and your staff . . . you all have high security clearances I'm assuming?"

"That's correct."

"Then you'll understand if I ask you to keep the events of this fairly vague in your reports."

Before the deputy consul has a chance to answer or even get out of the way, Pin-Up doubles over with nausea and roars vomit all over the diplomat's wing tips. The explosion of bile and particles of Pin-Up's breakfast that morning—scrambled eggs and cranberry juice—splatter pink viscous gruel across the deputy consul's shoes and the bottoms of his pleated Burberry trousers.

All onlookers step back as though avoiding radioactive material.

"So sorry . . . sorry . . . sorry," Pin-Up mutters breathlessly as Spur gently puts his arm around her, and helps her back across the room. He decides to take the stairs instead of forcing Pin-Up to scale down the elevator shaft.

6.

"It's morning sickness," Spur confesses to the group, dropping his bombshell as to the true cause of Pin-Up's embarrassing accident back at the embassy.

On the journey to Heathrow that night, Spur had convinced the others that he needed to tell them something important in a proper sanctuary so the Devil couldn't listen in, so they chose an empty country chapel, into which they gained entrance through the service door in the rear. Built in the nineteenth century, the modest little house of worship has a grand total of eight worm-eaten pine pews, four on each side. A scaffold from an ongoing rehab dominates one wall. The air smells of old candle wax, musty Bibles, and stale furniture polish.

For a long moment, the group just stares at Spur, silently processing this unexpected news. Spur glances over at Pin-Up, who is perched on the end of a pew, looking pensively down at the parquet floor. Perhaps she too is still processing the whole situation. It's hard to tell. All Spur knows for sure is that she looks almost angelic in the dusky light coming through a stained-glass panel, like a Raphael cherub.

The silence stretches, and it's excruciating to Spur. Both he and Pin-Up had feared that this inconvenient little development would cause a great disturbance in the cohesion of the Quintet. But neither knew how badly the others might react to the news.

Now Spur feels his blood pressure rising as he waits for someone—anyone—to say something.

CHAPTER TWO

To the Devil His Due

1.

At last Boo breaks the silence that grips the quaint little chapel, speaking up from an adjacent pew. "How far along are you?"

Pin-Up takes a deep breath. "Closing in on twelve weeks."

Boo grins. "And I thought it was Father Manny's cinnamon rolls," she says. "That's actually sort of wonderful. Congratulations, Pin."

Ticker turns to Spur and pats his shoulder, then vigorously shakes his hand, Spur grinning from ear to ear. For a moment, the news becomes a pleasant surprise that spreads through the group like a balm on their souls.

Finally Hack decides to speak up, a very subtle edge to his voice. "Do we know who the father is?" he says with a smirk. Is he jealous? Maybe. Does he hide his loneliness in morbid humor? Always.

Spur shoots a dirty look at him as the others snicker. "Wiseacre."

Hack glances at Boo and says, "Not to be presumptuous but I assume this means the moratorium on relationships has been officially lifted?"

Boo gives him a look. "Dude, if you knock me up I'm going to break your thumbs."

Ticker's smile fades as he says, "Uh . . . I'm going to have to go ahead and be the wet blanket for a minute. I'm delighted for both of you, really, I mean it." He takes a deep breath. "But if this gets out, we're going to be a thousand times more vulnerable."

"I'm aware of that fact, Tick," Spur says. "Believe me. We'll have to be a hell of a lot more careful."

Ticker looks over at Pin-Up. "The thing is, I would never dream of suggesting that you take maternity leave, and maybe stay out of sight for a while."

Pin-Up looks at him. "That's a relief, because for a moment it sounded like you were actually suggesting that I do exactly that."

"C'mon, Pin, at least until the baby is born."

"What am I, a snowflake now, just because I'm eating for two?"

"You could easily stay under the radar at the Cloister. Just for the remainder of the pregnancy. At least think about it."

"I did and I won't."

"Pin—"

"All right, everybody, just hold your horses." Spur paces in front of the altar. The chapel has a toylike quality, everything miniaturized, from the tiny bouquets flanking the little podium to the ornamental bishop's screen to the small marble Crucifixion diorama above the frontispiece. "This ain't 1822, folks." He glances at Pin-Up. "Women don't crawl into their shells anymore just cuz they're preggers."

Ticker: "And your point is . . . ?"

"The point is, in the field, Pin-Up can take care of herself and her baby-on-board until she tells us otherwise. Besides, the morning sickness is already tapering. Should be in the rearview by the second trimester."

Boo speaks up. "It's Pin-Up's body, it's her choice. By the third trimester, okay, maybe she'll slow down, settle in for the duration at the Cloister. But even then, I say it's her call. Hell, I once saw a lieutenant in the Navy fly F-16s over the Gulf of Sidra with twins in her belly."

Hack says, "Not to be sycophantic or to pander in any way but I agree with the ladies. Think about it. Who better to stay on top of her changing body than the neighborhood shapeshifter?"

Ticker sighs. "I understand where you're all coming from, I really do. And in concept I concur with everything you're saying. But think about it. We can't hide Pin-Up for nine months. How long will it take for news of this pregnancy to spread far and wide? And if that happens, I guarantee—"

Spur interrupts, finishing his sentence. "The Devil will get the news."

"Exactly."

"Wait a minute." Hack furrows his brow. "Should we be worried about that crazy woman at the website?"

Spur looks at him. "What website?"

"Transom. Transom dot com. The one that posts all the clickbait, trash tabloid stuff. Pretending it's news. You know the one."

"What about it?—What woman?"

"You know who I'm talking about, the one that thinks she's Rachel Maddow, the one who tried to track us down in Bethesda."

"I thought you wiped her article."

"I did but that's useless with these people. They're termites. Once you get one on your tail, you have to fumigate the whole house."

Spur pulls a plug of tobacco from his pocket, puts it in his mouth, and chews it thoughtfully. "What's she got on us, though, I mean, really, other than Silverback's little teasers?"

Hack shrugs. "Who knows? But she worries me, Boss. What the hell is her name?"

"Chasen?" Boo ventures.

"Close. Something like that."

"Chatham?"

"No. But you're getting warm. It's something like . . ."

2.

". . . Channing, name's Channing, Darby Channing," the woman in the paisley top, leather pants, and platform boots hollers into the intercom outside the front entrance of Transom Media Enterprises. "Here to see Mr. Soames."

The receptionist's voice crackles from the speaker, sounding like she's still in high school: "Um . . . okay, hold on a second."

A rustling sound follows, then a muffled voice yelling from a distance.

The receptionist returns. "He wants to know if you have, like, an appointment."

Darby Channing sighs. "Not exactly. The thing is, he said I could drop by anytime if I ever had anything he might be interested in."

"Um . . . okay, hold on." After more muffled conversation away from the intercom the kid's voice returns. "He wants to know if he said that to you in the bar at the Tech Fest seminar back in March."

"As a matter of fact he did, yes."

"Hold on."

Darby shakes her head with frustration, gripping her Stella McCartney satchel a little tighter as she waits for the prom queen to return. The black leather clutch bag with the embroidered stitching is the most expensive accessory Darby owns, a ridiculous splurge to which she treated herself the last time she was on assignment in Europe. A tall, willowy woman with raven-black Louise Brooks bangs over alarming amounts of eye shadow, Darby has the look of a stylish mod who has wandered into the millennium from the swinging sixties, like Twiggy if she were in the Velvet Underground.

The pubescent voice crackles: "He said he was drunk that night and doesn't remember talking to any chick journalist."

"Look. I don't mean to be rude. But you should tell him I'm onto something that is so hot it will make every other story he's ever published in his little online empire seem like Facebook posts, and also, you might add that if he refuses to see me I will me-too the fuck out of him on every social media platform that exists for trying to get into my pants that night."

A male voice comes over the speaker. "Jesus Christ, Darby, calm down."

The harsh noise of a buzzer accompanies the sound of the door lock clicking open.

3.

". . . [static] . . . nobody was more surprised by the phenomenon than I . . . [inaudible] . . . knew immediately it had something to do with . . . [static] . . . acquired skills . . . but there was very little time at that point . . . [static]."

Darby reaches over and pauses the playback on her digital recorder. She sits in front of Alec Soames's disaster area of a desk, her pulse quickening slightly as she lays out the evidence, or lack of it, depending upon one's point of view.

"According to my connection at the DIA," she adds with more than a trace of pride in her voice, "you're listening to an intelligence operative from a unit that was sent over to Karakistan a little over a year ago. They were sent over there to investigate a warlord named Abu Osamir, a real nasty piece of work who had allegedly gotten his hands on nukes."

"All right . . . you got my attention," Alec Soames says with a shrug, sitting in his high-backed ergonomic chair behind his desk, looking like a natty Oxford don in his corduroy, elbow patches, and greying temples. He puffs a pipe pensively. "Do we know this gentleman's name or is he a ghost like all these other agency people?"

"They all have code names, of course, but my guy thinks it's a former Navy SEAL named Samuel Johnson. Big brain, MIT grad, multilingual. He had a code name like Tick-Tock or Tick-Tick . . . my guy's not sure about that. We think the others in the unit were . . . uh . . . gimme a second." She scrolls down a screen on her cell phone. "Paul Candell, Maria Caruso, Aaron Boorstein, and an Asian woman . . . what was her name?" She finally locates the name. "Michelle Lin Chen."

Soames looks at her. "Why are those names familiar?"

"I don't know, you tell me."

"Hold on." Soames swivels in his chair, then starts madly pecking at his laptop. "Weird." He reads a line of text. "One of our reporters was suspicious about a leak at the DIA. Four operatives killed in action, buried at Arlington in a private ceremony, which is unusual for spooks." He looks up at Darby. "These were four out of the five people you mentioned."

Darby frowns. "Why did your guy think it was suspicious?"

"Because he's been in this business forever, and because they never name intel people who have died in the field. It smelled like a tactical leak to him, a plant, a form of misdirection."

An awkward pause ensues here, and Darby wonders if this is another piece of the puzzle.

Soames breaks the silence. "Play me some more of the audio."

Darby glances at the little oblong device with the tiny buttons at one end, a gadget that is growing more and more sinister with each passing minute. "I should remind you," she says before playing another excerpt, "you didn't hear these recordings from me. Okay? Also, they were made with primitive means by a mole in the DIA during a debriefing, a guy who no longer works there, hence the shitty quality. I think he found a way to tap into Bolling's security-camera audio."

"Let's hear some more."

Darby thumbs the play button. "[static] . . . what happened in that dungeon . . . [inaudible] . . . understand that none of us had any idea of what we were capable of yet . . . [unidentified noise] . . . powers . . . [static] . . . individual natures . . . [audible rustling]—"

"That's about it," Darby says, pressing the stop button.

"So whatever happened to Osamir?"

"Your guess is as good as mine. He's a missing person. Intel back in Karakistan lists him as 'at large' but you know . . . he could be anywhere. He could be dead. Maybe they wasted him but the powers back home didn't want to start World War Three over it so it's going to remain unknown."

"Darby—"

"Let me cut to the chase. I believe there's a deep-cover unit of vigilantes out there somewhere. Originally they went after Osamir, and somehow, for some reason . . . they acquired powers."

"Powers?"

"Yes, listen to the audio. I believe the 'dungeon' is most likely the sublevel of Osamir's compound in Karakistan. Something happened to these five operatives in that hellhole. And it has something to do with these powers that Johnson is talking about."

"Powers like Spider-Man? What are we talking about here? Like Johnson gets miffed, he turns into Ben Grimm?"

"Alec, I'm telling you, there is something going on with these five allegedly dead people, and I'm going to find out what it is and write about it. *BuzzFeed* gave me a five-hundred-word tease about it last month."

"Then go back there, go back to *BuzzFeed*."

"I can't."

"Why?"

"It's a long story."

Soames gives her a look. "You do realize that these banshees at the agencies are always cooking up stuff like this. Planting narratives, phony cover stories. Darby, you're a top-notch journalist—one of the best online. But I'm just not as convinced as you are that there is a story here."

"Are you fucking kidding me? What about the Cheyenne Mountain fiasco? We're talking about a code-red fuckup at a missile silo, one them even launching according to countless eyewitnesses in the Colorado sticks."

"Stoners and farmers?"

"C'mon, Alec, blackouts for weeks along the Eastern Seaboard and Europe? A U.S. sub put on high alert? Russia closing embassies? You don't think there's a story there?"

"It's still under investigation. It could be goddamn sunspots that crashed those satellites, and nobody at the State Department is talking."

"What about the eyewitness at SACCOM?"

Soames chuckles. "Some low-level schlub claims a guy does a David Copperfield and appears out of thin air in the missile control room? You're going to lead with that? Good luck. And while you're at it, don't forget to mention that Hillary Clinton is a cannibal pedophile from outer space."

"Alec—"

"We are a trusted web-based news source, Darby, with an emphasis on 'web.'"

"Alec—"

"We have to stick to the meat and potatoes and leave the stinky cheese and foie gras to the infotainment folks at Fox and MSNBC. Otherwise, we're going to go the way of Breitbart."

"It doesn't matter, Alec. I'm going after this one, with or without you."

Soames sets his pipe down, carefully canting it against an ashtray. "Maybe there's a reason that nobody from mainstream is tying these strands together. Did you ever think of that? Maybe you're traipsing into a minefield."

"That's a risk I'm more than willing to take."

"Most of this shit you're talking about happened a year ago. You know as well as I do that's an eternity in the news cycle. We've had floods, fires, riots, plagues, locusts, and rivers running red since then. Nowadays, people have the memories and attention spans of houseflies. I can't in good conscience pursue this with you."

Anger burns in Darby's belly as she pushes herself away from the desk.

She stands and digs a folded article of clothing from her satchel. She tosses it onto the desk. "I wonder if you have any idea what that is," she says somewhat rhetorically.

Alec Soames stares at the pair of baby-blue boxer briefs, size

M, lying on his blotter. "I was wondering what happened to those."

"You left them in my hotel bathroom at Tech Fest after you pulled a Harvey Weinstein on me and came out naked in a terry-cloth robe, trying unsuccessfully to get a hand job from me."

Soames frowns at the underwear. "I presume there's a point to all this?"

"You remember the guy at Tech Fest from 23andMe? Bragged he could analyze any source of DNA, tell you with one hundred percent accuracy who it is, and who all their ancestors are? Turns out there was a racing stripe in your shorts. Did you know that your ancestors in Scotland were sheepherders?"

"What are you doing, Darby?"

"What I'm doing is negotiating. This is my last card that I'm playing. If you don't become my personal House of Medici, finance my investigation, and publish every single word it yields, I will go to the state arbitration board and turn in the shit stain from your underwear, as well as the analysis, as well as my Pulitzer Prize–level reporting on your disgusting and dastardly sexual proclivities. Do I make myself clear?"

By this point, Alec Soames is slumping at his desk, head down, exhaling like a balloon figure losing all of its air. He softly says without even looking up, "Have a twenty-five-hundred-word kickoff piece on my desk by next Monday." The balloon man lets out the last of its air. "I'll direct-deposit your per diem into your account by noon tomorrow."

CHAPTER THREE

Reflexology

1.

The topography of hell resembles a barren, blasted, war-torn desert littered with garbage that stretches as far as the eye can see, its ground a dirty shade of grey, almost mildew colored, stirring and shifting in the intermittent whorls of rancid wind. Primitive roads, fossilized into the ground like scars, scattered with detritus, crisscross the land. Gargantuan heaps of un-identifiable human remains lie on the edges of embankments and in ravines, radiating unspeakable odors.

Together, five demonic entities assigned by the Devil to penetrate the human world and infiltrate the Cloister now travel across this malignant wilderness toward their destiny.

One of the entities—the greasy reptilian spirit known as Snakeroot—turns his leathery head toward the leader and declares in Aramaic, "This rotting vagina of an outskirt makes me ill, Wormwood. A fucking stroll down memory lane was not in the agreement."

Without breaking his stride, Wormwood turns his onyx, insect-like eyes toward the lizard prince. Wormwood's voice is a rusty nail penetrating stone. "The agreement, Snakeroot, was to keep your shit-stained anus of a mouth shut and do as you're told, or you'll end up in the ovens with the heretics."

This elicits a salvo of oily laughter from the other three demons.

"Such hostility," exclaims the flamboyant ferret-like entity in the garish harlequin attire, her long thin lips painted ruby red with baby's blood. She goes by the name Foxglove, and has a reputation for being a preening, sadistic trickster. Now, as she chortles and snorts with lascivious mirth, her entire being undulates and oscillates and recasts itself into myriad colors and shapes as though passing under milk glass.

On her flank walks the one known as Nightshade, a towering corpse-like figure in a black, hooded apocalypse robe, a denizen of hell's inner circle for the longest of the five. Nightshade is a demon of very few words but has annihilated more souls than the bubonic plague and all the World Wars combined. His low, sepulchral laughter is the sound of an ancient coffin lid creaking open, echoing throughout a deserted tomb. "The power of Christ compels him," he wheezes with amusement.

Another round of hyena-shrill guffaws echoes across the parched barrens.

Next to Nightshade walks the one known as Hemlock, her default shape a pale, featureless, naked banshee. More than a thousand years ago, she haunted the Highlands of Scotland, a shrieking ghost, ultimately enlisted by Satan and endowed with one of the highest demonic ranks due to her faculty with possession, as well as her flair for the work itself. The destruction of human souls is more of an art than a science, and Hemlock is the artiste of the group. The earthly realm is her palette. She once made a balloon animal out of a pensioner's intestines.

At the moment, however, Hemlock is wailing with laughter at the wisecracks, her contours wavering and changing in ripples of ghostly alabaster. Her eyes are flaming craters of yellow in her skull, ever simmering, ever swirling miasmas of evil. Like all the others, she was handpicked by Wormwood to undertake the most important mission of their immortal lives.

All at once, the five demons notice the Lake of Souls in the distance, barely visible behind the smoking mists, and all the laughter and camaraderie abruptly fades away to silence.

2.

The infamous, putrid body of inky black water lies like a great liquid corpse in a forbidden zone of hell, a place of high-level ceremonies and rites of passage. It is a sort of way station between the underworld and the human world, and it resembles a photographic negative of a placid mountain lake one might find in Nepal or Alaska. Vast and deep, rugged and fetid, it is an ugly serpentine of moldering, stagnant water reaching as far as the eye can see.

This cunning squad of evil spirits approaches it cautiously, crossing the final stretch of scabrous, scorched rubble gingerly, almost reverently. They pass through clouds of dense smoke and floating particulate, the air around the lake so polluted it would remind a human from the twentieth century of a television screen filled with electronic snow. The group reaches the threshold of the lake, and Wormwood raises his cadaverous black hand in a cryptic gesture that the others instantly recognize. The others fan out on either side of Wormwood, taking their places at the water's edge.

Wormwood recites the ancient incantation, then gazes down at the fine layer of cinders at his feet. The furnace wind blows the cinders away from a name in Arabic carved into the cracked earth. Wormwood absorbs the name, absorbs the life it represents, the man, the time, the place. It flows into him like a virus spreading through him. He can taste the bitterness of the man's soul. He can see the man's deeply lined face. He can hear the faint sound of him breathing, the heavy rasp of an old man. Wormwood is ready.

He calmly walks down the embankment and into the black mire of the lake.

The water rises up and engulfs him in its oily, cold clutches. The demonic have no use for breathing. They can see in utter darkness, and yet Wormwood has to concentrate carefully on the task at hand as he descends the slanted lake bottom, moving deeper and deeper into the murk. Behind him, the others have also uncovered their targets and are already on their descents into the cold, soupy darkness. The vibrations of their muffled, watery footsteps reverberate in Wormwood's ears. A moment later he has reached the bottom.

The Nadir.

The Pit of Despair.

Wormwood pauses, standing at the point at which the underworld connects like a magical circuit with the world above.

He gazes up. In the dark medium of the lake, he has to squint to see the bottoms of the feet. Human feet. Innumerable, busy, moving relentlessly like ants. Way up there, faint and fleeting on the surface of the lake. Some are clad in shoes, some in stockings, some bare. Some are old, some young, some rich, some poor, dirty, and coarse. Some are sick and hanging off the edges of hospital beds. Some of them are running, some dancing, some of them joined with others, poking out of bedsheets during coitus, making more human animals.

The soles of the souls. Wormwood hates them with eternal, undying passion, detests each and every one of them. They represent everything he despises about the human race—their life force, their instinct to keep moving, their drive to keep procreating, keep building, keep finding someone to love, someone to love them—all of it perfectly captured in those countless disgusting soles of those hideous feet, working, playing, scuttling, shuffling, hurrying.

The feet of Wormwood's host become visible, the demon fixing his baleful gaze on those gnarled, decrepit, aged soles, wrinkled and callused by time and wear, currently at rest, protruding from the bottom of a robe as the owner of the feet lounges before bed. These are soles that have walked countless miles in third world countries, feeding the poor, performing marriages, providing last rites and the rites of exorcism to the sick, to the afflicted, to the dying.

Wormwood silently mouths the Satanic litany, the invocation, while staring at the repulsive soles of an old man's feet as they dangle off his bed in his modest quarters.

Wormwood can feel himself beginning to levitate, his essence rising, rising, rising toward those hideous feet, coming closer, and closer, and closer.

Wormwood makes contact with the wrinkled, worn, revolting flesh, and a very old, very furtive, very subtle process begins.

3.

Father Emmanuel "Manny" Lawson feels a pinch on the sole of his left foot just as he is climbing into bed with his Bible in one hand and half a glass of whiskey on the side table. A stooped, balding little man somewhere in his eighth decade, the priest yanks his rimless eyeglasses off and lets out a hoarse little yelp at the sudden twinge on the bottom of his foot.

He tosses the eyeglasses on the table, sits up on the edge of the bed, and rubs the bottom of his foot. Lately he's grown accustomed to these aches and twinges. Two years ago he was diagnosed with tarsal tunnel syndrome in both feet, a condition he assumed was due to a lifetime of presiding over mass, standing on his feet for hours on end while delivering homilies and performing communions. But this sudden stitch of pain tonight feels different to him.

He searches for a bug or a spider that might have bitten him. The Cloister and most of its buildings have been around for centuries, and the Lord only knows what creeps and crawls in the crevices behind the walls or under the beds or in the seams of the floors. Father Manny remembers one incident several years ago when the floor in the east chapel caved in on one side due to a termite infestation. This part of Missouri, with all its ponds and marshes and tributaries shooting off the Mississippi, is notorious as a breeding ground for all manner of vermin and pests, including an abundance of ticks, one of which, years ago, had been responsible for the Lyme disease that gave Father Manny his slight limp.

But now the priest sees that the bed is free of any insects, or even the slightest speck of dirt. The previous day, the housekeeping staff had been in, and now the sheets still glow and smell of detergent.

Father Manny sits back against the headboard and lets out a pained sigh, rubbing the bottom of his foot. He remembers his podiatrist explaining once that many believe the sole of the foot is the gateway to the rest of the body, each portion of the sole corresponding to a different limb or organ. Massage therapists work on the theory of reflexology. They might address pain in the sciatic nerve by massaging the heel, or help with nasal congestion by rubbing the big toe.

The pain in his foot begins to fade, so he makes a mental note to call the podiatrist in the morning, pulling the covers over his frail body and turning out the light.

4.

The next morning, Pin-Up climbs out of bed, trying not to jostle Spur, who slumbers deeply next to her. She is well into her ninth month, and she feels like a water balloon about to burst. Even the simplest maneuvers—such as getting out of bed and getting dressed—have become an act of will. She grabs her robe and waddles into the bathroom.

Going about her business in the john, she avoids looking in the mirror, but not due to any sort of vanity or repulsion at the sight of her own body. On the contrary, she's proud of her enormous belly, and at thirty-three weeks it's getting more and more enormous every day. For Pin-Up, it's the kind of shape-shifting that comes from love, from intimacy, and from the urge to give birth rather than some Faustian deal made in the shadows. The sad truth, however, is that Pin-Up shuns her reflection out of guilt . . . and fear.

It started a few weeks ago, when Boo had told her that the way an expectant mother carries the baby is a sure indicator of its gender. Boys push straight out front, as though the mother had swallowed a basketball. Girls are much more all-around plump, like a serving of Jiffy Pop on a hot stove. Last week, the Cloister's visiting ob-gyn, Dr. Beckway, confirmed that the child is male, which made sense to Spur, who has interpreted the frequency of the kicking and moving as a sign the boy will be a football player just like his dad, hopefully for Texas A&M. All of which has made the experience much more real for Pin-Up, much more imponderable.

There is a fully formed human being inside her now, not just a conglomeration of cells. What was happening to it as it gestated? What will the baby inherit other than eye color and Spur's square jaw? What has her superpower done to her ability to safely bear a child? This is what keeps her up at night. This is why she looks away from mirrors and reflective surfaces.

But on this morning, if she did look, she would see a woman in full bloom, and as Spur would say, "as beautiful as a ripe peach." Her dark, exotic features have filled out, her breasts becoming fuller and heavier, her curves more accentuated. In fact, if she just glanced for one moment, she would see in that reflection her own mother, Mrs. Consuelo Caruso of Boyle Heights, California, looking back at her with those cinnamon-brown eyes and plump cheeks.

Instead of taking that glance, however, Pin-Up plops herself and her massive tummy down on the toilet to undergo the morning ritual of trying to pee. With the advent of the third trimester, and an extra-large baby inside her competing with her bladder for more and more room, urination has become an ordeal. She's either waiting for a trickle, or she's leaking every time she coughs or makes a sudden movement.

She's squeezing out a few drops when she hears the phone ringing in the other room, the sounds of Spur stirring, fumbling for the cell. And she knows all too well that a call on the secure line means one of two things: 1) It's Silverback calling with a new mission, or 2) the Devil's playing tricks again.

Over the last year, Old Scratch has been messing with them in the manner of a diabolical teenager, making the secure line ring at the oddest hours. When Spur answers it, all he hears is the Devil's voice reciting some ancient incantation in Latin, or the anonymous voices of people being savagely tortured, or the sound of Pin-Up moaning and squealing with orgasmic delight. Lately, it's often a strange pounding noise, like a single kettledrum booming in Spur's ear, three booms, always three—BOOM!-BOOM!-BOOM! BOOM!-BOOM!-BOOM! BOOM!-BOOM!-BOOM!—which Father Manny has explained is the Satanic signature, a sort of inside joke making fun of the Trinity: Boom!-The Father-Boom!-The Son-Boom!-The Holy Spirit.

But today Pin-Up can tell it's a legitimate call by the low sounds of Spur's Texas twang, followed by the rustle of his footsteps approaching the bathroom. He knocks twice and then gently pushes the door open. "Morning, sunshine," he says. "Y'all decent?"

"You gotta be kidding me." Pin-Up has noticed that Spur has started calling her "y'all," which is his little joke, a way of being mindful of the baby on board. "Not only am I not remotely decent," she tells him, "but I need to file for overtime just to piss."

"That was Silverback. Looks like we got a problem that needs addressing."

"I'm listening."

"You feel up to an early-morning meeting in the chapel?"

"We have any of those Depends left?"

5.

The campus of the mysterious and highly secretive complex of buildings known among an elite group as the Cloister is located on a leafy hilltop overlooking the Mississippi River just outside St. Louis, Missouri. Officially listed in the public records as a monastery, it encompasses over 250 acres of private land adorned with centuries-old Gothic towers and red-brick ramparts, all of it giving off the air of an exclusive Ivy League college. Unbeknown to most, however, it is the world headquarters of the Scarlet Order, a band of warrior priests dedicated to battling supernatural evil in all its forms.

From an aerial view, the Cloister's grounds are laid out in the fashion of the Templar cross, with the walkways among four discreet districts—operational, residential, ecclesiastical, and administrative—forming the celebrated cross. Since its inception in 1923, the Cloister has recognized the Knights Templar as spiritual forefathers. Founded in the year 1119, this mysterious medieval order consisted of highly trained military clergy who protected pilgrims on the road to the Holy Land.

Down through the years, the Cloister's leadership has come to believe that it is their sacred mission to carry on the work of the Templars. Which is exactly why, in 1965, members of the Cloister's rapid-response team escorted a group of civil rights activists to Montgomery, Alabama, after they'd been brutally attacked in Selma. It is also why paramilitary priests from the Cloister hunted down terrorists responsible for attacks on Christian churches in the Philippines in 1991 . . . and protected protestors in the general workers' strike in Paris in 1968 . . . and snuck a boatload of German Jewish refugees into the U.S. in 1939 . . . and on and on . . . many of the missions secretive and known only to the Cloister's leadership.

The compound has also unofficially become—thanks to Father Manny—a safe house and refuge for the Devil's Quintet, their meeting place a small auxiliary chapel on the northeast corner of the grounds.

Barely the size of a one-room schoolhouse, the little place of worship has stood on this land for generations. Rumor has it that it was here before the monastery was built over a century ago, a sanctuary for riverboat operators, dockworkers, and weary travelers. Over the past few months, the Quintet has personalized the tiny brick edifice with some of the comforts of home, although home for these people has been wherever the missions have taken them.

The personal items reflect each member's passions and obsessions. In one corner, Boo has arranged a miniature Shaolin temple shrine for praying and meditation, complete with figurines of the Buddha, a teapot, medicinal teas, and an incense brazier. Hack beefed up the Wi-Fi and brought in his computers. Ticker repaired the large regulator clock, and now the soft, persistent heartbeat of its pendulum is accompanied every hour on the hour by the melodious, comforting sound of its chime. Spur set up a coffee service, and Pin-Up equipped the place with a small refrigerator and hot plate for her unpredictable pangs of hunger.

It is their inner sanctum, the safest place on the Cloister grounds . . .

. . . or at least, that's the hope.

6.

"We got a problem on our hands," Colonel Sean McDermott—code name Silverback—announces to the others gathered in the chapel that morning. A tall, weathered, ruddy-complexioned man in a tartan plaid jacket and English riding cap, he paces back and forth across the rear of the chapel as the others sit at a conference table, looking on, their gazes following him back and forth as though they are watching a tennis match.

"Why don't you go ahead and sit down, Silver," Spur suggests from his seat at the head of the table. "Take a load off. You look as nervous as a whore in church. C'mon, relax."

"I'd rather stand. It's this gal reporter has me tied in knots."

"What's the problem?" Pin-Up asks around a mouthful of glazed doughnut. She's already polished off an entire breakfast burrito and a side of hash browns since arriving at the chapel that morning. "We've been through all this. She's just spreading your makeshift propaganda, Silver. We're just an urban legend, as far as she knows. Let her spread the bullshit."

"I wish that were still the case, Pin. It's not bullshit anymore. She's getting too close. Starting to know too much."

Ticker speaks up. "For instance . . . ?"

"For instance, she's got a recording of you, Ticker. Got it from somebody at the DIA, snippets of your debriefing after Karakistan. She knows about Osamir and the dungeon."

Spur gives Silverback a look. "She doesn't know about our little deal with—?"

"No. And neither does the DIA. Who would believe it, anyway? The thing is, though, situations like this, leaks, they tend to end badly."

Ticker purses his lips. "What did she do with the recording?"

"Nothing yet. Just wrote about it. It's in her latest piece on Transom. She's not exactly Tolstoy, but it's out there now."

Hack pipes in then. "I knew this was going to be a problem. I knew it. I knew she was going to keep going until she blew it all wide open."

Boo speaks up. "Slow down, hold on a second. Did she try and contact you for a comment, Silver?"

"She hasn't gotten to me yet. But it's just a matter of time. She's been following the kid around."

"Cthulhu?"

"Yup."

Spur sighs. Cthulhu is the code name for Silverback's administrative assistant, Hanley, a nerdy little chatterbox with high security clearance who could easily blow the cover. Spur thinks it over for a nanosecond. "You know, we should probably take this bull by the horns, get proactive on this sucker rather than just sitting on our derrieres waiting for her to come to us."

"What do you mean exactly?" Hack says then. "Like assassinate her?"

"Very funny. No. But maybe we should make contact, try to persuade her to be discreet, matters of national security, all that jazz."

Boo raises her hand like she's in school. "I'll go, Skipper," she says.

"No, no, it should be me," Ticker says. "I'm the voice on the tape. I'm the leak. I should be the one who goes and talks to her."

A tense beat of silence ensues, Spur licking his lips thoughtfully, eyeballing Ticker. "I don't know." He looks at Pin-Up, then back at Ticker. "Sending you out on this one, Tick . . . it feels like more exposure than we can afford right now."

Ticker shrugs. "Do we really have a choice, though? I mean, we have to—"

A noise from across the chapel interrupts. Someone is knocking furiously on the door. Silverback looks at Spur, and Spur gives a shrug. "Anybody expecting a pizza delivery?" He grins at Pin-Up. "You didn't order more doughnuts, did you, darlin'?"

"Hahaha." Pin-Up gets up and goes over to the door and answers it.

"I'm sorry to barge in like this, forgive me, I apologize," babbles the gangly young priest named Father Joshua. Clad in an old tobacco-brown monk's robe, wringing his hands nervously, the young man stands on the chapel's threshold. He's a sort of functionary around the Cloister, a Mr. Fix-It for the higher-ups, and it's strange to see him this unnerved. "I—I—Something's happened. Something's happened with Father Manny."

"Okay, no worries, come on in," Pin-Up says, and ushers the young priest into the chapel, shutting the door behind him.

"Father Manny's disappeared," Joshua blurts to the group.

The unexpected news ripples through the room like an electric current, Spur rising to his feet and cocking his head with incomprehension.

7.

Father Emmanuel William Lawson has become, in some ways, the sixth member of the Quintet—a trusted friend, a lovable elder, and most important, a sort of reluctant prophet whose visions and strange dreams have guided Spur and his unit over the last twelve months. It was Father Manny who foretold the formation of the Quintet itself, and who single-handedly saved the unit from a deadly ambush in an underground parking garage in Virginia. Most important, it was Manny who took the group in and arranged for their safety and anonymity behind the walls of the Cloister.

Born in a small river town along the Mississippi, Manny Lawson lost his parents in a house fire at an early age and was raised in foster homes and Catholic orphanages. As a young man, Manny was mentored by an elderly priest, Father Winston Bryer of Quincy, Illinois, who had visions of Manny's future accomplishments and convinced the young orphan to enter the seminary and study to be a priest. Manny took to the pious life and built a reputation for himself as a progressive man of the cloth.

By the time Manny had turned thirty, he had landed in Baltimore, where he became the youngest leader of a big-city parish in modern history. But sadly, he was soon to be removed by the archdiocese for his liberal ways, which, among other things, included allowing divorced people to receive communion, as well as insisting that he march in the annual gay pride parade.

Over the subsequent decades Manny was shuffled from parish to parish, but he didn't mind, because he had become a seeker, a man galvanized by visions that foretold he would one day meet five remarkable individuals who would fulfill a great and mysterious prophecy.

Now, in their sanctum sanctorum at the Cloister, this same group of people all turn their attention to Father Joshua, who stands near the entrance, wringing his hands.

Spur goes over to the young man and puts his arm around him. "Go easy, Padre. It's okay. Start at the beginning."

CHAPTER FOUR

Enter the Shadows

1.

Over those next critical days, no one suspects anything other than illness, encroaching dementia, or some benign pathological disorder driving the five subjects and their strange behavior. Most of them are in their late seventies, one in his early eighties, and the truth is, they've all been in the presence of Satanic forces throughout their careers.

In Morocco, in the dusty little village of Charlala, about twenty kilometers east of Marrakesh, Father Gordon Shamus would be the last person on earth one would expect to be vulnerable to such influences. In a country that's 98 percent Muslim, a Catholic missionary can be persona non grata in most situations. But Father Shamus has a calling—both figuratively and literally—to fight the holy war against the forces of evil in Morocco. It has become his life's work.

A tall, burly Irishman with a big laugh and a bigger appetite for bangers and mash, he had been summoned to the North African country years earlier by a member of the Peace Corps, who was concerned that a fellow aid worker could perhaps, maybe, in some way be under the influence of diabolical powers. The priest came immediately and, in due course, cleansed the troubled young woman through the rite of exorcism. At the time, the governmental pendulum had been swinging toward liberalism, so the country let Father Shamus stay indefinitely when the priest asked for a work visa. It seemed there were people lining up around the village to be cleansed by a holy warrior.

That was fifteen years ago. Now, on the morning of March

24, everything changes for the beloved priest. He dreams of stepping on a black crow and awakens with a sore foot and a skull echoing with voices.

He stumbles out of his tent and nearly knocks over a table laden with archaeological artifacts. He feels as though his eyeballs are too big for their sockets. He can't stop his palsied hands from making fists, from curling into claws, nor can he stop shuffling across the dig site with an awkward, fitful gait as though he's an enormous toddler just learning how to walk. One of the visiting paleontologists sees Father Shamus vanish over the eastern horizon, heading for parts unknown.

On that same day, similar scenes unfold at seemingly random places around the world.

In Johannesburg, an elderly Episcopalian priest and noted authority on the occult, Father Gabriel Warren, spends a tumultuous night tormented by horrible dreams in which he walks over burning corpses across an apocalyptic hellscape, watching his own feet turn black and deformed and almost simian. Upon waking, he shuffles out of his rectory mumbling a bizarre language that one of his fellow clergy manages to record with a cell phone and later discovers is Aramaic.

In Rome, Sister Mary Beth Malambri, a renowned and revered psychic healer—a women who has assisted Italy's most venerated religious leaders in the performance of countless rites of exorcism—comes awake with a start, an ear-piercing shriek in her ears that only the elderly nun can hear. Nightmares of a banshee devouring her feet had been gripping her all night, and now she sees her feet bleeding all over the sheets as though pierced with nails in a mock crucifixion. She crawls out of bed, the ceaseless shrieking turning her brain to mush. She staggers out of her quarters at the Subiaco nunnery, bursts out the rear exit into an adjacent alley and lumbers into the grey Roman dawn.

In the South of England, the much-loved and venerated leader of the St. Vincent de Paul Parish House and Food Distribution Center, Father Tommy O'Toole, awakens from a dream that a hooded figure was driving stakes into the soles of his feet. Now, corroded whispers speaking ancient tongues in his brain send signals to his arms and legs, directing him out of his room while still in his nightshirt, hastening him down the stairs of the vestry, and out into the briny air and early-morning light of Hastings on the Sea.

On a hillside overlooking the grey, roiling currents of the Mississippi, the sweet-hearted, tender, jovial priest named Father Emmanuel "Manny" Lawson finds himself hopelessly lost. He has no idea how he got to these rugged hills along the river. His arthritic knees ache, his feet burning with pain. He pauses to catch his breath, wheezing heavily, trying to figure out what's happening to him. The cold sun beats down on him.

To his left lies the tiny river town of Cape Girardeau, Missouri. Father Manny recognizes the leafy streets, the neat little brick buildings of merchants' row, and the proud stone steeple of the Centenary United Methodist Church. For years Father Manny had played occasional rounds of golf with the director of the church's ministry program until . . . what was it? What had happened to Dick Russell?

Father Manny searches his memory as the wind tosses his threadbare windbreaker and what's left of the grey hairs on the back of his skull. He feels faint. He can barely stand as he remembers years ago hearing that old Dick Russell had retired and was placed in a nursing home when dementia had set in. Father Manny begins to weep, his tears flung off his deeply lined face into the wind. This must be the reason he has wandered off to this wind-tossed ridge along the Mississippi—he's losing it. He's senile, has early-stage dementia, and has wandered aimlessly off the Cloister's grounds.

He falls to his knees and cries into his hands, and then looks up at the clouds in the sky, his vision faltering like a television broadcast losing its signal, the sight of the clouds flickering in his watery gaze. His brain begins to sputter, groping for purchase, the hiss of static crackling in his ears. The clouds have turned black. His equilibrium dwindles like a guttering candle flame.

Wait . . . wait . . . wait . . . this is precisely what happened earlier today when he first rose from a nightmare. Or was it yesterday? Or last week? How long has he been wandering?

He tries to stand, but his legs give way. He collapses onto his belly, eating a mouthful of dirt. He vomits into the weeds. He feels something growing within him, dark, spindly vines shooting up his ligaments, thorny tendrils of parasitic life pushing their way into his arms and legs and then into his hands. He rolls over onto his back, and he flexes his fingers, staring at his own hands as though they belong to someone else.

Isn't this exactly what happened earlier today . . . or yesterday . . . or the day before?

Father Manny feels himself shrinking inside his own skin like a seed retreating into its pod, the black, creeping branches growing within him with time-lapse speed, spreading across his vision until he's blind and something else occupies his body—

2.

—and now Wormwood picks himself up and brushes the dirt from the front of the shopworn windbreaker. He wipes the tears shed by the old priest from his eyes. He detests occupying the decrepit, flabby body of this disgusting piece of dung they call Father Manny. Father Mmmaaaaaannnneeeeee, Maaaanneeeeeeee—such an insipid name, idiotic, inane.

Shuffling off on the priest's knobby, feeble knees, moving in fits and starts, puppetlike, Wormwood wishes he could have possessed a younger man, or better yet a female, a woman with sturdy thighs. Younger humans are easier to possess, easier to keep from returning to consciousness. Clergy are such a pain, so much harder to keep quiet. They're always breaking through the spell, regaining control.

Wormwood will have to concentrate more intensely. He will also have to find a quicker mode of transportation if he is going to make it to the rendezvous point in time. He starts pushing the elderly body more rigorously along the high ridge . . .

. . . in search of railroad tracks, preferably on which a train is heading south.

3.

"Does that seem weird to anybody else?" Ticker points at the frozen image on the computer screen. "Can you go and get it again, Hack? Play it one more time."

Hack sits at a work desk in his private bungalow at the Cloister, his flesh glittering with the phosphorous glow of a hologram. His fingertips touch the laptop keys, a spark jumping off his cuticle. To the casual onlooker it would appear that he has become a ghostly doppelgänger of his physical body, a shimmering avatar that is suddenly sucked into the device.

Spur, Ticker, and Boo stand around the desk, arms crossed, looking on, waiting for the video to replay itself. It's been over a week since Father Manny disappeared, and since then Ticker, Boo, and Hack have conducted two separate searches, each time coming up empty. Everyone's on edge. Pin-Up has been confined to her room, and has been put on strict bed rest. The due date is still a couple of weeks off but apparently the baby could come any day now.

According to Dr. Beckway, Pin-Up's uterus is inflamed, the cause of which is unknown but Beckway thinks it could be stress. After the doctor departed, Pin-Up joked privately to Spur, "Stress, did he say? Does he mean the stress from being pregnant? Or does he mean the stress from being a member of a band of superpowered bounty hunters playing cat and mouse with Satan . . . and also being pregnant?" Spur laughed at the joke then but the humor has worn thin.

"Do we know for sure that's Father Manny?" Spur muses as he watches the blurry scene outside a 7-Eleven in the middle of the night. In the video a lone figure in a shabby windbreaker and baggy trousers trundles past the empty parking lot.

"That's him all right," Hack says with a nod, his body boiling with luminous benday dots as he nods at the screen. Hack has learned that his power enables him to journey anywhere inside the dark continent of the internet without leaving a trace, which is why he has chosen to use the power to discreetly search for Father Manny without drawing any undue attention. "The Monsignor confirmed it," he adds then. "I believe his actual words were 'Who else would be wearing such a crappy windbreaker.'"

Spur steps closer to the computer screen. "Let's see it one more time." Hack plays it again. Spur turns to Ticker. "What do you mean by 'weird' exactly?"

Ticker shrugs. "I don't know. Just the way he's walking."

"What about it?"

"I just . . . I've never seen him walk like that."

"Like what?"

"Stiff. I don't know. Like a toy Nazi."

"Yeah," Boo agrees, looking over Spur's shoulder. "I'm seeing it, too. Where is this place again?"

Hack informs her that it's Blytheville, Arkansas. About sixty miles west of Memphis.

Spur wonders, "Did we dig up any other surveillance footage of him?"

Hack sighs. "Not yet. Still working on it. We figured out he's heading south in this one, so I'm checking grids along that route."

"Southbound, huh?" Spur knows deep down this has something to do with old El Diablo but he won't let his thoughts go there yet. Geezers can get screwy in the head; dementia is so common at Manny's age. "I hate to say it, but it could be Alzheimer's . . . something like that."

This lands like a cement layer cake. Nobody says a word.

Spur takes a deep breath. "I gotta get back to the missus." He walks out, leaving the rest of them staring in abject silence at the screen.

Hack withdraws, and his body returns to its solid form. The screen goes dark.

4.

Kellington's Pub sits on the waterfront just off Canal Road at the end of a narrow little side street crammed with colonial-style brownstones. The joint is the worst-kept secret in D.C. since the tourist trade caught wind of the place a few years ago when *Food & Wine* magazine did a piece on Kellington's vintage cocktails. Nowadays the place is standing room only on unseasonably warm Friday nights such as tonight. Obligingly, the staff has opened the facade windows, so that the patrons can sip their wassails while watching the skiffs coming in off the Potomac.

The back of the establishment, however, is where the real action is.

Against a wall plastered with framed photos of past Washington barflies such as Harry Truman, Sam Rayburn, and Everett Dirksen sits a burnished hardwood bar warmed by Tiffany lamps and a massive potbellied stove at one end that sizzles and pops all night under the drone of insider conversations. Spooks from the CIA, functionaries from the Pentagon, even White House staffers are rumored to haunt this section. Getting a place at the back bar is nearly impossible after 6:00 P.M.

All of which is why the little runt of an administrative assistant with the horn-rimmed eyeglasses is brimming with pride that he not only arrived early enough to get a spot at the bar but has even managed to save the stool next to him for his impending tête-à-tête. For the past few months Drew Hanley, code name Cthulhu, has been receiving flirty direct messages, off the record, from a lady journalist.

As the front-office guy for Colonel McDermott, Hanley has a high security clearance, which among other things forbids him to talk to the press. But Hanley knows deep down in his gonads that this reporter is actually into him, and there is a good probability that romance will be in the air tonight, which is why Hanley nervously jerks with a start at the sudden sound of a voice next to him.

"What's a sharp cookie like you doing in a place like this?"

Hanley spins around and sees the source of the voice—a statuesque woman standing mere inches away. She is a vision. From her super-mod bangs down to her hourglass figure, which is currently clad in animal prints, leathers, and knee-high boots, she is the embodiment of Hanley's fantasies. "Darby Channing," she says with a killer smile, extending a shapely hand. "I'm gonna go out on a limb and assume you're Drew?"

Hanley shakes her hand, clearing his throat and making a big show out of glancing over his shoulder as though he's working under cover and there are multitudes of bad guys out there who would love to see him dead . . . but tortured first. Right now, though, nobody in the crowded bar seems the slightest bit interested in Hanley or his date. The dapper young black man sitting at the bar on the other side of Hanley is engrossed in the sports page of *The Washington Post,* and looks as though an atomic bomb could go off and he wouldn't notice it. Hanley nods, then smiles at Darby. "Yes, you've got the right guy but let's keep our voices down, if that's okay. But yes . . . I'm him . . . I mean . . . I am he . . . Drew Hanley, that is."

When Hanley finally stops shaking her hand, she takes a seat next to him. "Good to finally meet you."

"And I you . . . I mean . . . yes, it's good to meet you as well. Finally. At last."

"You don't have to be nervous."

"I'm not nervous."

"Okay, good."

"Why would you think I'm nervous?" He laughs nervously. "I never get nervous. I'm as cool as a cat. Calm as a cucumber."

"Okay. That's good. Good." The bartender comes over, and Darby orders a club soda with lime, and then pulls a digital recorder from her handbag. "I promise you, this'll be totally painless."

"Excuse me?" Hanley looks at the recorder and then looks up at her. "Painless?"

"You know." She smiles. "The whole Q-and-A thing?" She presses the record button. "I know interviews can be a pain."

"No, no, no." He turns the recorder off. "Um . . . I thought . . . No, no, no, no. You see, I'm not allowed to . . . No. Sorry. No."

She turns the recorder back on. "Listen. If you've signed an NDA, if something is classified, I totally get it. It's off the record. And I would never cite you as a source." Another smile. "I make it a point to protect my sources."

"No, no, no, no, no, no, no," he stammers, turning the recorder back off. "You don't understand. I thought you and I . . . I thought we were going to . . ."

He trails off. The well-dressed guy next to Hanley gazes up at the Baltimore Orioles game playing on a big screen TV. "C'mon!" the guy yells.

Darby turns the recorder back on, and then levels her gaze at Hanley. "You thought we were going to . . . what?"

He turns the recorder off. "Look. I thought we were . . . like . . . you know . . . this was going to be . . . like a date?"

Darby crosses her arms across her chest. "You gotta be kidding me."

"Well no, I'm not."

She puts the tape recorder back in her purse. The bartender comes over and sets her drink in front of her. She stares at it, murmuring, "You thought I was trying to pick you up."

"Well . . . that's not exactly how I would put it . . . but yeah."

"Jesus Christ." She digs in her purse for her credit card. "Unbelievable."

"Sorry for the misunderstanding." Hanley sees that she's going to pay for her drink and leave. "Let me buy your drink, please, it's the least I can do."

She shrugs.

Hanley puts a fifty on the bar, grabs his jacket, and climbs off his stool. "And please stay and finish your drink."

Another shrug from Darby.

"I'm sorry it didn't work out," Hanley says. "I hope you find what you're looking for." And with that, he turns and walks toward the exit, pausing once to turn around and sadly yet proudly wave like Nixon from the door of the helicopter as he left the White House lawn in disgrace in 1974.

Shaking her head, Darby goes back to her drink, and takes a sip.

She notices something odd out of the corner of her eye. The dapper African American in Armani, the one who was watching baseball two chairs over, has turned toward her and is looking directly at her with a weirdly expectant expression on his chiseled, handsome face. "Bad night?" he asks.

Darby sighs. "You could say that, yeah. Par for the course, I guess."

"Maybe it's time we had a little talk, you and I," he says.

Darby furrows her brow in confusion. "Do I know you?"

"Apparently, yes, you do," the man says, "a hell of a lot better than I know you."

Darby goes very still, almost paralyzed at the sudden realization. "Oh my God. I recognize the voice." She stares. "You're the tick-tock man."

CHAPTER FIVE
Saint Emmanuel of Delirium

1.

They take a cab back to Darby's place in Bethesda, a modest little bungalow on a tree-lined street, a home that Darby claims she inherited from her late mother. It's an art deco dollhouse filled with funky secondhand furniture and shabby-chic bric-a-brac. The front room features oddball items like antique hookahs, paper lanterns, David Bailey photos of Twiggy, a collection of James Bond lunch boxes, and even a death mask of Donald "Blofeld" Pleasance.

"Cozy little place you got here," Ticker says as he settles back on a tattered purple sofa. "I'm sensing an Anglophile vibe."

"Guilty as charged, gov'nuh," Darby calls out from the kitchen, the sound of ice hitting the bottoms of highball glasses, limes being cut, ice cold Bombay Sapphire being poured. She comes back into the living room and hands Ticker a cocktail. "I was raised in white bread Grand Rapids but my heart was always in Piccadilly Circus." She pulls a leopard-print ottoman in front of the couch and takes a seat as though she's a shoe salesman ready to fit Ticker with a new pair of wing tips. "So what about you? You a fan of the Empire or what?"

Ticker grins at her. "Sure, I love a good figgy pudding every now and then."

"Married, divorced, still window-shopping?"

Ticker's smile fades. "I lost my wife a long time ago."

"Sorry to hear that." She sips her drink. "Is that why you joined the unit?"

Ticker shrugs. "Who knows? Who knows why we do any of the things we do?"

"Thought you might see the world? Work through your grief, assassinate people?"

Ticker fixes his gaze on her now, half amused, half annoyed. "Always sniffing, huh? Always digging for a story?"

"Sorry . . . I'm just naturally nosy." She takes another sip. "What happened in that dungeon in Karakistan?"

"That's classified."

"You know I'll find out."

"Not from me you won't." Ticker takes a sip. "Doesn't national security mean anything to anybody anymore?"

"C'mon, give me something I can work with. Don't you want the facts out there rather than conspiracies, urban legends?"

Ticker thinks about it. "Tell you what. Let's play a little game—quid pro quo. I'll tell you something about me, you tell me something about you."

She grins at him. "Let the games begin."

"What do you know about us?"

"I know you and your pals are supposed to be dead, buried in Arlington, killed in action. I know something happened to you on that mission. Something off-the-scale weird."

Ticker gives her a poker face. "Okay, now it's your turn."

"Tell me what happened."

"We got ambushed, they tried to torture us, and we fought our way out."

"You're stonewalling again."

Ticker looks into her eyes. "My turn now. What will it take to get you off our backs?"

"Money."

"How much?"

"I'm kidding. Jesus. What kind of a skank do you think I am?" She sets her drink down on a side table and scoots closer to him. "Besides . . . that's two questions. Now it's my turn, and I get two."

Ticker shakes his head and grins. "Touché . . . go ahead."

"If you're dead, and you're buried in Arlington, what are you exactly . . . a ghost?"

Ticker sets his drink down. "You could say that, yeah, sure."

She touches his left knee. "You feel fairly substantial to me."

He looks at her hand patting his knee. "Is that a question or a statement?"

She smiles seductively at him, her hand now stroking his knee as though petting a cat. "I'm the one asking the questions right now. Remember? If I'm not mistaken, I get one more."

"Shoot."

"Is it against the rules of the unit for a member to fraternize with a reporter? I mean, after all, Superman did it."

Ticker smiles sadly to himself, closes his eyes, and freezes time.

2.

He has to work quickly now. He has a maximum of five minutes—in his timeline—before he will show the wear and tear of the Caesura when he comes out of it, which would give him away.

Darby has frozen in place, her hand on his knee, halted in the middle of the flirtatious stroking motions. Was she sincerely coming on to him? Or was this just another tactic, another form of manipulation in order to get information out of a source?

Just for an instant, Ticker feels a melancholy twinge of longing. Not since the death of his wife has he been this lonely. Darby's slender, sculpted face has congealed in front of him like a wax figure, her glassy, inscrutable stare fixed on him—

—as he gently disengages himself, slipping out of her grasp and climbing off the couch.

He crosses the room quickly. He is on a scavenger hunt now. He checks the little galley kitchen and sees nothing out of the ordinary, so he moves on down the narrow hallway. In the bedroom he rifles through the bedside-table drawer and finds pill bottles, lighters, vape pens, condoms, rolling papers, a sleep mask, a tube of K-Y jelly, a checkbook, but no thumb drives or data disks. Nothing on which she could store evidence.

He finds her office at the end of the hallway, a tiny, cluttered sewing room with a Steelcase desk pushed up against the window, hanging plants, and a large framed poster of a dashiki-clad David Bowie onstage. He hits the mother lode when he wakes up her laptop.

Ticker has learned over time that battery-operated devices will run for a brief moment during the Caesura on their residual juice, and he gets lucky when he discovers that she left her iTunes program open. He finds the audio from the Karakistan debriefing session—a total of three files—and traces them to an external hard drive on a shelf above the desk. Ticker erases the files—both on the computer and the hard drive—and does a search on both devices just to be sure all of it is gone.

A dog-eared binder marked "Candell, Caruso, Boorstein, Chen, and Johnson" sits atop a stack of congressional reports. "Sounds like a K Street law firm," Ticker mutters to himself under his breath, paging through the notes. Paper gets as stiff as tinfoil in the Caesura, and it takes a couple of minutes for Ticker to go through all the handwritten minutiae.

For a moment, he considers destroying all of it, but he has second thoughts when he realizes most of the notations reflect Silverback's strategic leaks and the making of an urban legend. There are no references to the Cloister, or the Devil, or superpowers. It occurs to Ticker that he might as well have stayed home tonight. Not a single one of these interventions will likely have any effect on Darby Channing's continued obsession with the Quintet. Nor will they stave off the eventual public disclosure of the existence of the unit.

With a sigh Ticker is starting to close the notebook when he notices the most recent entry—dated yesterday—written above a printout from *HuffPost* taped along the bottom of the page:

Disappearances of Renowned Religious Leaders
Have Authorities Baffled

WASHINGTON (AP)—Interpol announced Sunday that two prominent religious figures in different parts of the world have vanished on the same day.

"The confluence of events first came to the attention of our TransNational Crime Watch team," reports Amos Paoletti, chief information officer of Interpol Washington. "It's extremely rare for two different missing person cases to share so many attributes."

Among the many common denominators in the victimology are an expertise in the occult and a vast experience with exorcisms. "The similarities are extraordinary," Paoletti explains. "Each subject is Catholic, over seventy years old, and a trained and experienced missionary."

The names of the two individuals are listed at the bottom of the article, and Ticker's mind reels with dread. This definitely has the whiff of brimstone to it. But to what end? And is there a connection to Father Manny slipping away to parts unknown?

The tension closes in on Ticker, and he feels the weight of fatigue start to tighten his muscles, pressing down like a yoke on his shoulders, stiffening his joints, and making each breath heavier and more labored. He has come to think of it as Pause Fatigue. He needs to disengage the Caesura ASAP. He leaves the office as he found it and hurries back down the hallway to the living room.

Darby is still perched stone-still on the ottoman, her hand extended, frozen in midstroke where only minutes ago his knee had been. It takes some careful maneuvering but Ticker manages to climb back into his original position before the Caesura, carefully sliding his knee under her outstretched hand so that it gently makes contact with her delicate cupped fingers.

Then he closes his eyes. He imagines playing a dissonant chord on a piano, then imagines lifting his fingers off the keys.

Darby suddenly jerks her hand away from his knee with a start. "Wha . . . ?"

Ticker plays dumb. "What is it? What's wrong?"

"What just happened?"

"What do you mean?"

Her face fills with alarm. "What did you just do?"

"When?"

She springs to her feet, starts backing away from him as though he's an explosive device. "Look at you, you're sweating. You look . . . drawn . . . pale all of a sudden."

"That's ridiculous," Ticker says, looking up at her, wiping his brow. He feels slightly wobbly, faint. "I didn't do anything."

"You're lying! I saw it. Just for an instant. You moved slightly. Like a cartoon that's out of sync . . . or . . . or . . . a bad edit in a film."

"You're high." Ticker climbs to his feet and approaches her. "I swear to God, whatever it is you think I did, I didn't do it. You're seeing things."

She crosses her arms against her chest, eyes cold with anger. "You did some kind of voodoo on me just then, didn't you."

"Darby—"

"Some kind of Jedi mind trick. I saw it. What the fuck did you do?"

Ticker lets out a long, pained exhalation of surrender. He looks into her eyes and then very softly says, "You're right. I did do something."

"What did you do?"

"I stopped time."

3.

"Should I be afraid?"

An hour later they sit side by side on Darby's front porch swing, shrouded in darkness, Darby's voice drained of all its hard-boiled bravura. Fireflies spangle the shadows of the front yard. The tip of the joint they're sharing glows like a caution light each time one of them takes a toke.

"Honestly?" Ticker says, passing her the joint. "I'm the one who should be scared."

"How's that?"

"Telling you everything I just told you? It could get me executed for treason."

"C'mon . . . really? You really believe that? I mean, something this off-the-scale weird under the auspices of the government . . . I don't know." With a trembling hand she snubs the roach out in an ash can next to the swing, the glider squeaking softly as they compulsively rock to and fro. "Seems to me there's no way you could plug every last leak. It's bound to hit the public sooner or later—with or without me nosing around."

Ticker shrugs. "Maybe . . . maybe not. You'd be surprised, all the crazy shit the government has going on behind the scenes, especially the DIA."

"Yeah but a deal with the Devil?—Satan?—Please. That's smacks of some smart-ass at the agency cooking up a goofy cover story."

He looks at her. "You have to remember, though, most of the folks over at the Pentagon, functionaries in the DIA, congressional committees, they've all been given a basic cover story that has nothing to do with supernatural evil."

"Right, the radioactive thing."

"Exactly."

She smirks. "Smacks of comic books, though, guys in capes. Would it have killed you to come up with something more plausible?"

He gives her a sidelong glance. "What would you suggest? Alien abductions? An ancient curse? You got something better, I'm all ears."

She shakes her head. "You know, I always thought Satan was basically just a concept—a pretty creaky and archaic one at that. I mean . . . I was raised by Jewish intellectuals. You know? It's a lot to swallow."

"You're telling me," Ticker mutters softly, more to himself than to Darby.

"I mean, I believe in God as much as the next person," Darby goes on. "But if you unpack the whole myth of the fallen angel, it seems like Satan is basically working hand in hand with God. You know, like punishing sinners? Like he's God's prison warden, or sergeant at arms, or something like that. I don't know. Does any of this make sense?"

Ticker smiles at her. "Sure it does." He thinks about it for a second. "Let me ask you something. You say you believe in God?"

"I do. Yes."

"Do you by any chance keep any religious icons in the house?"

"What do you mean? Like a cross?"

"Yeah, or a Bible, a menorah . . . a holiday crèche. Anything like that?"

"Yeah I guess." She narrows her eyes. "Why do you ask?"

4.

In her bedroom, sitting beside her on the edge of her brass bed, Ticker measures his words. "Okay, so, now you're going to definitely think I'm crazy if you don't already . . . but this is how we speak in private."

He gestures to the items that he has just positioned in a neat little row across a shelf above the bed. They include a tiny brass menorah, a Bible, a pocket Torah, a chipped and faded ceramic Star of David from Darby's days in Hebrew school, and an old tarnished crucifix from St. Francis Primary in Alexandria. Darby's Jewish mother, Rachel, had always believed that the Catholic schools in Virginia had better resources and curricula than the public schools.

Darby gazes up at the row of memories, and says, "'Private' meaning . . . what?"

He looks at her. "Okay, again, this is going to sound insane but we've found that the Enemy eavesdrops constantly . . . unless we're in a church, a synagogue, a place of worship . . . or even something totally makeshift like this."

"By 'the enemy' you mean the Devil?"

Ticker nods. "Our friends in the clergy call him the Adversary."

"I'm really trying to take this seriously." She gives him a hard look. "This isn't some elaborate ruse to throw me off the scent, is it?"

"I wish it were." He raises his hand. "My hand to God, scout's honor, and I swear upon the most beautiful ceramic Star ever made in any Hebrew school . . . everything I'm telling you is the truth and nothing but the truth."

"So help you God?"

"Yes, absolutely. Look, I'm sorry I went through your notes behind your back but it was imperative that I learn how much you know about us."

"Which turns out to be bupkis, I'm starting to realize."

"Let me ask you something else. I know this is probably against every ethical standard of good journalism, but by any chance, would you consider working your end of the block exclusively for us?"

"Okay, first off, I have never been accused of being ethical. Secondly, I have no fucking clue as to what you're talking about. Working my end of my block? What is this, a business plan for hookers?"

"I'm sorry. That didn't come out right. Let me try again."

"I wish you would because my head is spinning, and it ain't the gin and tonics."

"First of all, we didn't know about those two missing priests. That could be an extremely important detail, missed by a lot of people, or it could be nothing, a coincidence. Regardless . . . that's what I'm talking about. You have a knack for digging things up, making connections, putting two and two together so it adds up to five. Plus, you can move around and get access that we can't get."

"I thank you for the kind words, but what in God's name would I be able to contribute to a team of badass superheroes with a bone to pick with Satan?"

"You could be our intel, our bloodhound, our person on the outside."

A pause intervenes as she thinks it over. She looks deep into Ticker's eyes. "You're not just trying to keep a leash on me, are you?"

"Of course I am. What do you expect? You haven't given me much of a choice."

"You're not just keeping your friends close and your frenemies closer?"

"Stop it." Ticker reaches up and touches her shoulder. "Whatever you decide, you have my utmost respect and my deepest admiration. If you say no, I'll get out of your hair and that'll be that."

"And if I say yes?"

He gives her a warm smile. "It'll be the beginning of a beautiful friendship."

"And I can keep doing my freelance work, keep my career going full blast?"

"As full blast as you want."

She purses her lips pensively. "And when the day comes that you go public, I get exclusive rights of first of refusal to do the book?"

He shrugs. "If that day ever comes, I'm sure we can work something out. All we ask is that you back off on the investigation—for the moment, at least—and work with us, not against us. What do you think?"

She takes a deep and girding breath, a diver about to jump

off the high board. "Here's what I think." She leans forward and plants a kiss on his lips.

Ticker flinches at first, taken aback, but then the heat rises in him, and he kisses her neck and her jawline and her parted lips, their arms intertwining, their bodies falling sideways onto the bed, until they are lost in each other's scent, each other's flesh, each other's intimate places . . .

. . . and as elegantly and inevitably as fingers lifting off the keys of a piano, they lose all sense of time.

5.

The rumbling vibrations bring him back to consciousness. He comes awake with a start in a foul-smelling enclosure lined with moldering hay and greasy metal. He lies on the floor in a fetal position and detects the reek of livestock.

Father Manny sits up, looks around, and realizes that he's in a ramshackle freight car, the dilapidated conveyance clattering and thumping as it thunders through the night. The blur of signal lights flickers and streaks through the slatted walls. The priest sees a few emaciated cows huddled near the front of the car. He tries to stand but the swaying movements of the speeding train along with his aching joints conspire to keep him on the hay-strewn floor.

He rolls over onto his sore hands and knees. He feels as though his body has been stretched on a rack, every tendon panging with agony. His old windbreaker is soaked to the skin, his priest's collar torn and hanging by a thread. He's starting to make another attempt to stand up when he sees something beneath him that makes him freeze with terror.

In the flickering darkness, a puddle of cow urine reflects his face. But the face doesn't belong to him.

He sees a creature from the depths of hell looking back at him, its face as dark as crude oil, putrid and inhuman, a cross between a mutated bat and the face of a corpse that's been dead for millennia. It shifts and refracts the light, changing its shape at will like a denizen of the deepest part of the ocean. It takes Father Manny's breath away, and he has to will himself to look away from it.

Rolling onto his back, the priest realizes what has happened, and the revelation cleaves him down the middle like a knife. He knows the signs. Now he knows with utter certainty that his condition has nothing to do with aging or dementia or Alzheimer's or any other prosaic malady of mankind. He knows all too well the ancient process that has infected his soul.

The face in the puddle of piss is the face of a superior demon.

Now Father Emmanuel Lawson realizes he is engaged in a very old, very mysterious, very secretive battle for his own soul . . . and the odds are stacked against him . . . as the shade pulls back down over his consciousness, and Wormwood takes back possession of the feeble little body.

6.

At the break of dawn, the cell phone starts chirping from out in the living room where Ticker had left it on the coffee table.

In Darby's bedroom, tangled in sheets, clad only in a borrowed terry-cloth robe, Ticker stirs awake from a deep sleep.

"Duty calls?" Darby Channing murmurs groggily next to him. She wears only his boxer shorts, the sheet pulled up to her neck. "Cat up a tree needs rescuing?"

"That's my secure line." Ticker climbs out of bed, instantly wide awake. He ties the robe around his slender waist as he walks briskly out of the bedroom without another word.

He answers the phone on the third ring. "Spur, go ahead."

The voice on the end is tense, uncharacteristically businesslike. "Tick, I'm gonna need you to go ahead and come back home."

"Everything okay?"

The slightest pause precedes the reply: "The baby's decided to join us today."

"What? Wait . . . today? The baby's coming this morning?"

"This afternoon or later tonight. Gives you just enough time to grab Silverback and take the Blackhawk express. I gotta go, Tick. Just get your ass back here on the double."

"Wait, Spur, wait. Just tell me, is Pin-Up okay? Is the baby all right?"

Another pause. "Sure, I mean I guess so. What do I know? I'm just a dumb hillbilly from East Texas. Just get your skinny butt back here."

The call clicks off.

CHAPTER SIX

On the Tallulah Docks

1.

That night, in a mobile birthing room bathed in soft white light, on a gurney situated under a chandelier of antique crucifixes, Pin-Up slams her eyes shut as another contraction rocks through her. Her stocking feet wedged into stirrups, her face beaded with perspiration, she hyperventilates furiously, edging along the precipice of unconsciousness, but somehow hanging on, her rigid body drenched in sweat, mucus, blood, and steely determination.

"Breathe, darlin'—breathe through it," Spur whispers in her ear.

He's on his knees next to the gurney's headboard. He wears a sterile gown and a surgical mask, his hands clad in rubber gloves. Throughout his remarkable career he has been known to hold off entire battalions with a pair of .50-caliber machine guns and a roll of duct tape, but this—this is the hardest thing he's had to endure. He desperately clutches Pin-Up's right hand and adds, "Remember, darlin,' the bar's open. All you gotta do is give us the word and—"

"N-no!" Pin-Up's admonition has a breathless wheeze to it, a voice corrupted by pain.

Spur squeezes her hand. "There's no shame in it. We can order you a nice tall glass of fentanyl and nitrous oxide . . . or . . . or . . . maybe something stronger like a tequila epidural."

"Stop it! Spur, stop it. I told you—"

Another contraction rocks through her, cutting off her words. She tries to breathe through it but they're coming more frequently and more fiercely now, invisible tsunamis sending wave after wave of agony through her solar plexus. The previous night she had baffled both the internal and external medical teams when she announced as she reached four centimeters that she was going to go the distance without painkillers.

What she neglected to tell them is that she's terrified that her shape-shifting power will somehow go off the rails during labor, and maybe hurt the baby. It took quite a bit of convincing to get Spur to go along with it, but now the big man is having second thoughts, turning away at the advent of each contraction, staring at the floor with tears in his eyes as each wave of torturous pain shudders through his beloved.

"Looking good at eight centimeters now," Dr. Steven Beckway murmurs to the nurse as he softly palpates the cervix, feeling for the crowning of the baby's head. A tall, stocky man with a boyish face partially obscured by his mask, he gives off the air of an academic. The man reminds Spur of a different kind of superhero, the kind of white-hat savior in scrubs and booties who will never give up on a human life. Spur watches the man's skilled, stained, rubber-clad fingers busily probing, measuring, and palpating.

Pin-Up's pale, exposed belly is visible in the halogen over heads, a bulbous full moon undulating with the baby's every twitch. An ornate henna tattoo of a Guadalupe cross entwined with flowers runs down the length of Pin-Up's tummy. One of the Cloister's beloved nuns designed the cross and carefully applied it early in the first trimester, and it has already started to fade. Initially Pin-Up had wanted permanent ink, but Spur had to draw the line there, worried about toxicity.

Luckily, Beckway never once commented on all the religious icons, nor did any member of his obstetric team grouse about all the spiritual accouterments festooning the birthing room. They seemed to take in stride the countless votive candles flickering in every corner, the prayer shawls under the bedding, and the rosary beads hanging from the vital monitors.

"Okay . . . that's interesting." The tone of Dr. Beckway's

voice has changed very subtly, a studied way of avoiding the impression of alarm or urgency. "Hit a little roadblock at ten centimeters."

The nurse, an older, greying women with cat's-eye glasses resting above her mask, glances at Beckway. "She's fully dilated."

"How's the O$_2$ saturation?"

The nurse shoots a glance at the monitor. "She's at ninety-two, mild hypoxia, not too bad, holding steady."

Beckway looks at the ultrasound monitor. "That's odd."

"W-what was that?" Pin-Up cranes her neck suddenly, trying to see what's going on. "Is there a problem? What's the matter?"

Spur and the doctor exchange a strange, fleeting glance.

"No worries, honey," the nurse says in a reassuring tone. "Very common for the baby to pause at the birth canal."

"Absolutely right," Beckway says with a nervous little nod. "Going to need you to go ahead and push now, dear, give him a good shove."

Pin-Up moans and tenses and pushes as Beckway stares intently at the ultrasound. Spur feels the dynamic in the room change, as palpable as the air pressure dropping. Something is wrong. "Doc, talk to us," Spur says. "What's going on?"

"One moment," Beckway mutters, feeling for the baby's head.

The nurse stares at the monitor. "Is that shoulder dystocia?"

Beckway shakes his head. "No, the baby's position is fine. Fine and dandy. Heartbeat's strong. He's presenting like a champ. Keep pushing, dear."

"Placenta previa?"

"Sharon, would you please stop trying to diagnose something that's not there."

The nurse mumbles under her breath. "There is something there, though."

"Sharon, please!"

Beckway's anger flaring wakes everybody up, including Spur, who feels a feathery chill creeping down his spine. He squeezes Pin-Up's hand. He hears her whispering the Lord's Prayer.

"The placenta is exactly where it's supposed to be," Beckway is saying to the nurse. "Little guy's just taking a breather."

". . . Our Father, who art in heaven . . ."

"C'mon now, Maria, push. You can do it. Get him going again."

". . . Hallowed be thy name . . ."

The nurse gazes at the ultrasound monitor. "What in the name of . . . ? Is that . . . is that the perineum?"

". . . Thy kingdom come, thy will be done . . ."

The doctor swings the ultrasound monitor away from Pin-Up's view—

—but not before she catches a glimpse of the object blocking the baby's path.

2.

The phantom hand has a pale, vaporous, translucent look to it on the sonogram, as if a ghost has reached into Pin-Up's uterus and splayed its fingers wide in order to halt the baby's progress. But the murky image is so detailed, so specific, it spot-welds itself on the back of Pin-Up's midbrain, to the point that she knows she will never unsee what she has seen.

Pin-Up lies back on the gurney and tries to breathe and keep pushing . . . as another lightning bolt of fiery pain shoots up her spine . . . and the terror threatens to strangle the life out of her.

The Devil has very distinctive hands. Pin-Up remembers them well from her encounters with the Beast in the dungeon in Karakistan, and also at that lonely crossroad in Missouri the previous year. The long, crooked fingers, the gnarled untrimmed nails, and the strange, antique signet rings with their pentagrams nestled in ornate settings . . . all of it unmistakable.

Satan's hand is blocking the progress of her baby down the birth canal.

Spur is saying something to her, whispering in her ear, but Pin-Up barely registers it now, the horror transforming into quiet rage as she settles back into the pillow and closes her eyes. He will not stop her baby from being born. He will not hurt her baby. He will leave her body in the name of Jesus Christ and all the saints and all that is holy.

She sees herself as a ghost, a wraith, a revenant haunting her own anatomy. She slips though the pores of her skin, through her organs, past a Fallopian tube, through the walls of her uterus, down her birth canal, and into the mind of her unborn son.

Fight it!

The message fires from one synapse to another, penetrating the prenatal brain of her baby, her son, her beautiful, beautiful boy whom she and Spur had agreed to name Paul, Jr.—although Spur has simply called him Junior since the second trimester, when they saw the first sonogram of his little space-alien body—so Junior it shall be, and Junior shall be how she now addresses him in her mindspace, her innerspace.

Fight it, Junior!—FIGHT IT!

The sudden commotion in the birthing room yanks Pin-Up back to consciousness.

"Would you look at that," the nurse is saying now, standing behind the ob-gyn.

Beckway is nodding. "Okay, that happened." He turns the ultrasound screen back around so that it's within Pin-Up's and Spur's view. "Now let's get this young fella into the world."

The ghost hand has vanished. The baby begins to crown as Beckway gently ushers the child out of the birth canal and toward the light.

"Ladies and gentlemen," Spur exclaims, wiping his tears, half crying, half laughing, as he squeezes Pin-Up's hand, and the caterwaul of the baby fills the air. "Put your hands together for the star of the show!"

3.

Outside, behind the Cloister's front gates, Hack paces across the shadows, chain-smoking and checking and rechecking his cell phone. He has a Beretta semiautomatic pistol holstered under his leather jacket, and with his porkpie hat he looks like a nervous jazz musician waiting for his stage cue, or perhaps a bank robber casing the place. He's supposed to be guarding the north entrance of the Cloister but instead he's fixated on the impending arrival of Paul Elliot Candell, Jr., Esquire.

Besides, it's a pretty sure bet that if an evil spirit chose this moment to invade the Cloister they would most likely not arrive via Uber.

Boo watches him pace from her perch on an adjacent stone wall. She glances through the enclosure of the gates at the deserted entrance road, the wind rattling the trees along each side. She figures this is the part of the movie where the cowboy says it's quiet . . . a little too quiet. But she keeps that observation to herself. She hates clichés. And to make matters worse, she's starting to feel like a cliché herself, falling in love with a man as cynical and tightly wound as Hack. Plus, there's that question she keeps meaning to ask him and keeps chickening out.

She feels her cell phone vibrating suddenly in the pocket of her long coat. She checks it and sees that it's a text from Ticker, who's positioned on the other side of the compound, at the south gates with Father Josh. She reads the message and lets out a little yelp of excitement:

THE EAGLE HAS LANDED

"What is it?" Hack wants to know, stopping in his tracks, tossing his cigarette to the pavement, and grinding it out with the toe of his boot. "What's wrong? What's the matter?"

"Nothing's the matter, hotshot." She grins as she pushes

herself off the fence. "Baby train just pulled into the station. C'mon!"

They hustle across the commons, hurrying past the administration building, past the chapel, past the tree-lined barracks and rectory, until the massive semitrailer comes into view at the top of a grassy berm on the edge of the quad. The trailer is gunmetal silver, unmarked, and shimmering under the glare of sodium-vapor light.

They knock on the rear doors, and the nurse lets them in.

They find Pin-Up in the far corner of the birthing room, curled up on a padded armchair, nestled in blankets, cradling her baby in her arms. The baby—his eyes still glued shut with afterbirth, his pink skin as delicate as rose petals—nuzzles and coos, completely at home in his mother's embrace.

Pin-Up's face glistens with tears in the white light as she says in a thin, reedy voice, hoarse from all the pain and pandemonium, "Meet Paulie the Second . . . Junior for short."

Boo drops to her knees by the chair. "Oh, sweetie, he's beautiful."

"Well done, Skipper," Hack says to Spur, who stands proudly behind the chair, trying not to cry, but failing miserably.

"Pin and Junior did all the work," Spur manages in a wobbly, teary voice. "I just did the cheerleading."

"He's a chip off the old block."

Spur laughs through his tears. "Lucky he didn't get my hairline."

"He's got Pin's eyes, though," Boo says, softly stroking the baby's thin, downy hair. "Lucky kid. He's just edible."

The sound of knocking emanates from the rear doors, and the nurse lets in Ticker and Joshua.

The two men approach cautiously, as though walking on thin ice. On the opposite side of the trailer, Beckway watches from his desk, a proud smile tugging at the corners of his mouth, the strange anomaly on the sonogram long forgotten. Father Josh immediately starts to silently cry, genuflecting as his tears roll down his cheeks. Ticker kneels next to the chair.

"What do you think, Tick?" Spur asks.

"I . . . I . . . don't have the words." Ticker brushes a tear from the corner of his eye, swallowing the lump in his throat. "He is . . . perfect. Just perfect."

"Takes after his daddy," Spur says with an exhausted grin.

Another commotion at the door, and the nurse admits Silverback. The big, burly Irishman takes off his riding cap and approaches reverently, grinning a huge joyous grin.

"Okay, folks," the nurse announces, her hands on her hips as she surveys the crowd. "That's it, no more visitors."

Silverback looks around the room and sees that every member of his beloved Quintet is crying. "Why all the waterworks?"

4.

The next morning, just north of Baton Rouge, the rising sun filters through the red cedars and bald cypress along the Mississippi. The clean, early light ignites the cattails, weeds, and sodden pilasters of the Tallulah docks, the brilliant, fiery beams stitching through clouds of gnats and cottonwood fluff, reflecting like embers off the muddy, churning surface of the river.

The crickets and bullfrogs are still singing their burbling night chorus as a figure approaches from the north road.

The diminutive man in the tattered windbreaker and clerical collar casts a mile-long shadow in the hush of early dawn as he descends the litter-strewn banks, his Florsheims making smooching noises in the mud. He sets his sights on an immense, greasy oil tanker docked and idling at the pier. To a casual observer, the man would appear to be a harmless clergyman, an old shaman who has perhaps lost his way and is looking for directions home. Very few onlookers would suspect something malevolent going on inside the little padre.

Wormwood steers the old man's body toward the massive

mooring rope attached to the fore section of the tanker. The demon has been practicing Father Manny's expressions in restroom mirrors along the way, rehearsing the timbre and rhythms of the old man's voice, his choice of words and turns of phrase.

As he waddles along the length of the vessel, he hears the drone of voices beneath the rumbling monotone of the tanker's engine—most likely the crew having breakfast inside the bridge cabin near the stern. If the Eiffel Tower were laid on its side, the tanker would come up short by only a few feet. The chimney-red hull is pocked and battered by decades of weather. The fore section resembles a small encampment, the containers draped in ancient tarps.

Careful not to injure the priest's aged body, Wormwood lifts himself up onto the mooring line—a gnarled, ancient rope the size of a rhinoceros leg—and carefully traverses the length until he's close enough to the ship's iron bulwark to hop onto the deck. He hears a whistling noise and heavy footsteps coming toward him. He hides behind one of the tented containers.

A crewman comes into view along the vessel's port side.

A bear of a man with a Dutch Masters beard and a massive belly contorting his grease-spotted T-shirt, he whistles an off-key version of a country waltz and ambles up to the edge of the deck. Wormwood peers around the end of the container and watches the behemoth pause, unzip, and begin to pee off the side of the boat. His stream is so profuse it looks as though it could put out a burning building.

Wormwood does not wait for the torrent of urine to subside.

He lowers himself to the floor of the deck and begins to feign physical distress, moaning and holding himself as though his appendix is about to burst. The piss stream abruptly halts as the beefy crewman whirls around suddenly toward the moaning sounds. "Who the fuck . . . ? Who's there?"

Wormwood uses Father Manny's vocal inflections and precise phrasing. "Over here, young man . . . dreadfully sorry to sneak up on you."

The big man zips up and comes around the side of the container. "What in the blue blazes?—Where the fuck did you come from?"

"I'm a little under the weather, my son, to be honest, got turned around, got lost."

"You a preacher?"

Wormwood delivers an Oscar-worthy performance as he replies, "Last time I checked, yes, a humble priest, if you want to get specific. Although my preaching days are probably behind me."

The crewman kneels by the old clergyman. "Let me give you a hand there, Padre."

Wormwood strikes with the speed and authority of a cobra.

The crewman stiffens as Wormwood clamps an ironclad stranglehold around the man's thick neck. The crewman clutches at wrinkled fingers. Wormwood increases the pressure. The crewman shudders and seizes up, clawing at the old man's unremitting grip. Father Manny's eyes turn as pale as egg whites. And this is the last thing the burly crewman registers—his own eyes bugging with shock, his face turning ashy blue—before Wormwood finishes him off with a sharp twist.

The torquing of the man's upper cervical vertebra snaps the brain stem and brings death like a curtain dropping.

5.

The next few seconds are critical to the success of Wormwood's mission. He drags the massive, hairy, inert lump of a human across the bow. And then, with every shred of strength he can muster out of the old priest's feeble limbs, he gently pushes the crewman over the railing and drops him in the water.

Wormwood sits back, lets out a sigh, and allows his shell of wizened skin and brittle bones to rest, relieved that the splash of the crewman hitting the water had most likely not made a big enough noise to alert the other members of the tanker's crew.

In this age of automation and mechanization, the crews on these vessels are usually small—maybe half a dozen at the most. In his research, Wormwood has learned that some tankers can operate with a crew of one. He has also absorbed the inner workings of the pilothouse through a combination of book learning and the kinetic dark magic that allows him to move objects, read minds, cause stigmatic wounds, make noises, shape-shift, and generally make life a living hell for any human of his choice.

Wormwood hears something odd then, which causes the old man's head to cock itself so suddenly it makes an audible crack.

Like a dog reacting to an ultrasonic whistle, he flinches at a low, thin, atonal moaning coming from somewhere close by. He looks around the bow of the great tanker. He sees nothing other than tarps, iron bulwark, paint-chipped railings, and an overcast sky empty of birds. The moaning deteriorates to sobbing noises. Wormwood looks over the railing to make sure the big crewman has not revived in the water.

Nothing but the grey, filthy lapping of waves against the hull can be seen.

The sobbing noises intensify—sloppy, human, tortured, not unlike the sounds of the damned in hell. And all at once Wormwood identifies the source of all the racket. Instantly disgusted, deeply annoyed, and perhaps even a tad surprised, he rolls his eyes with withering disdain. Once in a great while, a human comes along with a soul strong enough to maintain consciousness during possession.

The weeping sounds are coming from inside the old bag of flesh currently being commandeered by Wormwood. The moaning and crying are emanating from the priest himself, from his pathetic, frail soul, which, apparently, is still conscious enough to be a spectator to the festivities unfolding before his eyes.

Wormwood sees a puddle of oil on the deck a few feet away.

He goes over and looks at his reflection in the puddle, and he sees a double image. He sees his own demonic visage, the monstrous, simian, feral face of pure evil, its serpentine yellow eyes devoid of mercy. But he also sees the ghost of a face overlying the demon face, a human visage in utter agony, a tearstained, tortured face, a face that believes in goodness and light and the grace of God.

Wormwood finds this hilarious, and he bursts into laughter, robust and belly-deep laughter, enjoying one of the great cosmic jokes.

At last, between gales of guffawing and chortling, Wormwood thinks of the secret objective, the ultimate purpose of the quest, and it fills him with pride, and that's when he manages to render in a human voice, in the mongrel language of English, in the vernacular of the day, addressing the grief-stricken face in the puddle, "Just wait, preacher man . . . you ain't seen nothin' yet!"

CHAPTER SEVEN

Thy Kingdom Come

1.

With each passing mile marker it becomes more obvious to Hack that something is eating Boo. He can tell by the dearth of conversation, by her pensive gazing out the window at the passing landscape. She's never been this quiet. Boo is a champion conversationalist, but today she seems sullen, brooding.

At last, somewhere around Edwards, Mississippi, on a barren stretch of Interstate 20, Boo breaks the silence. "What are we missing?" She gazes out at the ocean of soybean fields, brown and seared in the raw winds of spring. "We knew he was heading south for a while but then . . . shit. Nothing. No sign of him. He could be anywhere."

"Let's face it. We're just extrapolating at this point. He could be in Tijuana by now, Poughkeepsie, the fucking moon. This is fast becoming a wild-goose chase, if you ask me."

Boo turns back to the window and stares out at the patchwork fields and ramshackle barns passing in a blur, and Hack drives in excruciating silence for what seems like an eternity. He considers putting on some music. Maybe that would bring Boo around. Silverback's government-issue Escalade comes stocked with a fabulous stereo and an impressive collection of midcentury bebop CDs. But then Hack decides against it.

Better to just stew in his private thoughts and insecurities.

They've been searching for Father Manny for nearly a week now without any results. At every city in their path, every wide spot in the road, every little two-bit farm town or trailer park, they exit the interstate and do a sweep. Hack enters the grid and checks traffic cameras or surveillance videos (if the town has the infrastructure for such things). If there is a sheriff's office or police station, Hack finds a back door into their database and checks recent dispatches or reports of drifters or suspicious strangers, or anything even remotely like an old, arthritic, lonely priest out trying to get back to nature or discover himself or whatever the hell he's doing.

Every time Hack calls in to Spur to give an update, the situation seems more hopeless. Spur is too busy doting on his newborn son behind the walls of the Cloister to offer much help, and Silverback is spending his days contacting local authorities and FBI offices along the Mississippi—in confidence—for updates, calling in favors, pressuring colleagues, and getting as many eyeballs as possible on the case.

At the Cloister, the Monsignor has been making inquiries throughout his network of clergy across the middle South. But no clues have yet emerged. A big, boisterous bull of man with the beard of a medieval wizard, Monsignor Charles McAllister is the Cloister's North Star, its guiding voice of reason, but Father Manny's disappearance has stymied even him. Plus, the Monsignor hates publicity. He prefers to handle issues such as this internally. But now it's becoming more and more obvious to everyone involved that they're looking for the proverbial needle in a haystack. And the length and width of this particular haystack encompass thousands of square miles.

But they have to do something. They can't just let their beloved Father Manny up and vanish.

"You okay?" Hack finally asks Boo.

She turns to look at him. "Yeah, of course, why do you ask?"

"No reason. Just wondering."

"C'mon."

"You've said like two words since Vicksburg. Would it kill you to shoot the shit with me now and then?"

She shrugs. "I'm just . . . frustrated, you know, trying to figure out if there's anything we missed."

"You sure that's all it is?"

"What does that mean?"

"Nothing, nothing. . . . Call me paranoid, I just feel like something's up."

She gives him another shrug. "Nothing's up, okay, I'm good."

Hack lets out a sigh. He throws a glance at her sitting there like a porcelain doll in her long duster and spandex top, her coal-black hair pulled back tight. The late-afternoon sun glows around her sculpted profile, sending a twinge of melancholy down Hack's chest. He feels like the more he falls in love with her, the more cryptic and mysterious she gets. Is that what he finds so intriguing about her? Is that what turns him on—the stereotypical inscrutable Asian thing? Is he that shallow and racist? Finally, he says to her, "Did you see something?"

"What do you mean?"

"You know what I'm talking about."

"No, I actually don't."

"Your circuit cable to the Other Side."

"I don't think that's—"

She stops herself, jerking her gaze back to the window.

"Boo?"

If she were a cat, her back would be arching right now; her hair would be standing on end.

"Boo, what is it?"

Stone-still, eyes wide, she gapes at something out there in the Mississippi hinterland.

Visions like these can terrify her but they are also the cross she must bear—her connection to the Great Beyond.

2.

Born and raised in a small fishing village in China's Hubei Province, Michelle "Boo" Chen grew up plagued by visions. This psychic affliction only worsened when her family moved to America and settled in a suburb of Oakland. Nightmares, waking dreams, ghostly figures following her . . . all of it turned her inward, and preoccupied her with death and the afterlife. In high school, she became obsessed with martial arts, which served her well a few years later when she enlisted in the U.S. Marine Corps. She was groomed to be a sniper, but what her superiors soon learned was that she was deadly efficient in up-close-and-personal combat, which had earned her the nickname "Boo" . . . as in, "Boo, you're dead."

After a few years in the Expeditionary Strike Group 3, she was granted upper-tier security clearance, and served as a go-to government assassin for over a decade. She often saw visions of those she had killed, which earned her the reputation among her fellow spooks of Tormented Genius—haunted by her deeds—right up until the day Spur invited her to join his team of outliers.

But Boo would one day learn that her fate was inextricably linked to her relationship with death.

This was how the superpowers had been meted out by the Devil in that dungeon back in Karakistan. The dark magic from hell had hooked into the individual personality of each team member. Boo, being the psychic medium, the bringer of death, who ushered unfortunate souls off this mortal plane, was bestowed with the ability to be a human pipeline between this world and the next. She was given the power to communicate with the dead, and even die herself and continue to roam the earth, undead, recovering from all but the most catastrophic injuries—or so it appears. She has already returned from the grave once, but is in no hurry to find out if she can do it again.

Like all superpowers bestowed by the Devil, however, Boo's is as much a curse as it is a blessing.

This very day, in fact, as the Escalade roars past the old country cemetery, Boo sees another disturbing apparition, standing on the edge of the property between two calcified stone markers half sunken into the earth. The ghost of the old man wears a moldering, ragged nineteenth-century burial coat. His cadaverous face is fringed with moss, and filled with dread, as he stares at Boo, slowly shaking his head back and forth.

The gesture brims with portents, a forewarning of something terrible coming. And as the Escalade rumbles on down the road, leaving the little boneyard in its dust, the look of that ghost, the very power of that decaying figure appearing so rattled, so fearful, delivering that simple yet disturbing gesture, stamps itself on Boo's mind's eye.

"Boo? What's going on?" Hack stares at her from behind the wheel. "What did you see?"

"I—I don't know—it was—"

A few hundred yards ahead of them, on either side of the interstate, more ghosts appear in the distant cotton fields, haloed by the setting sun. Male, female, old, young, in varying degrees of decomposition, some in the tattered, worm-eaten clothing of the grave, others in their formal burial attire, they slowly trundle toward the highway like supplicants bringing in sheaves of wheat. Their dead, sharklike gazes rise in unison to meet the passing Escalade.

Hundreds, maybe thousands of lost souls begin shaking their heads in unison—*no, no, no, no, no, no*—as the SUV roars past the sea of early cotton.

Boo slams her eyes shut and gasps, the faces of the deceased flickering and crackling in her mind's eye like afterimages burning into photographic paper. NO!—NO!—NO!—NO! Boo spasms against her seat and holds her ears and cringes at the psychic warnings bouncing around her brain, sparking synapses like a battery of firecrackers unleashed behind her eyes.

"*Boo!*"

She feels the gravitational force of the Escalade coming to a sudden stop on the shoulder of the southbound lanes. The g-force throws her forward, her shoulder belt digging into her chest. She opens her eyes in a series of fitful blinks.

The ghosts are gone.

But the premonition that something horrible is about to unfold remains like a cancerous tumor growing in the depths of Boo's brain.

3.

That next morning, around 4:00 A.M. central standard time, an unauthorized vessel whispers into Lake Borgne, fifteen miles east of the Port of New Orleans. Its running lights turned off, its engine purring softly, the hundred-foot-long fantail cruiser is in the final leg of a long and arduous voyage across the Atlantic, enduring several storms that would have demolished a lesser boat and killed a lesser group of passengers. But this craft has a special history and pedigree known to very few.

Once in the possession of an infamous Moroccan crime lord, the boat is outfitted with bulletproof glass, reinforced bulwarks, racing engines, and a high-capacity fuel reserve that enables it not only to cross the Atlantic without having to refuel but also to outrun most international authorities.

At the moment, in fact, the unsanctioned vessel is on the radar of the U.S. Coast Guard out of Metairie, Louisiana, which has sent a patrol after it. But chances are the patrol will never find the cruiser that night, owing to the fact that it takes a sharp turn as it approaches the marshy thickets of the bayou at the Old Spain Fort Dupré. Moments later the boat vanishes into the shadows of the swamps. The motor dies, and the cruiser floats for another fifty yards or so until it comes to rest beneath an enormous cypress swathed in Spanish moss. The ripples in the estuary disturb the stillness, and a sleeping mallard suddenly erupts in a flurry of feathers and squawks as it flees the scene.

Just beyond the cypress tree, in the shadows, a lone figure awaits in a stolen skiff.

Out of the cruiser's lower cabin four shadowy figures emerge like ancient revenants rising from the grave. They now stand on the upper deck facing the smaller boat, which is anchored in the water a little less than thirty yards away, softly pitching in the currents. On the skiff's fore bench, Wormwood sits watching impatiently, his human body wrapped in a shawl to stave off the predawn chill. The demon's eyes glow like embers within the sockets of the old priest's skull.

On the cruiser's deck, the demon Snakeroot—now in the body of the burly Irish priest known as Father Gordon Shamus—turns to the woman next to him. "You have the honors, my dear. Do not fuck it up or I will peel off every inch of that skin you inhabit!"

The beloved Roman nun, Sister Mary Beth Malambri—now possessed by the banshee demon Hemlock—wears a long raincoat still dappled with the remnants of an oceanic storm. She waves her plump right hand, and the sound of metal and fiberglass rupturing fills the still air. A gaping hole forms in the cruiser's starboard hull, water roaring into the midsection now. And the boat begins to sink.

The four possessed souls remain standing on the surface of the water as the massive steel vessel descends beneath their feet in a heaving display of foam and bubbles. As all evidence of the cruiser—including the corpses of the captain and navigator—vanishes in the darkness below, the disturbance stirs up the swamp for a moment, and then gradually settles.

The demonic foursome now calmly walk side by side across the water's surface toward the skiff. Inside Father Gabriel Warren of Johannesburg, Foxglove cannot contain her amusement at the irony. "Look at us, Wormwood, walking on water just like Christ."

"Thy kingdom come," Hemlock giggles maniacally as she strolls across the shimmering surface of the marsh. "Thy will be done, on earth as it is in hell."

On the right flank, within the gnarled body of old Father O'Toole, the demon known as Nightshade lets out a deluge of oily, lascivious, obscene laughter. "Just like Christ, that's rich, if only—"

"Enough!" Wormwood hisses at them, concerned about engaging with human authorities. "We haven't the time for this!"

They pile into the skiff. Wormwood switches on the tiny outboard motor. The little boat pitches and rolls slightly with the extra weight. The motor groans as Wormwood steers the craft northward . . . toward their rendezvous with the tanker.

4.

Just before dawn, the rhythmic blinking of pink neon shines through the cheap curtain of the roadside motel room ten miles south of Natchez, feeding Hack's sleeplessness. Sharing a broken-down double bed with Boo, he lies next to her, wide awake, staring at the slowly rotating ceiling fan, stewing in his angst.

"I know you're awake," he says at last, tired of playing games.

Over an hour has passed since she once again refused to tell him what's wrong, and since then Hack has been obsessing over the sound of her breathing. He knows the sound of Boo sleeping peacefully, and he knows the sound of her having a dream, and he also knows the sound of her insomnia. She sleeps on her side, and tonight she has offered him only her back—another first, and a gesture that has exacerbated the situation.

Now, by the low, soft sound of her breathing, he knows she's still awake, probably worrying about whatever the fuck it is that has her worried.

"I'm asleep." Her voice sounds strained, thin, distracted. "Leave me alone."

"C'mon, Boo, this is ridiculous, and if I may be completely candid, it's unfair. You haven't let me touch you in days. You've said three words since we pulled off the highway. Don't do this to me. It's me, it's Hack. C'mon."

She rolls over and gives him a stoic look. The fuchsia-colored light on her girlish face makes her look injured, vulnerable, soft—all the things she isn't. "What do you want me to say?"

"I want you to say . . . something. Anything. I want you to be with me. I want you to be present. And I want you to treat me like something other than a skin disease you're trying to shake."

She sighs. "It's complicated . . . I don't have the energy right now."

"You saw something on the road. What was it? What's going on in that big brain of yours? Why haven't you shared it with the rest of us?"

"I am seeing visions, but I don't know what they mean yet. I'm getting all kinds of signs, messages, but I can't figure out what they have to do with Father Manny . . . if anything."

Hack looks at her. "That's it? That's why you've been treating me like cold liver and onions? Really?—Seriously?"

"That's it, Hack. What can I tell you? That's what's been keeping me up at night."

Hack says nothing, just shakes his head with dismay. He doesn't see the faint, delicate arteries of darkness spreading throughout the room. Like desiccated veins of black mold, they spread between the cracks of the old plaster ceiling, branching behind the yellowed cabbage-rose wallpaper, spreading and metastasizing with the wildfire speed of poisonous creeping vines growing and dividing and multiplying under the malodorous carpet. Cancerous, malignant, putrid, these are the strands of Satanic influence invisible to most. These are the seeds of anger, hate, resentment, and recrimination that the Devil plants in the hearts of family members, friends, and lovers.

It may be true that Satan cannot directly cause the death of a human being, but he certainly *can* sow the seeds of disaster that have already begun to eat away at the Quintet.

5.

That night, in that squalid motel room, after trying unsuccessfully to fall asleep for nearly an hour, Hack lets out a frustrated breath, climbs out of bed, and goes over to his pack of cigarettes on the desk blotter across the room. He lights one up and paces in his boxers, compulsively puffing on a Marlboro.

"You're not being straight with me. I can tell. I know you. You're holding something back."

Boo sits up against the headboard, and wearily rubs her eyes. "Okay. You're right. That's not the whole story."

Hack turns toward her. "I'm all ears."

"The other day, I was helping Spur get the nursery ready, cleaning out the temporary office. Ran across some classified documents from the Karakistan mission. They were supposed to be shredded. I guess they got mixed up with some legal papers in Spur's briefcase. It doesn't matter. Anyway. Point is, sometimes numbers stick in my head. I saw the tally—Osamir's rainy day fund. I don't think anybody else caught it."

She pauses and gives him a look. Hack is nonplussed. What in God's name is she talking about? It was over a year ago that they ended up captured by the warlord Osamir, got thrown in the dungeon, made the deal with the Prince of Darkness, and started this surreal new chapter in their lives. "I'm not following," Hack says, stubbing out his Marlboro after only a few drags.

"The total amount in the numbered accounts changes from one day to the next."

"And . . . ?"

"Osamir and all his cronies were either dead or in custody by that point."

"Where are you going with this?"

She burns her gaze into his face. "When we left Karakistan it stood at ninety-seven million, two hundred and three thousand, three hundred and three dollars and seventeen cents American. Like I said, for some reason numbers stick in my head."

"Wait a minute, you don't think that I—"

"I'm just going according to the statements. Okay? When we landed at Dover Air Force Base it stood at eighty-seven million, two hundred and three thousand, three hundred and three dollars and seventeen cents."

"Stop it. All right? Just stop it."

"Tell me I'm crazy."

"You're crazy."

"Explain it then. You were the only one who had a laptop on the C-130, and had access, et cetera, et cetera. You're the guy. You can traipse into the digital world, move shit around, fuck with shit. It doesn't take Sherlock Holmes to figure out where the money went."

Hack stares at her. "You were in a goddamn casket at the time, if memory serves."

The reference is harsh to Boo's ears. A year and a half ago, in the chaotic aftermath of Karakistan, during a struggle in an air transport, Boo parachuted out of the plane but her chute failed and she appeared to die at sea. She was shipped home and buried at Arlington before anyone learned that she was actually, thanks to her superpower, *undead,* and able to claw herself out of the grave. It was not a pleasant experience for her, to say the least.

"Numbers don't lie."

"It's a fucking clerical error! Nine looks like an eight on a shitty scan. I don't know. I didn't take the money, Boo. Period. Full stop."

She gives him a shrug. "I don't care if you hocked Osamir's collection of Rolls-Royces and spent the money in Vegas. It's the fact that you didn't tell me, you didn't share the wealth."

"Are you fucking serious?!"

She climbs out of bed, angrily pulls on her robe, and walks over to him. "We all put our lives on the line every day, every mission, and now it's worse because we're saddled with these powers, and dude, this ain't no comic book, this ain't no disco, this is real life-and-death, souls-in-peril shit we're dealing with here. And you keep the cash for yourself?"

"Goddamn it, I didn't take the money!!"

The force and volume of his voice barely fazes her. She just stands there, hands on her hips, her gaze fixed on him.

Hack shakes his head. "You don't believe me? Fine. But I can't stay in this relationship—or whatever you call it—if I'm not trusted. You understand what I'm saying? I'm out!"

She cocks her head. "What the hell does that mean? You're out? You're breaking up with me?"

"I'm breaking up with the whole goddamn team. I can't be in this crazy fucking unit anymore. Not if the trust is gone. That's how we survive!—Trust!—Look into it, Boo. I'm *out*!"

"Out?!—There's no fucking 'out'!"

He grabs his pants and hurriedly puts them on. Then he pulls on his boots, grabs his backpack, his jacket, his gun, and his wallet, and heads for the door. He pauses, considers saying something else, thinks better of it, and leaves . . . slamming the door behind him.

6.

Inside the derelict tanker—now anchored in a remote area of the Tallulah docks—the demons gather in the shadows of the lower decks.

In a cavernous open area just in front of the engine room, the naked corpse of a crew member hangs upside down, its ankles hooked to an ancient block and tackle connected to the high ceiling. In life, the victim was a heavyset man, hirsute, with a full beard and long greasy hair, the lifeless remains now slowly turning in the dusty air like a side of beef waiting to be butchered.

While Wormwood softly recites the Satanic invocation, speaking in the glottal grunts and sighs of Paleolithic Aramaic, the demon Hemlock climbs a stepladder next to the cadaver. Inhabiting the skin of the nun, the banshee commands the youngest of the five bodies, the one most fit for such a strenuous task. In her right hand she clutches a long railroad spike, found in a toolbox in the ship's pilothouse.

As Wormwood reaches the crescendo of the prayer, the banshee stabs the spike through the crew member's carotid artery.

In the absence of a heartbeat, the blood leaks out as if from a hole in a cistern. The rivulet falls through a large circular opening in the floor, mingling with the thousands of gallons of thick, obsidian-black oil in the reservoir beneath the deck.

The sacrificial exsanguination lasts for endless minutes until the corpse gives up most of what it has to give.

The demons step back from the opening as a rumbling noise reverberates up from the bowels of the reservoir. The ship shudders, the hull quaking as though from a gathering storm. Those inhabiting older bodies are forced to grab hold of the side beams in order to brace themselves.

Something begins to disturb the pool of black oil visible in the opening. Ripples tremble across the oil's greasy surface as twin ram horns slowly rise out of the onyx muck, followed by the elongated, lupine face of Satan, now dripping with thick, viscous fluid.

"It took you pathetic children long enough to get here!" the Devil snarls in Aramaic as the rest of his wondrous and terrible body levitates out of the oil with its regal bearing, its massive insect-like wings folded against the ridges of its spine. He rises into midair, dripping, the oil sluicing off his breastplate and epaulets. His long, spindly fingers angrily shake off the fluid as he hovers like an enormous dragonfly.

The demons reverently lower their bodies to one knee, bowing their human heads in supplication to their great and powerful leader. Wormwood speaks up, using the dead language. "Please forgive us, Master, for we have each traveled a great distance in order to—"

"Silence, imbecile!" The Devil hovers over them, still dripping. "See if you are able to do one thing correctly."

"Yes, Master."

"The fateful transformation must be carried out without fail."

"Of course, Sire."

"As the magicians say, misdirection is your central objective."

"Misdirection, my lord, yes," Wormwood says with Father Manny's gravelly, aged vocal cords, kneeling on Manny's arthritic knee.

Floating above the five human shells, the Devil raises his long arms in a grandiose gesture of baptismal significance. "The five of you shall be hell's antidote to these five impertinent troublemakers who have the gall to call themselves the Devil's Quintet. . . . You five shall be the antidote to their vanity. . . . You five shall change the nature of the universe as prophesied in the Great Satanic texts."

In unison the voices of the possessed rise up in response: "Hail Satan!"

"I hereby bestow on you five the infernal name of the Shadow Society."

"Hail Satan!"

"Go forth now, and infiltrate their realm in the guise of holy men and women."

"Hail Satan!"

"And bring about the end of mankind's rule on the earth forevermore!"

"Hail Satan!"

PART II

THE UNVEILING

The sun and the moon grow dark
And the stars lose their brightness.
The LORD roars from Zion
And utters his voice from Jerusalem,
And the heavens and the earth tremble.

—Joel 3:15–16

CHAPTER EIGHT

Simulacrum

1.

That morning, several hours before significant events will begin to upset the calm of the Cloister, Spur's cottage sits silent and tranquil in the genial hush of dawn. Beams of brilliant sunshine cant down from the high windows, the dust motes drifting softly through the light. The crib sits empty by the changing table, the little homemade mobile of paper stars that Pin-Up crafted out of construction paper and glitter slowly revolving in the air currents above the crib.

Presently the baby lies sound asleep between his mother and father on Spur's bed, the child cradled in Pin-Up's arms, his tiny hand clutching at Pin-Up's breast. Both Pin-Up and Spur are awake, listening to the faint and lovely noise of their child's breathing, still somewhat of a miracle to Spur. The day the baby was born, Spur held him for over an hour, counting each breath with the same pang of astonishment. In a way, this was Spur's true superpower—to play a role in bringing a living, breathing human being into the world. It is a gift that far outweighs Spur's ill-begotten superpower.

Many years ago, as a young man named Paul Candell, feeling trapped in the small East Texas hamlet in which he grew up, Spur dreamed of seeing the world, of making a difference, of fighting what his dad had called "the good fight." He had been in the ROTC in college, and decided to enlist in the Navy after watching the World Trade Center go down. He chose SEAL training, and proved himself a prodigy on the obstacle courses and in the underwater demolition training programs. Part of it was his time playing linebacker for Texas A&M,

being a team captain, and motivating his fellow players. He instantly became a leader in the SEAL program, to the point that instructors at the Great Lakes training facility started calling him Spur . . . as in *"We'll put the Spur to 'em, that'll get 'em off their asses."*

Flash-forward to Karakistan, a dungeon stained in blood, and a ragged, unearthly shadow figure appearing as a last-minute reprieve. On that fateful day, the Devil knew something about Spur that very few people knew. The Devil knew all about Spur's warrior soul, and his strength on the battlefield, and his ability to triumph over stronger men than he. Spur often used his enemy's strength as an advantage. In judo, they call it "the gentle way"—using an opponent's superior strength and weight against them—but in the dark magic of the Devil, the skill becomes a superpower.

Terrifying in its simplicity, the power given to Spur by Satan that day enables Spur to destroy any enemy by mirroring their strongest attribute and turning it back on them.

But today, in the genial hush of his cottage, in the warmth of his bed, with his baby and wife cuddled against his shoulder, the only thing that matters to Spur is family.

Is he being paranoid and overprotective to have nanny cams installed in the nursery? The tiny digital cameras cost a fortune, and they took Hack a week to wire up and install. Early on, Spur would compulsively run checks during the day, watching different angles of the child napping in his crib, marveling at the little life unfolding before the cameras. To this day, in fact, Spur is still trying to wrap his head around the arrival of Paul Candell, Jr. Is it fate? Is it truly a blessing? Or is it a huge mistake to bring a child into this violent cat-and-mouse game that the Quintet is playing with the forces of darkness? All Spur knows for sure, as he watches the tiny creature slumber in Pin-Up's arms, is that he has never felt a love this pure, this unconditional.

"Gotta admit, the kid's a champion sleeper," Spur whispers.

"I know, right," Pin-Up says with a languid smile, stroking the downy softness of the baby's head. "Not even two months old yet and the little shaver sleeps straight through the night."

"I remember my mom telling me stories of me being one hell of a colicky baby. Keeping the poor gal up all night, screaming to beat the band."

Pin-Up gives him one of her patented looks. "You're still pretty goddamn colicky, you ask me . . . keeping me up all night."

Spur grins at her. "It's a thankless job but somebody's gotta keep you up."

"That's not all you keep up."

He laughs. "Hey, watch the innuendos. There's a child present."

Her smile fades. "It's been a while, though."

"What?"

"Since you've gotten it up, I mean, and I have to say I don't blame you."

He sits up against the headboard. "What in the Sam Hell are you talking about?"

"Believe me, I wouldn't want to have sex with me right now if I were you."

"You've gotta be kidding me."

The baby stirs. Pin-Up gently climbs out of bed, the child still cradled in her arms, squirming a bit, his eyes still closed. Padding across the room to the crib, Pin-Up carefully lowers the child into it and builds a little wall of blankets around his tiny body. She does all this with a strange kind of practiced quality that makes Spur wonder if she's been secretly preparing herself for motherhood for a long time.

"He'll be starved when he wakes up," she says, sitting down on the armchair across the room. Her midsection is thick and soft from the pregnancy, her face plumper than usual. The pink tracks of stretch marks on her belly become visible as she sits back, pulling her T-shirt up above her breasts. "But these big jugs won't wait, they're killing me." She grabs a suction bottle off the end table and attaches the funnel to one nipple. "Gotta make a trip to the dairy, relieve some of the pressure."

Spur watches her as she begins to express milk from her breast.

She doesn't make eye contact as the milk flows, just gazes off with a faraway stare as she pumps the little bottle. Spur gets out of bed and comes over to her, kneeling by the chair with a strange kind of reverence. "You are more beautiful than ever," he says, stroking her arm, kissing her knee. "And you don't even know it, which makes you even more beautiful." He gently takes the pump bottle from her and sets it on the side table. "C'mere, we need to have a little ol' board meeting of the Candell/Caruso Corporation."

She looks at him as he cups his big, callused hands around her chin. He leans down to plant a kiss on her lips.

He doesn't notice the idea sparking in her eyes as they begin to make love.

2.

By the time they make it to the bed, Pin-Up has already begun the process of reading his secret desires.

As he tenderly lays her on her back, shoves down his boxers, and climbs on top of her, Pin-Up begins to transform, triggered by his touch. Either due to the gates of his feelings being opened by their intimacy, or perhaps the familiarity of his lips and hands, his memories, fantasies, and fragments of stolen moments flow into Pin-Up's satellite dish of a brain on a tsunami of fractured images.

She sees naked women from the pages of girlie magazines through Spur's feverish teenage point of view, hourglass figures and prominent derrieres and big busts that would make Jessica Rabbit blush streaming into Pin-Up's consciousness, changing the cellular makeup of her skin and tissues with the speed and efficiency of a chameleon. She absorbs the erotic triggers of Spur's later years, the stolen glances at sweater girls at Texas A&M, the furtive glimpses at cashiers with zaftig figures at the grocery store.

Pin-Up's shape shifts beneath him, her loose skin tightening, her stretch marks fading.

"What in the blue blazes?" Spur jerks away from her with a start. "What are you doing?"

"C'mon, big boy," she purrs in that fake sex-symbol patois heard in every spicy one-reeler since the dawn of the peep show, her body a simulacrum of every cheesecake model since the advent of *Playboy,* her face sculpted now with high cheekbones and plush lips and electric-blue eyes. "We both know this is what you want, this is what you need."

"No, no, no, no, no, no . . . whoa there, Tonto. C'mere, rewind, go back."

Pin-Up is confused, scattered, her skin now starting to tingle. "What are you—?"

"C'mere, I want my gal back." He reaches out for her and pulls her into his arms. He holds her, tenderly stroking her hair. "This is not what I want," he says softly into the simulacrum's ear. "I want my sweet Maria, I want her back, and I want *only* her, forever and ever and ever."

"I don't—I—I thought—"

She gropes for purchase, her head spinning, her body reconstituting, returning to its swollen, milk-sodden, stretch-marked default form.

He kisses her ear, her jawline, her chin, her nose, her abundant cleavage, her loose tummy. He whispers, "I don't want anybody else but you, Pin. You are the most beautiful woman on earth."

"Oh my God, I'm so sorry. I . . . I thought . . . I didn't want to . . ." Somehow she staves off her tears. "I love you, cowboy."

They fall into a full embrace on the bed, their lips coming together so softly, so tenderly, the sensation feels new, it feels fresh, like a secret place they didn't know existed. Something preternatural and invisible flows out of Spur and into Pin-Up.

She senses it as palpable as mulled wine on the back of her tongue, flowing down into her, warming her, easing her fears and her insecurity and her secret pain.

Now his strong, sinewy arms have wrapped around her and his hands have found the small of her back, and she feels him girding her, positioning her with such reverence, such aching love that it feels as though she's being restored, revitalized, recharged. All the doubt and dread and angst suddenly drain out of her and she presses her engorged breasts against his broad chest and threads her fingers through his hair as he gently enters her and softly thrusts until they're both rising toward a beatific, shattering climax.

They collapse onto their backs, side by side, catching their breaths, and staring at the plaster swirls in the ceiling.

3.

A moment later, in the tranquil silence of the bedroom, Pin-Up feels a new sensation entering her consciousness. Sudden and inchoate, it would be impossible for her to put into words but it has a physical effect on her, the hairs on the back of her neck standing up, her flesh prickling with nervous tension. She sits up and looks around the room.

"What is it?" Spur asks softly, still half smiling in the afterglow.

"Oh my God." Across the room the baby has moved in his crib, his little cherubic face now visible between the slats of the crib. "Oh. My. God."

"What?!"

"Spur, look. Look." She pulls a blanket around herself, climbs out of bed, and shuffles across the room on bare feet. "Look at Junior!"

Spur sits up, completely taken aback. "Well, butter my ass and call me a biscuit."

Pin-Up kneels by the crib, peering through the vertical slats at the little pear-shaped face. She can smell baby powder and fresh sheets. "You see this, Daddy? You see what's going on here?"

Spur comes over and stands in front of the crib. The child awkwardly raises his head with the shakiness of a newborn bird in a nest seeking food. Spur grins. "I'll be doggone if he ain't looking right at me, making eye contact."

"I told you he was a gifted child." Pin-Up wipes her eyes, but she can't wipe the ridiculous smile off her face. She's giddy. She knew this milestone would eventually come but she wasn't fully prepared. "His eyes are stunning, aren't they?"

Spur strokes the baby's head. "Takes after his old man."

"Junior?" Pin-Up gets the baby's attention. "Look at me, Junior."

The baby coos and bobbles its head back down to the familiar female face hovering outside the slats of the crib.

Pin-Up gets very still, kneeling by the crib, studying those pale blue eyes. The baby has Spur's eyes, clear and stalwart eyes. But caught in the path of that innocent gaze—that clean, soft, guileless gaze—Pin-Up feels a strange sensation washing over her, a feeling of being vulnerable, as well as a memory deeply buried in the hidden compartments of her brain.

She hasn't thought of Hannah—her younger half sister—for years. Back in East L.A., the two girls had lived in the same house for eighteen months while Hannah's father did a stint at Chino for grand theft auto. Pin-Up became a doting big sister, and was crushed when the younger girl was killed in the cross fire of a gang skirmish.

The experience changed Pin-Up's life. She left home shortly afterward and kicked around Hollywood for a while, trying to be an actress-slash-model-slash-whatever, and then decided to go to nursing school. She needed to help people. It was that simple. Was it to assuage her loss and her guilt over Hannah's death? Maybe. One thing was certain: The pain was always there. It drove Pin-Up. It defined Pin-Up.

And ultimately it led Pin-Up to the military and Spur's original SEAL team.

"Everything all right?"

Spur's voice shook Pin-Up out of her daze. "Yeah, I'm good." She glanced away from the baby's stare as though breaking a circuit. She rose and looked at Spur. "Can I ask you a question, though?"

"Shoot."

"When Junior first looked at you, first made eye contact, did you feel something . . . I don't know . . . something weird?"

"You bet your boots I did."

"What was it? What was the feeling?"

Spur sighs. "Let's see . . . um . . . disbelief that I had a hand in bringing this little tyke into the world . . . and also the sheer terror of realizing that he would be driving someday."

"Very funny. That's not what I mean."

"Where are you going with this?"

She shrugs. "When his little eyes first met mine I felt something. I mean, not just unadulterated love. Yeah, I felt that for sure. It's overwhelming. But I also felt . . . I don't know." She looks back at the baby, strokes his head, and grins at him. "I don't know what I'm talking about. I'm imagining things, postpartum dementia or something. Who knows?"

Spur comes over to her, takes her in his arms, and kisses her forehead. "You ask me, you seem to be functioning just fine."

She grins and returns his kiss, and soon they're making out again . . .

. . . as the baby calmly watches.

4.

Late that afternoon, the unraveling starts with a phone call.

At the time of the call, Spur is outdoors with Father Josh, repairing a fence along the northern edge of the property. The day has turned blustery. Spur wears a denim jacket with a G19 holstered under it on a chest rig. Storm clouds have rolled in from the west, the sky turning the color of black lung disease in the waning dusk, when the cell phone in the back pocket of Spur's jeans begins to vibrate.

The caller ID tells him it's Boo.

"Boo, for Chrissake," Spur hisses into his cell. "Where the Sam Hell have you two yahoos been? When I said go search for the padre I didn't mean take the week off and go to Vegas."

"Something's happened." The voice on the other end says this in a low, exhausted utterance. "I need to talk to you about it. But privately. Can you get to the chapel and call me back?"

Spur discreetly walks away from the fence so that Father Josh won't hear the conversation. "You were supposed to check in on a daily basis; it's been over a week."

"Skipper, I need you to get to the chapel. I'll tell you all about it then."

Spur lets out an exasperated groan. "All right, don't get your knickers in a knot. I'm heading over there now, call you back in five."

He tells Father Josh he has to run a quick errand and off he goes.

5.

"Hack quit."

Inside the dusty little sanctuary, Spur pauses in his angry pacing and stares at a narrow stained-glass window depicting Jesus and the casting out of demons into pigs. The dwindling daylight filters down through the mosaic and refracts shattered rainbows across the old hardwood floor.

"That's a good one," Spur finally replies. "You oughtta audition for a spot on *Jimmy Kimmel*."

"It's not a joke, Skipper."

"What does that even mean? 'Hack quit.' Quit smoking? Eating pork?"

"It's a long story, but I have to tell you, I think I'm right behind him. I need some time to figure some things out, get my head screwed on straight."

Spur stops in his tracks. "Come again? What did you just say?"

"We're both out, Skipper. For the time being, at least. Maybe we're both going to hell. So be it. I can't do this anymore."

Spur lets a beat of silence pass. He takes a deep breath, trying to control his temper. "Okay, maybe I'm having issues with my hearing, I need to blow the wax outta my ears—"

"I'm sorry."

"'Sorry' don't cut it, soldier."

"I don't know what else to say."

"Okay, let me say a few things then. Let's start with the fact that you two monkeys must be a few pickles short of a barrel. Nobody gets off this train. Hack knows this better than anybody. In perpetuity, Boo. We're talking a lifetime membership. You walk away from this gig, it's walking away from your own shadow."

"Skipper—"

"Boo, listen to me. Whatever is going on, we can work it out."

"That's not in the cards, Skip. The problem is—"

"I don't give a good goddamn what the problem is! You realize how vulnerable we are right now? Diablo knows about the baby. There's no doubt in my mind about that, and there's nothing we can do about it. The child can't live behind a church pew, Boo. We need all hands on deck, now more than ever."

Spur runs out of breath for a moment. The silence on the other end worries him. He paces and tries to measure his words.

His tone softens. "I know the work takes its toll. I know you and Hack were both looking to rotate out pretty soon. Before Karakistan, you two were talking about taking that mental health time and whatnot. I get that. But we got a situation now. Force majeure, Boo. I can't let you do this."

After a long portentous pause, the voice on the other end says, "Look. I wasn't going to tell you about this. But Hack skimmed off the funds recovered in Karakistan."

Spur stares at the stained glass. "Run that by me again."

"It's all there in the documents. It's pretty clear he skimmed cash off Osamir's war chest."

"Are you serious?"

She tells him about the discrepancy in the numbered accounts, and the fact that Hack had twenty-four hours to cook the books. "You probably think I'm an asshole to rat him out," she says. "But I can't deal with it, I can't be with somebody who has the gall to do something like that when we're putting our lives on the line."

Spur is shaking his head. He takes a deep breath and struggles to keep his emotions in check. "You gotta be kidding me. I don't blame him. I wish I had thought of skimming money off that son of a bitch's nest egg. The shit we go through on these missions, we deserve a cut of every goddamn shekel we recover."

"Spur, stop it."

"No! You stop it, Boo. I don't mind you ratted out your teammate. That's your business. In this line of work relationships are complicated. Especially now with all the expectations, all the black ice on every road. Bad juju everywhere you turn. But goddamn it, Boo, you gotta do this now?"

The voice on the other end of the line darkens, Boo's anger flaring. Outside, distant thunder rumbles as the rain starts up. "For God's sake, Skipper, at least I'm filing a fucking report. Hack just skipped on us, just walked out. No two weeks' notice, no goodbyes. At least give me that much."

"What do you want from me, missy, a goddamn medal of honor for a phone call? You're fucking AWOL!"

"Really?" The voice has turned icy cold. "That's all you have to say to me? After all the shit we've been through, all the years I've had your fucking back?!"

"You don't seem to understand, soldier, you're leaving me, Pin-Up, and the kid in the lurch!—*You're fucking us royally!*"

"I'm hanging up now."

"Fine! Hang up the fucking phone! What do I care?!"

Click.

Spur's scalp crawls with anger, his guts clenching, the rising noise of the storm synchronized with his rage. He winds his pitching arm back and prepares to hurl the cell phone as hard as he can at the stained glass, but something stops him. Perhaps it's the sacrilege of it, the prospect of destroying something as precious to him as a depiction of Christ casting out demons. Or maybe it's the intermittent gusts of wind blowing rain against the window. He furrows his brow at something outside, a ghost peering through the stained glass at him. He moves closer to the window.

He sees the boyish face of Father Josh, the hood of a rain slicker over his head, water dripping from its bill. The young priest is saying something inaudible, his voice drowned by the storm. He points to his right, mouthing something about the door.

Spur hurries over to the entrance and unlocks the door only to find a rain-soaked, nervous Josh wiping the moisture from his face. "Sorry to interrupt," he says. "But I saw something . . . in the lightning . . . I think I might be hallucinating."

Spur lifts his collar. "Show me."

6.

By this point the storm has brought darkness with it as they hurry across the grounds, the rain coming down in sheets. Josh trots alongside Spur, holding an umbrella over their heads. Thunder rattles the sky, and intermittent blasts of lightning turn night to day. The arrhythmic flashing makes their movements appear in jerky slow motion, which strikes Spur as reminiscent of an old silent movie. But he finds no humor in it. Ever since Boo hung up on him he feels as though he's caught in a nightmare from which he cannot awaken.

"There, along the road, on the edge of the woods," Josh points out to Spur after they have climbed the steps of an old gatekeeper's shack situated just inside the southeast gates.

Spur peers over the gate's wrought-iron finials. "I don't see anything." Wiping the rain from his face, he stares into the distance. "Wait . . . okay, yeah . . . now I see it."

A little over fifty yards away, in the swaying shadows of rain-swept pines, a crumpled body lies on its belly on the road's shoulder, at first appearing to be unconscious or even dead.

But the longer Spur stares at it, the more he realizes the body is that of an old man dressed in a filthy windbreaker and tattered priest's collar, struggling to crawl toward the entrance.

CHAPTER NINE

The Valley of the Shadow

1.

Spur carries the semiconscious little man across the north quad to the Cloister's infirmary.

Father Joshua fetches the staff medic—Brother Brian—and they get the shivering priest into a dry gown and lay him down on a gurney in a fluorescent-drenched examination room with portraits of Raphael the archangel and Jonas Salk on the walls. They cover the patient in an electric blanket, and immediately start treating him for extreme exposure, hypothermia, malnutrition, and exhaustion. They hook him to a pulse-ox monitor, and then start an IV drip of electrolytes, glucose, and two kinds of antibiotics.

All through this, the portly little minister keeps murmuring deliriously—mostly nonsense—his speech slurred and hoarse. With eyelids at half-mast he moans something about the coming of the End Days, and something about visions of the Messiah, and God's master plan. The nurse-practitioner, Sister Amy, removes the man's little round eyeglasses, which are shattered and bent. She also applies balm to Father Manny's jowly face, which is severely sunburned, blistered in places, and drawn from starvation.

At one point the priest opens his eyes and smiles, and manages to say in a cracked, thin voice, "My dear, dear friends . . . I prayed I would see you again . . . and the Lord has answered."

"Father Manny—?"

"Please, sir." Brother Brian steps between Spur and Manny. A spindly young man in a white coat who is all Adam's apple and nervous tics, the medic raises his hands in a cautionary gesture. "You'll have plenty of time to catch up with the man . . . but for now we need space and time for observation and treatment."

"Of course," Spur says, backing away. "My bad, sorry." Spur has not quite gotten used to the clerics calling him "sir" or worse yet "Mr. Spur."

Father Manny has already drifted back into semiconsciousness, his eyelids drooping, his head lolling to one side, when all at once the sound of muffled knocking can be heard across the room, and all eyes turn toward the door.

Ticker and the Monsignor peer into the room with looks of concern. "Is it true?" the Monsignor says softly, his rich baritone filled with awe. A grizzly of a man with broad shoulders and a big belly, he wears a St. Louis Cardinals baseball cap and a hockey jersey over his vestments. "Are my eyes deceiving me?" He smiles with delight, and with his long white beard and braids framing his deeply lined face, he looks increasingly like a roadie for a country rock band. "Has the prodigal son actually returned?"

Spur grins, and then shoots a quick glance at the fastidious Father Brian. "Can the patient have two more visitors?"

Before the medic can answer, Ticker pushes the door open and says, "Three more, actually." He nods toward the fashionable woman lurking behind him. "You all know Darby."

Darby Channing wears her standard mod attire—lizard boots, leather skirt, and velveteen blazer—and gives everybody an awkward little bow, as well as her trademark coy grin. She's been a fixture at the Cloister for weeks now after making a deal with Spur that she would confine her duties to doing research and snooping around the periphery of society for signs of occult and/or Satanic influence. She was also asked to keep her affiliation with the Quintet a secret, and refrain from writing any more profiles about the unit. "I'm just being nosy again," she explains. "Forgive me, may I come in?"

Sister Amy shushes them all, giving Darby a look. "As long

as you keep your voices down." Then she rolls her eyes with exasperation. "Come one, come all, the more the merrier."

They gather around Father Manny, who's still drifting in and out of consciousness. Ticker gently strokes the old man's gnarled bare foot, which sticks out of the bedding. The foot is lacerated, filthy, and swollen from God knows how many miles it has on it. Ticker lets out a sigh of relief. "Thank God, he's back in one piece."

The Monsignor pulls his rosary out, kneels by the bed, and silently prays.

Spur takes a deep breath. "He's a tough old buzzard, though, isn't he?"

Darby speaks up. "Did he say anything about where he's been all this time and why?"

"All right," the medic says with great irritation. "I'm going to have to ask everybody to go ahead and vacate the room for the time being while we stabilize the patient and do some tests."

Reluctantly, one at a time, the visitors slowly turn and file out . . .

. . . while Darby's question hangs in the air, unanswered.

2.

"For lack of a better phrase, it was a vision quest."

The next day, Father Manny sits in the cozy front room of Spur's private quarters. Wrapped in a blanket, holding the slumbering baby in his lap, the fragile little priest is nestled in an armchair next to the window, a space heater buzzing next to him.

"You mean like a Native American sort of thing?" Spur asks, sitting next to Pin-Up on the sofa. He hasn't yet told his fellow members of the Quintet about Boo and Hack bailing. The knowledge of it presses down hard on him. It has stolen his sleep and occupied practically every thought. He has no proof that it has any supernatural origins, but he finds it strangely apropos of the Devil somehow to take apart the Quintet piece by piece. It reminds Spur of the Russians and their sowing of discontent through cyber warfare, weakening the U.S. from the inside out, driving wedges and turning the citizens' prejudices and paranoias against each other.

The Monsignor listens from the other side of the room, settled into an armchair, thoughtfully fiddling with his beard. Ticker paces, and Silverback stands by the far window, gazing out at the overcast day as he absorbs what's being said. Darby wanted to be present that day but Spur decided it might be better if she wasn't there, since she had never met Father Manny, and her presence might inhibit the old priest's recounting of his experiences.

"Yes, in a way, it was the same kind of thing," the priest finally replies, gently handing the sleeping baby back to Pin-Up and sipping his tea. His face has regained some of its color, but he still looks frail in his little cocoon of blankets. "I had a dream, and in the dream I was barefoot and walking across hot coals. I could see a beautiful mountain stream, birds singing, a lovely forest just ahead of me, just out of reach. And I knew, somehow I just knew, if I could only cross the smoking embers that were burning my feet and causing me terrible pain I could enter the Promised Land."

Nobody says anything. But Spur can tell everybody is processing.

Spur looks at the priest. "Go on, Padre."

"So . . . maybe this was heaven in the distance, this mountain paradise, or a heaven on earth, I'm not sure. You know how dreams are. I'm getting up there in my years, so heaven is probably in the forefront of my mind more than not. But I do remember vividly in the dream I saw out of the corner of my eye a lovely deer walking alongside me. Or maybe it was a wild goat. Who knows? I remember it was almost regal with these enormous curved antlers like ram horns." He pauses, pondering, getting a strange faraway look on his face as though he's re-creating the dream in his mind's eye. "Perhaps it was an ibex. Anyhoo. I believe the Indians call this a spirit animal. The creature looks at me and says, 'You can do it, old friend. You can make it. You just have to travel the miles, put in the time . . . do the work.'"

He pauses and looks around the room as though it should all be self-explanatory.

The Monsignor says, "I'm guessing you woke up then and lit out on your journey so filled with the spirit you forgot to tell anybody?"

"Guilty as charged. I was . . . I was . . . ennobled by the dream. That's the word. I was ennobled. Galvanized. Beset by it. I admit I should have notified you of my departure, and I will confess I had no clue as to my destination, or where paradise lay for me. But I knew I had to go. I had to try. I had to see if I could make it to that sweet mountain stream; wherever it took me, I had to go. I had to."

The old man trembles with emotion, and then stares at the floor, catching his breath. When he looks back up, Spur can see that the priest's old grey eyes have welled up.

"God led me on this journey, and I felt His presence at every turn. I was guided by His love, and His righteousness. The truth is, I had begun to lose my passion for the Word, my faith, my commitment to a life of Christ. This journey may have had no map but it had a purpose—to restore my spirit. It has prepared me to be a better shepherd, to love my fellow man and life itself with more gusto, to be ready for the End Days. Jesus said, 'If ye are prepared, ye shall not fear.' I saw so much pain and misery out there. I walked through the valley of the shadow of death. But I feared no evil because He was with me every step of the way." The priest pauses for a breath. He looks down. His voice softens. "Every step of the way . . ."

In the silence that ensues, Spur exchanges glances with the others.

The awkward tension in the room is palpable now. The old

rascal Emmanuel, the man who once told dirty jokes late at night in the rectory after too many glasses of port, is nowhere to be found in this new version of Father Manny. His original personality has been left behind along the side of the road like a discarded candy wrapper. This new, denatured version of the old beloved priest is fraught and grave and pious and dour.

Spur is having a hard time wrapping his brain around this, despite the fact that he has come to accept many things over the last year, things that he thought were fairy tales, myths, or urban legends. It was less than two years ago, in fact, that he and his team narrowly shut down a possible nuclear holocaust coaxed into being by the Devil. But the End Days? The Rapture? He looks at the old man. "Father, I'm as happy as a hog on ice that you've gotten rejuvenated on this little jaunt. I truly mean that. But let me ask you something. As long as I've known you—and I realize it ain't that long—you've always been, let's say, *galvanized* by the idea of Armageddon. Now, I don't want to steal your thunder, and I don't want to get into some kind of philosophical pissin' match, but you don't really believe that the apocalypse is coming down the pike any time soon, do ya?"

The smile that appears on Father Manny's face could melt the polar ice caps. "My dear, dear friend, you are a good man, a decent soul, and now enjoying this glorious blessed event." With a nod he indicates baby Paul, who is just beginning to stir in his mother's arms. "I am better off for knowing all of you. But what you people don't realize is that the end is indeed nigh."

"Father, all I'm saying is—"

"Think about it," the priest goes on, undeterred. "We have new plagues every few months now, a pandemic for every occasion. In East Africa hundreds of billions of locusts are swarming the landscape. You can look that up. Wildfires are ravaging Australia and Europe and much of North America as we speak. Terrorism and political violence and social unrest are at all-time highs. Global warming is swallowing every continent and causing biblical storms and droughts around the world."

"But Father, do you really—?"

"Countless signs are being presented every day. Just last year, an earthquake in Italy shook St. Peter's Basilica from its foundation to the top of its capital. It literally caused the crucifix at the crest of the steeple to break off and fall to the ground. I've been following the signs for years now, Spur. But another thing about it that most people don't realize is that a biblical apocalypse is not only the end of the human race."

Spur sighs. "Okay, I'll bite. What else is it?"

"I can help you with that," the Monsignor says from across the room, his voice taking on a weary tone as he sits forward in his chair. "The word itself in Greek—*apokalypsis*—means an unveiling, a revelation. Religious scholars believe the end of mankind will help us see something that has been hidden since the dawn of time."

Father Manny is nodding vigorously. "And I welcome that. I do."

Now Pin-Up chimes in. "But Father, how in the world can you say these things, and be happy about all this, and at the same time see this sweet little innocent soul here in my arms?"

Father Manny's smile widens. "But don't you see, Pin-Up, that's just it. The child will be lifted up by God into heaven with all the other innocent souls. It will be a glorious day."

"Yeah, well, I'll guarantee you one thing," Spur comments with a trace of melancholy in his voice. "Odds are, that ain't gonna be the place I'm taken to when the shit comes down."

Nervous laughter spreads around the room, but nobody really finds it very humorous.

3.

At first, not a single person present notices the baby coming awake in Pin-Up's arms.

Initially the process unfolds in the natural way. Eyes still closed, yawning, the child squirms and writhes for a few moments. His little hands clench and unclench, his tiny lips smacking, involuntarily seeking nourishment from his mother's breast. He makes faint cooing noises as he stretches and yawns again . . . and his eyelids begin to flutter open.

Now the baby starts focusing on the world around him. Still at the tender age at which focus is tricky, he first registers the ceiling. He sees pinpoints of light, the revolving blades of a ceiling fan, and even the faint trowel marks in the plaster. Now, with his big blue eyes fully open and alert, he looks around the room, seeking the source of the aged, gravelly voice currently filling the air.

Spur notices the strange phenomenon first. He doesn't say anything. He doesn't draw any attention to it. He merely watches the baby as Father Manny continues babbling about the joys of Armageddon, and how wandering aimlessly in the wild has inspired him.

* * *

"If I may cut to the chase," the priest is saying now. "The Devil exists. Alas. We all know that now. We've encountered him together, we've seen him with our own eyes as well as witnessed his deeds. He is the eternal enemy. And like, say, the Nazis in the thirties and forties . . . he has his own 'final solution.' The thing is, I experienced what I would call a transformative moment out there in the elements. I had an epiphany. And I hope you'll keep an open mind when I tell you what it is."

Spur watches the baby's gaze, which is now locked on to Father Manny.

From across the room, Ticker stops pacing and says, "Don't keep us in suspense, Padre. What is it?"

Father Manny looks at his superior. "Monsignor, I propose we have a symposium, and hold it in absolute secrecy here at the Cloister, a conference of high-ranking religious figures, an exchange of ideas, all of it in the interest of discussing and understanding the coming of the End Times."

Spur is now mesmerized by his child's gaze, which suddenly

changes as it absorbs and processes the sight of the old priest. The baby's eyes widen with primal fear. The child's flawless little alabaster face furrows and creases into an infantile mask of horror, his tiny mouth forming a perfect, toothless oval of terror that reminds Spur of that iconic Edvard Munch painting, *The Scream.*

"Skeptics will be welcome, of course," the priest is saying. "No point of view will be suppressed. All opinions will be treated equally. I propose that this gathering be hosted soon, very soon, because time is of the essence, and knowledge is power, and understanding God's plan is paramount to us all if we—"

Little Paul Candell, Jr., starts caterwauling with the volume and intensity of an animal being tortured. Some of the people in the room jerk back with a start, the crying is so loud and sudden.

Spur puts his arm around Pin-Up as she comforts the baby, gently bouncing him in her arms and telling him everything's going to be okay, Mama's here, it's going to be all right.

Pin-Up looks at the others and raises her voice to be heard over the shrieking. "Sorry, folks, he's been dealing with diaper rash, and he's probably starved, so if you'll excuse us . . ."

She carries the child back into the bedroom and shuts the door behind them.

The muffled crying does not subside for what seems an eternity.

4.

Over the next two weeks, the Monsignor makes a concerted effort to convince Father Manny to drop his grand scheme, but the little priest is resolute and determined to host an unprecedented roundtable examination of the coming End Days. He explains to the Cloister's leadership that he believes the gathering is part of God's plan. He claims that the Lord planted the idea in his head during the vision quest, and he believes that the conference is God's will. He also makes a case that the gathering is organic to the Cloister's mission: to provide a bulwark against evil, to maintain a continual watch over potential disturbances and assaults upon the forces of good and the kingdom of God. He asks the Monsignor for twenty thousand dollars as an emergency endowment from the educational fund in order to finance the event. The Monsignor reluctantly agrees to ten thousand.

During this time, the weather turns mild over much of Missouri—even for late spring—and the grounds of the Cloister come alive with new greenery, buds on the trees, and tendrils of young flowers peeking up through the soil. In anticipation of the big event, fences are repaired and painted. Even the belfry tower in the center of the campus is renovated and given a shiny new bell, the object handcrafted by an artisan in Chicago and express-delivered to the Cloister. Father Manny supervises the landscaping team in an effort to spruce up the courtyards, hedgerows, and fruit groves that border each sacred quadrant.

The Conference on Revelations and the End of Days, as Father Manny has christened the event, will span a week of presentations, panels, and special events. The programs—curated, of course, by Father Manny—are scheduled to take place in the grand meeting hall in the rear of the St. Augustine chapel, which sits like a godly fortification in the center of the Cloister's campus. The exterior is a monument to great cathedrals down through the ages. Ornate stained-glass arches and gilded mullions line the towers, and steeples and pinnacles rise up over a hundred feet above the ground, the finials standing guard like stone sentries against the sky.

Inside the great edifice, behind the high altar, a side corridor leads attendees to the great meeting hall. The vaulted ceiling features ornate chandeliers of decorative lamps blanketing the burnished space with soft angelic light. Enormous portraits of past monsignors and administrators line the flagstone walls. Father Manny arranges for round tables and high-backed chairs to be placed throughout the hall, and a stage and po-dium to be positioned at the far end of the room, draped in greenery, and equipped with a PA system. The event will be attended by invitation only, and will host no more than a cou-ple of dozen of the foremost clerics, experts, and leaders in the field of religious studies.

Suppers will be a high point. Father Manny believes a re-laxed atmosphere, a little wine, and full bellies will yield hon-est conversation. Guards will be down. Fruitful interactions and a sharing of ideas will flow naturally into the evenings. The old priest spends hours going over the menus with the Cloister's kitchen staff. Rich comfort food will be the fare each night: Swedish meatballs, shepherd's pie, braised short ribs, roast duck with plum sauce, spaghetti Bolognese, lobster mac and cheese, and beef bourguignon. The finest wine in the cel-lar, vintage brandy, and excellent cigars are chosen for after-dinner confabs.

All preparations go according to plan, and the days pass without incident, until the night before the attendees are sched-uled to arrive and check into their guest rooms.

5.

Father Manny is in the great dining hall, dressed in his clerical collar and coat, busily putting out name placards, one at each place setting, still limping slightly from his long trek to enlight-enment, when Spur, Ticker, and Darby barge into the room.

With its dark oak trim, high vaulted ceiling, and exposed brick walls, the dining hall brings to mind an old German rathskeller, albeit an enormous one. The air smells of malt and woodsmoke. There will be a total of nineteen attendees arriv-ing in two days for the orientation dinner, all of them looking forward to participating in such programs as "It's the End of the World as We Know It . . . Now What?" and "God's Great Finale: Should I Stay or Should I Go?"

"Padre, we've been looking all over for you," Spur says as he approaches, Ticker and Darby on his flanks, expectant looks on their faces.

Father Manny puts down his stack of embossed placards and gives them a warm smile. "I promise I wasn't hiding from you."

Ticker speaks up, holding up the guest list that Darby flagged as though offering an exhibit in a criminal trial. "I don't know if you're aware of this but two of your VIPs scheduled to attend tomorrow have been listed by Interpol as missing persons. Darby discovered this earlier today."

Father Manny cocks his head as though attempting to process the statement, which, at first, seems to take him by surprise. "May I see the names?"

Ticker hands him the list and points out the two dignitaries, Fathers Warren and Shamus. Father Manny pulls a new pair of eyeglasses from his shirt pocket, puts them on, and takes a closer look. He starts to chuckle, and his chuckling builds to full, robust laughter. He laughs and laughs as though it's the best joke he's heard in a long time.

Spur and the others stare at the old man, nonplussed by his reaction.

"I apologize," the priest says at last, getting his laughter under control. "It's just that the term 'missing person' strikes me as hilarious. No, they are not missing. They, too, have been on vision quests, not unlike my own. They are the first colleagues I contacted, and we are so fortunate to have them."

Spur and Ticker look at each other. Spur looks at the old man. "I'm going to need to mention this to Silverback; he's going to want to follow up on it."

"Is that necessary?"

"Padre, these priests have friends, families, congregations that are going to want to know they're safe and sound."

Father Manny smiles. "Of course, Spur. You're right. I don't know what I was thinking. Please inform all interested parties that these two preeminent men of the cloth are alive and well and will soon be providing brilliant insights at this important gathering. And in case I've been remiss and have not invited you and your Quintet to the conference, I would like to extend that invitation now. You are welcome to join us tomorrow for dinner, and afterward attend any program that strikes your fancy. You as well, Miss Channing."

Darby smiles back at him. "That's lovely of you, thank you." She glances across the length of the dining hall, and sees several place settings that are missing placards. "Can we help you finish putting the final touches on the tables?"

"That's a lovely offer, but I'm almost done, just a few last things to do."

"It's no trouble," Darby says. "Right, guys?"

Spur is nodding. "Absolutely. Put us to work, Padre. Make us earn our keep."

"All right, well, let's see." The old priest glances around the hall. "Spur, would you and Ticker kindly go fetch some extra firewood so we'll have a full pile for the week?"

The two men give a nod, and exit the hall through a side door.

"Why don't I finish up placing the placards," Darby says.

"All right, excellent, so, here are the rest of them." Father Manny picks up the stack of remaining placards, and hands them over to her. "There are two more tables to go, there and there." He points out the large round tables in the corner. "You can set them out in any order. In the meantime I'll go get the wine goblets."

6.

Nobody notices the Devil watching from inside the massive fireplace.

Situated on the far wall, over twenty feet wide with a firebox as deep as a spare room, the fireplace features a mosaic hearth and a gilded mantelpiece imported from Bavaria decades ago. At this hour, embers still smolder in the ashpit between the andirons, sending thick smoke wafting up the enormous chimney.

Behind the column of woodsmoke, camouflaged by the haze and the charred firebrick, an inky black humanoid figure crouches, apelike, peering through luminous yellow eyes at the action in the room. The Prince of Darkness has taken on the form of an onyx phantasm, a monstrous smudgy stain on the fabric of the world, watching and waiting and savoring every moment of this great deception.

Tonight he is almost childlike in his utter delight, deeply amused by Wormwood's performance as the venerable old priest Emmanuel. How delicious it is to see the demon puppet master inhabiting the very same human soul charged with protecting the innocent from evil. And how amusing it is to watch the ingrate Spur stumbling around without a clue as to what is really about to happen.

The faint yet robust laughter that issues from the flickering darkness behind the smoke is like rusty knives scraping bone.

It is time to proceed with the next item on the agenda.

CHAPTER TEN

The End of the World as We Know It

1.

In his modest bungalow on the northeast corner of the Cloister, Colonel Sean McDermott, code name Silverback, paces across the room in his civvies and slippers, broodingly puffing on his meerschaum pipe after placing a secure call to the home of a former colleague at the Special Expeditionary Section of the Defense Intelligence Agency. At six feet four inches in his stocking feet, with flaming red hair turning to grey and a college-football physique settling into paunch more and more every year, the big Irishman cuts an imposing figure against the cozy ruffled curtains and quaint colonial furniture of his bungalow.

The man has been the Quintet's only conduit to the government for practically two years now, perhaps one of the only people in the world trusted implicitly by the five operatives.

"Jesus, Sean, you know what time it is?" The voice on the other end of line belongs to Captain John Massamore, former head of the U.S. Navy Chaplain Corps, now retired and living outside of Detroit. An old college chum of Silverback's, Massamore is one of only about a dozen people who know where Silverback currently resides. "Is this business or personal?"

"Sorry, Johnny, I got something going on, needs a delicate touch."

"I'm listening."

"Without going down a rabbit hole with all the details, just suffice to say I need somebody from the clergy, somebody who can keep their mouth shut, either active military or somebody with military experience. Need them to do a little reconnaissance for me over the next twenty-four hours. I know it's short notice, and it might lead nowhere, but I gotta try. Does that make any sense?"

"Sean, you never make any sense, that's why I love you."

"Back at ya, brother. So here's the thing. And I know it sounds like the beginning of a dirty joke, but I promise it's not. There are these two priests, each an American on a mission overseas, that have been listed as missing persons by Interpol for several weeks. Now I have reason to believe they're in my neck of the woods."

"Missouri?"

"That's right. I'm thinking they gotta be within a hundred-mile radius by now. Need to check hotels, hostels, and all rectory residences in the area. They might be arriving tomorrow, possibly through Lambert International. It's all a guessing game at this point."

"What's the hurry, and why all the cloak-and-dagger? You suspect these two of something?"

"I don't know, Johnny. Could be somebody posing as them, could be anything. They're due here for a conference on Friday. I just want to make sure they are who they say they are."

"You sound nervous, Sean."

"You know me, Johnny, I'm always nervous. But something doesn't smell right to me about this whole thing. We also had one of our folks up and vanish for a time, then just materialize. Due diligence is all I'm after. You think you can give me a hand with this?"

"Tell you what. I know a bloodhound, we were in the 101st together, Airborne, a million years ago, used to work with one of my chaplains. I can put them both together on it. It's so last-minute, though, it's gonna be expensive."

"That's fantastic, Johnny. Really. I appreciate it. Whatever it ends up costing, send me the—"

All at once, Silverback freezes in midsentence, gripping the secure cell phone tighter, hearing a telltale beep in his ear, which he recognizes instantly as an alert telling him an encrypted call is coming in from the DIA. "Gotta bounce, Johnny, call me if you need anything else." Silverback thumbs the END button, cutting off the original call, and then thumbs the TALK button on the encrypted line. "This is Silverback," he says, and then he hears the buzz of an automated voice.

"Pin number, please."

Silverback recites the six-digit pin that he long ago committed to memory.

The line clicks, and the voice of the assistant to the director of tactical operations says, "Sean, it's George Dunmore. Got a redball situation up in Chicago. Delicate as hell and active as we speak. Mayor's office wants it handled under the radar. I'm thinking it's crying out for your ghost unit to tackle for us."

"I'm listening, George, go ahead."

2.

That night, sixty-three miles south of the Cloister, in a small town not much more than a truck stop, a few mom-and-pop businesses, and a trailer park along Highway 61, Boo lies sleepless and unnerved on a moldering bed in a dilapidated roadside motel room. Since she placed her fateful call to Spur two weeks earlier, essentially handing in her pink slip, her world has come undone.

The dead are trying to tell Boo something that she doesn't want to know. Every cemetery she passes calls out to her. Every dead relative going back multiple generations has tried to warn her. She's not a big drinker, but she's been numbing herself, ignoring the signs and portents, pretending that she's nothing special, and she has nothing to offer, and it will all pass if she can just stop the voices and apparitions and omens.

The evidence of her crusade to hide from her fate sits all around the room now: a brown paper sack with three empty pints of vodka in it, a half-full bottle of cheap merlot on the floor next to the bed, a vial of over-the-counter sleeping pills lying on its side next to the wine. The TV lies facedown on the floor, unplugged, powerless. The clock radio next to the bed is covered in a pillowcase. Even the electrical outlets are stuffed with paper from the wastebasket. Hack has been relentless in his attempts to communicate with her through the grid, to reconcile, to find her and reunite. He sounds a bit unhinged to her, riddled with guilt, lonely, desperate, maybe even suicidal. But at the moment, Boo is in no shape to do anything but lie on the slumped, shopworn bed in her tawdry motel room and moan.

That night, after drinking the rest of the merlot and taking two more Unisom tablets, she eventually manages to drift off despite the constant knocking and creaking noises and muffled voices inside the walls of the room as the restless spirits of the dead continue to try and reach out to her and deliver their warning.

In a half-dream, half-trance state, she finds herself wandering a barren, featureless, scourged wasteland. The sky is low and parched, and as grey as ash, and the ground is cracked and scarred, a salt flat that extends forever in every direction. At first Boo wonders if this is hell. But deep down she knows the truth. She knows exactly what this is.

Purgatory.

Is this her destiny, her comeuppance for making a deal with the Devil? Did she accidentally kill herself in that squalid motel room by drinking herself to death or taking too many sleeping pills? Is this how she'll spend the rest of eternity, wandering in limbo forever and ever? She abruptly stops. She sees something in the far distance—an object sitting on the horizon line, too far to make out, a dark shape against the ashen landscape.

She starts toward it, and as she draws closer she begins to recognize the shape. A needle of fear pierces her. The closer she gets to the thing, the more certain she is that the object means something important. She comes to within fifty feet of it and freezes in abject horror. Her heart hammering in her chest, her throat closing up with terror, she can barely force herself to creep closer to the thing. At last she stands over it and looks inside it.

Her scream is silent and as powerful as a sudden earthquake.

She comes out of the trance, awakening with a start, drenched in sweat.

3.

Back at the Cloister, in the wee hours of that night, Sister Lucy June, one of the organization's longest-term residents and closest confidantes of the Monsignor, is fully caffeinated and knocking on the door of Spur and Pin-Up's bungalow.

A heavyset, handsome woman just entering her sixth decade, she wears a long beaded Mexican serape over her denim shirt, embroidered skirt, and worn-out cowboy boots, all of which completes the picture of yet another refugee from the 1800s inhabiting the Cloister. The gunslinger effect is not lost on her colleagues in ecclesiastical circles. Sister Lucy June has presided over or assisted in countless cases of demonic possession, and has served under some of the Church's most iconic exorcists over the years in the performance of the ancient rites. She also has a lovely, gentle way with children and animals, to the extent that she has become the Cloister's go-to babysitter.

"Sorry about getting you out of bed in the middle of the night, Lucy," Spur says with a warm smile after answering the door. He already has part of his regalia on—his gauntlets around his wrists, and his Kevlar vest—and he's a strange sight in the doorway of a quaint little bungalow at this time of night.

"No worries, Tex. Duty calls. I get it." The chubby little elfin nun is the only human being other than Pin-Up that Spur allows to call him the lame and hated nickname. "Always happy to babysit whenever Mom and Dad have to go off and save the world again."

Spur opens the door wider and ushers her inside the bungalow.

The nun finds Pin-Up in the armchair by the fireplace—also

partially dressed in her regalia, her chain mail and leather, her combat boots and scabbard—busily nursing Junior. It's an odd thing to see, this badass female superhero in such a tender domestic scenario, but it's something the people of the Cloister seem to be growing accustomed to. "There she is," Pin-Up says with a grin, covering up her exposed breast with the top edge of her bustier. The baby's eyes glance up at the nun and twinkle with recognition.

"I swear that child has the oldest-soul eyes I've ever seen," the nun marvels, winking at the baby, stroking the child's tiny chin with her gnarled, chubby finger as he suckles. "Looks right into your heart."

"Gets that from his daddy," Spur boasts as he shrugs on his medieval longcoat.

"Figured I would give the little duffer a big breakfast before we go off to work," Pin-Up explains to the nun. "In the fridge there's a half dozen bottles that I expressed earlier, and there's formula in the pantry in case he goes on a binge. Diapers are in the bedroom next to the crib, and you remember how to operate the baby monitor, I'm assuming."

"Piece of cake, Pin. No worries."

"Help yourself to anything you need. Hopefully we'll be back tonight in time for dessert, you know, unless the End Times come."

Sister Lucy June lets out a yawp of laughter. "That's a good one. I got this, Pin. You two just have fun saving mankind."

"Yeah, I'm sure it'll be a blast." Pin-Up hands over the baby and then cleans herself up, hurriedly zipping and buckling her otherworldly garb.

"C'mon, wiseass," Spur says, holding the front door open. "Don't want to be late for the end of the world."

4.

Forty-one miles farther south, just before dawn, two men enter the lobby of the Pheasant Run Inn. Located just a stone's throw from the Mississippi, the inn is a fixture in the sleepy little river town of St. Mary, Missouri. The younger of the two, Chaplain Alex Jorgenson, is a balding, scrawny little man with a boyish face, presently clad in a dark coat, a clerical shirt underneath it featuring a pocket protector brimming with pens and other ministerial tools.

The older man in the leather jacket is a former Department of the Navy cop, now a member of an elite group of skip tracers and private investigators known as the Dog House. His name is Bill Fulbright, and he's a brawny little fireplug of a man with a flattop crew cut and cunning eyes. He's known for finding people in a hurry, which is exactly what he is about to do. He takes the lead as the twosome walk up to the front desk.

"Morning, ma'am," Fulbright says to the blue-haired old woman behind the counter. "Can you possibly do me a huge favor and ring the room of a Father Gordon Shamus? That's S-H-A-M-U-S."

The woman thumbs through the register, finds the room number, and prepares to dial. She pauses and looks up at Fulbright. "Uh . . . who shall I say is here to see him?"

"Officer Fulbright of the Department of the U.S. Navy, ma'am." He indicates Jorgenson. "And my buddy here is Navy Chaplain Alex Jorgenson."

The old woman dials. "Yes, uh, Father, there are two gentlemen here to see you . . . an Officer Fulton—"

"That's Fulbright, ma'am," the investigator corrects her.

The woman takes a breath. "One is a Navy officer, and the other is a chaplain." She hears a response, nods, and hangs up. "Second floor, room number 213, the stairs are next to the vending machine."

5.

The first light of dawn that morning bruises the horizon east of the Mississippi, turning the clouds into smoldering embers, igniting the runways at Scott Air Force Base with radiant sunbeams. By 6:00 A.M., the blinding rays have cut across the tarmac and hit the Air National Guard barracks windows with a blitzkrieg of magnesium-bright daylight.

Hustling across the sun-blanched runway, Silverback reaches into his breast pocket, rooting out his aviator sunglasses and putting them on as he leads Spur, Pin-Up, and Ticker across the lot outside the main hangar operated by the 932nd Airlift Wing.

"Good news is," Silverback is saying in a loud voice as they approach an idling Blackhawk helicopter, "the Chicago field office has managed to keep a lid on any media coverage . . . so far, at least . . . but time is of the essence."

The three members of the Quintet draw curious stares from the mechanics and ground crew now finishing up their third shift. A Blackhawk scrambled at this hour, on this particular tarmac—it's not something they encounter every day. Nor is the sight of three mysterious figures carrying road cases and clad in longcoats with chivalrous garb visible as the wind tosses the coattails.

"So at the moment it's just another day on the Windy City Elevated," Spur ventures, his gauntlets and medieval body armor covered by his longcoat. "At least as far as the local gentry is concerned."

"Exactly. Except we got more than wind today. It's raining to beat the band up there."

Pin-Up chimes in as the backdraft gusts from the chopper momentarily flap the tails of her raincoat up and apart, revealing her chain-mail stockings and her black wasp-waist Kevlar corset: "And they don't have a positive lock yet on which train it is? Is that what we're dealing with here?"

"Affirmative."

"Hostages?"

"That's one of the many unknowns."

"Demands?"

"Unknown."

"Inside job?"

"What do you mean?"

Pin-Up shrugs as she hurries along toward the big bird. "Somebody who works for the Transit Authority maybe? Somebody . . . works at the reserve center?"

"Unknown."

"Lone suspect or a group of hostiles?"

"Who the hell knows," Silverback says, the sun glaring off his shades. "Only one brief communication was sent to the commanding officer at the base by an encrypted email after the explosives turned up missing. This was around oh three hundred hours." Silverback hardly breaks stride as he pulls his cell phone from his pocket and thumbs the insinuating text into view on the tiny display. "'The Wrath of God will be delivered to Sodom and Gomorrah on the L. May He have mercy on all your souls.'"

"Seems odd to me," Ticker says now as they approach the aircraft, ducking down instinctively under the furious squall of the main rotors. He also has his regalia on underneath his duster—his shamanic coat of black crow feathers and panther teeth—and he has to yell now in order to be heard. "Suspect breaks into the armory at the Philip H. Sheridan Reserve Center on the west side of Chicago!?—Absconds with enough RDX to blow the top of the Willis Tower clean off!?—And yet no demands, no hostages texting their loved ones, no crazy extremist group taking credit?!"

Silverback pauses under the rotors. "And it's raining, too."

Everybody else pauses. Spur hunches down under the noise and agitated air. "Okay. So. The plan here is to find this train among about a bazillion other trains, take down this yahoo who's hijacked the thing, do it quietly, defuse the bomb if necessary, and hightail it out of there before anybody sees us? That about it?"

"That's correct," Silverback says at the top of his voice. "And don't forget to let the feds take all the credit."

Pin-Up speaks up: "A minute ago you told us the good news

was that the whole thing was still under wraps, no leaks, no media yet."

"That's right."

"What's the bad news?"

Silverback sighs. "Everything else."

Spur leans in toward Silverback's ear so he's sure that he's being heard: "If we're not back in time for the big shindig tonight, make sure things go smoothly and nobody pees in the punch bowl."

"Copy that," Silverback hollers. "Now get your asses up there and save the day."

Ticker circles around the front of the fuselage and tells the pilot that his services will not be needed for the duration.

6.

At that moment, a mere fifty-three miles to the west, two men take the stairs to the second floor of the Pheasant Run Inn slowly, deliberately, not exchanging a single word. Neither man is certain about what they should say to the priest in 213. They reach the second floor and start down a narrow corridor lined with brass sconces and a purple carpet that looks like it was installed in the Vietnam era. For Fulbright, the assignment is a nuisance—a high-priority track-down, what field agents call a sniff job, mostly keyboard work. You go find the guy, check him out, make sure he is who he says he is, and if everything looks copacetic you apologize for the inconvenience and be on your way.

They start to detect the weird odor halfway down the corridor. The smell intensifies as they pass 209, 211, and finally pause in front of 213. They look at each other. The odor reminds Fulbright of the time he was stationed in Texas, and he had to patrol the most foul-smelling part of the San Antonio River. Each day he would have to walk along the place where all the bottom-feeding catfish were dying due to toxic waste, and then washing up onto the banks and decaying in the sun.

That rotten black smell is now emanating from room 213.

Probably out of habit more than instinct, Fulbright reaches inside his jacket and unsnaps the holster strap holding his Glock. He steps forward and knocks on the door. "Father, it's Officer Bill Fulbright of the Department of the Navy, and Navy Chaplain Alex Jorgenson here. If you'd be so kind as to open the door, we'll explain why we have to bother you for just a couple minutes."

The sound of an animal—a dog, most likely, a big one—comes from behind the door, a deep buzz saw of a growl that rises and fades. Another glance between Fulbright and Jorgenson follows. Fulbright knocks again. "Father, I need to know if you have an animal in there with you."

No answer.

"Father, if you don't open up, we're going to be forced to go ahead and break down the door."

Still no answer other than thick, feral snarling noises.

"Stay behind me, Chappie," Fulbright instructs the chaplain. The investigator draws his pistol, and thumbs off the safety. Two-handing the gun, he steps back and slams the sole of his combat boot into the door, causing plaster dust to cascade.

CHAPTER ELEVEN
The Thing in Room 213

1.

Established in 1921, the Pheasant Run has good bones. The floors are solid, and the seams are tight, and the rooms have been well tended over the years. Fixtures, windows, and doors have been regularly repaired and eventually replaced. But Bill Fulbright is a tightly wound bundle of muscles and anger, and the door gives on the third kick, nearly swinging off its hinges.

The moment the weird atmosphere of that room greets the two men through the open doorway, Navy Chaplain Alex Jorgenson remembers where he learned about such smells and sounds. Descriptions of the rotten-meat odor, and that low, deep contrabass growl, are woven through every narrative of every exorcism Jorgenson ever studied in seminary. But the realization is fleeting and, quite frankly, comes too late to help matters, because an abomination of nature hangs from the ceiling across the room.

Father Gordon Shamus hangs upside down from the ceiling like an enormous hibernating bat, eyes shut, the soles of his patent leather shoes impossibly adhering to the rafter as though welded there. He looks lifeless, bloodless, his chiseled face as white as porcelain. Fulbright approaches the body cautiously, his gun pointed downward at his side, and he's gotten only about halfway across the room when the priest's upside-down face opens its eyes. For a moment, Fulbright freezes, mesmerized, as does Jorgenson, who is still standing in the doorway, covered in gooseflesh, because the priest's eyes are merely black sockets, empty craters in his skull, and yet they seem as expressive and full of lascivious hunger as the eyes of a man watching porn.

Then the priest's upside-down face grins and reveals teeth as black as pitch. Fulbright has just started moving again when a slimy forked tongue suddenly bursts from the cleric's grinning mouth.

It is the demon Snakeroot's prodigious talent—thanks to this long, slimy, flexible appendage—to rope and bind a fleeing human with the skill of a seasoned member of the rodeo. Now the tongue lashes out directly at Fulbright, who barely manages to raise his gun when the tongue lassos his neck and strangles him with the pressure of an iron vise. Fulbright's body seizes up, the Glock slipping from his frozen fingers, clattering to the floor.

A loss of consciousness takes Fulbright down next to the fallen weapon.

Near the doorway, with trembling hands, Chaplain Jorgenson fumbles for his vial of holy water, which is caught in his pocket protector. He stammers and babbles the preamble to the rite of exorcism—"Saint M-M-Michael the Archangel, d-defend us in b-b-b-battle"—as every fiber of his soul becomes mortified by what has been inhabiting room 213. Shivering with terror, the chaplain can barely force himself to look at the noose-like tongue drawing back from Fulbright's purple ligature-scarred neck, retreating back into the upside-down mouth of the Honorable Father Gordon L. Shamus.

Jorgenson drops the vial of holy water, the blessed liquid splattering across the floor, the water sputtering and steaming as though being fried on a skillet. The chaplain digs in his pocket for his crucifix, still stuttering: "P-p-protect us now against the w-w-w-wickedness of the D-d-devil so that we m-m-m-m-may—!" But it's all for naught as the tongue bullwhips toward him, strikes his throat, and cuts off his words.

He collapses to the floor, shuddering in the throes of cardiac arrest.

He dies within seconds.

Bill Fulbright is still breathing . . . barely . . . just barely.

2.

Snakeroot, the dark reptilian god, the superior demon from hell's core, the wisecracking lizard king, the thing that goes bump-bump-bump in the night, retracts his oily black tongue from the neck of the ridiculous young holy roller, and fixes his sights on the cop lying in a heap across the floor, still clinging to life.

The process of possessing a human soul can be slow and tedious. The prelude can last for weeks, and involve the triggering of nightmares; the kindling of fear and repulsion of sacred things such as Bibles and churches; the causing of spontaneous abilities to speak in dead languages and to know things the victim could never ordinarily know; to psychically move objects; and on and on, ad nauseam. But a superior demon can bypass all the boring foreplay. The superior demon can instantly inhabit a human soul through touch, through sexual penetration, or through some sort of injury.

The fact is that Snakeroot has always preferred a combination of the three.

The oily black tongue slithers and shimmies across the floor with a flourish, forcing its way into the slackened mouth of the dying cop, and then plunging down the man's gorge. No conscious human observer is present that night to see the miraculous transformation as the remainder of Snakeroot's scaly, grey, reptilian mass is vomited out of the body of Father Gordon Shamus, who is left hanging upside down from the ceiling like the empty husk of a chrysalis, his human soul muted and catatonic within the disgusting skin-sack of his hulking body.

The rest of Snakeroot invades Fulbright's body through the man's insensate mouth and throat.

Fulbright's eyes suddenly flicker open, and his body spasms and jerks into a sitting position. His head pivots and he sees his cell phone on the floor a few feet away, the device having fallen from his jacket during the commotion in the room. He rises robotically and walks over to the phone, then snatches it up and dials a number that Snakeroot retrieves from the man's memory.

As the call connects to a secure number with a Michigan area code, Snakeroot clears his throat and practices a few words in the voice of Officer Bill Fulbright.

3.

"Goddamn son of a bitch," grumbles Captain John Massamore, awakened out of a deep sleep by the chirping of his cell phone. He reaches over to his bedside table and sees that the caller is Bill Fulbright. He thumps the green ACCEPT icon and gruffly answers: "Talk to me, Bill, what's the situation? Did you find the guy?"

There's an awkward pause on the other end of the line. "Yes, we found the . . . guy."

Massamore blinks. "You okay, Bill? You sound weird. What, are you hungover?"

"No, I am not hungover. I am just calling to tell you that we found the priest, and everything looks good. He is who he says he is."

"That's great, Bill. Well done." Right then, Massamore notices that, on his bedside table, next to his medicine bottles and water glass, his iPad is displaying the score from the previous night's game between Massamore's beloved Detroit Tigers and the Los Angeles Angels, the fifth straight loss for the Tigers. "Damn them to the burning pits of hell!"

After a brief pause, the voice on the other end says, "May I ask who it is you would like damned to the burning pits of hell? That can certainly be arranged."

"Haha, Bill, that's a good one, sorry, it's just these damn Tigers, once again they're looking like a bunch of candy-ass amateurs."

"Oh."

"Anyway, I'll let my associate know all is well, and let's meet on Monday for a debriefing."

"Boss, if it is okay with you, I would like to tail the priest to the Cloister, just to make sure he is on the level and nothing goes awry."

Another pause. "How much is that going to cost me, Bill?"

"Nothing. I will do it as part of our original arrangement. I just want to make sure everyone there is safe." There is the slightest pause. "Because you cannot be too careful nowadays."

4.

By seven that morning, the Cloister bustles with activity. Outside the main entrance, valets prepare to welcome dignitaries. Members of the kitchen staff busy themselves with prep work. Groundskeepers make last-minute checks of the walkways and common areas, sweeping, hosing, leaf blowing, and primping.

Like a whirling dervish, Father Manny flits from checkpoint to checkpoint, building to building, vestibule to vestibule, checking and double-checking directional signage, orientation materials, and miscellaneous amenities. Father Joshua harbors concerns about Father Manny's health.

"He's as pale as a ghost," the young priest confides to the Monsignor that morning around the coffee service in the front room of the rectory.

"He marches to the beat of his own drum, that's for sure." The bearded sage is still in his sweatpants, down jacket, and high-tops after an early-morning jog, and is now devouring a cheese Danish. "He's a sturdy old soul, though."

"I don't know," Joshua frets. "I'm seeing twitches and shaking that I've never seen before."

"Twitches and shaking?"

Father Josh nods, his boyish face full of troubling emotions. "Like palsy or something."

"Perhaps I should see to it that we schedule a checkup for him after the conference."

"I don't want to be a worrywart."

"No, listen. Father, you are a caring soul concerned about a friend."

"Thank you, Monsignor. I just . . . I think something is wrong."

"Healthwise, you mean."

Joshua sighs. "More than that. I don't want to be an alarmist, or speak out of school."

"What is it? There's something else bothering you. Tell me."

"This morning, early, before sunrise, I went to his quarters to make sure he was up, and see if I could get anything for him. I knew it was the big day and all. I was about to knock when I stopped myself. Monsignor, I heard him crying."

"Crying?"

"Sobbing. Mumbling to himself. Moaning and mumbling."

The Monsignor puts down his pastry. "Maybe a dream he was having? The man does dream a lot. Maybe another prophetic dream?"

Joshua swallows hard. "I don't know, I don't think so, Monsignor. I heard him say, 'Please stop, please, I beg you!' And then there was this pause, and I heard his rapid breathing. I know I should have knocked again, I should have called somebody, should have fetched the paramedic, but I . . . I just . . . stood there on that front porch, listening, sort of paralyzed." The young priest pauses for a moment, glancing over his shoulder to make sure they're alone, and nobody is eavesdropping. "I heard his voice change, Monsignor."

"Change? How do you mean?"

"I heard his voice go low, deep, and . . . I guess maybe 'gravelly' is the word? And I heard his sobbing turn to laughter. Monsignor, it was the worst sound I've ever heard. If it was a dream, it must have been a terrific nightmare, because this was the laughter of madness. No, that's . . . not exactly it." He broods for a moment. "Monsignor, I was teased unmercifully as a kid. I don't know if I ever mentioned that. Kids can be very cruel. If it wasn't my looks or my clothes, or my cheap tennis shoes, it was my bad haircut that my mom gave me every school year."

"Sounds familiar," the Monsignor says, thoughtfully devouring the last of his Danish. "With me it was these awful earmuffs my mother made me wear at the first sign of a chill."

"With me it was constant. I was always getting picked on, bullied, laughed at. But see, Monsignor, the thing is, that was the exact tone of this laughter coming from behind Father Manny's door."

The older man pensively pulls on his iron-white beard as he thinks it over.

In his dark suit coat, clerical collar, braided ponytail, and derby hat, the Monsignor—also known as the Right Reverend Charles David McAllister—looks like a transplant from another century. The telltale bulge under his coat, just above his left hip, is caused by a silver-plated .357 Magnum revolver, its grip engraved with a cross. He finally gives the young priest a pat on the shoulder and says, "I'll go see him later this morning before all the festivities start."

5.

By 11:30 CDT that morning, up in northern Illinois, the rains have intensified.

A cold front has rolled in from the north, crashing into a warm front from the southeast, causing tornadoes in Indiana and torrential rains across the Great Lakes. The storms have slowed the Blackhawk's progress, and now Ticker finds himself flying a high circle around the edges of the Chicago metro area, the rain practically horizontal as it whips across the aircraft's windshield and buffets the chopper's fuselage. The day has turned as dark as night. Thunder booms overhead. Lightning sutures the wall of black rain with it luminous needlepoint. The aircraft shudders.

"Delta Quebec, niner-niner-seven, on approach," Ticker says into his neck mike, radioing the tactical unit on the ground. "Coordinates: forty-one-point-eight-November, eighty-seven-point-six-Whiskey. Over."

The chopper lurches and thumps over bumpy air as the voice in Ticker's ear gives him the coordinates of the best part of the storm to penetrate in order to land somewhere near the Loop, where the elevated train circles the city's business district. "Delta Quebec," the voice sputters and crackles. "You're thirty-five miles south of Gardner Field—[static]—there's a pad down there on the—[static]—clear to land if you need to get out of the—[static]."

Ticker makes a slight correction to their course, the Blackhawk banking in the storm, nearly slamming Spur into the gangway hatch in the rear. In an effort to keep the aircraft steady, Ticker has bound his right hand to the stick with a bungee cord, and the constraint has begun to send stabbing pains up his arm. He gazes down through the glass turret embedded in the cabin floor. Several thousand feet below the Blackhawk's belly, veiled under the churning sea of storm clouds, the faint ghosts of suburban street grids blur past them. Ticker says into his mike, "Copy that, Tac Com, will advise. Stand by."

Ticker shoots a glance across the cockpit at Pin-Up, who sits strapped into the navigator's seat, her muscles coiled and taut from the turbulent journey northward. She has her iPad in her lap and is thumbing secure texts to Silverback's contact within the bureau. She looks up at Ticker and shakes her head. "According to Ellison, they don't have anything yet. Nothing out of the ordinary on the L platforms, nothing going on in the subway, no terrorist demands, just a shitload of trains running back and forth as rush hour sneaks up on us, one of the trains with a madman and a boatload of—Hold on, wait!—Wait a second!"

Pin-Up taps the Bluetooth in her ear. "It's Silverback again on the secure line." Pin-Up listens. "Okay, got it." She glances over her shoulder at Spur, who's now strapped into a jump seat in the back.

Pin-Up's voice goes cold all of a sudden, calm, like the voice of an assassin. "They figured out which train it is."

6.

The Monsignor makes it over to the south rectory by noon. He enters through the main entrance, crosses the dusty vestibule with its tattered armchairs, and outdated *Catholic Digest* magazines on stained secondhand coffee tables. He says hello to Helen, the desk clerk.

"And a blessed morning to you, Monsignor," says the slender, greying nun with the Coke-bottle glasses and a perpetually revolving line of garish sweaters with kittens embroidered on them.

The Monsignor strides to the end of the hallway, and knocks on Father Manny's door. No answer. He knocks a second time, and again gets no response. He puts his ear to the door. Nothing but drips of water ringing off a stainless-steel sink can be heard.

"Emmanuel the Tender, it's Charlie," the Monsignor calls out. "You're needed for a cleanup in aisle six-sixty-six." Over the years the two priests have jokingly spoken in code with each other. "Cleanup in aisle six-sixty-six" is a play on the Satanic number 666, and sometimes refers to an exorcism, but more commonly some intractable problem that's going to take a while to fix.

Still no reply comes from the small apartment. The Monsignor considers trying again later but decides to try the doorknob. No luck. The door is locked. "Father Manny, you in there?"

Nothing. With a sigh, the Monsignor turns and walks away. He gets halfway down the hall when he hears a strange and unexpected noise coming from behind him—the squeak of door hinges. He whirls around. He sees Father Manny's door rapidly opening on its own power.

7.

Priests who have had many battles with the dark forces in the universe experience a sort of innate, involuntary reaction to demonic activity. Like dogs hearing an ultrasonic whistle, the exorcist will feel a prickling of the scalp, gooseflesh, and hairs standing up on the arms and neck when encountering supernatural evil. One renowned exorcist confessed once that he feels his testicles rise up into his groin when he comes across a demonic infestation.

The Monsignor certainly has had more than his requisite ten thousand hours of fighting the good fight against Satan, but there are mitigating factors now in his life that can distract him from his war footing. He often jokes that priests who can exorcise do . . . and those who can't get desk jobs in the clergy house. After his decades of being an administrator at the Cloister, his "Spidey sense" when it comes to identifying the work of demons has been dulled and buffered.

All of which is why, at that moment, in that deserted rectory corridor, the Monsignor's concern for the safety and well-being of his friend gets the better of him. He can hear a rhythmic creaking noise as he slowly walks back to Father Emmanuel's door.

Inside the room, the old priest is sitting on a bentwood rocker in a tidy little parlor with Early American furniture and doilies on the arms of the wing-back sofa. On the walls are old, framed, hand-tinted pictures of Christ. Father Manny's back is turned to the door, and he's rocking, and making that creeeeeeak-creeeeeeeak-creeeeeeeak noise, as the Monsignor cautiously enters.

It doesn't occur to the Monsignor to pull his crucifix out. Nor does it strike him as an appropriate moment to draw his

.357 Magnum. But as he approaches the old priest in the rocking chair, he sees that the back of Father Manny's head is shaking ever so slightly, as though it were caught in a machine or riding in a vehicle going far too fast for conditions. His flesh is the color of bread dough, the veins in his neck as dark as ink blots.

The Monsignor gently lays a hand on Father Manny's shoulder.

In one sudden and abrupt movement that knocks over the rocker, the old priest springs to his feet, spins around, pulls the larger man into an embrace, and plants a kiss on the Monsignor's lips. The larger man struggles. Something cold and slimy slithers down the Monsignor's gullet, spreading through him with the virulent speed of radiation poisoning.

CHAPTER TWELVE
Time Running Out

1.

For over a century now, the Chicago Transit Authority's rail system has been constantly repaired, renovated, retrofitted, and rendered larger and larger with each passing decade. Nicknamed the "L" due to the fact that much of it is elevated twenty-five feet above ground level on scabrous iron girders and stanchions, it encompasses over a hundred miles of ancient rails snaking through canyons of skyscrapers and neighborhoods like a main circuit cable keeping the city in motion. Over three hundred thousand impatient Chicagoans ride the L every day, getting on and off at 150 stations in a 250-square-mile crucible of glass, steel, concrete, and carbon monoxide.

The command and control center for the CTA operates out of a secret location on Racine Avenue in the bowels of a nondescript building that looks more like a huge, innocuous dentist's office than the heart of a major American city's transportation system. Inside this heavily guarded edifice, the main control room bustles 24–7 amid a beehive of CRT screens, virtual maps of train and bus icons that are constantly in motion, and a battalion of overcaffeinated, overworked tech-heads in shirtsleeves and pantsuits pecking away at keyboards, executing track switches, lane closures, and emergency announcements.

"Harriet, pipe that visual into the big guy's office, please, right now," Larry Steagall, the day-shift manager, says to one of his terminal operators. The dowdy, middle-aged woman at the keyboard taps out the commands, unaware that the rogue train that she discovered a mere thirty minutes ago approaching the Loop from the west is laden with death and destruction.

Steagall tears a spreadsheet from her printer and pats her on the shoulder. "And take the visual off the big wall, will you, please? And keep this to yourself for the time being."

The keyboard operator vanquishes the visual and gives Steagall a nervous nod as he turns and hurries across the control center to the corner office. He knocks on the door marked DIRECTOR OF OPERATIONS, and a booming voice says, "It's open!"

"Train number 3247's in the Loop now," Steagall announces as he enters the room, shutting the door behind him. Two men already occupy the room.

Carl Bressler, the CTA's head honcho, is a heavyset man with a double chin and a comb-over sitting behind a cluttered desk. The armpits of his short-sleeved dress shirt are dark with flop sweat. "One second," he says, thumbing an icon on his Android. "Sir, I'm putting you on speaker so you can hear this from the horse's mouth."

Ticker's voice crackles out of the black box on the desk, the background clamor of the Blackhawk and the storm sounding like Niagara Falls. "Go ahead."

The other man in the room, Special Agent Scott Ellison of the local field office, stands in the corner keeping tabs. He's well dressed and groomed, his square-jawed face that of an engineering professor or an accountant. His voice is deep and sonorous. "To whom are we talking?"

Ticker's voice cuts through the ambient roar: "You got three members of Sean McDermott's unit on approach in a Sikorsky Blackhawk, about thirty miles south of the city. Talk to me. Can you give us the train's twenty?"

Steagall speaks up. "It's in the heart of the city now. Fact is, it's going in circles, making no stops, just circling the Loop."

A noisy pause ensues, the thrumming of thunder hissing from the speaker.

Aboard the Blackhawk, in the pandemonium of the storm—the lightning, the savage gusts of rain strafing the windshield, the drumbeat of the rotors—Spur holds on tight to a ceiling beam and leans forward. He has to yell to be heard. "Get the coordinates or a street address for the GPS . . . where they estimate the train will be in . . . what? What's our ETA?"

Ticker looks at the console. "Little less than ten minutes."

"Ask them to give us a guess as to where the train will be then. Just ballpark it for us."

Ticker nods and asks the question.

It takes Larry Steagall less than ten seconds to calculate the L station that the train will be passing in ten minutes at its present rate of speed.

"Copy that," Ticker says. "Keep the frequency open. We'll get back to you when there's something to report." He switches off the radio, turns to Pin-Up, and says, "Punch in the Harold Washington Library station, State Street and Van Buren."

She does so as the sea of rooftops two thousand feet beneath them becomes faintly visible through the dense, shifting, swirling curtains of rain. The tops of tall buildings loom and blur past them. Ticker pushes the stick forward and the aircraft descends into the Chicago Loop. A necklace of headlights becomes visible down below, a traffic jam on the Eisenhower Freeway. Ticker cuts back further on the throttle, and threads the needle down between the spires of two highrises.

Meantime, Spur and Pin-Up have unbuckled. They open a road case and pull out a pair of TEC-9 machine pistols, a tool kit, extra clips, coils of mountain-climbing rope, scabbards, friction gloves, broadswords blessed in holy water, zip ties, carabiners, and tension clamps. They switch their dusters over to rain gear, and quickly climb into their harnesses.

By this point Ticker has banked the Blackhawk between two smaller buildings. Myriad windows pulse past them, glassine ghosts in the storm, almost close enough to reach out and touch.

"So much for the media blackout," Ticker wisecracks into his two-way.

Neither Spur nor Pin-Up offers a response; they're too busy

securing their harnesses. Ticker eases the throttle back further and carefully flies the bird along the route cut between buildings by the famous State Street thoroughfare.

"Got a visual on the station roof," he announces, tamping back the throttle, taking the aircraft down to four hundred feet . . . three hundred . . . two hundred . . . one hundred and fifty . . . and finally at one hundred feet he hovers the aircraft, the big bird pitching and yawing in the furious winds.

Spur unlatches the gangway door and attaches the end of each rope coil to the chopper's steel beams. In his earpiece, he hears Ticker say, "And here comes the disaster express."

Spur glances out the rear canopy and, behind black sheets of rain, gets a glimpse of Pink Line train number 3247 rumbling toward the Harold Washington Library L platform, looming closer and closer, sparks jumping off the wheels as it rattles along. The train consists of three rectangular cars like glorified shipping containers with huge windows lining the sides. In the gloomy light of the storm it's impossible for Spur to see how many—if any—passengers are on the train.

"You set?" Spur says to Pin-Up through the two-way, glancing at her across the gangway as she clips the harness around her midsection and straps the satchel and machine pistol tight over her shoulder.

Spur secures a backpack full of gear over his broad shoulders, tightening the buckles, unaware that his pulse has barely risen above its resting rate of sixty beats per minute as he slides the gangway doors open. Rain and wind erupt in his face, the wet slipstream whirling through the Blackhawk as it hovers over the roof of the L platform and lists to the side slightly, the g-forces tugging Spur toward the open gangway.

"Gonna wait for the train to come out the other side of the platform," Spur says into his mike.

"Copy that," Pin-Up's voice crackles.

Down below, in the squalls of rain, train number 3247 hurtles into the station.

"On three," Spur says, his gaze now locked on the platform's rooftop shelter. The lead car suddenly bursts out the north side.

"Three, two . . . *one!*"

They jump in tandem, the cables singing high opera as they plummet. The rain engulfs them. Thunder booms as they plunge toward the moving train, controlling their descent rate with their tension clamps. The train cars zoom northward.

Spur lands hard on the rear car, tumbling across wet metal, sliding on his belly, closely followed by Pin-Up, who lands on her shoulder, rolls, and slides. Spur grabs her arm just as she careens off the back end of the rear car.

She dangles there for a moment, enveloped in rain, hanging from the umbilical, sparks jumping off the third rail all around her, her big combat boots slamming into the rear window. She tries to kick the glass in, the automated wiper blade continuing to swing back and forth, the window seemingly impervious to her blows.

Pin-Up uses her bootheel, and the glass gives on the third blow.

The window implodes, and both Pin-Up and Spur swing through the jagged opening and into the car.

2.

The atmosphere inside the speeding, vibrating train smells of death-rot and decay. On the floor, crunching in the broken crumbs of glass, Spur and Pin-Up detach their tethers, and the ropes whip back out the open window and into the storm. The throbbing, percussive din of the Blackhawk following the train can be heard above the metallic shriek of the steel wheels.

The two warriors climb to their feet, getting their bearings in the swaying, shuddering train, unsnapping their harnesses and dropping the rigs to the deck. Pin-Up's satchel still clings to her back, strapped tight. They draw their TEC-9 pistols, attach silencers, thumb the safeties off, and gaze down the full length of the car's narrow interior.

The car appears to be empty. The contour benches along each side of the cabin are unoccupied. The report from the FBI stated that the train had been commandeered while in service at some point in the wee hours, stolen by persons unknown. At that time of night there would be very few riders, maybe some street people, homeless individuals, second-shift workers, but at the moment the train looks deserted as it keens noisily through the storm.

Cautiously they move single file, Spur in the lead, down the aisle toward the forward door leading into the next car. Without warning a figure darts out from behind a seat back.

The ragged homeless man is dressed in tatters, his facial features deformed, contorted, his eyes pure white orbs in his skull. Clearly in the grip of some sort of demonic influence, he pounces on Pin-Up, sending her reeling backward, stumbling over her own feet.

She lands on the small of her back, the machine pistol slipping out of her hand and skating across the floor, hitting the wall and going off, sending a slug into the opposite wall, puckering the metal near the exit doors. Meanwhile the attacker tries to bite Pin-Up's face off, but she gets her hands around his scrawny neck, and knees him in the groin. The pain registers in the attacker's eyes, and he's convulsing, rearing back, when all at once a boot smashes into his skull.

The attacker is thrown sideways off Pin-Up. He slams into the side window, his face smashing into the glass, sending hairline fractures through the pane. Spur moves in to finish him off, but something happens then that causes Spur to balk, freezing in his tracks, staring in awe with his fist already clenched and poised to deliver a knockout punch.

The homeless man's head rotates a hundred and eighty degrees, and that horrible face looks directly at Spur with a toothy grin. The voice that comes out of it is the Devil's voice. "Your time's running out," the voice says, and that haggard face laughs in Spur's face with inhuman malice. "Tick-tick-tick!" The voice giggles. "Tick-tick-tick-tick-tick-tick-tick!"

"No worries, old hoss, we got plenty of time," Spur says with casual disgust, and delivers a battering ram of a punch to the possessed man's jaw, the uppercut spinning the attacker into a steel support beam. The impact knocks the homeless man unconscious, his body going limp as it slides down the pillar and sprawls to the floor.

Spur goes over to Pin-Up, who's still brushing herself off, shaking off the momentary shock. She picks up her gun.

In Spur's earpiece, Ticker's voice crackles: "Was that a shot fired? You two good?"

"Affirmative, we're good."

Pin-Up shrugs off her raincoat, revealing the dark wonders of her regalia, her chain mail and leather. She checks her scabbard. "That voice coming out of that dude . . . sound familiar?"

"You bet it did. Had a feeling Ol' Diablo was behind this somehow."

"Correct me if I'm wrong, but we need to get to the lead car, find out who's behind the wheel."

"Roger that," Spur says. "I'll take point, you stay close, and stay frosty in case we meet up with any more nasty-ass commuters."

"Copy that, cowboy. After you."

They make their way through the forward door, into the wet wind and sparks, then across the catwalk, plunging into the middle car. The overhead lights flicker wildly as thunder shakes the heavens. The air reeks of charred flesh and decaying meat.

They get a third of the way down the aisle when Spur freezes and shoots his hand up. Pin-Up comes to a sudden halt.

Directly in front of them, a lanky figure in nineteenth-century garb, who may or may not be an apparition, has materialized, blocking the door to the lead car. He is at least seven feet tall, and with his frayed waistcoat, spats, and bowler hat, he would bring to mind a villain in a Charles Dickens story if it weren't for the twin ram horns spiraling out from under his hat, or those unearthly eyes, which are completely black, with tiny crimson embers of evil burning in their cores.

Or so he appears to Spur.

3.

Pin-Up sees a different figure standing before them at the far end of that train car. Her version is a tattered, shopworn, scorched revenant of a B-movie Lucifer, a sort of sleazy, nightmare carnival attraction clad in an ancient cinnamon-colored silk suit with tiny horns protruding from his onyx, pomaded, slicked-back hair. She doesn't flinch. She doesn't back down. In fact, both she *and* Spur square their shoulders and face this Beast from the netherworld with almost involuntary fortitude, like two gunslingers with nothing left to lose. And it's no surprise to either of them that the Devil can read their minds.

"Oh, my foolish, foolish signatories," the creature says to them now. "You have no idea how much you have to lose." Then the sepulchral voice lowers an octave and taunts them in barely a whisper. "Tick, tick, tick, tick, tick, tick, tick, tick—"

"Cute, very cute," Pin-Up says, taking a step closer. She and Spur now stand side by side less than ten feet from the Devil. Pin-Up can smell the char, the ember smoke, the dusty ancient brimstone in the tight quarters of the swaying, rattling, vibrating train car as it circumnavigates the inner city. "You're just so adorable, Lou, as always."

The Devil's smile is rancid, lascivious, filled with malice. "Do you hear it? Tick-tock, tick-tock, tick-tock . . . that beautiful music . . . the sound of your time running out?"

Right then, Pin-Up hears the crackle of Ticker's voice in her ear. "Should I stop the clock? Please advise. Freeze time now?"

Spur murmurs into his two-way: "Negative, no, negative, we'll handle this. Stand by."

Then Pin-Up and Spur each take another step toward the Great Adversary, raising their guns, lining up the front sights on Satan's grotesque face. "You want to hear another beautiful sound?" Pin-Up asks, and she jacks the cocking lever on the TEC-9.

The Devil shrugs dramatically, playing the game to the hilt. "You would kill me in a heartbeat, I'm well aware of that, but you would only be killing the messenger. When all I'm attempting to do is warn you of the dangers facing your mutant baby."

"DON'T YOU FUCKING DARE SPEAK OF OUR CHILD!!" Spur's booming cry pierces the din of the storm and the steel wheels and the third rail zapping and sparking beneath the undercarriage, making even Pin-Up jerk slightly with a start. Then Spur's voice cools, lowers an octave, and becomes cobra-calm. "Not with that disgusting, filthy, rotten thing you call a mouth will you ever utter another word about our child."

The storm-ravaged city blurs past the windows as Pin-Up realizes that Spur's superpower has begun to kick in. In its early stages it can be subtle and inchoate, but it's clear to Pin-Up now that Spur has begun to reflect the horrifying bloodthirsty hate that radiates off the Devil *back at the Devil . . .*

. . . as the train suddenly thumps over a gap in the third rail, and the overhead lights flicker off for a moment, plunging the car into grey darkness.

A second later, the light returns, and the Devil's face has changed. His grin has enlarged, ratcheting his jaws apart into a gruesome deformity, revealing rows and rows and rows of piranha-sharp teeth. His voice now is barely a voice. It has the dark overtones of the lowest string of a piano being plucked. "The ticking of a time bomb is a poignant metaphor, though. Don't you think? For what will become of you and your—"

"Awwww, come on, you can do better than that," Spur interrupts. "These cheap theatrics, man . . . they're beneath you . . . and also sort of disappointing, if you want to know the truth." Spur takes one last step toward the Prince of Darkness, drawing close enough now to press the muzzle of the TEC-9 machine pistol against the Devil's forehead. "C'mon, man, you're supposed to be hell's head honcho, gimme something to work with." Spur's face changes now, mirroring all the Devil's ugly malevolence. His flesh curdles, his eyes becoming luminous yellow pilot lights as he snaps the lever back on his pistol. "I'm beginning to think we got a situation here where the lady doth protest too much. What do you think, Pin?"

"Copy that, cowboy," Pin-Up says, taking a step forward, and pressing the muzzle of *her* TEC-9 against the *other* side of the Devil's forehead. "A bunch of fucking sound and fury signifying shit." She drills her gaze into the Devil's black, lupine eyes. "I believe Lou here has forgotten one crucial fact. He can't hurt us. He *created* us." She spits the word at him. "In *perpe-TU-ity.*"

The Devil laughs then . . . and his laughter rises above the noise of the L and the rain and the throbbing of the Blackhawk in the sky . . . laughter from the grave, glacially cold, as cruel as death itself. He tosses his head back and laughs and laughs and can barely get the words out. ". . . Tick-tock . . . the mouse runs up the clock. . . ." He chortles and guffaws and convulses with uncontrollable mirth at the barrels pressing in from either side. ". . . Better go catch it . . . time's running out . . . oh . . . oh . . . where did it go . . . ?"

"Fuck this," Spur says, and squeezes off a single point-blank blast into the Devil's skull at the exact moment the train hits another gap in the rail, and the lights go off.

In the momentary darkness, Pin-Up fires off five rounds into Satan's head. In each brilliant flare of silver light from the muzzle blasts, like the flash frames of a nickelodeon, a different version of the Devil flickers for a scintilla of a second: BOOM!— The demonic, decomposed Asian demon called the mogwai. BOOM!—The fire-breathing, three-headed djakata of African folklore. BOOM!—The skeletal, emaciated dybbuk of Judaic mythology. BOOM!—The seven-headed dragon-beast from Revelation. BOOM!—The oily, black humanoid snake from the Garden of Eden.

The overhead lights return, and both Pin-Up and Spur flinch as though slapped.

The Devil has vanished. No trace of him ever being there remains. The odor of death is gone. The heavy weight in the air has lifted, and the only evidence of what just happened consists of five bullet holes in the forward wall, and the stench of cordite from the gunfire.

Pin-Up looks down at her satchel, which has come loose in all the excitement and now lies on the floor at her feet. She remembers the defusing gear she brought along.

She looks up Spur and says, "Holy fuck, the *bomb!*"

4.

Inside the small operator's booth, situated at the front end of the lead car, they find the corpse that will soon be identified as Staff Sergeant Brian Workman—the armory's night manager at the Philip H. Sheridan Reserve Center—lying on the floor, covered with blood, tangled in a makeshift bondage of rope and duct tape, a single, apparently self-inflicted bullet entry wound above his right temple.

His left hand still clutches a .45-caliber pistol. His right hand, even in death, even as rigor mortis begins to set in, appears to still be reaching up to the control panel to operate the train. Closer scrutiny will reveal that he apparently duct-taped his hand around the train's throttle.

Across the floor, under a tarp, Pin-Up finds the improvised explosive device. She sees the digital timer, which is taped to an igniter box, which is taped to a steel canister presumably filled with the stolen RDX, an abbreviation that stands for royal demolition explosive. Pin-Up had served for a short time as a technician with a bomb-disposal unit in Afghanistan, and had some experience with both RDX and IEDs similar to this one.

According to the countdown being displayed on the digital timer, she has less than three minutes to defuse the device before it goes off and destroys what will likely be an entire square city block. "Hand me the tool kit," she says without even looking up.

The time continues counting down: 00:02:37 . . . 00:02:36 . . . 00:02:35.

Spur hands her the tool kit, and then says into his two-way, "Tick, you read me?"

In their earpieces, Ticker's voice sizzles: "Copy, go ahead."

"Found the device, working on disabling it, which is plan A . . . plan B is we hit that bridge over the north branch of the river before the IED goes off."

Ticker's voice: "Copy that. We're on the opposite corner of the Loop at the moment."

Spur shakes his head. "Fuck me and the horse I rode in on."

Ticker: "Don't fuck the horse yet, I'm doing the calculation as we speak."

"Bad news," Pin-Up says, looking up, wiping beads of sweat from her brow. "It's a lockout. I can't get to the wires."

Ticker's voice in their earpieces: "Gonna be a close shave at this speed."

"How close?"

After a beat: "Down to the quick, Spur. I don't know."

The digital display on the device says 00:01:53 . . . 00:01:52 . . . 00:01:51.

Pin-Up rises to her feet and chimes in: "If we cut the car loose, can the bird lift it? Maybe haul it into the lake?"

"Negative. Sorry. Too much weight."

Outside the windows, other train cars zoom past them in the opposite direction. Down below, at street level, headlights are backing up on State Street in the rain as rush hour builds.

Ticker's voice. "Skipper, is it time to press the pause button?"

"Negative, absolutely not," Spur says into the mike. "I don't want you risking your butt climbing down here. Don't worry about it. I'm gonna just throw the dad-burn thing in the river . . . if we can get there in time, that is."

A splash of static fills the earpiece, and then Ticker's voice returns. "Get ready to heave that mother because I got a visual on the bridge. It's just up ahead around the bend."

"ETA?"

"At the rate you're going I'd say under a minute."

"Pin, what's the timer down to?"

Pin-Up's voice crackling over the air: "A minute and change, cowboy. If you're going to do something, better do it now."

CHAPTER THIRTEEN
The Last Supper

1.

Carefully lifting the device off the floor requires more time than Spur would have guessed—practically twenty seconds—since both he and Pin-Up have learned over the years that you never know what booby trap is doubly booby-trapped. They saw a group leader of a bomb unit once bite the dust after casually digging up a land mine that was rigged.

Thankfully, Spur and Pin-Up find themselves still in one piece after lifting the canister off the floor. Spur uses up another eleven seconds cautiously hauling the device out of the booth and down the aisle to the double side doors.

He glances down and sees that the timer has ticked down to 00:00:41 . . . 00:00:40 . . . 00:00:39. He eases the double doors open. Gales of rain and carbon monoxide punch him in the face. He flinches at the wind, and doesn't notice the hundreds—maybe thousands now—of onlookers, peering out of high-rise windows, or on the streets, in cars, craning their necks to see this madness involving a military chopper and a runaway train unfolding along the L tracks.

Clutching the canister as though holding a newborn, Spur leans out and has to squint against the onslaught of rain in order to see the bridge looming in the middle distance.

In the north Loop, the bridges that span the Chicago River look like structures that time forgot. The ancient, riveted trestles, so oxidized by the brutal weather they've turned the color of old tobacco, feature double decks for vehicular traffic below and L train passage above. At each end of each bridge stand Gothic bridge tender's towers, rising up from the water's edge like miniature citadels, giving the structures an almost medieval air.

The one currently looming directly in the path of train number 3247 overhangs a wide swath of the river, the gunmetal surface of the water below presently churning and roiling, agitated by the storm. Spur girds himself in the open doorway, ready and steady as a rock as the train shrieks around a corner near the bridge entrance.

A mere thirteen seconds remain as a strange, unbidden memory zaps across Spur's mind, casting him back to his days playing football at Texas A&M, and the greatest moment of his athletic career. It was in the Big 12 championship against Nebraska, and there were only forty-one seconds left on the clock, and the score was tied, and Nebraska had the ball on the Aggies' eleven-yard line, and Spur was the anchor of the Texas defense, playing middle linebacker. On the third down, the Cornhuskers ran an option and Spur saw it coming, and he intercepted the pitch.

Halfway to the opposite end zone, about to be tackled as the clock ran out, Spur tossed an expert lateral across the width of the field to his cornerback, Leon Briggs, and Leon carried the ball all the way to a winning TD. But on that glorious day it was Spur who the team lifted up on their shoulders and carried off the field in victory.

Now the train careens onto the bridge. Spur executes a perfect toss, hurling the canister in a gorgeous arc through the rain to rival that perfect lateral which won him MVP honors against Nebraska. Now the device splashes down into the murky currents, bobbing for a moment, and then sinking below the surface as the time ticks down . . . 00:00:03 . . . 00:00:02.

2.

Up in the Blackhawk's cockpit, banking sharply to the north, Ticker pulls away from the river at the last possible instant before the enormous flash convulses a square block of murky water. The explosion—muffled at first—sends a vast geyser the size of a house up into the storm, blossoming fifty feet above the river into a gargantuan fireball.

The shock wave slams tsunamis of filthy river water in all directions, crashing into the facades of adjacent buildings, sluicing down perpendicular streets, and coursing through the tunnels of Wacker Drive. It will not be until much later that Spur and his unit learn of the massive property damage caused by the submerged explosive going off.

But the best part will be learning that the single loss of life involved in the incident was the staff sergeant from the army base who had obviously become a puppet of diabolical influences.

This day, however, as train number 3247 passes over the far terminus of the Lake Street Bridge, Pin-Up carefully cuts the sergeant's dead right hand from the throttle, and brings the conveyance to a full stop. Out of respect, she gently lays the man's remains on the floor, and closes his eyes.

The storm continues to rage outside the train's windows, and due to the noise of the encroaching sirens and the wind and the rhythmic throb of the Blackhawk, Pin-Up doesn't hear the sounds of applause coming from the windows of buildings and cars.

3.

By four o'clock that afternoon, back in Missouri, the bluster of midday has calmed down, and the late-afternoon sun has softened, and all the pieces have been put into place for the beginning of the conference. The attendees have been escorted from their guest rooms to the veranda on the west side of the great chapel, where they are scheduled to enjoy a meet and greet with their fellow conference-goers. The patio area has been decorated with grape arbors strung with tiny white Christmas lights. Round pedestal tables have been positioned across the herringbone brick deck, and a canopy of pear trees provides a convivial swath of shade under which long tables are set with hors d'oeuvres, bottles of pinot noir, sauvignon blanc, mineral water, and freshly made iced tea and lemonade.

For his part in the festivities, Father Manny is doing his best to appear as cordial and normal as possible, but he carries a heavy weight on his shoulders on this night, and not merely because of nerves. Earlier that day he was found wandering the grounds, mumbling to himself, and stricken with profound amnesia. Father Josh had to rescue the man, giving him nourishment in the rectory and explaining what was scheduled to occur that night. It all had slowly come back to Father Manny like pieces of a puzzle being put back into place. But there were still missing pieces, and the cognitive dissonance was plaguing the man.

Minutes before the meet and greet is scheduled to begin, Father Josh decides to have a heart-to-heart with the Monsignor. Josh finds the old lion in his stately rectory quarters, among the artifacts of a life in service to the Lord—Renaissance oil paintings, bookcases brimming with first-edition Bibles, fragments of stained glass from famous cathedrals. The Monsignor stands at a mirror near the door, adjusting his silk ascot. "What's on your mind, young Father?"

Joshua measures his words. "It's just a feeling, mind you, but I'm not too thrilled about this event tonight."

"Sounds ominous."

Joshua lets out a sigh. "What's the word? There's something . . . *diabolical* going on? I can feel it, Monsignor. I know that sounds crazy, but I had to tell someone."

The Monsignor turns and gives the young priest a thousand-kilowatt smile. The old bear of a man looks like a geriatric rock star in his long velveteen cape and midnight-blue vestments. His iron-white beard is braided, and his lustrous silver hair is pulled back in a ponytail. His smile widens, revealing yellow teeth as he utters the word with great amusement. "Diabolical, huh?"

"That's the word, Monsignor, yes, that's what I'm sensing here tonight."

"Josh, I'm beginning to think you worry too much. Is that a symptom of youthful inexperience?"

"Ha-ha, you got me there," Joshua says with a nervous chuckle. "Thing is, Father Manny's been a little . . . indisposed today. Confused. Now, maybe it's stress, or age . . . I don't know. But it's just adding to this feeling we might want to reschedule."

The Monsignor gives his walrus-sized mustache one last stroke of his brush. "No can do, my son. Sorry. Wheels are in motion." He tosses the brush on an end table and gives Josh a wink. "This is going to be a night for the ages."

The old man exits the room, leaving Father Josh to mutter under his breath, "That's exactly what I'm worried about."

4.

Among the first of the nineteen attendees to arrive for cocktails is Father Sanderson Wilkins, a stooped little priest in a black cape and clerical collar somewhere in his early eighties, who says a quick hello to Manny and the Monsignor, and then trundles with his cane over to the wine selection. Wilkins is one of the world's foremost authorities on spirit infestations, a man on whom the Discovery Channel has based an entire reality show. Other early arrivals include Father Homer Wexler, a portly old Episcopalian from Minneapolis–St. Paul who holds the world record for the most exorcisms performed in a single year . . . and close on his heels, the great Lorraine DeForest, the former child prodigy and celebrated psychic medium, now confined to a wheelchair, but still as spry as ever . . . and behind her, the world-famous Father Rafael Gasperi, an orphan left on the doorstep of the Vatican, a man who became Pope John Paul II's most trusted advisor and was the Vatican's official exorcist for over two decades, now retired and closing in on ninety years old.

One after another, they arrive at the meet and greet, each one a leader in their field, each one a battle-hardened veteran of the war against the Kingdom of Darkness, each one galvanized by this unprecedented gathering.

The last four attendees make their entrance at the veranda as though freshly released from a sleep clinic. They walk in an awkward cluster, brushing elbows with each other, blinking at the dusky light in their eyes. The lead sleepwalker is the honorable Father Gabriel Warren of Johannesburg, South Africa, his hunched, aged body clad in a cardigan sweater and clerical collar. His deeply lined face furrows with confusion as he gazes around the patio as though he were just air-dropped here for reasons unknown, the demon Foxglove hiding deep in the folds of the man's soul. The Brit, Father Thomas "Tommy" O'Toole, shuffles along on the right, garbed in a funereal charcoal-grey suit and fedora, teetering and wobbling like an escapee from a nursing home, the demon Nightshade lurking in the shadows of the man's subconscious.

Behind the doddering twosome waddles the little chubby Roman nun, Sister Mary Beth Malambri, clad in her dowdy black pantsuit and scarf, her short, stocky legs hastily trundling along in order to keep up. Inside her, the demon Hemlock looks through her bewildered eyes as though operating a periscope. On her flank walks the former military cop and bounty hunter William Fulbright, currently exhibiting a sickly pallor, infected with the parasitic member of the Shadow Society known as Snakeroot.

At that moment, unbeknown to the rest of conference attendees, seventy-five miles southeast of the Cloister, in the far reaches of a remote cornfield, the corpses of Father Gordon Shamus and Navy Chaplain Alex Jorgenson lie in a shallow trench, not yet cold, covered with leaves and corn silk. Dumped there earlier that day by the demon Snakeroot, the two victims have families and congregations that will try in vain to find their missing loved ones.

Alas, owing to the weather and the insects, as well as the foxes and stray dogs in the area, there will not be much left of the remains to find.

5.

The dinner that night begins with an aperitif of Italian Amaro and a cold salad of roasted beets, walnuts, and goat cheese. It takes several minutes for the waitstaff to roll the drink cart and salad caddy into the room, and serve each of the nineteen dignitaries. From their table in the far corner of the room, Darby and Silverback are both hyperalert, jittery, surveying the dining hall with the attentiveness of security guards at a bank scanning the lobby for anybody or anything that looks out of the ordinary. Each for different reasons feels a low, smoldering sense of unease in their guts.

At the moment, the only thing that Silverback can see that doesn't feel right is the behavior of the Monsignor, who sits in the center of the dais in his magnificent vestments. He is flanked on each side by the Cloister's executive branch—Fathers Hoscheit, McCready, Steadman, and Reeves—as though the Monsignor were Christ at the last supper. He has a strange grin on his face—more of a smirk than a joyous expression—and his eyes don't look right.

The sound of a spoon clinking against a wine goblet fills the room.

The Monsignor calmly pushes himself back from the table, rising to his full imposing height. "Friends, fellow toilers in the field, honorable guests, I am the Right Reverend Charles David McAllister, and I have the distinct pleasure and privilege to welcome you to our little sanctuary."

The room quiets down, the soft chatter among guests hushing immediately.

Silverback's hackles are up. He glances over at Darby. She meets his gaze with a strange, expectant look on her face that's both bemused and jittery. Silverback can tell she feels the odd energy in the room, too, a weird tension like a low sixty-cycle hum from an overloaded transformer. The others around them listen intently to the Monsignor's welcome speech.

"For centuries, this land has been the home of a spiritual fortress, and we continue this tradition today—and with all of you tonight—in the eternal conflict between the forces of good and the forces of evil. Now, I'm no historian, but I believe this gathering is unprecedented in its scope and variety of very important people in our midst, and I thank all of you from the bottom of my heart for gracing us with your presence. I also want to extend a special thank-you to our own Father Emmanuel Lawson for dreaming up this very special week. Tonight, we celebrate this summit meeting with fellowship, good food, and hopefully not too much wine."

A smattering of chuckles and whispers circulates around the great hall.

"And now, if I may," the Monsignor is saying, "I would like to offer a humble invocation before we enjoy this excellent meal prepared by our magnificent kitchen staff headed up by Sister Laura Derricks." He pauses here for dramatic effect, as heads bow all around the hall, and the silence deepens. "Our father . . . who art in hell . . . darkness be thy game."

Silverback shoots a look at Darby as one might glance at a seatmate on an airliner if suddenly, without warning, the oxygen masks drop from the ceiling. He had a feeling that something like this—whatever it is that's happening—would happen. Which is why his right hand slowly fishes inside his jacket for his gun, his thumb carefully flipping the safety off.

"Thy kingdom of heaven," the Monsignor goes on, starting to giggle. "Thy will be fucked, as all of you are shit out of luck!"

The Monsignor starts laughing uproariously now, chortling, cackling, wailing with amusement, his entire enormous body beginning to levitate off the ground as though hooked to invisible guy wires, the eyes of the guests widening around the dining hall as they gape at the spectacle of a huge elderly man rising into the air. Frantic whispers surge like a rainstorm in the room. Silverback stands up and draws his pistol so fast his chair flips backward, cartwheeling into the wall.

"Give us this day our daily lies!—And forgive us our pathetic tribes!—As they practice their graft and greed and bribes!"

Rising slowly toward the high ceiling, the Monsignor guffaws and shudders with delight. His laughter is that of a hyena—predatory and taunting. This is apparently the funniest thing he has ever encountered, and his mirth is uncontrolled as other figures around the room begin to levitate as well—Sister Mary Beth, Father Warren of Johannesburg, Father O'Toole, Officer Fulbright—each of them slowly rising as though filled with helium, their faces beginning to contort as if made of melting rubber, their eyes bulging and distending.

Some of the attendees have now sprung to their feet, looking around the hall with panic twisting their faces. The waitstaff—each one an experienced layperson who has assisted in many Catholic rites—begin to back toward the kitchen pass door. Some attendees have reached for their crucifixes or their Bibles, while still others have started backing toward the exit, because they now see that the familiar dark power has taken over, a power with which many in attendance are all too familiar.

6.

At the corner table, Silverback grabs Darby by the nape of her blouse, pulling the stupefied woman away from the table. Darby tries to say something, but the words won't come, her eyes as big as silver dollars. She backs away until her rear end hits the wall. Her lips are moving, but no sound comes out of her.

Silverback moves instinctively in front of Darby to protect her, to block her from whatever is happening, whatever is coming their way. The chivalrous instinct is innate. When Silverback was only seven years old, his parents and sisters and he emigrated to America from their home in Dublin, but the family clung to their Catholicism, and Silverback never really lost the old beliefs, the old dogma, the old conceptions of supernatural evil. He knows what this is. He recognizes it like an odor.

"Everybody down on the floor!" Silverback's piercing cry galvanizes the stunned attendees. *Do it now—now-now-down—down!!"*

One by one the guests drop to the floor as a series of loud booms makes Darby jump, and she sees the storm shutters on the high windows slamming shut under their own power. One after another, the windows seal themselves with such force that each impact is followed by the crack of the frame nearly bursting inward, the noises as thunderous as successive gun blasts.

Across the hall, near the exit doors, about a dozen fleeing guests and staff are met with a similar manifestation. The two sets of double doors bang shut in their faces with such force that the floor trembles beneath them. One of the doors slams on an elderly priest's hand, severing the gnarled appendage clean off.

The hand lands on the floor as the old man convulses and wails, reeling backward, finally collapsing in a miasma of arterial spray. A nun rushes to the old man's side and starts working on a makeshift tourniquet, while others back away in shock, trying to process what is happening before their very eyes.

Meanwhile, up in the rafters, the laughter has intensified into a chorus of hyenas singing atonal arias. The five afflicted humans now resemble sinister parade balloons looming overhead, their demonic, bloated faces stretched to the breaking point. The thing that was once Sister Mary Beth convulses with hilarity, her eyes turning fish-belly white, her cheeks expanding. Father Tommy O'Toole hoots and hollers and sprays black saliva through the air. Father Warren's body undulates and contorts, a forked tongue wagging out of his greasy, blackened mouth.

Silverback manages to turn the big round table in the corner onto its side, allowing other guests to take cover behind it, all of them huddling close together. Among those cowering now behind the table next to a terrified Darby are Father Sanderson Wilkins, the renowned ghost investigator; Lorraine DeForest, the famous psychic medium, who is still slumped down in her wheelchair; and Father Rafael Gasperi, once the Vatican's demon hunter, who trembles with emotion.

"These entities that have possessed these people, they're uncommonly powerful," Father Gasperi wheezes in a strained, heavily accented voice to Silverback, the old man speaking very quickly as though on a field of battle, raising his voice to be heard above the monstrous laughter. "I'm afraid these are no ordinary demons."

"He's right," the woman in the wheelchair concurs. "I'm feeling echoes of the Devil's voice. These are what is known as superior demons. Very dangerous."

Silverback looks up at the buoyant creatures from hell floating above them, the taunting laughter, the stench of death pressing in. "This is above my pay grade. I'm essentially a glorified cop." He reaches into his suit jacket for the .38-caliber revolver tucked into a shoulder holster. "What do I do with this? What are the rules of engagement here?"

"There is only one rule of engagement," the elderly priest says cryptically, rising to one knee, his wrinkled, emaciated hands crossing his scrawny chest. He fishes in his pocket for a tattered, leather-bound liturgical book. Above him, the abominations laugh and laugh, their voices like knife blades scraping stone, the laughter and singing transforming into howls.

At first, the five possessed figures wail in unison as they hover, their spines pressed up against the high vaulted ceiling. Their ear-shattering yowls soon resolve again into lunatic choruses of atonal, dissonant singing. To the modern ear the song is garbled nonsense. But to the old exorcist, Gasperi, who now holds his old dog-eared Bible in one hand and a tarnished crucifix in the other, the lyrics are familiar, ancient Latin, profane and scatological, and highly sacrilegious.

> *Erat quidam sacerdos, qui debacchatus est*
> (There once was a priest who raved)
> *"Mortuam meretricem in antro meo servo!*
> ("I keep a dead whore in my cave!)
> *"Cum incipit olere, dico quod infernum.*
> ("When she starts to smell, I say what the hell.)
> *"Cogitate pecuniam salvare!"*
> ("Just think of the money I save!")

7.

By this point, the stalwart old Gasperi has had enough. He has begun to recite the ancient litany. "Christ, hear us!" he cries out over the piercing song of dead prostitutes and perverted priests.

Undaunted, Wilkins and the DeForest woman, side by side behind the table, call out the response in unison. "Christ, gloriously hear us!"

Gasperi goes on. "God, the father in heaven!"

Wilkins and DeForest respond: "Have mercy on us!"

Gasperi: "God, the Son, Redeemer of the world!"

Wilkins and DeForest: "Have mercy on us all!"

Gasperi: "God, by Your name save us, and by Your might defend our cause!"

Wilkins and DeForest: "God, hear our prayer!"

Fifteen feet above them, the dynamic suddenly shifts among the possessed.

As though a switch has been thrown, the hellish singsong wailing ceases, and the facial features of each entity begin to transform as though their flesh is aging in time-lapse. Eyes sink into hollows. Lines deepen, wrinkles spreading, lips blackening and receding, teeth yellowing, incisors turning fang-like, pupils narrowing, becoming lupine, alien, and monstrous. Wormwood fixes his multifaceted eyes on the old priest beneath him, and booms: "THERE IS NO GOD TO HEAR YOUR

PITIFUL ENTREATIES!! YOU'RE ALONE, PREACHER MAN! ALONE IN THE COLD, COLD, COLD, EMPTY UNIVERSE! AND YOU SHALL DIE ALONE!! AND YOU SHALL SPEND ETERNITY ALONE!—ALONE!!"

The other demons join in: "ALONE!!—ALONE!!—ALONE!!—ALONE!!—ALONE!!—ALONE!!"

Undeterred, steadfast, defiant, old Father Rafael Gasperi continues the litany, still shuddering and quivering with emotion: "God, let these enemies have no power over these servants!"

Wilkins and DeForest together call out: "And let these sons of iniquity be powerless to harm them!"

8.

Up in the rafters, the Right Reverend Charles McAllister, better known as the Monsignor, now ripples with the most deformities, the big man's torso undulating and twisting, shoulders audibly dislocating with a series of nauseating cracks, arms pinning themselves back behind his huge body like wings. The Monsignor's jaws gape open to the point of fracturing as the demon's thunderous baritone pours out of its black maw: "YOU PITIFUL HOLY WHORES YOUR WORDS ARE WORTHLESS, AND YOU ALL ARE FECKLESS IMPOTENT MAGGOTS IN THE AFTERBIRTH LOWER THAN ROTTING PUS IN THE ASSHOLE OF THE UNIVERSE, AND YOU ARE ALL WEAK AND SMALL AND LESS THAN NOTHING, AND I *EXSPUE MORTUUM PROPINQUOS TUOS ET EXCREMENTUM TUIS POSTERIS EGO EXSPUE!!*"

"Do not look into his eyes!" Father Gasperi warns, his voice crumbling, strained by exhaustion.

Above the fray, in the body of the corpulent Sister Mary Beth Malambri, the demon Hemlock starts shrieking, her banshee scream so piercing, so keening, that many of the attendees start cringing, and dropping to their knees, and holding their hands over their ears. Even Father Gasperi is taken by surprise at the volume of the demon voices. He slowly backs away from the chaos, wiping his hound-dog eyes with his vestment scarf, coughing furiously, and trying to continue his recitation of the exorcism in fitful, mumbling, garbled bursts. He starts choking. He falls to his knees. He can't breathe.

Across the room, the sight of the elderly clergyman gasping for breath is like a slap across Darby's face. She rises up behind the sideways table. She calls out to Silverback: "The old man! He's—he's having a—he's having *a heart attack!*"

From the rafters, the demons all latch their luminous gazes on Gasperi as the old man coughs and gasps for breath on the floor, barely able to stay upright on his wobbly knees. The monsters float toward him, searing their horrible gazes down upon him. The eyes of a superior demon are poisonous, cancerous, and lethal—they can destroy, they can scour a person's soul—and right now, five pairs of these phosphorus-yellow eyes have fixed themselves on the old man from Rome.

"DIE!—DIE!—DIE!—DIE!—DIE!—DIE!!" Their ugly, grating, feral voices pour out of them as they begin to circle above the dying man like giant, ghastly buzzards. "DIE!—DIE!—DIE!—DIE!—DIE!—DIE!—DIE!—DIE!—DIE!—DIE!!"

Silverback raises the .38, thumbing the hammer back, not sure who or what to fire upon first; then he hears a noise that stops him cold. Faint to begin with, but rising over the demonic din and the cries of the guests. Rhythmic, incessant, the pounding of helicopter rotors intensifies outside the building.

Silverback gazes up at the high windows and realizes what's happening. He lowers his gun.

CHAPTER FOURTEEN

The Flames of Hell

1.

A moment later, three shadows materialize like ghosts—one behind each high window—and the sound of bootheels shattering wooden shutters and window glass pierces the pandemonium below.

Spur appears first in his medieval regalia, leaping through one of the jagged openings, harnessed to a rappelling rope. The rope sings as he quickly lowers himself to the dining hall floor, detaching the harness, followed closely by Pin-Up and Ticker, each of them hurtling through a gaping window, zinging down to the floor, and detaching their harness. Each enters the chaos with a machine pistol poised to roar.

"Thank Christ!" Silverback says to himself, shoving the pistol into his holster and signaling to Spur.

The demonic horde hovering over the dying priest barely notices or acknowledges the late arrivals. The demons just keep hovering over Gasperi, snarling their taunting chorus: "DIE!—DIE!—DIE!—DIE!—DIE!—DIE!—DIE!—DIE!— DIE!—DIE!!"

"What in the Sam Hell is going on?" Spur wonders aloud, his voice hushed with awe, as he and the others circle around the sideways table to where Silverback and two other attendees are huddling. "Got a frantic call en route from Father Manny," Spur says to Silverback. "Said something about the dinner being a 'trap'?" Spur's gaze rises to the ceiling. "The *fuck*?"

"Hold that thought, Spur!" Silverback says, and grabs Pin-Up's arm, and frantically gestures toward the elderly Roman priest on the floor fifteen feet away. "Pin, Pin!—Father Gasperi's coding out, can you help him?"

Pin-Up's nursing instinct kicks in immediately, and she vaults across the gap between her and the priest, the lunatic chanting continuing unabated, echoing up in the ceiling beams. She kneels by the old man, palpates his neck, feels his feeble and fibrillating pulse, and rips open his shirt.

Meanwhile, Spur and Ticker come over and kneel on either side of Pin-Up, guarding her as she presses her hands down against the middle of Gasperi's breastbone. She starts pushing down and lifting up, pushing down and lifting up—a hundred times a minute—to the beat of the Bee Gees' "Stayin' Alive," as she had learned in nursing school a million years ago.

2.

At the same time, across the room, Silverback is panicking because he can't find Darby or his gun. His holster is empty. In all the excitement, did he drop it? Did it slip out of his holster? Frantically looking around the hall, he finally sees Darby on the other side of another overturned table, moving directly under the floating squadron of chanting demons. She holds the .38 with both hands, trembling as she aims it up at the possessed mortals.

"Darby, no!—NO!" Silverback makes a leaping charge toward her, but it's too late. She starts squeezing off wild shots.

The demonic chanting intensifies as .38-caliber slugs chew through the beams of the ceiling, puffing sawdust and debris into the air. Darby keeps firing even after Silverback reaches her and tries to gently wrestle the weapon away from her. She is gripped now with rage and bloodlust, and shrieks as she fires more wild shots.

Finally, one of the rounds strikes the possessed Monsignor in the leg, the bullet passing through the meat of his thigh, puffing out the back of his leg in a gout of pink tissue. The impact slams the big, lanky body into an adjacent rafter, the blood-puff swathing across the timber.

The chanting ceases instantly, as though a circuit breaker has popped. The face of the Monsignor—once a kindly, bearded visage reminiscent of that of an old prospector, friend of child and stray dog alike—now collapses into the face of Wormwood; as dark as crude oil, putrid and savage, the face brings to mind a mutant insect, its iridescent flesh refracting the light, wavering and undulating like a denizen of the deepest part of the ocean.

This is the face of the field marshal, the commander in chief of all the superior demons that serve the Kingdom of Darkness, and right now it focuses all its hatred of the human race, all its supernatural evil upon Silverback and Darby. Wormwood snarls at them, his deep growl of a voice reminiscent of the sound of sewage flowing through a subterranean culvert, and with each utterance the ancient words seem to deform the unholy face into gruesome permutations: *"Morieris . . . solus tu morieris . . . morieris in dolore!!"*

The Monsignor's gushing blood transforms, igniting into a luminous, white-hot stream of pure hellfire.

3.

A mere six minutes has passed since the remaining members of the Quintet arrived in a thunderous whirlwind of pounding rotors and xenon searchlights, landing safely in the quad just outside the dining hall and breaking into the locked building via the high windows, the noise rousing the skeleton crew currently overseeing the rest of the Cloister.

Under the command of Father Joshua, the three-person security team that was hunkered down in the control room on the other side of the campus had been cautioned by the Monsignor that they should "give attendees at the dinner the utmost privacy." In the words of the Monsignor, "Debates can get pretty heated when you're in the throes of such an important and controversial summit." But when the massive helicopter came out of nowhere, landing on the Cloister's grounds, Joshua could no longer ignore his suspicions that something had gone awry, and it probably was connected in some way to the strange behavior earlier that day of Father Manny.

Now Father Josh springs into action. He arms his two lay assistants, and alerts the skeleton crew of medics, security guards, administrators, and janitorial workers present that night that he will be heading over to the dining hall to investigate, and wants everybody on high alert until he gives the all clear.

At the same time, neither Joshua nor his two lay assistants notice the shadowy figure slipping onto the Cloister property. Joshua is too busy working up the nerve to investigate the commotion in the great dining hall, marching across the grounds with his men, taking deep breaths, and brushing his fingertips across the Taser gun holstered on his hip.

Nobody sees the figure sneaking into the building on the northeast corner of the property, locking the door after them, vanishing into the shadows of the armory.

4.

In the pandemonium of the dining hall, Darby has run out of bullets. Above her the demon roars—"*IGNES INFERNI!!*"—as the flaming rivulets of blood from the Monsignor's leg strike the floor within inches of Darby, spreading across the hardwood like a brilliant serpentine river of fire. As if on cue, the banshee demon Hemlock—inside the twisted, contorted body of the nun—roars flaming vomit as incendiary as napalm. The fiery sputum ignites wooden chairs and tablecloths and spilled liquor.

At the same time, startled cries rise up from the guests crowding the jammed doors along the side of the dining hall as the fire spreads wildly through the room. The flames gobble the drapes, crawling up the walls in brilliant tendrils of light, crackling and popping loudly, the smoke and fumes intensifying. The harsh odors of burning fabric and brimstone fill the air.

Up along the ceiling, the other demonic entities follow suit, spitting fire now with the force of flamethrowers, catching the wallpaper and carpets, and gobbling the overturned tables and chairs. Magnesium-hot backdrafts engulf the windows and doors, sending many of the attendees staggering backward, coughing profusely, many tripping over their own feet and falling to the floor only to attempt to crawl out of harm's way.

By this point Ticker has rushed to Darby's side and is trying to pull her away from the gathering flames. He doesn't worry about the massive figure looming above him . . . until the former Right Reverend Charles McAllister pounces. The monster lands on Ticker with the impact of a two-ton elephant.

Ticker's breath is knocked out of him. Wormwood grabs the man's neck—utilizing the Monsignor's two large, gnarled hands—and squeezes with all his supernatural might. Ticker gasps and struggles to get air into his lungs, but it's no use. The superior demon is bloodthirsty and relentless, and strangles the man to within a hairsbreadth of his life . . . when all at once an enormous crash rings out along the east wall, surprising even Wormwood.

A cold wind swirls through the room, fanning flames, sending sparks across the floor.

The demon's grip on Ticker's throat falters suddenly. A dark strap has wrapped around the Monsignor's neck from behind. It seems to have appeared out of nowhere, and Wormwood is as shocked as anyone by the abrupt, sharp yank that snaps the huge man's head backward. The Monsignor's massive body tumbles off Ticker and lands on the floor . . .

. . . revealing a slender, masked figure standing over the two men. She holds a dark velvet curtain sash, which she had torn free from the wall during her dramatic entrance. She shakes her head now at Ticker and says, "I leave for a few weeks and everything goes to hell."

5.

It was the vision that brought Boo back into the fold. Sure, she was guilty of going AWOL on her fellow warriors. And she felt awful about her breakup with Hack. But it was a Technicolor prophecy in that seedy motel room along the Mississippi River that had convinced her that she had to return and rejoin the Quintet. Most important, she had to deliver the message to Spur that was conveyed to her by the dead in the vision. The last image in that waking dream, presented in brilliant high definition, provided a terrifying clue regarding the Devil's true objective. It had stamped itself on Boo's midbrain, and had haunted her. But there had been so many questions left unanswered. The truth was, Boo had no idea how she would be received by Spur and the others, or for that matter, what she would find at the Cloister when she returned. She knew it would be bad. It had to be in order to fulfill the prophecy. But she had no idea it would be a conflagration on the order of this.

She now stands in the flickering yellow light and heat of a growing maelstrom, draped in her phosphorus-green Shaolin monk's robe, her face partially obscured behind a hand-painted Kabuki mask, her katana sword sheathed in its shoulder harness. The flames have spread up the walls, sparks catching the ceiling beams. A warning siren has begun to wail in the distant night, the sounds of frantic footsteps and voices echoing outside the high windows as Joshua and his men close in. Boo is taking a step toward Ticker, who is still incapacitated on the floor, gulping air, holding his neck, when the Monsignor springs forward off the floorboards as though on a catapult.

The enormous possessed man pounces on Boo, but she is too fast and too skilled to be knocked off her feet.

She slips free and simultaneously spins and draws the katana blade from its sheath. The blade slices across the Monsignor's ankles and wrists so quickly that the cuts are almost invisible to the naked eye. The gashes, permeated with holy water, are so deep, and so invasive, that the big man staggers backward on spumes of his own blood, which instantly ignite into florets of sparks, his damaged tendons causing him to trip over his own feet.

Across the room, the thing that used to be Officer Fulbright attacks Pin-Up.

The two of them engage in a deadly embrace, spinning, spinning, and then slamming into an overturned table. On the floor, Fulbright makes a forceful attempt to bite into Pin-Up's carotid artery, but Pin-Up rolls at the last moment, and then executes a perfect martial arts counterhold on Fulbright's left leg, fracturing it with one quick, sharp kick. Rising quickly to her feet, she slams the table down on Fulbright's head, which concusses the brain enough to inhibit Snakeroot's ability to do any further puppeteering.

Pin-Up whirls around and sees, across the room, the plump old nun, Sister Mary Beth, dropping from the ceiling directly onto Spur.

Spur throws the monstrous mutation of a woman off him, but Hemlock, inside the nun, is relentless and thirsty for blood. The nun crab-walks up the adjacent wall behind Spur. When Spur spins around, the nun lurches at him cobra-quick, latching on to him and nearly biting his nose off.

At the last moment, right before the nun's fangs sink into Spur's face, he gets his hand between his face and the nun's gaping blackened mouth. Razor-sharp incisors puncture Spur's hand, and he lets out a loud grunt before kicking the nun's legs out from under her. Both combatants tumble to the floor. Arms and legs tangle. The twosome rolls wildly across the parquet floor.

They collide with a neighboring table. They come face-to-face.

Hemlock snarls and emits a hell-born voice through the nun's aged vocal cords, breathing deathly horrible breath in Spur's face: *"Tempus mori!—TEMPUS MORRRRI!!"*

Spur feels his central nervous system shifting, as though a jolt of high voltage is coursing through him, changing him, reflecting his adversary's strength. Spur's face becomes a mirror, transforming for one brief instant into a clone of Hemlock's, growling back at the demon, *"TUUM RURSUS AD MORR-RRRRTEMMMM!"*

The nun's eyes widen suddenly. Shocked. Vexed. Enraged. Spur takes advantage of the pause by immediately clenching his right fist and delivering a bone-crunching roundhouse punch to the nun's face, knocking out the human part of her unconscious . . . and for a moment, at least, incapacitating the demon.

6.

By this point, the fire is raging out of control, the smoke starting to permeate the hall, the blaze curling past the high windows, scorching the rafters and skylights as dark as lampblack. The heat has intensified tenfold. Silverback has dragged several attendees back toward the wall, where most of the guests are pressed up against the doors and railings, coughing and covering their mouths with handkerchiefs.

Silverback has some experience with wildfires and has started hollering at the attendees, "Everybody down, down on the floor! Stay down!—*Down!—Down everybody!*—DOWN!-DOWN!-DOWN!"

Most of the attendees follow his cue, knowing instinctively without being told that the heat gets worse the higher you are. But few notice the figure in the far corner of the hall, curled into a fetal position on the floor, softly crying as the smoke starts to swallow all the light.

Only minutes ago Father Manny had sunk to the floor, weeping, reeling from the dark epiphany that had struck him earlier. Through fragments of memory, disturbing images, and the sounds of demon voices, he now realizes he is victim zero. Perhaps others had suspected this, but the realization hits Manny hard: that he is the one who first became possessed, and like a modern Typhoid Mary, he brought this conflagration upon the Cloister. He had prayed it was all a dream, but the nightmare was all too real.

Outside the high windows, the sounds of Joshua's frenzied instructions, the banging of battering rams, and the creaking of crowbars are apparent now over the freight-train roar of the blaze, as staff people frantically try to crack open the jammed doors. But the dark magic persists. The doors and windows remain wedged tight, and the great hall now becomes as dark as deep space from all the smoke.

Darby suddenly snaps out of her daze when she sees something moving above her behind the dark haze. She screams. Foxglove and Nightshade emerge from the veils of smoke like revenants, crawling upside down across the ceiling, moving toward the attendees. Their host bodies—Fathers Warren and O'Toole, respectively—are so burned now, and malformed from the attack, that they look like giant black centipedes.

Nightshade pauses and opens the distorted mouth of Father Tommy O'Toole, and a black, oily, reptilian tongue shoots out toward the crowd, eliciting a dissonant symphony of shrieks.

While this is happening, twenty-five feet away, Spur looks at Ticker, who is still on the floor, trying to recover from the strangulation attack. The two men exchange a knowing glance. Spur does not have to say a word. He simply nods at Ticker, and Ticker nods back at him.

Ticker then bows his head, closes his eyes, and over the course of a single instant imagines that he's ten years old again and he's taking piano lessons—

—his cruel Italian teacher yelling at him again for playing the cantata *Jesu, Joy of Man's Desiring* all wrong. "Where is the caesura mark?!" she shouts at him, making him jerk with a start. He points to a symbol at the far end of the staff—two parallel diagonal lines, commonly known among musicians as "railroad tracks"—and the ruler freezes above the boy's hand as though caught in a tableau, a snapshot, a moment in which time loses all meaning. "Correct!" the old woman squawks with the brusqueness of an angry crow. "And what does it mean, this symbol of the caesura?—explain to me!"

"Railroad tracks mean stop," the boy murmurs. "And then start again."

Nearly three decades later, in the grip of a smoke-bound prison of a dining hall, he feels the fragments of the jigsaw puzzle in his brain click into place:

Click! A little boy's slender brown fingers playing the notes of *Jesu, Joy of Man's Desiring* on the keyboard of a battered spinet piano back in Chicago, the same instrument for which his mother scrimped and saved before purchasing it from a pawnshop . . .

. . . and now the fingers abruptly lifting up.

Click!

CHAPTER FIFTEEN

The Frenetic Motion of Molecules

1.

The abrupt silence in the great dining hall is overwhelming, as though a wet skein of fabric has been pulled down over Ticker, who lies on the floor, still blinking fitfully, getting his bearings. The second thing he notices is that smoke in the Caesura looks like the grain in old photographs.

From Ticker's point of view the room has seized up into a sepia-grey still frame, a tableau that might be a page from a dog-eared book on a shelf in some dusty old historical society. The scene might bear the title *The Great Dining Hall Showdown and Fire Circa Late 1800s,* and the casual reader might pause on that page and study the picture.

The reader of such a book might be disturbed when they notice in the picture the bodies on the floor. They might linger on the image of Father Gasperi lying in the foreground, his arms and legs akimbo, his deeply lined face pale and bloodless, a casualty of cardiac arrest. They also might notice the heavy-set nun lying limp and unconscious on the other side of the room while blossoms of flames the size and shape of a Christmas tree form a weird backdrop behind her, sprouting billows of smoke that look like dirty blots of eiderdown. They might experience a shiver of revulsion when they see the monstrous abominations of people clinging to the ceiling, twisted and deformed by Satanic magic, a long serpentine tongue protruding from the mouth of the one once called Father Tommy O'Toole.

Ticker picks himself up off the floor, his ears ringing. He sees Spur standing a few feet away, barely visible behind pixels of frozen smoke, his expression stuck on his face—that square-jawed Texas certainty that *it's now up to you, Ticker, to unravel this mess, and fix everything in the Great Pause. Get to it. Time's a-wastin'!*

Taking a deep breath, rubbing his sore neck, Ticker gazes around the grainy still life of the dining hall. The flames have a tarnished, metallic look to them, like stalagmites made of golden tinsel. But the smoke is far more pervasive, bathing the hall in the darkness of an underexposed negative. In the gloom Ticker sees the mob of attendees pressed up against the east wall, some of them clawing at the doors, some of them frozen in utter horror as they gaze up at the ceiling, where a pair of immolated, scorched, mutated humans slither toward them.

Next he notices the remains of the Monsignor lying supine on the floor between two overturned tables, the ligature of the curtain sash still tight around his throat. Did the demon inside the Right Reverend Charles McAllister escape in the throes of death? The thought of Boo killing such a beloved member of the religious establishment sends a feather of dread down Ticker's spine. That's when he notices Boo standing next to Pin-Up, her katana gripped in both hands, her eyes narrowed, her diminutive body in battle posture.

Over by the east wall, he sees Lorraine DeForest lying on the floor by her wheelchair, gaze upturned as though she is seeing visions. Silverback is next to her, paused in midshout as he directs the attendees to get down where the temperature is cooler. This is the next thing Ticker notices: The intense heat of the blaze has lessened in the Pause.

Ticker has been studying the phenomenon of the Caesura for almost two years now, and he believes that the molecular motion of objects other than himself slows down to an almost undetectable level. The molecules keep moving, but very slowly. Hence the frenetic motion of molecules in a fire slows down to the point of causing the temperature to drop.

He's processing all this when he sees Darby. She is caught in midscream, her eyes wide and hot, her feverish gaze locked on the monstrous figures clinging to the high ceiling above her. The sight of her utter terror rattles Ticker, and he starts working on his breathing exercise—in through the nose, out through the mouth—as he struggles to ignore the grim reality of the situation, the self-doubt, the daunting proposition of facing this Herculean task by himself in the loneliness of the Caesura.

One thing at a time, Ticker tells himself, morbidly amused by his inadvertent pun. He looks at the dining room differently for a moment, analyzing his options, clarifying his objective of either neutralizing or removing the demonic entities. But how does one man do this—especially a man of science, a man of left-brain orientation, a man who is also oriented toward agnosticism? Also, there's the secondary goal here of extracting the innocent guests from the peril of the fire.

Walking around the periphery of the frozen darkness, Ticker runs down a quick checklist in his mind of things that will not work in the Pause—engines, electric current, wireless devices, clocks, gauges, lighters, magnets, echoes, and radio waves. More important, Ticker has his own physical limitations within the Pause. After a few hours in the Caesura, he starts to succumb to a strange type of exhaustion. It's almost systemic, like a faint malignancy that radiates out from his bones, and drags him down until he surrenders and takes the world off pause. He has not tested the limits of this yet, but he's fairly certain that after seventy-two hours he probably would drop dead.

He also has learned that—just as the universe itself is finite—the Caesura has an outer boundary, beyond which time continues unabated. Again, he has yet to explore this discovery, but he has gathered circumstantial evidence here and there that proves such a wrinkle exists.

It takes several minutes (in Ticker's solitary timeline) merely to labor back up a rappelling rope to one of the upper windows, and then climb through the jagged opening.

2.

Ticker emerges from the building and moves across an overhanging section of the ancient roof. There are no night breezes to greet him, no drone of crickets, no nocturnal animals rattling branches. The crystalline night sky looks strangely cold and inert, devoid of any movement, as though someone has painted it. The moon has an opaque quality, chalky and static, yet still luminous enough to faintly light his way. As he traverses the length of the shake-shingled roof, his footsteps crackle so loudly the sound pangs painfully in his skull.

He is as alone as alone can be, and the world around him is dead silent and still. He climbs down an access ladder embedded in the steeple's turret.

At ground level he encounters another eerie diorama of people reduced to frozen action figures. He sees Father Josh with a horrified expression on his boyish face, standing behind a group of staff people and security guards, some of them with large timbers that are serving as battering rams. For an insane instant Ticker is reminded of the famous statue of Marine Corps flag bearers on Iwo Jima, their struggle to raise the American flag solidified in bronze for eternity.

He crosses the dark, still grounds of the Cloister buzzing with ideas, passing silent tableaux of emergency workers hauling firefighting gear toward the dining hall with frantic expressions on their faces, now as still as statuary. Ticker weaves between motionless trucks laden with ladders and hoses. He passes clusters of rescuers on foot, some of them carrying hand extinguishers, some with axes, some in utility vehicles heavy with sandbags—all of it immobilized by the Caesura.

These bizarre displays of people in midrescue add to Ticker's sense of urgency.

The library is situated on the north edge of the commons, behind the administration building. Since it's after hours, the small redbrick cottage is closed and dark and locked up tight. Ticker climbs in through a window near the service entrance. He is immediately swallowed by utter darkness. He can't see his hand in front of his face.

He feels his way through the storage room, bumping into racks of cleaning supplies and boxes of books, until he finds himself in the main room. By this point, his eyes have dilated enough to see faint outlines of shelves brimming with religious texts. A tall arched window above a reading desk lets in enough moonlight for Ticker to make out the titles on the spines lined up along the shelves. He hastily chooses a couple of thick volumes on the Catholic rites of exorcism. In a drawer he finds paper and a pencil, but as soon as he sits down at the moonlit desk, he realizes this is insane.

Who does he think he is? He has no time to take a crash course in the rites of exorcism. And besides, even if he could absorb centuries of tradition and case studies, and memorize litanies and prayers, how could he hope to do a better job than Fathers Gasperi and Wilkins? It is the very definition of insanity—doing the same thing Gasperi did and expecting different results—and he instantly discards the idea.

He glances over at the corner coffee service, a small table with cups and a brew pot half full of black coffee as petrified as onyx. But something else catches Ticker's eye. Above a tiny stainless-steel sink, he sees a droplet of water in the dim ambient light, captured by the Pause on its plummet toward the basin—a tiny pearl frozen in midair an inch below the mouth of the faucet—and it gives him an idea.

3.

During his postgraduate years at MIT—on the fast track to becoming the youngest person in the history of the school to earn a Ph.D.—he supported himself as a night janitor. He worked the graveyard shift at the Maclaurin Building, where he was studying applied physics, and during that time, he learned more than he ever wanted to know about the inner workings of an ancient, drafty study hall. By the time he received his degree, he knew more about heating and air-conditioning than he did about quantum computing or electromagnetic propulsion.

Now he flashes back to those days in Cambridge, sweeping the floors and cleaning out gutters. He remembers keeping the plumbing updated and operational, and the memory sparks a connection. He feels his way across the room to the main stack of reference books. In the gloomy light, he strains his eyes to read the spines of old, musty tomes stacked to the ceiling.

He finds what he's looking for, and he pulls it off the shelf. The book is so old the gilded corners crumble in his hands as he carries it back over to the desk by the window.

He sits down, and starts taking notes. He writes down a step-by-step procedure recorded in the late nineteenth century by a Franciscan monk. He copies the words from the Roman Ritual, and he notates specific directions, such as making the sign of the cross in the water as the salt is added, and simultaneously reciting the blessing.

The next phase of his plan takes nearly an hour in his timeline.

He takes his notes with him as he exits the library and heads back to the great dining hall and chapel building. In a toolshed behind the loading dock, he finds a wheelbarrow and a crowbar. He throws the crowbar in the wheelbarrow and pushes it over to the rear service entrance behind the kitchen.

The doors are jammed, and the window next to the loading dock is still so tightly shuttered the seams around the frame have cracked. He pries the shutters open with the crowbar and squeezes through the window into the dark, smoke-bound kitchen.

Pots and pans are strewn across the greasy floor, and the air is thick with veils of frozen smoke. He detects the odor of burning flesh, and notices the motionless silhouettes of staff people pressed up against the far wall, some of them keeled over, some caught in midcough, all the faces distorted with terror.

In a walk-in pantry he finds boxes of kosher salt and a fireplace lighter. He shoves the lighter in his pocket and gathers as many salt boxes as he can carry. He then shimmies back through the window. He pours all of the salt into the wheelbarrow.

4.

Due to all the physical exertion, as well as the length of the Caesura thus far, Ticker starts feeling the familiar fatigue as he pushes the wheelbarrow around the side of the building. The exhaustion radiates out from his neck, and every breath now is accompanied by a dull ache in his lungs. It's as though the weight of the Caesura is pressing down on him, a thousand-pound yoke on his shoulders. He ignores the sensation and searches for the HVAC housing.

Under a jungle of ivy he finds the grey metal enclosure.

Using the crowbar to clear away the tangled vines, he locates the rusted hatch. It takes him several minutes to loosen it, but it finally gives way and creaks as it stubbornly swings open. He recognizes the valve on the sprinkler reservoir from his days in Cambridge. He finds that the valve is as jammed as the building's doors and windows. Is this why the sprinkler system malfunctioned in the great dining hall? Were the spigots disabled by demonic influence? He opens the cap on the reservoir and peers down into the tank.

The reservoir is full, the water within mere inches of the top. Ticker recognizes the pressurized valves and pipes snaking off into the building. He knows that normally the heat of a fire inside the dining hall will break the glass sensors on the sprinkler heads, and the pressurized water will be released. There's no guarantee the sprinklers will work after the Pause, but he doesn't have the luxury of worrying about that right now. He proceeds with his plan.

He takes the folded piece of paper from his pocket with the words of the Roman Ritual, and lays it on the housing next to him. Then he lifts the wheelbarrow up across the edge of the reservoir, slowly pouring the salt into the water.

He recites the blessing, his voice sounding almost alien to his own ears as the salt mingles with the water: "O water, creature of God, I exorcise you in the name of God the Father Almighty, and in the name of Jesus Christ His Son, our Lord, and in the power of the Holy Spirit. I exorcise you so that you may put to flight all the power of the Enemies, and be able to root out and supplant those Enemies with their apostate angels—through the power of our Lord Jesus Christ."

He makes the sign of the cross as he finishes pouring all the salt into the water.

"May this salt and water be mixed together, in the name of the Father, and of the Son, and of the Holy Spirit. Amen."

Next he blesses the holy water with the final words of the Roman Ritual.

"Blessed are you, Lord, Almighty God," he reads aloud with great reverence, "who deigned to bless us in Christ, the living water of our salvation, and to reform us, and assure us that we who are fortified by the sprinkling of or use of this water, the youth of the spirit being renewed by the power of the Holy Spirit, may walk always in the newness of life. In Christ we pray. Amen."

5.

It takes him quite a while to pry a door in the dining hall open far enough to accommodate a body. All the hinges and latches and doorframes are fossilized by both the Caesura and the dark magic that had originally jammed them shut in the first place. At length, Ticker manages to force a service door open in the back of the room, and then, from the hall of frozen smoke and stillborn flames, he begins to drag one guest after another across the floor and out the exit.

Removing all the innocent victims of the attack uses up another hour of his timeline.

Some of the attendees are frozen in tense, horror-struck poses, others crouched near those on the floor requiring medical attention. All of them are dead weight, as though they are wax figures being hauled away from a deserted museum exhibit, each one an exhausting ordeal for Ticker. It's as if the Caesura has turned the world into a macabre outer planet with three times the gravity of earth, and with each successive extraction Ticker's energy flags even further.

Finally he comes to his fellow warriors from the Quintet. Their eyes burning with rage, their bodies caught in battle postures, he carefully drags each one of them across the hall as if removing statues from a memorial commemorating some great and historic conflict. Outside, in the moonlit night, he positions his comrades-in-arms under the trees, in the cool shadows, where they will be safe.

Now, reentering the great dining hall, he sees only the five monstrous mutations of what used to be human beings suspended within the frozen flames. In the dead stillness and unearthly silence, Ticker pauses to catch his breath. Every muscle in his body aches. Every joint pangs with stiffness and pain. A sudden dizziness threatens to send him to the floor, but somehow he stays upright, taking deep breaths, and gazing up at the abominations that once answered to the names Father O'Toole and Father Warren, now stuck like bats to the rafters.

Ticker turns away and notices the Monsignor lying on the floor in a heap near the spot where the big man nearly strangled Ticker to death. Across the room, the beast that once was a plump little nun named Sister Mary Beth Malambri is curled into a fetal position on the exact spot where Spur had delivered a massive battering ram of a punch. And not far from there lies the thing that used to be Officer Fulbright, his skull fractured, his torso sprouting a luminous bouquet of flames caught in suspended animation.

6.

The final phase of Ticker's plan involves sealing the room, which he does now with his last scintillas of strength. He goes back over to the rear service door and yanks it shut. The latch catches with a dry click that sounds far too loud to Ticker. The noise throbs like a migraine behind his eyes. Another deep breath, and he's able to push a table under one of the malfunctioning sprinklers. The fixture is still at least fifteen to twenty feet above the surface of the table. Ticker remembers seeing a stepladder in the kitchen, in the walk-in pantry.

It takes what seems like an eternity for Ticker to return to the kitchen, fetch the ladder, drag it back out into the dining hall, lift it up onto the table, and steady it. By this point he is barely able to move. His joints have stiffened as though filled with cement. His muscles ache, and the pain radiates down his spine to the bottoms of his feet as he climbs the ladder practically in slow motion. His wheezing breaths come on labored gasps with each step as he slowly, painfully ascends the ladder to the topmost rung.

He is trembling convulsively now with pain and fatigue. He has no idea how long he can keep this up, or how many more minutes in his timeline he can endure in order to maintain the Caesura. He reaches for the fireplace lighter in his pocket.

A drop of sweat falls in his eye, and he wipes it away with the back of his hand. The silence is excruciating. It presses down on him and melds with the bone-deep loneliness that's been eating at him throughout his solitary mission.

He takes one last deep breath and exhales before attempting to trigger the sprinkler. The timing has to be perfect. He knows he'll be attacked by the demonic entities the moment he lifts the Pause. He places his thumb on the lighter's flint wheel and raises it toward the sprinkler. His arm pangs with agony, his muscles trembling as though the lighter weighs hundreds of pounds. He manages to bring the business end of the lighter to within an inch of the igniter tube.

An unexpected noise rings out across the dining hall, sending an icy chill down Ticker's spine.

Someone is knocking on the front door.

CHAPTER SIXTEEN

The Hell Chord

1.

Ticker jerks toward the sound.

The abruptness of his movement causes the footing of the stepladder to slip, sending Ticker careening to the floor.

He lands hard on his shoulder, and the ladder lands on top of him. The fall knocks him senseless for a moment. He rolls over onto his belly, and gasps for breath, his vision blurring, mind swimming with confusion. Did he imagine the knocking sound?

Someone knocks again on the hall's front double doors, harder this time—knock!-knock!-knock!—knock!-knock!-knock!

Ticker pushes the stepladder off of him, and sits up, a sharp, knifing pain stabbing the small of his back. He blinks at another salvo of knocking.

Knock!-knock!-knock!—Knock!-knock!-knock!—Knock!-knock!-knock!

Rising to his feet, brushing himself off, swallowing air, he realizes he's shivering. He sees his own breath. The air pressure in the hall has changed. He can feel his skin crawling.

Knock!-knock!-knock!—Knock!-knock!-knock!—Knock!-knock!-knock!—Knock!-knock!-knock!

The noise has intensified, grown impatient. Crossing the hall seems to take forever, as though he's walking in slow motion, the front door stubbornly receding from him as he approaches as though in a dream. Terror constricts his throat.

He opens the double doors.

The corpse of his late wife Laura stands there on the landing.

2.

It is the central trauma of Ticker's life. He and Laura Johnson (née Simmons) had been married for only a year and a half when the slender, doe-eyed former ballet dancer had left their apartment early one morning for jury duty. A brilliant social worker who had hung a shingle on one of the meanest streets in Chicago, Laura Johnson was not only fearless but always believed in civic duty—hence serving as a juror on a complex murder trial was not something to be taken lightly.

At the time, Ticker had just accepted the post of associate professor at Northwestern University's Physical Engineering Anomalies Program, spending most of his time interviewing test subjects and slicing cross sections of laboratory mice brains. He had come home late that night to dozens of messages on his voice mail from the Chicago Police Department regarding the whereabouts and physical condition of his wife.

The drive-by shooter had not been aiming for a member of the jury (as early reports misconstrued). Laura had simply been in the wrong place at the wrong time. But it wasn't until a few minutes after midnight that Ticker managed to get himself down to the morgue at Cook County Hospital to identify the body. At first, they wanted him to view the remains on a video screen, but he insisted that they let him see the body in person.

It was a moment that he would never eradicate from his memory—the zipper on her body bag sticking, the pallor of her flesh, the swollen, puffy aspect of her face, the tag on her big toe, and the three heartbreaking gunshot wounds along her sternum that had been hastily cleaned like a spill on a kitchen counter.

This same corpse now stands on the threshold of the dining hall's front entrance, aiming her milky, opaque, fish-belly stare accusingly at Ticker. Her voice is a death rattle, reverberating inside Ticker's skull more than in his ears.

"Why . . . ? Why did you leave me there?"

Ticker backs away as though from something wild and poisonous. "I . . . I . . . I . . . I . . . I . . . I . . . I . . . I don't . . ."

She tilts her head, the tendons in her neck creaking like old straw from the rigor mortis. When she speaks, her voice is out of sync with her lips like motion picture film slipping from its sprockets. "Why, Sammy . . . why would you leave me down there on that cold slab in the dark with the dead . . . Why?-Why?-Why?-Why?"

Ticker feels the wound of grief opening inside him, hemorrhaging in his chest, choking him. He tries to speak, but has trouble forming words. The woman's face has started decomposing, the sockets of her eyes drooping as though melting, her lips withering and peeling back away from a rictus of yellowed moldering teeth. Her flesh turns as grey as lung disease, maggots appearing in the cracks, her hair drying into a brittle white nimbus of spiderwebs.

Ticker stumbles backward over his own feet and falls to the floor, scooting away on his scrawny ass as a frightened child might back away from something feral and rabid.

The thing in the doorway starts vibrating like a tuning fork, the trembling so furious, so unhinged, the dead woman begins to blur in the moonlight. She lifts her cadaverous head and lets out an ugly, coarse cry of rage and disgust—partly sardonic laughter, partly a gut-deep howl of pure agony—and then the dead face snaps down and fixes its vacuous gaze on her husband. "Hypocrite!—You never loved me!—Fucking that bimbo lab assistant in the ladies' room while I was working the goddamn night shift!"

Ticker stares at the apparition for a long moment, blinking, his hectic breathing gradually settling down, his expression changing from white-hot terror to something more like revulsion . . . as the dynamic in the doorway abruptly changes.

3.

"You're not Laura," Ticker says to the entity on the landing in a cold, flat, knowing voice. "You're a second-rate magician—a lousy mimic—you wouldn't survive five minutes in a battle with my late wife Laura. How dare you impersonate such a beautiful human being!"

"What an impudent worm you are," the apparition says calmly.

The ghost points at Ticker, and a shock wave lifts him off his feet and hurls him back across the dining hall with the force of a hurricane-level wind. Ticker lands on the floor and skids wildly backward, banging into tables and inert bodies strewn across the hall.

He slams into the back wall, all the air knocked from his lungs, the impact concussing his skull and sending a cascade of stars across his line of vision. He rolls over and tries to rise to his feet, but his arms and legs buckle. "Did I . . . did I . . . s-s-strike a n-nerve?" Ticker mutters breathlessly, the pain shooting up his spine, his body practically shutting down now.

The thing in the doorway has shape-shifted into the shetani.

Eight feet tall, draped in shadows, with scaly black skin and phosphorescent eyes, this version of Satan appears to have come from another dimension, its head half the length of its body, its horns scraping the lintel above the massive doors, its fangs the size of tusks. Ticker's Tanzanian grandmother had first planted the image like a malignant seed in her grandson's imagination. She told him old East African folktales of this horrifying incarnation of the Devil . . . and now Ticker hears its baritone growl oozing out of its hideous craw: "You are the epitome of human duplicity, convinced that you are innocent, pure, angelic even. . . ."

Ticker struggles to a kneeling position, noticing figures in his peripheral vision, emerging from the shadows, closing in around him. The Devil lets out a guttural laugh as he goes on in his wood-chipper drone of a voice: "It is the narrative you tell yourself when the truth is you are as evil as my minions, as wicked as the damned. . . ."

Twenty-five feet away hangs the main sprinkler head, beckoning to Ticker as he painfully rises to his feet, the ghostly figures approaching him from all corners of the room. Shambling, drooling black bile, some of them are diplomats, double agents riddled with bullet holes . . . others are foreign intelligence operatives, military men and women, political attachés.

"Look around you, hypocrite," the shetani snarls from the doorway. "Meet the human beings whom you have slaughtered in your illustrious career as a glorified assassin, a gentleman killer, a scholarly sociopath. You believe employment with me is a sin? You have convinced yourself it is righteous to defy me?! You have no idea what is about to happen here on this very night at this feckless, pitiful anthill of shit . . . what is truly about to commence. . . ."

With his last soupçon of strength, Ticker lurches toward the ladder, reaching for the lighter lodged in his pocket. He heaves the ladder up on top of the table and climbs the wobbly structure with lighter in hand, already simultaneously thumbing the tiny flint wheel, kicking up a spark in the thick atmosphere of the Caesura, the business end of the lighter coming to within inches of the glycerin-filled glass tube.

From the doorway, the Devil laughs and laughs, as though enjoying this hopeless display by such a pathetic insect of a man.

Ticker closes his eyes. He presses the muzzle of the lighter against the sprinkler tube. He imagines his own slender fingers poised over the keys of a spinet piano. He sees in his mind's eye his imaginary fingertips plunging . . . plunging toward the keys.

He lights the tube.

In his imagination his fingers strike the keys—a full, fat, ominous C-major triad chord—the sound ringing out in his ears.

4.

"Jesus H. Christ!"

Spur flinches backward, banging his head against the massive old weeping willow behind him one nanosecond after his world abruptly jumps to a new locale. One moment Spur is trapped in a burning dining hall and the next he's out here in the cool shadows. It dawns on him instantly what has happened—Ticker performing his little magic trick—but no matter how many times Spur is on the receiving end of it he will never get used to it.

"Pin?!—Pin?!—You okay?—You good?" He sees Pin-Up on her hands and knees to his left, Boo staggering to his right.

In his peripheral vision he notices the rest of the attendees along the front walk, across the lawn, and scattered among the boxwoods. Some are groggily looking around as though they were just hit with a ball-peen hammer. Others are trying to stand but struggling with wobbly legs and sputtering central nervous systems. Others are genuflecting and praying and murmuring softly to themselves.

Father Joshua and his guards are completely flummoxed, blinking as though awakening from a dream, looking around at the sudden and inexplicable appearance of nearly twenty attendees. Some of Josh's laymen still hold fire extinguishers, others are gripping the ends of battering rams, the doors dented from the continual ineffective bashing. Darby is among them, at the moment sitting in an adjacent flower bed, looking dazed and vexed.

Pin-Up begins to comment: "You ask me, Ticker just inadvertently—"

She pauses, her words interrupted by the sudden din of screams emanating from within the building. It sounds like a slaughterhouse in there, as though livestock are being skinned alive, all of it accompanied by the jet-engine roar of water flowing.

Spur looks at Pin-Up, who rises to her feet and looks at Boo. For one tense moment, the three of them just stand there, processing. Then Spur and Pin-Up spring into action, charging side by side at full speed toward the front entrance.

"Hold up!—*Wait!*" Boo runs after them. "I have news!—Something I have to tell both of you, something important!—*Damn it!*"

5.

The front entrance is still lodged shut, cracked along the edges, jammed . . . until Joshua and his men snap out of their collective stupor and deliver a single blow of the battering ram to the double doors, cracking them open. "Stay back, Josh, let me check it out first," Spur warns, and steps into the vestibule, encountering a scene worthy of Hieronymus Bosch.

Pin-Up and Boo are right behind him, both of them coming to a sudden halt on Spur's flanks, both staring wide-eyed at the swirling cauldron of smoke and water forming a vortex around the four bodies on the floor, each of them now being soaked by the very special liquid spraying down upon them from the ceiling.

The howls of pain coming from this foursome defy description—keening, ululating, alien shrieks of torment pouring out of the four unfortunate victims that were possessed by superior demons from the underworld but now seem to be purging the evil in gouts of vomit and paroxysms of pain and shuddering, spewing, gagging vocalizations from some other world. It brings to mind a pack of dying hyenas, but Boo realizes, as she listens more closely, that much of what is being howled is a dead language.

But Spur—an instant before lurching headlong into the fray—notices two other strange and perhaps even more disturbing aspects to the lurid spectacle unfolding before him. He sees the fifth victim of the demonic assault—the beloved Monsignor—now lying in a heap, motionless, seemingly unaffected by the torrent of water erupting from the sprinkler system. And not far from the big man a second figure lies stone-still amid the violent inundation.

"Ticker!"

Spur calls out to his friend and then plunges into the storm of smoke and water, rushing past the quivering bodies of the possessed, all of which are now quaking and wailing and flopping in the onslaught of water with the spasms of fish speared and yanked from the ocean and tossed on the deck of a ship. Spur is immediately soaked, and starts coughing from the noxious fumes. He kneels by Ticker and feels the man's neck for a heartbeat and gets a pulse—albeit a faint one—which elicits a nod to the two women in the foyer.

Pin-Up then hurtles across the hall to where the body of the Monsignor lies in a simmering pool of his own blood. Hacking and coughing, she palpates the man's neck for a pulse, but can't find one. She tries again to no avail. She reaches down to his wounded wrist, which has stopped bleeding, and cannot find a pulse there either. She administers CPR for a moment, frantically trying to revive the man, her saliva mixing with blood and tears and holy water.

At length, her shoulders slump with anguish. She looks up at Spur and slowly shakes her head.

Spur nods sadly, then carefully pulls Ticker by the shoulders across the sodden floor, through the rain of healing water, and out the door.

"Let's get some medics in there stat," Spur says to Joshua as he gently lays Ticker on the landing in front of the building. The young priest is still a bit stupefied, and seems as though he might be going into shock. "Joshua! Padre! Look at me! Snap out of it!" Spur finally gets his attention. "We need doctors A-SAP! Now! Move your ass!"

The young priest gets his bearings, pulls a walkie off his belt, and hurries down the steps as he radios the clinic.

"Is he okay? Spur, is he all right?" Darby Channing has

rushed to Ticker's side. Her eyes have come back into focus as she kneels by him. "Spur? Talk to me.—What happened to him?—Is it the time thing, the stopping of time?"

"I don't know for sure what it is," Spur says, reaching down and gently thumbing Ticker's eyelid open. The man's eye has rolled back in its socket, and all Spur sees is bloodshot white. "The Pause takes a lot out of him. Let's hope this is just temporary."

Darby lays her head on Ticker's chest and starts to pray.

CHAPTER SEVENTEEN
Worst-Case Scenario

1.

By this point, inside the smoke-bound dining hall, the other four victims of the Shadow Society have fallen silent and still. Pin-Up motions to Boo, waving her into the hall. "Boo, help me check their vitals!"

Pin-Up's voice is barely audible over the noise of the water and the hissing of the dying embers. She hunches over for a moment, coughing and hacking, and tears a piece of her chiffon scarf off and wraps it around her mouth. She gives the rest of the scarf to Boo, who ties it around the lower part of her face and then follows Pin-Up to the other side of the room, where the cop, the nun, and the two priests lie strewn across the floor in various degrees of injury.

The cop, Fulbright, is barely breathing but still alive nonetheless, his face battered, his skull fractured from Pin-Up's explosive assault. The two priests who had levitated and terrorized the guests are badly burned, their pulses barely registering to Pin-Up's touch, their heartbeats slow and faint, but again, both are alive. Boo examines the body of the nun, her breathing thick and sporadic, her jaw dislocated from Spur's counterpunch, but again, she seems as though she will survive. Will she be permanently disabled from the ordeal? That's unknown at this point. It also goes unspoken that the whereabouts of the demonic entities that infected them are unknown. Boo looks up from the nun. "Pin, I have to talk to you about something."

"Hold that thought," Pin-Up says. "I have an idea. C'mon."

Pin-Up heads for the door, and Boo chases after her. "Pin, listen to me—"

"Hold on." Pin-Up exits the building, and she sees Spur and Darby across the landing, crouched near an unconscious Ticker, as Brother Brian, the medic, examines Ticker's eyes, stethoscopes his heart, and palpates his neck.

Joshua's lay assistants are now pouring into the building with chemical fire extinguishers and oxygen masks. Voices have risen across the parkway, many of the attendees now praying, some of them recounting the tribulations in the dining hall to curious groundskeepers and night watchmen. Brian's assistants and nurses are treating some of the attendees for first-and second-degree burns.

Pin-Up sees a figure being carried away in a black body bag, and she knows that it's poor, brave, steadfast Father Gasperi, the one who would not back down, the one whom Pin-Up could not bring back to life. Boo's voice barely penetrates Pin-Up's racing thoughts. "Pin, seriously, listen—"

"Hold on!" Pin-Up finally sees the person she was seeking.

Lorraine DeForest sits slumped in her wheelchair under a tree, her crooked, arthritic, palsied hands clasped reverently. She trembles as she silently mouths an ancient Lakota Sioux prayer: "Oh, Great Spirit, whose voice I hear in the winds, help me remain calm and strong in the face of all that comes—"

"Ma'am?" Pin-Up's voice interrupts her concentration, and the older woman looks up. "Ms. DeForest? May I ask if you would do us a huge favor?"

"Of course, honey, I'd be happy to help in any way I can."

"I should warn you, it would involve going back inside the dining hall."

The woman's expression does not change. "Just make sure the door at the top of the accessible ramp is open."

2.

Inside the ruined dining hall, from the padded seat of her wheelchair, she leans down and puts her hand on the damp forehead of Sister Mary Beth Malambri, who still lies unconscious in an inch and a half of holy water. The psychic closes her eyes. "The entity in this one is gone," she says softly, and opens her eyes. "Gone with the wind."

Pin-Up stands nearby, looking on with intense interest. "Can you tell if the demon has jumped into someone else? Is that a possibility?"

"It's a possibility, honey. Anything's possible. But I doubt it."

"Why's that?"

"Because Father Gasperi did a number on them, bless his soul . . . really kicked their ass . . . and your buddy Ticker finished them off."

Now she examines the others, rolling herself from victim to victim, while Boo, Brother Brian, Father Joshua, and two lay assistants with gurneys and oxygen masks wait in the background, looking on with morbid interest. The psychic feels each forehead, closing her eyes and absorbing the essence of each victim as a prospector might use a divining rod in the search for water. Each one is free and clear of the superior demon that had so tormented their soul.

"They've all gone back to hell where they belong," Lorraine DeForest explains. "All of them except one. That one." She points at the massive remains of the Monsignor. "That one is still skulking around here somewhere."

Boo steps forward. "I'm sorry to interrupt, but this is important."

With a sigh, Pin-Up says, "Go ahead, Boo, what is it? What have you been dying to say?"

"When was the last time you checked on the baby?"

An awkward pause ensues, and Pin-Up blinks as though slapped.

3.

As the crow flies, the distance between the great dining hall and the quaint little cottage that Spur and Pin-Up call home is a little over three hundred yards. That's a thousand feet—a fifth of a mile, or roughly three city blocks. An Olympic sprinter could run the distance in less than a minute. A vehicle moving at a safe speed, maybe thirty-five miles per hour, could make the trip in approximately thirty seconds. But right now, with her cell phone glued to her ear, and a series of buildings, cul-de-sacs, fences, parking lots, and elaborate landscaping in her way, Pin-Up takes quite a bit longer to complete the journey than she would prefer. "C'mon, c'mon, answer the phone . . . c'mon, Sister Lucy June . . . answer the goddamn phone," Pin-Up mutters under her breath as she sidesteps a statue of Saint Joseph holding a baby in swaddling cloth, the horrible sound of continuous ringing in Pin-Up's ear.

Again, the recorded greeting crackles: "Hello, blessings and gratitude to you all on this lovely day; you've reached the cell phone of Sister Lucy June; I'm unavailable at the moment but please feel free to leave as long a message as you'd like at the sound of the beep, and I promise I will get back to you forthwith!"

Again the awful beep drones far too loudly and far too long in Pin-Up's ear as she hustles along a hedgerow, running as fast as she can, recording her third message in the last five minutes between gasps: "Sister Lucy June . . . it's Pin-Up again . . . please, please . . . let me know you're there . . . and the baby's okay . . . *please!*"

A familiar voice calls out from the darkness behind Pin-Up: "Pin, wait up! We should tell Spur about this!—*Pin!—Wait!— Wait up!*"

Now Pin-Up can see the cottage in the middle distance behind a grove of apple trees. The porch light is on, and the front door is open. The window shades are drawn, and Pin-Up's pulse quickens, her heart pounding painfully in her chest as she weaves through the trees, forgetting that the recent spring rains have softened the mulch and wood chips in the grove. The loss of traction slows her down. She realizes she left her pistol in the dining hall. Her brain sputters and she loses her balance on a muddy patch, and she careens to the ground.

She pulls her hands from the mud and struggles to her feet. Boo's voice echoes over the treetops: *"Pin-Up, wait!—Wait!"*

Heart racing, gut tightening with panic, Pin-Up starts toward the cottage and suddenly wavers, nearly falling again, dizziness washing over her as she stares at her little house in the distance. Like an image in a backward telescope, the cottage has begun to recede into the distance, the little pool of light illuminating the porch growing smaller and smaller as the place slides away from Pin-Up.

"No—*No!*" Pin-Up slogs through the mire, half running, half trudging toward the retreating cottage. Like a scene from a nightmare, the little homestead with its flower boxes under the windows and homey picket fence lining its tiny yard keeps retreating into the dark distance no matter how hard Pin-Up races toward it. She lets out a furious cry of frustration as she labors through the unforgiving mud, making zero progress toward the home, which keeps drifting farther and farther away.

"Pin-Up!!!!!!"

Boo's cry reverberates on the rising wind, a sense of unfinished business in her voice, something important that Pin-Up needs to know.

4.

A little over fifty yards away, Boo can see Pin-Up in the shadows of the apple grove, staggering, struggling through the muck. Something's very wrong. Boo is starting to call out again when a cold wind kicks up out of nowhere, and the gusts begin to buffet the trees.

A barrage of dry leaves and detritus swirls around Boo, blinding her, stinging her, scourging her face. She surges forward against the wind. Inexplicable gales begin ripping the boughs off of trees. Boo staggers backward amid the onslaught, ducking when a jagged piece of a limb nearly strikes her between the eyes. She tries to keep pushing forward but the wind doesn't want her anywhere near Pin-Up or the cottage.

The violent squalls lash at Boo, forcing her backward, but Boo refuses to relent and keeps laboring forward with every last ounce of strength.

All at once, a phalanx of twisted, misshapen weeds and stalks burst from the ground around her. The withered black tendrils reach for her, winding around her ankles, tripping her, sending her to the ground. She struggles to rise back to her feet in the demon wind. She pulls her katana and lashes at the hungry stalks that refuse to let go.

Out of the corner of her eye, she sees something dark and shadowy moving toward her.

The Cloister's younger staff members have a nickname for the head gardener. It's a tad cruel, and they're careful not to use the moniker in the old man's presence, but it certainly fits his appearance. With skin as brown as tobacco, and a wiry frame as gaunt and bony as a wooden marionette, the man known as Scarecrow—real name Carlos Lombordini—has worked at the facility for decades, as long as anyone can remember, and is legendary for having the greenest thumb this side of the Mississippi.

Tonight, however, as he emerges from the shadows of the orchard, he is obviously under demonic influence, wielding a large, curved, rust-pocked scythe, his normally kind eyes now completely black, like vacant sockets in his skull. Boo spins toward the gardener as the old man lets out a garbled, otherworldly growl, swinging the razor-edged scythe at her with preternatural speed.

Boo deftly dodges the blow, the scythe embedding itself into the trunk of an adjacent tree. Crumbs of bark and pith go flying, swirling up and away in the wind. Boo counters with a graceful lash of the katana, the blade slicing through the gardener's shirt and lower midsection. Blood erupts and instantly soaks the old man's lower half but has little effect as he yanks the scythe from the tree. He whirls and lashes out at Boo.

The two blades—katana and scythe—crash and clang and send plumes of sparks into the supernatural winds.

The gardener, a puppet now, driven by diabolical forces, incognizant of his own innards spilling out of his midriff, swings the scythe at Boo's face again and again and again, driving her back against the oldest and largest of the apple trees. Her tailbone slams into the massive trunk, sending stabbing pain throughout her body. She may be undead, but her central nervous system is more alive than ever, sensitive to every wound. She cries out, and the tree begins to move.

The tree's ancient branches reach down to her, their brittle appendages clutching her, imprisoning her. The scythe swings at her face. She manages to get the katana blade up just in time. Steel meets steel. Sparks fly across Boo's line of vision. Boo slashes the limbs, cutting through the marrow of the boughs, freeing herself. She trips and falls.

The scythe looms over her. She's blocking her face with the katana when a sudden shot rings out, its booming echo audible over the roar of the wind. The front of the gardener's face opens up, an exit wound blossoming as wet brain matter showers Boo and the tree, vaporizing in the wind. The gardener manages to stay upright for a brief and horrible moment, his jaws working as though he is gumming his food . . . and then he collapses.

Boo wipes her face as footsteps quickly approach. Spur appears out of the shadows, holstering his Beretta.

"You good?" he says while gazing over his shoulder, searching the wind-blasted darkness for Pin-Up.

"I'm good," Boo says as she struggles to her feet. She sees Pin-Up's shadowy form in the distance.

5.

The spell broken, Pin-Up manages to reach the cottage. She leaps over the low picket fence lining the parkway, charges across the little postage stamp of a front yard, and then plunges through the front door.

She is greeted by a persistent whistling noise coming from the empty kitchen.

Breathing hard, scanning the deserted living room, Pin-Up immediately senses the worst-case scenario. All the lights are on, and the air prickles with the aftershock of a struggle, the residue of invasion. The odors of woodsmoke, scorched metal, and rotting meat press down on her. Pin-Up darts across the room and down the hallway to the former office that is now the nursery.

The ceiling light is on. Pin-Up tosses blankets from the empty crib.

The baby is missing.

"Pin?"

Spur's voice from the living room is a splash of cold water. It's followed by Boo's voice: *"Pin!"*

The three of them practically crash into each other in the hallway. "The baby's gone, *gone!*" Pin-Up raves at Spur. "The baby's fucking *GONE!!*"

Boo starts to say something when Spur chimes in: "Okay, take a breath . . . think with me . . . think." He holds Pin by the shoulders, and speaks directly into her face. "Could the sister have taken him on a walk? Did you look for the stroller?"

"You guys—?" Boo tries to jump in but Pin-Up is inconsolable.

"Fuck no!—No!—He should be sound asleep by now, Spur. Sister Lucy June knows that."

"Pin, this is—" Boo again begins to explain something but Pin-Up is beside herself, fighting the tears.

"God damn it, damn it, *damn it!*" Pin-Up's eyes have welled up, but her expression remains stone cold, as though she's in a firefight on a battlefield. "This has never happened before." She shoves Boo aside and storms back out into the living room. "Lucy knows better than to take him out at night." She bites her fingernails. "What is that fucking whistling noise?!"

Boo goes into the tiny galley kitchen and turns the front burner on the stove off. The whistling teapot slowly quiets down as though running out of breath. The silence tightens around the room like a vise. Boo calls out to them. "Come in here, you two. I've got to tell you something important about what's going down."

6.

"I was told in a vision that this would happen." Boo stands next to the stove, her gaze downturned, her voice soft and filled with emotion. "I was told Junior would be kidnapped."

Spur paces the kitchen like a caged animal. Pin-Up stands in the archway, her arms crossed against her chest, an incredulous frown on her face. "What the fuck are you talking about?"

Boo swallows hard. She returned to the Cloister ostensibly to deliver this message. But now that she has finally gotten their attention, and the nightmare has begun, she can hardly get the words out. "It took place in a parallel universe, a purgatory, but it was vivid and important, and I knew what I was seeing and what I was being told was prophecy."

Spur stops pacing. "What is it you were being told? C'mon. We're burning time here."

Boo looks at Spur and then at Pin-Up, and she says very softly, in a defeated voice, "I was told the whole assault in the dining hall would be staged as a form of misdirection. And the real target—of the demons, of the Devil basically—was the child."

Pin-Up and Spur exchange a mortified glance. Then Pin-Up looks back at Boo and asks, "Who the hell told you this?"

After a long anxious pause, Boo says, "It was Joseph Lister."

PART III

ANTICHRIST

Evil enters like a needle and spreads like an oak tree.

—Ethiopian proverb

CHAPTER EIGHTEEN

The Sacred Machine

1.

Arturo, the second-shift attendant at the county morgue, is a heavyset man with a shaved head that resembles a ripe melon. With his gore-splattered black apron, his rubber gloves, and the halogen light strapped to his forehead, he brings to mind a Hasidic mohel with questionable hygiene. He also resents getting a call in the middle of a shift from the mayor's office with orders to show a John Doe to some government asshole with connections.

Earlier that evening, down in sublevel C—aka the Ice Box—the disgruntled Arturo reluctantly pulled open a stainless-steel drawer, and then stepped back so the visitor could get a good look. Drew Hanley, code name Cthulhu, gazed down at the pale, naked remains of a man who was officially declared killed in action nearly two years ago. But now the man's death is apparently no longer a cover story invented by Hanley's boss.

"They're not going to believe this back at the swamp," Hanley muttered as he gaped at the corpse.

In life, the deceased was a brilliant polymath with a wicked sense of humor, a tech wiz who could take apart and put back together the mainframes at the Defense Intelligence Agency, but was also a badass warrior who completed SEAL training at the ripe old age of twenty-three. Now his remains lay blood-less, pasty, and stone-still in a drawer at the St. Louis County morgue.

"Unbelievable," Hanley murmured.

"What?" Arturo was looking askance at Hanley.

"Oh, nothing," Hanley muttered. He wore a surgical mask and rubber gloves, all of which, combined with his ill-fitting sport jacket, Neil deGrasse Tyson T-shirt, khakis, and Crocs, made him look like an absent-minded internist from some university medical center. "Is there a time of death?"

The attendant let out an impatient sigh, and pulled the toe tag off the cadaver. "Not really my job," Arturo grumbled under his breath as he checked the TOD on the tag. "Let's see . . . says 5/11 . . . so that would be . . . uh . . . what?"

"Yesterday," Hanley says.

"Right. Between midnight and four A.M. central standard time."

"Cause of death?"

"Um—"

2.

Unseen, unbeknown to the two men standing over the body, the latent energy in the deepest folds of the dead man's brain, in the core of the most tangled ganglia, in the nucleus of a single cell, a memory, not yet guttered out, like a candle flickering its final sparks, reenacts the previous evening.

In a tawdry, fetid motel room with moth-eaten curtains, rattling heater, and sagging trundle bed, the man slumps in an armchair and reaches rock bottom with an empty gallon jug of cheap vodka slipping from his hand and thumping onto the worn carpet. Being a nonobservant Jew, the man had never really believed in the supernatural before the incident in Karakistan, but now its presence looms as real and palpable as death itself.

The man tries to stand, but the manifestation intensifies both internally and externally. The room darkens and crackles with evil, and in the man's brain, in his thoughts, in his heart of hearts the realization that he has fucked everything up—his responsibilities, his relationships with his closest colleagues and friends, even his one true love—all of it devours him like a cancer.

Across the room, something glints in the shadows, a pair of yellow eyes, a long, ghostly, emaciated arm, its gnarled, crooked hand pointing at the wall just above the scarred, ancient base-board. There, a single duplex pair of plugs are embedded, just waiting, a hundred and ten volts of household-type current, calling out to the man in the chair: "Wait . . . hold on . . . with your powers . . . with your skills . . . your ability to cross the boundary between the real world and the virtual world . . . why not electrical current itself?"

Why not? Why not become pure, unfettered, boundless current?

In his final moments, the man slips off the armchair and falls to the floor, and he crawls . . . he crawls toward the wall outlet . . . urged on by the whispering of the Devil himself . . . whispering . . . "You can do it" . . . "You can become pure and righteous and invisible" . . . "You can become pure current."

The man reaches the wall, and he reaches down, and he tears the faceplate off the outlet, and he rips the live wires apart . . . and he licks his fingers . . . and he touches the fires of oblivion—

3.

"—electrocution, self-inflicted," the morgue attendant explained to Hanley with the nonchalance of a man describing the ingredients of a sandwich.

"Self-inflicted?"

"Yessir."

"Suicide by electrocution?"

The attendant shrugged. "Honestly . . . you see all kinds of shit down here, crazier than this."

"Really?"

"I shit you not. This is nothing. I had a DOA once, drilled a hole in his head with a Black and Decker."

Hanley sighed. "Well . . . if you knew who this guy was, you would find this pretty damn crazy."

"Who was he?"

Hanley looked down at the body one last time. "That's classified."

"Huh?"

"Unfortunately I'm not at liberty to identify this body; he'll have to remain a John Doe."

Arturo thought about it. "Let me ask you something: How did you find out about this guy offing himself?"

"Colleague of his, said she was worried about him, asked me to start a search."

"But you can't identify who he is, even though you know?"

Now Hanley was the one thinking it over. "I've already told you too much. But I'll just add this . . . in the way of a eulogy for this dude. He was one of the most talented, brilliant, and dangerous people who ever worked for the government."

"No kidding."

"Yes, he was. And he was hilarious, funny as hell. Trust me, this guy was one of a kind."

Now he had Arturo's attention. "You mean like he was some kind of a spook, CIA assassin, that kind of thing?"

"Let's just say he was a member of a . . . I guess you could say a very special team."

"Yeah?" Arturo looked down at the body. "What kind of team?"

Hanley shook his head wistfully. "Close it. We're done here. Thank you for your help."

4.

At exactly 7:13 P.M. central standard time, that evening, from the vantage point of the security camera mounted eighteen inches above the morgue's double entrance doors, which was at that time recording a bird's-eye view of sublevel C, an unexplained pulse of electromagnetic energy—technically known as adenosine triphosphate—had coalesced in the coils of the camera's coaxial cable.

This collection of atoms, which in some circles would be known as an entity, since it has consciousness and is, for all intents and purposes, a sentient being, had traveled across great lengths of high-tension wires, cables, radio waves, and wireless signal at the speed of light to arrive at this grim, dour, depressing place, only to watch with great melancholy the steel drawer containing the remains of what used to be its body slammed shut by a chubby morgue attendant.

"Would it kill this guy to lose some weight," the entity remarked to itself as it watched the attendant turn out the lights and usher Cthulhu out of the facility. "Maybe take a pass on the doughnuts in the staff lounge once in a while . . . or he's gonna end up in the drawer next to mine."

These were the thoughts running through the mind of Hack 2.0 (as he had come to think of his new self), as he held this lonely vigil over the morgue. Hack 2.0 may have been a disembodied spirit trapped for eternity in the digital universe . . . but he was no dummy. He knew this was all a result of a fateful accident in a motel room engineered by Satan. He also knew that he could turn these lemons into lemonade because of one particular wrinkle in the small print of Hack's deal with the Devil.

In perpetuity.

The phrase is most commonly used in legal documents, and essentially it means "for all time," as in "The land shall be the property of the Cartwright family, the ownership of which shall be passed on from one generation to another, in perpetuity." In other words, "in perpetuity" means forever, always, permanently. And back when this superpower of jaunting through the information highway had first been bestowed upon Hack by the Prince of Darkness himself, it had been made clear that, no matter what, contractually, this skill would be Hack's for all time, forever and ever . . . amen.

All of which galvanized Hack to accept his fate, and become what he imagined in his wildest childhood daydreams: the gremlin on the wing, the invisible monkey wrench.

The ghost in the machine.

5.

Interstate 55 between St. Louis and Memphis in the dead of night is a vast desert of shadows broken only by the occasional sodium-vapor glare of a truckers-welcome twenty-four-hour diner. The tangled ancient wetlands along the Mississippi press in on the sporadic passing headlights of lonely travelers, and the chill air smells of possum spoor and fish rot. Now, into this dead world of droning freight trains and boarded-up way stations comes a single southbound vehicle filled with hermetically sealed secrets and the high tension of a C-17 filled with paratroopers girding themselves to jump into enemy territory.

"Just start from the beginning, Boo, and don't leave anything out," Spur says from behind the wheel of the Cloister's tricked-out Escalade. The vehicle is adorned with countless religious icons, crucifixes hanging from every hook and strap, Stars of David, prayer cards taped here and there for protection and privacy from the prying ears of the Devil.

Spur now wears his Quintet regalia—Kevlar-impregnated, formfitting longcoat and gauntlets modeled after medieval sentries, all of it designed to terrify and intimidate adversaries. He has the accelerator pinned, the heavy vehicle hovering around eighty miles per hour, the speed jibing with Spur's racing thoughts. The baddest of the bad now have his baby, and he's going to get Junior back by any means necessary. He'll put blood on the walls if it comes to that.

But right now, he needs as much intel and information as he can get.

"Okay, so . . . it starts with the vision," Boo says from the darkness of the rear seat, the ambient glow from the dash painting her Shaolin robe and sculpted face in Rembrandt shadows. "At first I'm just wandering . . . moving through this sort of purgatory landscape. Desolate. Like the end of the world. But I see this object in the distance. Just a speck at first . . . but as I close in on it, I realize it's a baby carriage."

She pauses. She can see the back of Pin-Up's head in the front passenger seat, the tension apparent in her rigid posture. Her hair is pulled back tight, and she's suited up in her matte-black wasp-waist corset, chain mail, and bandoliers. She's loading an extra magazine, but Boo can tell she's hanging on every word. "Go on," she says without looking over her shoulder. "It's a baby carriage . . . then what?"

Boo takes a deep breath, and continues, speaking calmly and rapidly, as though on a battlefield, reporting the results of her reconnaissance, which, in a way, is exactly what she's doing. "I look inside it, and I see Junior, and he's got black eyes."

Spur speaks up. "Black eyes like bruised, like they're injured?"

"No, they're just black, all black, and he looks at me and his look goes right through me."

"Is this an actual dream?" asks Pin-Up. "I still don't understand exactly how this works. Is it a vision? Is that how you communicate with the other side? Or were you asleep?"

"It's kind of both," Boo replies. "I was kind of in a trance. But I'd been drinking so who the fuck knows. But when I saw the baby's eyes, I sort of came out of it with a start, like I was waking up, and I thought it was over, and I go into the bathroom to puke and there's another face in the mirror behind me. And it's Lister. At least I'm pretty sure that's who it was."

"What do you mean, you're *pretty* sure it was him?" Spur asks, remembering Joseph Lister being the lowest of the low, a denizen of the backwaters of New Orleans who had run a small criminal empire as well as a Satanic cult before his death. Acting on orders from the Devil himself, Lister had organized an assault on a missile silo two years ago, an operation that the Quintet managed to shut down with extreme prejudice. But now, hearing his name even remotely connected with their child is making Spur livid. He struggles to keep his cool. Losing one's cool is not in the playbook of dog soldiers like Spur and his unit. The moment he learned his baby had been kidnapped, though, he needed to be moving, despite the fact that they had not yet uncovered any leads as to the details of the kidnapping—the who, what, when, where, and why. The nanny cam had conveniently stopped working. But Father Manny had painful fragments of memory of his own possession and his subsequent ordeal. He remembered heading south, and for some reason, Spur thought that was a good place to start. All evidence pointed to the physical intrusion into the cottage at the Cloister taking place only minutes before Ticker had triggered the time pause. So whoever had snatched the child did not have much of a head start. "How could you not recognize Joseph fucking Lister?" Spur wants to know with more than a trace of incredulity in his voice.

"He was badly burned, Spur," Boo explains. "Almost a skeleton. His time in hell had not done him any favors in the looks department. But that voice. I'll never forget that creepy Southern-dandy accent. Anyway. He tells me he's been keeping tabs on the Devil in the underworld, following him, listening in. I guess Lister has a bone to pick with the Devil for not being more grateful for his services and for damning him to hell without so much as a thank-you. Anyway, he could tell something major was going down from all the rumors and whispers among the damned."

6.

"I shall never forget that day," the burned face in the mirror reported, *"when I saw those two imposin' figures havin' their little chat at a café table under a canopy made of dried human flesh. I instantly recognized both figures.*

"The larger one I knew all too well, the one with the great

insect-like wings folded behind him, pressed between his spine and the back of his chair. The Devil has a regal kind of bearing in that onyx breastplate and those epaulets of petrified human fingers. His elongated lupine face is the color of ox blood, those ancient ram horns sprouting above each canine ear. If it's possible to be simultaneously monstrous and elegant, that's my description of the Devil.

"The thing sittin' across the table from Satan, hangin' on every word, was also a monster . . . but was . . . well . . . merely monstrous. As dark as crude oil, putrid and otherworldly, he is a cross between a giant bat and some sort of mutant insect, and his body shifts and refracts the light, changin' its shape at will like a denizen of the deepest part of the ocean. This is the archetypal version of a demonic entity, in its default state of being. If anyone remembers the flyin' monkeys from The Wizard of Oz, imagine one of them, a big one, exposed to radiation and terminal illness and severe decomposition, and you might, you just might begin to get the picture. I knew this beast's name, Wormwood—the most superior of all demons, and the Devil's right hand. Wormwood functions as field marshal and commander in chief of all the superior demons that serve the Kingdom of Darkness.

"I had to know what these two were discussin'. I can't explain it. Maybe it's just my natural curiosity, or maybe my affinity for gossip. Or perhaps it's just because I'm bored out of my wits in this place, persistently being tormented by my agonies and exile. But whatever the reason, I carefully circled around the covered seating area, my movement hidden behind the veils of haze and toxic vapors, until I found a suitable vantage point, crouchin' down behind a pile of human skulls, from which I could safely listen.

"I got very still then. From the tone of their basso profundo murmurs, I heard them discussin' something of extreme importance, speakin' some long-dead language—perhaps it was Aramaic, perhaps an even older one, Sumerian dialect maybe—which I quickly, feverishly transcribed phonetically with a stick into the dirt.

"Later, after they had finished—each of them vanishing into thin air—I went and found a gentleman I had met in the netherworld sometime earlier, a man that had been in hell for so long he was not much more than a moving skeleton, his bones blackened from the ages. But he was alive during the second millennium BC, and when I showed him what I had scrawled into those hellish cinders that served as the ground, he got very still. His head jerked slightly before he began to speak, and by this point I had retrieved my pencil and parchment from my modest hovel.

"I wrote down everything he said as he translated the dead language into English, and there was so much to be learned between the lines before I wiped the marks away with my scorched feet.

"Only the most ruthless and resourceful," the Devil was saying at the beginning, speaking, according to my associate, in Sanskrit.

"I understand, my lord," the superior demon replied with great reverence.

"With the greatest sense of urgency."

"I understand."

"Only the most unclean."

"Yes, Master."

"You will choose your four."

"So it will be a total of f—?"

"SILENCE!"

There was a slight pause here, during which time it seemed that Satan was about to banish Wormwood to the lowest circle. "I detest that diabolical number," the Devil finally snarled. "Do not utter that hideous figure aloud in my presence . . . ever."

"Of course, my lord. I beg your forgiveness. Please go on."

"You will recruit these four superior demons and you will join them in the earthly realm where you will commence with the theft of souls."

"The possessions."

"Yes."

"Of the clergy."

"Correct."

"I have the names, Master."

"Good."

"I am ready."

"Wormwood, for your sake, I truly hope that is the case because the possessions are only the beginning. Do you understand?"

"Yes, Sire."

"Do you recall the ultimate objective, the true nature of the undertaking?"

"Yes."

"Tell me."

Now . . . here was where the demon's voice dropped into a lower register. And according to my translator, the language became garbled, a mixture of Sumerian, Aramaic, Akkadian, and Latin. Whatever the demon was describing here—the actual goal of the operation—the translator could tell it was extremely secretive, not only of the utmost importance but unprecedented.

7.

Pin-Up chimes in. "Wormwood? Like the poison? Cute." She clicks the final bullet into the magazine, and then stuffs the mag into her belt. "I'm betting he's the entity that originally hijacked Father Manny."

"Right," Spur says. "Must have jumped into the body of the Monsignor when the big man went to have a powwow with him."

"Be that as it may," Boo goes on, "this demon Wormwood—he's a real charmer. One of the nastiest in hell. Powerful. Way at the top of the pyramid. According to Lister, the Devil wanted to create a doppelgänger unit. A shadow of the Quintet. Named it the Shadow Society. Five of the meanest motherfuckers in hell. All of them superior demons. But now we come to the real purpose of the Devil's mission, the real reason to go to all this trouble."

Spur glances at the rearview. "Obviously it's to kidnap the child, right? He stages this grand grotesque assault on the dinner guests but it's all a diversion. He's really after the baby. And it's all designed to destroy us. If he can't take our powers away, he'll take the most important thing in our lives."

"It's more than that, Spur." Boo's voice has dropped an octave, softened, become less confident. She no longer sounds like a soldier in the field reporting back findings to a superior officer. She sounds for the first time a little unnerved. Maybe even scared. Which is completely out of character for Boo.

"We're all ears. Tell us."

She takes another breath, girding herself before replying, "Okay . . . apparently the Devil wants Junior for himself, for what Lister calls 'grandiose purposes.'"

"'Grandiose purposes'?"

"The guy's a lunatic, a drug addict and pedophile, and God knows what else. I don't know what he's talking about. It's bugfuck crazy. But it's also good for us if you think about it. If it's true it buys us time. It makes it easier—"

"Slow down," Spur says. "Lister didn't explain what the grandiose purposes were?"

Boo measures her words. "Look. I'm not the one you should ask about this part. Some members of my family, my aunt, they were very devout, but I'm no Christian, Spur. God knows. Lister said something about all this being prophesied in the Bible. He said it's mentioned five times in the New Testament, and in the Gospels, Matthew and Mark, it's in there, too."

"What is? Boo, what in the blue blazes are you talking about?"

For a long, unnerving moment, the only sound is the drone of the engine and the hum of the tires on the weathered pavement as Boo gropes for words, for a way to explain the inexplicable. At last, she speaks very softly, almost inaudibly. "'There will come a man, the son of destruction, who exalts himself above every so-called god or religion.'"

"Excuse me?"

Boo took a deep breath and said, "The Devil wants to groom your son to be the Antichrist."

8.

The Cloister's modest little clinic bursts at the seams that night with patients requiring immediate attention, mostly victims of the dining hall debacle, most of whom are being treated for smoke inhalation and second-degree burns. With only one doctor and three nurses on-site, it's tough going for attendees still in pain. Brother Brian, the attending physician, goes through six thousand milligrams of Vicodin in the first hour. Some of the patients with more serious injuries—such as the old priest whose hand was severed in the slamming door—are transferred via ambulance to Old De Paul Hospital north of St. Louis. But the most baffling case of all that night is sequestered in a private treatment room at the end of the main hallway.

"Look, I know you're anxious, but I'm telling you it's hard to predict outcomes on something like this."

Brother Brian says this in a low, tense voice outside the treatment room. Silverback paces, hardly listening, his brain swimming with panicky to-do lists. He has yet to set up a command center in the search for the kidnappers. He already alerted the local field office of the FBI but has held off in bringing in the tactical group from the U.S. Marshals Service. Spur had begged him to allow the Quintet a few days' lead time before the cavalry came in and fucked everything up, perhaps even getting the baby killed in the process. Silverback had reluctantly agreed to give Spur and his team twenty-four hours to go after the kidnappers their way, on their own, without the intrusion of the feds. But now Silverback is starting to regret his decision.

"He's doing fine," the medic adds. "So far so good. I've done everything I can right now. We got a specialist coming in tomorrow morning."

Silverback peers through the half-open door and sees Darby Channing sitting at Ticker's bedside, holding his limp hand, her head down, maybe praying. Who knows? Maybe asshole reporters have hearts like everybody else, Silverback silently muses. Ticker lies supine on the bed, nestled in blankets, his head and shoulders slightly elevated, a nasal cannula under his nose, helping him breathe. "How did the MRI go?" Silverback asks, turning away from the room.

"It was negative, which is a really good sign." Brian crosses his arms against his chest. His white lab coat looks two sizes too big for him, which is, perhaps, why the nurses had started calling him Brother Doogie Howser behind his back. "His brain shows no abnormalities, no injury, and his blood work is normal. Best of all he's at fifteen on the Glasgow scale."

"Remind me what that means."

Brian takes a deep breath. "It's more good news, Colonel. The Glasgow coma scale measures involuntary motor responses, eye dilation, stuff like that. If you're above, let's say, ten or eleven, you have really good odds of recovering fully."

Silverback gazes back into the room, muttering to himself. "Thank God for small favors."

His cell phone buzzes in his pocket. He looks at the caller ID and sees that it's Cthulhu. He thumbs the ANSWER button. "Go ahead, Hanley. What's up?"

"Boss . . . I got some news. Is this secure? Can you talk?"

Silverback covers the phone and says to the doctor, "Thanks,

Brian, I have to take this." Then Silverback finds a private space in the coffee room down the hall. "Okay, talk to me."

"Boorstein is dead."

Silverback's scalp crawls. "Wait . . . what did you just say?"

Cthulhu's voice lowers, becomes deferential. "I'm so sorry, Boss. I know you were good friends, and it's a major loss for the program."

"You're talking about Hack? Aaron Boorstein? What are you talking about?"

"You remember he dropped off the grid, and Boo asked us to do a search. He showed up as a John Doe in the St. Louis County morgue. Blood alcohol level was off the charts. And there's something else . . . about his death . . . you should know."

"Jesus . . . go on."

"Coroner's ruling it a suicide."

"Good Lord . . . what happened?"

Cthulhu tells him, and Silverback listens, aghast, unaware that his eyes have begun to well up.

9.

Highballing southbound at eighty miles per hour with no real destination, just a bunch of hunches and vague extrapolations, Spur keeps the Escalade on course while chewing on the very idea of an Antichrist. It was one of those convoluted sidebars of Christianity that Spur never really understood: an evil human being who comes along and decides to substitute himself for Christ right before the Second Coming?

"Junior . . . the Antichrist?" he said. "Not going to lie. I'm having trouble wrapping my head around that."

From the back seat, Boo speaks up. "Then let's set aside the whole Antichrist thing for the moment. What's the mission here? What's the protocol?"

Pin-Up doesn't even look at her, just wipes her eyes. "It's a hostage situation and we're the extraction team. We've done them before. Like the National Christian Resistance Movement kidnapping back in Johannesburg, or that cult deal in Sri Lanka, took that kid from the missionaries. What about the diplomat's daughter in Syria? Think of these kidnappers same as those—insane in the membrane. That's how we treat this. We get in, we get out. That's all we're doing, Boo. Extraction. Nothing more. Nothing less."

Spur is slightly stung by her words but he lets it slide, and backs off on his Sunday school rant. He steals a sympathetic glance at Pin-Up across the dark interior, patting her arm, and murmuring softly, "Sorry, babydoll . . . just a little jacked up."

Pin-Up slowly nods and dries her eyes with a wadded Kleenex. Since learning that her baby had been snatched by a wolf pack of demons, she's been vacillating between tears and white-hot anger, at times simultaneously. She knows she has to bite down on all this emotion, but she can't do that right now. The emotion keeps her sharp. This is her baby, her precious child. She feels the loss, the danger, the helplessness like a hot poker twisting in her guts. "Look," she says, her voice softening. "I know I'm supposed to be a professional, a career soldier, an army nurse who stays calm in the . . . I don't know . . . the heat of battle. But this . . . this is a different sort of battle. Right? This is fucking personal, and there's nothing we can—"

Spur's cell phone starts chiming, the telephone icon appearing in Technicolor on the big multifunction screen embedded in the center of the dash. It's eleven minutes past one in the morning central standard time when Spur presses the TALK icon.

"Go ahead, Silver. What's the latest on the task force? Any leads yet?"

There's a weird, awkward pause, during which time Spur at first thinks they lost the signal. "Silver? You there? Did we lose you?"

"Spur, Pin-Up, Boo," the voice of Silverback finally crackles from the JBL surround-sound speakers, bringing to mind the voice of God. "I've got more bad news. I'm sorry to pile up on you right now but I figured you'd want to know about this as soon as I knew about it. It's . . . it's about Hack."

"What about Hack?"

Boo scoots forward on her seat, her ears pricking up, her hands making fists as Silverback breaks the news to them.

CHAPTER NINETEEN

That Which Dwells in the Hive

1.

Boo takes the news hard, and for the first time since Spur and Pin-Up met her back at the naval support facility at Bolling Air Force Base, back when dinosaurs roamed the earth, she weeps openly, uncontrollably, alone with her grief in the darkness of the Escalade's rear seats.

For the next twenty-five miles, they pay homage to Hack, trading hilarious stories of his Borscht Belt comic sensibility, his one-liners and barbs. They talk of his genius with computers, and his skill in the virtual world that had developed long before any superpowers had been bestowed upon him.

But mostly they discuss whether or not it was an accidental death . . . or a suicide . . . or foul play . . . or God forbid Satanic.

"Boo, look at me," Pin-Up says at one point, gazing over the seat back at her friend in the shadows of the rear seats. Boo is staring out the window at the passing desolation of wee-hour river towns and ancient boat docks. "This is important, Boo. Look at me. Please."

Boo yanks her gaze away from the passing nightscape and looks up at Pin-Up with bloodshot eyes. "What?"

"This had nothing to do with your dustup. Trust me on that."

"What do you mean?"

"The whole situation with you catching Hack breaking into Osamir's cookie jar, skimming some for himself?"

"Yeah, I know."

"I'm not gonna sit here and watch you blame yourself."

"I don't blame myself."

"You sure?"

"I'm sure, Pin. Look. Hack would have done the same thing if he caught wind I had gone astray. He would have confronted me." She lets out a sigh. She has burned her tear ducts out. She's numb. She looks at the back of Spur's head. "It just doesn't make sense. He's just not the type."

Spur notices that the fuel level is close to empty. "I'm sorry, folks, but we have to grab some gas pronto or we're gonna be hoofing it."

2.

They pull off at the next exit, the meager little filling station located at the top of the off-ramp, on the northeast corner of the intersection. Its small cement lot is deserted and bathed in sodium-vapor light. Under a dilapidated metal canopy sit two rust-pocked pumps, one with regular and premium and one with diesel. The ramshackle office is the size of a toolshed, the restrooms located outside around back. Spur pulls the Escalade up to the regular pump, turns off the engine, and says, "Let's make it quick."

They cover their regalia with overcoats, and the women go inside for the key to the ladies' room while Spur fills up the tank. He tops it off, puts the cap back on, pays with a credit card, and then locks up the Escalade. Then he goes inside, and asks the heavyset teenager behind the register—who is currently absorbed in a *Hustler* magazine—if he can borrow the key to the men's room.

With a grunt the kid shoves a key on a piece of old balsa wood across the counter.

Spur takes the key outside and tends to his business, and when he emerges from the men's room, he notices Pin-Up and Boo standing outside the door with puzzled looks on their faces.

"What's the matter?" he says, looking from one bewildered face to the other.

Pin-Up looks at him. "You think it's a good idea to leave the car running while you take a pee?"

"What?—What are you talking about?" The building is blocking his view of the SUV. But he can hear the telltale sound of the big engine idling, and he can see the high beams shining off an adjacent fence.

Spur's hackles go up instantly. He tosses the restroom key to the ground, one hand instinctively fishing inside his pocket for the Escalade's keys. He holds up the keys and shows them to the women. His other hand is reaching into his coat, his fingers slowly wrapping around the grip of his Beretta pistol, which is holstered on his belt. Pin-Up and Boo react with the involuntary muscle memory of career soldiers. They instantly back up against the wall, reaching for their weapons, crouching down in defensive postures. "What the fuck?" Pin-Up utters as she cranes her neck to see the Escalade, now lit up like a fireworks display, parking lights blinking, interior light flashing rhythmically.

Spur lifts his hand up, signaling for them to stay put.

Then he points at himself, then points at the Escalade, and then makes a fist signal and yanks it downward, all of which means that he's going in and they should cover him.

3.

Hectic with blinking lights, the sole vehicle in an otherwise deserted lot, the Cloister's Escalade looks like a pinball machine on tilt, its headlamps flashing, its exhaust vapors visibly pluming out of its tailpipe into the chill air. Spur doesn't see anybody inside the vehicle but plays it safe, crouching beneath the level of the windows as he approaches, carefully peering into the vehicle's interior.

He sees only empty front seats, empty middle seats, and an empty rear cargo bay. Then he duckwalks around to the driver's-side door, and, using his left hand, cautiously reaches for the door handle. Before opening the door, he looks over his shoulder at Pin-Up, and then at Boo. With a nod he silently signals he's opening the door. Then he holds up his left hand, with three fingers raised, and he counts down . . . three, two, one.

He opens the door.

A large green face peers out at Spur from the ten-inch multifunction screen in the center of the dash. "What, you were expecting a terrorist organization?" the face says with a voice not unlike an electronic beehive. "Boko Haram perhaps, al-Qaeda maybe lurking in your SUV?—Put the iron away, Spur, you may need the ammo later."

Spur gapes, paralyzed, vexed by the hallucinatory thing he's seeing on an infotainment screen most commonly used for navigation and finding wonderful oldies on SiriusXM.

He lowers the gun.

"Look, Spur, old buddy, old pal, I realize this mode of communication here is not the most terrific way to introduce you to my current, shall we say, state of affairs, but be that as it may, we don't have much time," says the face, which belongs to the late, great Aaron Boorstein, code name Hack. And a handsome face it certainly is: boyish, deep-set brown eyes, nifty smile—all of this despite the ghostly effect of being hewn out of chartreuse vapor. Spur stares and stares, mesmerized. "Spur, say something already," Hack 2.0 pleads. "Your lips are moving but no words are coming out."

"Can you . . . can you . . . see me?" It's all that Spur can manage at the moment, as he shoves his pistol back into its holster.

"That's it? That's all you have to say at a moment such as this?" the face chides him from inside the screen. "After all we've been through? I mean . . . not to be unctuous or insecure or needy in any way, but a little love would be nice at time like this. Yes, for God's sake, yes. To belabor a point, I can see and hear you just fine, Spur, thank you very much. I've had my eyes checked recently by a licensed ophthalmologist, for which I'm happy to say my Defense Intelligence Agency insurance was kind enough to reimburse me. As a matter of fact I'm still alive and well in what you would call the grid, which is how I got here, jaunting from the morgue attendant's cell phone to a local tower, and from there a few side trips into the wireless Bluetooth connections of key surveillance cameras. From there it was an easy hop, skip, and jump into the radio-wave matrix, and into the Escalade's shark fin antenna, and finally into your vehicle's computer—which could use some service, if I may be totally candid with you—all of this in spite of the fact that I watched my body go kaput before my very eyes, electrocuted, a little practical joke played on me by Guess Who. But never mind all that, here's the most important part, and I apologize in advance for dropping this in your lap in such an abrupt fashion, but if you recall what I said a minute ago, time is of the essence, so here goes."

The face vanishes, and a grainy black-and-white night-vision image from a surveillance camera replaces it, filling the multifunction screen. The viewpoint is high above the floor of the Cloister's great dining hall—flames licking up the walls, general chaos. "Let me review the timeline for you," Hack's buzzing voice drones. "First, I was tapped into the dining hall surveillance cam the moment the parasite inside the Monsignor meets his match in our dear Miss Boo."

The screen cuts to a close-up of Boo in her Shaolin regalia, two-handing the katana, adeptly spinning and slashing the Monsignor's wrists. "The big man hits the mat, out for the count, at exactly 9:17 P.M. central standard time, as you can see from the time code in the corner."

Now the image cuts to "nanny cam" footage from Spur and Pin-Up's cottage. Grainy, black-and-white, from the point of view of a ficus plant in the nursery, the image shows little Junior asleep in his crib, thumb in mouth, and Sister Lucy June nearby, dozing on a rocking chair next to the crib.

She abruptly springs to her feet as though on a catapult.

"As one can plainly see, at this same exact moment—9:17 P.M.—our beloved babysitter Lucy June is hijacked by the same piece-of-shit evil spirit that apparently was inside the honorable Monsignor."

Moving robotically now like a puppet on invisible strings, Lucy June scoops the baby from the crib and charges out of the room.

"Meantime, we got more visitors slipping into the Cloister to assist in the kidnapping, as you can see here on the east parking surveillance cam, at precisely 9:23 P.M. CST."

Now the screen cuts to a skinny hoodlum in leather using a slim jim on the door lock of a Ford Taurus parked in the lot.

"Which brings us to the last stop on the travelogue. Take a look."

Spur moves in close to get a better look at an overhead shot of a lonely truck stop parking lot drenched in sodium-vapor light, a car visible at the bottom of the screen that matches the vehicle reported stolen from the Cloister's motor pool only hours ago. The moment Father Josh reported the car missing, the bureau's rapid-response team immediately sent out bulletins on a 2018 Ford Taurus SEL in Kodiak Brown with beige interior and Missouri plates, Alpha-November-Eight-Baker-Five-One, and now, at this moment, Spur watches live footage of Sister Lucy June sitting rigidly on the front passenger side of the stolen Taurus, waiting, a partial reflection of her face in the rearview, obscured in shadow, her features distorted like a corpse's, while, outside the car, an emaciated man in a leather jacket hastily unscrews the rear license plate and swaps it for a different, presumably stolen plate. In the back seat, the silhouette of a slender woman hovers over a small object that may or may not be a cradle or car seat; it's hard to tell in the grainy surveillance footage, but the very sight of it thrusts a knife into Spur's solar plexus.

He leans forward, putting his hands on the screen as if he is about to dive into the image. "Hack, where is this?—Is it live?—Where is it?!"

The face returns to the screen. "Yes, it's live, and it's south of here, and if you could possibly convince our illustrious female members of the Quintet to get their asses back in the Escalade, I'll give you directions so we can go save your baby."

4.

Wormwood—the Devil's right hand, hell's field marshal—has no idea how to drive a modern automobile. He was born Agrippa Maledetto, a human, in the year 79 BC, the child of a prostitute who died from a hemorrhage during his birth. He was raised by a band of thieves, and grew up to become the most vicious soldier in the Imperial Roman army, which channeled and honed his innate cruelty into monstrous proportions. In time he developed a reputation for wickedness that caught the attention of the Devil himself. When Wormwood was slaughtered by his own men in the year 48 BC, Satan welcomed him into the underworld, and groomed him to be the most superior of all demons.

But driving a car had not been part of the mentoring process.

Which is one of the myriad reasons Wormwood has planned all along to utilize surviving members of Joseph Lister's Satanic cult to assist him during this glorious escape phase of this great and epochal mission.

"Left," the demon voice says in a flat, cold baritone that emanates from the plump little nun in the shotgun seat, as the man behind the wheel pulls the Taurus out of Simkins' 24-Hour Service Center of Perryville, Missouri, turning left, and heading south on Highway 67.

"That new plate ain't gonna get us very far, Your Excellency," says the man behind the wheel. A scrawny, withered, rail-thin heroin addict with an acne-scarred face and the eyes of a possum, Johnny Prast used to be a second-tier NASCAR driver, as well as a principal moneymaker in Joseph Lister's occult gang, right up until Prast got pinched by the NOLA PD, and got five to seven years for parole violations.

"Silence," the voice coming from the shadows of the passenger seat instructs.

"Sir, I'm just sayin', if they got an APB out on a turd-brown Taurus, the wrong plate ain't gonna keep the jackals off us; plus, last time I checked, kidnapping was a federal issue, so I guarantee they got the entire bureau bustlin' as we speak."

"SILENCE, PHILISTINE!"

The booming, otherworldly quality of the voice nearly makes the skinny junkie swerve off the road. In the rear seat, the baby whimpers . . . and then begins to caterwaul.

"Awright, folks, that's enough now," the woman in the rear seat protests in her deep Southern drawl, fishing in the baby's makeshift cradle for the pacifier. "You're disturbing the little one."

The woman is also a former member of Joseph Lister's circus of the occult. A madam from a Bourbon Street bordello who dabbles in Satanism, she's a late-stage meth addict and former exotic dancer who goes by the name Esmeralda Villainous. Emaciated, with purple hair and a goth corset, she's in her midforties but looks twenty years older. Most of her teeth are either gone or not doing very well, and her facial tics bring to mind the movements of a lizard or a mongoose. She is also a prolific killer of innocent women, some of the victims over the years earmarked for human sacrifice, some murdered just for the fun of it.

It was only a week ago that Esmeralda received the mysterious note written in what appeared to be human blood inviting her to come to St. Louis for a landmark ritual that will "change the future of mankind." Rumors among the Satanic underworld started surfacing that the Devil himself was involved. Which is how Esmeralda convinced her favorite thug—the lanky, tattooed man currently behind the wheel of the Taurus—to accompany her to Missouri for what could turn out to be the experience of a lifetime.

"Right turn at the intersection," the voice coming from

the nun directs the driver. The words have their own strange accent—ancient, cryptic, unidentifiable—and are nearly drowned out by the piercing squalls coming from the baby.

The voice galvanizes Johnny Prast as he makes a right turn at the light and heads down a deserted blacktop two-lane that wends through a stretch of unincorporated woods, the head-lights brushing past endless palisades of pines and river foli-age. Their route to the sacred place—the place at which the great ritual will unfold—is more of a zigzag than a straight shot, but that doesn't bother Johnny.

At that moment, in the shadows of the rear seats, Esmeralda finds the pacifier and gently lodges it into the child's wide-open mouth. The baby instantly quiets down, suckling furiously. But what Esmeralda doesn't see is the manner in which the baby fixes its watery eyes on the woman for a long time.

It is the beginning of a process that no one—not even the Devil himself—could have predicted.

5.

"Found them!" The voice burbles up through the buzzing hive of the power grid.

From the shadows of the Escalade's rear seats, the trained assassin known as Boo wrestles with her emotions as she watches the face of the only man she ever loved wavering in and out of a pixel storm on the Escalade's front screen. Hack's handsome visage distorts and stretches like taffy as he says, "Thank God this piece-of-shit Taurus we're searching for—a vehicle of which Father Manny is so fond—is a late enough model to have a 5G console."

"Whatever the hell-or-high-water that means," Spur com-ments.

"It means," replies the undulating face on the Escalade's screen, "that we can now track these muthafuggas with ex-treme prejudice."

From the front passenger seat, Pin-Up's voice is a tense murmur. "How much of a lead do they have on us?"

"At the risk of being glib," says the face, "it'll be a hell of a lot easier to just show you on their GPS. Take a look."

On cue, the image of Hack's ghostly face on the Escalade's screen dissolves into a crystalline image of a GPS landscape rendered in primary colors, with pop-ups, street names, and a speed indicator along the bottom at 73 mph. The pirated display shows the outside temperature at 63°F, the direction south, and the arrival time 1:37 P.M. EST.

From the rear seats, Boo sees the big glowing blue arrow in the center of the screen gliding along a back road labeled HWY C.

Her eyes well up again as another wave of grief mixed with anger crashes through her. She has not completely processed what has happened to Hack, or what her relationship with the man will be in the future. She can barely face the reality that she will never hold him again, never run her fingers through that thick mane of hair, never make love, never see him as anything other than an avatar, a digital phantom, an animated memory. She tries to push aside her feelings and think of the baby in harm's way, in the clutches of a superior demon from hell, and the realization braces her.

"Highway C, that's a back road I would guess," Spur says.

"I'm looking it up," Pin-Up says, pulling out her cell phone and opening up her GPS.

"Don't bother," the voice of Hack says, now deep and modulated and coming out of the Escalade's best-in-class JBL surround-sound system. "It's forty-three miles from here; best route is probably staying on 55, then getting off at Perryville."

"Copy that," Spur says.

"Should I call it in?" Hack asks. "Get some backup on the front burner?"

"Negative."

Boo feels the centripetal force pushing her deeper into her

seat as Spur puts the pedal to the metal. Boo reaches around to the back of her belt, draws her Beretta, ejects the clip, and checks the magazine. She does this more out of habit than necessity—a Major League Baseball player entering the batter's box and tapping the mud off his cleats when there is no mud there in the first place; in other words, it's all ritual, a girding, a rebooting of focus.

Spur apparently notices this in the rearview. "Look, everybody, listen up. We're not calling in any backup. We're not starting a firefight. We're not engaging with the kidnappers unless it's absolutely necessary. Everybody got that?"

Pin-Up gives him a look. "Then what the fuck are we doing here, Spur, making a reality TV show?"

"Listen to me, Pin. Junior is in that car. Our baby is in the back seat of that fucking car. I'm not going to draw down on them and get everybody killed."

"Then what are we doing?"

"Getting as close as we possibly can without getting made."

"Yeah? Then what?"

Spur lets out a sigh. "I don't know. I guess keep an eyeball on them and assess."

"Assess?"

"Pin—"

"Assess this, Spur. I'm going to get Junior back safe and sound by any means necessary. If I have to track these animals to hell and back, I'm going to save my baby. And that's all there is to it."

In the awkward silence that follows, Spur reaches over and touches her arm, and she lets him. They exchange a brief glance and an even briefer nod. From the back seat, Boo recognizes the signal. It is a gesture born of the battlefield. It is a silent acknowledgment that the odds being stacked against them have become irrelevant.

Boo leans forward finally, and poses a question. "Is there any way we could figure out where they're headed? I mean, we can extrapolate from their direction and their arrival time. Right? Ten hours, straight south . . . it says New Orleans to *me*."

"Why New Orleans?" Pin-Up wants to know.

"Lister was from there. I mean, if you had to pick a city where the Devil lives, and where the Antichrist would be born . . . New Orleans would be a top contender."

Another beat of silence grips the Escalade.

Spur focuses on the road, and gaining on the kidnappers. He keeps the SUV roaring down Interstate 55 at ninety miles an hour for nearly ten minutes before they see a blue flashing light in the mirrors. Glancing over her shoulder, Boo mutters, "Fuck me."

A state trooper on a tricked-out police Harley is closing in on them.

6.

"Can't we just let him pull us over?" Pin-Up asks rhetorically, already knowing the answer. "Maybe explain we're under-cover, working for the government on a classified mission or whatever?"

"Yeah, sure," Spur says, his voice laden with tension and sarcasm. "We can just have him give Daddy a call. I'm sure Silverback can straighten everything out with the boys in blue."

From the multiscreen, the voice of Hack buzzes like a digital wasp. "Let me see if I can jaunt into his radio, maybe find the archive of all the recent dispatches, figure out if it's just a speeding ticket in our future or something more serious."

Pin-Up glances over her shoulder and follows the faint glimmer of Hack's astral body as it zips off the Escalade's antenna. The pale glow of pure signal skates along the length of an adjacent high-tension wire, and then shoots like a lightning bolt down the Harley's whip antenna.

Meanwhile the trooper has closed the distance, the motorcycle drawing to within a few car lengths. Now, in the red glow of the Escalade's taillights, Pin-Up can see behind the cop's helmet visor a telltale face: as white as porcelain, eyes like black craters in his head, lips curled away from his teeth as the Harley bears down on the SUV.

"Spur—" Pin-Up starts to say, reaching for the Beretta pistol wedged under the map case.

Through the speakers, Hack's voice returns. "Not to be the bearer of bad news but I'm gonna play you the most recent dispatch received by this highway rat."

The Harley looms closer, engine screaming, its rider emotionlessly drawing his pistol.

Out of the Escalade's sound system comes a stream of ancient Church Latin, an incantation spoken in a guttural drone, an esoteric spell being cast on the cop. Right at that moment, the first shot rings out, sparking off the Escalade's front quarter panel. Spur yanks the wheel.

The SUV swerves. Spur puts the pedal to the floor. Pin-Up rolls down her window, leans out into the furious wind, and empties a magazine into the slipstream. The flash of the Beretta's muzzle provides a fireworks display. One of the rounds hits the Harley's windscreen and shatters it, grazing the possessed trooper.

The man barely flinches as half his shoulder rips free, the blood gush atomizing in the wind.

"Hold on!"

Spur's cry girds everybody as he jacks the steering wheel to the left. The Escalade lurches across the median. An oncoming semi roars directly at them. High beams flash. The trumpet roar of the horn accompanies the squeal of air brakes as Spur sends the SUV across the opposite shoulder and down an embankment.

Bone-rattling vibrations shake the SUV as it clamors wildly across a soybean field.

"Son of a bitch!" Pin-Up cries out as the trooper's Harley soars over the embankment behind them and then digs into the bean field, the glare of its headlamp relentless, unyielding on the backs of their necks. Spur wrestles with the wheel, the Escalade chewing through the field. More shots ring out. In the rear seats Boo ducks down as the rear window implodes. She reaches for her sniper rifle.

In the darkness dead ahead, Spur sees a dirt access road cutting between two farms.

"Wait! Am I hearing things?" Pin-Up says from the shotgun seat, slamming a fresh mag into her Beretta as she peers out the jagged opening of the rear window. The air has begun to reverberate with a rhythmic drumbeat. Up in the night sky, a light has appeared behind the clouds. The nose of a police Huey emerges, the helicopter swooping down at them, its searchlight magnesium-bright silver reflecting off the rearview.

The Escalade bursts out of the bean field, Spur turning sharply, the SUV fishtailing down the narrow farm road. In the rear seats, struggling to load the rifle, Boo shoves a magazine into the stock. She twists around and braces the weapon on the seat back. "Let me take the trooper out of the equation," she says in a cold, flat voice.

"Do it quick, Boo," Spur says, guiding the Escalade down a narrow road between two cornfields.

Boo fires once, knocking out the Harley's headlamp, then a second time, missing the front tire by less than an inch, and the third round is the grand slam. The blast punctures the front tire, and the thing blows, and the sudden loss in traction flips the possessed cop head over handlebars. His body—as stiff as cordwood—rolls in the dirt and comes to a stop, consciousness knocked out of him.

Almost instantly, as if in answer to the trooper's fate, a torrent of high-powered gunfire rains down on the SUV from the light in the sky. Puffs of dirt and dust erupt along the side of the road, a few of the rounds clanging off the Escalade's quarter panels.

Spur swerves again. The Escalade goes into a spin in the

dirt. The g-forces suck Pin-Up toward the door. Outside the windows, the darkness blurs with fiery ricochets, some of the bullets piercing the hood and the roof, embedding into the floor, barely missing Boo, who now holds on tight.

Spur straightens the vehicle and floors it. He hits the high beams and he sees through a veil of smoke and cordite ahead of them the access road passing over an irrigation culvert. He yanks the wheel and plunges the Escalade into the sea of cornstalks. Tassels and leaf particles and dust erupt in the SUV's wake as Spur circles around the hill and then steers the SUV directly into the culvert. Splashing through stagnant standing water, the Escalade skids to a stop in the moldering darkness of the culvert. Spur kills the lights.

The Huey hovers over the tunnel, the gunfire momentarily ceasing. Pin-Up sees the brilliant, harsh searchlight passing back and forth from one end of the culvert to the other. "Okay, cowboy, what's the plan here?" she says. "Correct me if I'm wrong but they're just going to wait us out."

Spur glances at the rearview. "Boo, how many rounds left in the mag for the M82?"

"Five left . . . if I'm not mistaken."

The drumming of the helo's rotor nearly drowns his voice. "I want you to exit the vehicle when you're not in the spotlight—stay low—hide in the corn, and then—"

"—blow the tail rotor off?" Boo interrupts, finishing his sentence. She knows the exact result Spur wants and how to get it. With a nod, she cracks the rear door open and carefully slips out of the SUV. On her hands and knees, she creeps through the well water toward the mouth of the culvert with the rifle strapped tight to her back.

She pauses just inside the opening, watching the beam of silver light from the chopper sweep across the threshold. She times how long the searchlight takes to sweep back and illuminate the opposite end of the culvert. She counts five seconds. Outside the mouth of the culvert she can see the edge of the cornfield about twenty feet away—close enough to reach within five seconds, depending upon how fast she can crawl.

The pool of silver light sweeps down again across her side of the ditch, and she braces herself, reaching for her rifle's stock, clenching her teeth. Again, the light drifts away. She bursts out of the tunnel on hands and knees and quickly crawls through the shadows, and then stealthily slips into the cornfield. Darkness swallows her in a sea of stalks.

The air is thick and musty. Crickets scatter as she crawls deeper into the vegetation. She sees thin tendrils of light from the chopper's xenon lamp slicing through the cornstalks, piercing motes of corn silk and dust. She sees the searchlight circling again.

What she doesn't see is the figure leaping from the helo's midsection into the darkness of the cornfield.

CHAPTER TWENTY
Purgatory of Darkness

1.

The newer Huey UH-1 helicopters favored by most police departments nowadays are larger than the older models, with heavier skids for difficult landings, more powerful hydraulics for lifting rescue gurneys, bigger blades for higher speeds, and longer tail booms for stability. The tail rotors are bigger as well. All of which provides an easier target for Boo, who now opens the rifle's bipod, lies down on her belly in the fusty darkness, steadies the weapon, rotates the safety off, pulls back the bolt, injects a round, flips open the scope's lens cover, and lines up the crosshairs through the jungle of cornstalks. She squeezes off a single shot.

The full-metal-jacketed .50-caliber round hits the bull's-eye. The Huey's rear rotor erupts, and the blades disintegrate in the backdraft. The aircraft goes into a wild spin, engine wailing, fuselage tilting left and right. Finally gravity intervenes. The chopper slams down to earth, shaking the ground, and sending a thunderous shock wave rolling across the fields. Thankfully, the fuel tank remains intact, so, with any luck, the lives of the cops on board—currently under the influence of demonic forces—have been spared.

Boo works quickly in the darkness, folding the bipod shut, thumbing the safety back on, pulling the rifle's lockpins, disengaging the receivers, and strapping the weapon back against her spine. All through this she can hear the sick whining noise of the Huey's motor, the crackle of radio voices, and the wrenching sound of twisted metal being moved. She rises to a kneeling position, and is in the process of turning back toward the way she came when a dark figure leaps out of the under-growth and pounces on her.

A pair of gloved hands instantly wrap around her throat. Struggling to escape, Boo sees that the tactical officer from the Huey is young in years but his facial features are corpse-like, cheeks sunken, flesh pallid, eyes as black as tar. His liver-colored lips move, forming a litany in a dead language hissed like spit on a skillet. He squeezes harder, his grip supercharged by the demonic engine inside him.

All at once, the tactical officer gets very still, blood starting to leak from his gaping mouth. His grip falters. He looks down as though checking to see if he remembered to zip up his pants, and makes eye contact with the hilt of a shimmering katana sword that has been thrust up inside him from his solar plexus to his throat. He doesn't see the razor point of the blade pro-truding from the cervical vertebra behind his neck, but he feels the life leaking out of him right before he collapses to the mulchy ground.

"I'm sorry this was your fate," Boo whispers to the human soul fading away in front of her.

An instant later, she retracts her sword and slips away with-out a sound.

2.

Back on the highway, Spur and the others continue southward in the damaged, rattling SUV for a few miles, arguing over whether it was pure Satanic intervention that had sent those local county mounties after them, or if it had started with a leak out of the DIA.

"Does it really matter?" Pin-Up says at one point. "The clock is ticking, and we're gonna get made by somebody at some point."

Spur shakes his head. "You make it sound like we're up to no good, Pin. Keep in mind we're technically working an ex-traction for the goddamn government."

Hack's voice buzzes through the sound system: "Yeah, and killing members of law enforcement and destroying millions of dollars of equipment while we're at it."

Spur tries to tamp down his anger. "Hack, I don't mean to diminish in any way the miracle of your resurrection, but do you think you could possibly stop your yappin' and get off her ass and boot up the kidnappers' GPS again? We gotta be closer to them than white on rice by now."

The multiscreen flickers. The bright colors and pop-ups return.

"There they are!" Pin-Up points at the virtual landscape. The glowing blue arrow is gliding down Highway 61, still southbound, zipping along at precisely eighty-seven miles per hour, according to the little square indicator in the corner.

Boo glances out the window at a road sign blurring past them, then peers over the seat back at the Escalade's speedometer. She sees that Spur has the SUV roaring southbound on I-55 at eighty-four miles per hour. "Wait a second," she says, noticing something critical on the kidnappers' GPS screen. "We're going to run right into them." She points at the multiscreen. "Look!"

"Holy Jumpin' Blue Jesus, you're right," Spur says. "Sixty-one and 55 intersect. Looks like maybe five miles to go. Just south of . . . what is that, a little podunk town in our path I'm looking at?"

"Fruitland, Missouri," Pin-Up chimes in. "Population who-the-fuck-knows."

"Four and a half miles to the crossroad," Hack's voice announces from the hive, buzzing in their ears.

"Looks like there's an overpass at that point," Boo says, watching the screen. "Sixty-one goes under us."

"Four miles to go."

"Okay, listen up." Spur's voice lowers into that clipped, economical war-footing monotone he acquires on the battlefield. "Hold your fire. No matter what happens. Hostage protection is the priority."

"Copy that," Pin-Up says.

Spur changes lanes. "What we're gonna do is we're gonna let them pass under us."

"Three miles to go."

Spur slows down just a tad. "Gonna exit a few car lengths behind them."

"Two miles."

"Gonna put a tail on them," Spur says. "Nice and easy. Stay back as far as possible."

"Copy."

"One mile."

"Here we go." Spur puts his blinker on. "Keep your safeties on."

"Point-five."

"Got a visual on the Taurus!" Pin-Up says, nodding toward the east.

In the back seat, Boo cranes her neck to see down the embankment, the converging blacktop highway looming out of the darkness.

"Five hundred feet."

"Easy does it," Spur says, steering the massive SUV down the exit ramp.

"Here they come!"

Spur applies the brakes, easing down the ramp.

The Taurus passes under the ancient cement viaduct above them.

"Wait—!"

"What the fuck?" Hack's voice sizzles from the speakers, suddenly taken aback.

On the multiscreen, the kidnappers' GPS has gone blank—no roads, no pop-ups, no mileage or temperature indicators, just a barren virtual world of flat beige nothingness.

Spur slams on the brakes as they reach the bottom of the ramp, the SUV grinding to a stop.

The sudden halt throws Boo forward, her face hitting the seat back so hard the impact knocks a tooth loose. She shakes it off and glances over her shoulder, a bit dazed and nonplussed.

"I'll be a goddamn monkey's uncle," Spur utters, peering into the side mirror as the dust and carbon monoxide clear. He can see under the overpass, and the road leading up to it.

The Taurus has vanished.

3.

The last human being to check on Ticker that night is a certified nurse anesthetist, formerly on the staff of St. Mary's Medical Center in Belleville, Illinois. A slight, tidy, bespectacled little woman in her midfifties who found God a decade ago and joined the Cloister staff as a novitiate nun, Nurse Nancy Pellegrini swishes through the door at 1:47 A.M. CST in her crepe soles and white headscarf, unaware that in addition to herself and the patient, the room has a third occupant invisible to the naked eye.

The Devil sits on his haunches in the corner like a mutated dragon at rest, his long, shimmering black insect wings like crinoline folded into bolts along his scaly back. His serpentine eyes fix themselves on the nurse as she takes readings from the pulse-ox monitor, empties the urine bag, and makes notes on the clipboard hanging off the end of the gurney near Ticker's pale, bloodless toes. She notes that the patient is stable, does not appear to be in any pain, and exhibits normal blood pressure and sodium levels. The last item on her agenda is to take a tongue depressor from a bedside jar and softly scrape the bottoms of Ticker's feet with one end. She does this, and is satisfied when she sees Ticker's legs involuntarily twitch with each scrape.

On her way out, the Devil plants a thought in her head that she should kill her ex-husband so that she can be free to marry

Jesus once she takes her vows. Unbeknown to Nurse Pelligrini, the seed of this idea will haunt her the rest of her life. She turns out the lights, and the door clicks shut behind her, plunging the Cloister's treatment room into silent darkness.

Now the Great and Terrible Adversary rises to his full height of seven feet, his wings undulating as he strides over to the bed, and gazes down at his subject, this thorn in his side, this ingrate. The only light in the room comes from the softly huffing and beeping machines, illuminating Ticker's sculpted, handsome, tawny face in a faint orange glow. The Devil realizes that if he is bound contractually to allow this cretin to retain his power of manipulating time, the best corrective would be to imprison him in his current state.

With a single wave of his long, crooked, cadaverous hand, he plants an illusion in the mind of the comatose man. Then the Master of Lies leans down and plants a cold, poisonous kiss on the man's forehead, turns, and exits by passing through the wall, leaving Ticker to his endless dream.

In the silence, the monitors continue to register normal vital signs.

But deep in the folds of Ticker's brain, a malignant dream has sprung to life.

4.

He finds himself lost, naked, and alone, in a place most Christians would instantly recognize. They would recognize the boiling flames on the horizon, the barren, blasted, war-torn desert, the primitive roads, fossilized into the ground like scars, scattered with detritus, crisscrossing the land, and the gargantuan heaps—which Ticker first misidentifies as trash—lying on the edges of embankments.

In the distant hills rise great and ugly towers belching black smoke and flame, some of the pinnacles sprouting girders that dip and bob with the irregular pulse of oil derricks. He sees innumerable lights shining up on the plateaus, perhaps the infrastructure of ramshackle cities, some of the lights arcing with the brilliance of spot welders. He notices the silhouettes of immense wheels and millstones and generators turning languidly against the sky.

Now he sees that the dark, ragged objects, which he first misidentified as garbage and wreckage—on the ground, in the ditches, and along the crests of adjacent hills—are human souls. Some sit and stare at the horizon in dazed vexation. Others crawl through the mire without purpose or destination. Some of these putrid apparitions seem to take an interest in Ticker, some of them looking as though they might be hungry for a taste of Ticker's organs or soft tissue. To make matters worse, a bizarre column of flame appears on the horizon, almost as if on cue, a fireball with a mind of its own, and it seems to be changing course and coming straight for Ticker.

He runs.

Ahead of him, in the side of a volcanic berm of ash, he sees the mouth of a tunnel. He quickly ascends the hill and plunges into a labyrinth of man-made passageways reinforced with prehistoric rebar, reeking of human decay, ancient feces fermenting, and the inside of taxicabs. He stumbles through the passageways without direction, without purpose other than to hide. Soon a methane-like glow as blue as a blood clot begins radiating off the tunnel walls, the result of either natural gases or Ticker's imagination.

In the gloomy light, the naked, frantic Ticker barely registers as solid matter. In a state of complete undress—as he is now, filmed in grit—he resembles an emaciated panther.

He doubles over in the darkness, a searing pain blossoming out from his guts—a nameless pain, an agony unlike anything he has ever experienced. Far worse than the ruptured appendix that almost took his life, far worse than the worst day of SEAL training, during which he thought he would die choking on his own vomit, this pain twists like a tightening fist inside him. Relentless, inexorable, terminal, it steals his breath and intoxicates him with agony. He has not yet identified it as late-stage starvation.

In fact, Ticker has only now begun to come to terms with where he is, where he has ended up, where he must belong because he has squandered his life . . . because for years he has served as a paid assassin for the U.S. government . . . but worst of all, because he has allowed his beautiful wife to die at the hands of anonymous gangbangers in a Chicago alley . . . alone, suffering, lost. Just like he is now.

Here.

Ticker gazes around the tunnel, the low ceiling of stone fanged with icicle-like formations of limestone. He begins noticing signs of previous inhabitants, including a single word, in English, scrawled repeatedly on the blackened basalt walls. Someone has written it over and over, in progressively messy, disordered letters, as though the very meaning of the word were sinking in . . .

ENDLESS ENDLESS ENDLESS ENDLESS

5.

3:00 A.M. approaches along the Mississippi as the Escalade creeps down the weathered blacktop two-lane, still heading southward, but now barely going forty miles an hour, the slowness reflecting Spur's frustration and nerves. He has fought guerrilla insurgents with bloodthirsty vendettas, homicidal maniacs masquerading as private security forces, and professional mercenaries with nothing left to lose, but he has never gone after the kidnappers of his own child. It is an emotional ladder he has never climbed.

"You think this thing inside Sister Lucy June has the power to just . . . teleport them to wherever they're headed?" Pin-Up's voice is thin, tight with barely contained terror for her baby. "I mean, if they can do a Houdini under an overpass—like they just did—why would they even bother driving, you know, if beaming somewhere else were an option?"

From the front screen, Hack's milky ghost of a face appears. "Still checking security cameras posted along the southbound exits, state trooper radio chatter, police dispatches . . . nothing yet."

Spur nods, white-knuckling the steering wheel. "What about their GPS?"

"Blank as a test pattern. It's as though they vanished off the face of the earth."

"Don't say that, Hack," Pin-Up admonishes him. "It could be a distinct possibility in this case."

Boo speaks up from the rear seats. "They can't take the child to hell, if that's what you're referring to. Only the damned can be sent to hell. The child is innocent, and pure. That's what they want. It's like currency to them."

Pin-Up glances over the seat back at the slender, owlish face of Boo. Almond eyes still wet, her wiry body clad in its ninja regalia, Boo looks like a specter that just stepped out of a Chinese folktale. The tracks of her tears shimmer on her cheeks in the intermittent flashes of each streetlight they pass. "Where do you get all this stuff, Boo?" Pin-Up asks her. "How do you know all this about the demons and the protocols?"

"I learn it from the dead."

"Can you summon them when you need information? How does it work?"

"It depends," Boo says. "Most of the time they come to me in visions, sometimes they pop up in mirrors, looking over my shoulder."

"Do they naturally have insights about stuff like this?"

"Again, it depends on who they were in life. Some of them haunt the living. That's where they get information."

"They eavesdrop."

"Exactly. Trust me on this, Pin. The demon has not absconded with the child to hell. He needs the baby alive. The rites that they want to perform on Junior have to be done in the human world."

"Why is that?"

Boo measures her words. "Because the Antichrist, when he appears . . . he'll be human. Lister told me this. Like it says, 'Lo and behold, the false prophet comes forth on the earth.'"

With one hand on the steering wheel, his chain-mail gauntlets jangling, Spur digs in his pocket with his free hand for a plug of tobacco to help him think. He plants it between his cheek and gum, and says, "What are we supposed to do with all this shit?"

"There's a place, a cursed place somewhere, a haunted place. According to Lister, that's where the ritual will be performed. Like I said, judging by the direction they're going in, and the arrival time on their GPS, it's a pretty good bet it's about six hundred, maybe six hundred and fifty miles from here. Straight shot south. Gotta be New Orleans."

"You think we can get there before them?" Pin-Up asks Spur. "Find the place, and ambush them? Maybe we can get Silverback to scramble a Blackhawk."

"Wherever the fuck they are," Spur says, chewing his cud, "I don't see how we can find the place without following them."

In the silence that follows, Hack's image returns to the screen, his voice buzzing out of the speakers. "I did take the money."

Boo sits up straighter and stares at the multifunction screen. "Excuse me?"

"You were right all along about me taking a chunk of the warlord's rainy day fund. Osamir didn't need it where he was going."

Boo swallows her anger. "Why didn't you just own up to it?"

"Full disclosure, I don't have a fucking clue what I was thinking. It's not my finest hour, to be perfectly candid."

"What were you going to do with it? Open up a retirement account? Invest in a . . . in a . . . chinchilla farm?"

"I got rid of it."

"What?!"

"I gave it away."

"To whom?"

"A third went to the Karakistan Refugee Rescue Mission, a third to Doctors Without Borders, and a third to the Red Cross."

Boo stares at the screen and tries to muster up a response but can't come up with anything.

Spur is nodding. "Poetic justice, Hack. Not too shabby."

"To be perfectly frank I just figured Osamir had a lot of victims and—"

He stops himself.

"—Wait, hold on, we got the GPS signal back from the Taurus."

Spur nods. "Show it to us."

The two-dimensional landscape returns to the screen with all its pop-ups, indicators, animated caution signs, and big blue arrow gliding along Highway 61. "Okay, if I may jump in here right off the bat," Hack's voice sizzles in surround sound. "Somehow they managed to fall back behind us."

Spur frowns. "Behind us?"

"According to their navigation screen they just passed mile marker 101."

Spur chews harder, thinking, punching the accelerator, the Escalade speeding past 50 mph . . . then 60 . . . then 75. He notices a stick blurring past the edges of his headlight beams. It says MILE 111. "They're ten miles behind us," Spur announces to no one in particular. "How the hell did they . . . ?"

"What's the play here, cowboy?" Pin-Up wants to know, her voice strained as she glances over her shoulder. All she can see behind them is darkness.

"Gimme a second, Pin, and I'll think of one. Did you burn all the rounds in the M82?"

"Negative—still got a full cartridge."

Hack's voice reverberates in the air: "They've already closed the distance to six miles."

"What? You sure about that? Do the math. That doesn't sound right." Spur reflexively shoots a glance at the rearview but sees nothing but his own brooding eyes framed by pitch darkness. He looks down at the kidnappers' GPS and sees the luminous blue arrow now racing down the red glowing abstract highway, moving faster and faster. The speed indicator shows 165 mph. "What, are they in an F-15 now?"

"Question, Skipper."

"Go ahead."

Boo takes a deep breath, fiddling with her loose tooth. "Let's say they get close enough for us to shoot the tires out."

"That's what I was thinking."

Hack's voice: "I don't want to be an alarmist but they're now at four miles and closing fast."

"What in the hell and a hootenanny is going on?" Spur looks at the kidnappers' GPS and sees that the little speed indicator in the lower left-hand corner has risen to 179 mph and is rising like a furnace , , , 183 . . . 191 . . . 204 . . . 211.

Again Hack's voice crackles out of the speakers: "Not to belabor the point but at this rate—"

"I know, Hack, I get it." Spur shakes his head. The indicator on the enemy GPS now has risen past 230 mph. "Boo, get the 82 warmed up again, on the double."

Boo finds the Barrett on the floor, partially disassembled. She quickly slides the top receiver in place and pushes in the lockpins.

"They're a little over a mile away," Pin-Up announces in a jittery voice barely above a whisper. "You're not going to shoot their tires out from under them at this speed, are you? Liable to send them into a roll."

Boo doesn't answer. She's laser-focused on ejecting the mag, checking the round, shoving it back in, and rotating the safety off. She pops the covers off the scope, snaps the bipod open, and positions the weapon on top of a road case in the way-back.

"We'll fire a warning shot over the bow," Spur says, thumbing a switch on the dash. "Put the fear of God into that old demon. Boo, wait until you get an eyeball on them. Don't fire until you get a good enough angle to give them a haircut. You understand? You copy?"

"Copy that, Boss."

Hack's voice sizzling: "They're now at eight hundred meters and closing."

Boo jacks the rifle's slide. She looks through the scope, adjusting the focus knob. She has a clear shot through the jagged opening of the broken rear window. "Got a visual," Boo says softly, her voice barely registering over the rumble of the Escalade.

"Six hundred meters."

She unsnaps the trigger guard. Spur has almost unconsciously sped up to around eighty miles an hour. The road looks like it's being gobbled up by the Escalade's undercarriage.

Boo puts her finger on the trigger. "Holy fucking shit," she utters under her breath.

What she sees in the crosshairs will likely live in her nightmares the rest of her life.

6.

At first, through the optics of her scope, Boo sees the Taurus looming out of the darkness, twin supernovas erupting in her field of vision, the headlights a nimbus of magnesium-silver fire. The car approaches so rapidly it seems as though it has leapt out of the frames of a poorly edited motion picture, coming at her with the jittery speed of jump-cut splices in celluloid. But Boo does not react, does not budge one centimeter from her sniper's station as the light engulfs her. The flat-line state of her pulse, respiration, and circulatory system—as well as her training as a master sniper—all contribute to her cobra-stillness. And in that terrible instant when Boo realizes the Taurus is going to ram into the Escalade, she does not waver, does not flinch, but instead drills her gaze into the blinding white light. She centers the crosshairs of the scope on the area just below the left headlamp, where the front tire lives, and she squeezes the trigger.

The resounding boom causes ears to ring inside the Escalade's interior and the aftershock to echo out above the tree line.

"W-wha—?"

Boo jerks back with a start because the Taurus has vanished.

It happens so abruptly that it practically knocks the air out of her. She lowers the rifle, and she swallows her shock. She frantically looks around in every direction, gazing through every window, seeing nothing but the blur of a desolate wooded landscape rushing past them. She tries to formulate a reaction, tries to say something, but Spur speaks up first.

"What did you do?"

Boo keeps looking around. "What did I do . . . nothing, I didn't do shit, didn't hit anything but the fucking pavement."

From the front passenger side Pin-Up keeps her gaze locked on the dark stretch of highway receding into the night behind them. She blinks. "Where the fuck did they go?"

Boo's throat has gone dry and tightened up, making it difficult to speak. "H-hallucination? Projection of some kind?"

Spur keeps the SUV roaring along the highway at 80 mph. The multiscreen has gone dark again. "Stay frosty. Everybody. If they're playing some kind of Jedi mind trick on us, so be it. They gotta come out of hiding sooner or later."

"Sorry, folks," Hack's voice crackles. "I got nothing. They just disappeared off the grid."

Boo mutters, "They were there, though, as sure as I'm sitting here, I could smell the oil burning."

7.

Inside the rarefied world of the Ford Taurus interior, Johnny Prast clutches the steering wheel as though it were a life-preserver ring on a sinking ship. Outside the windows nothing but darkness envelops the car. Where are they? At the bottom of the Mississippi? In the ninth circle of hell? Prast's teeth are clenched in horror, his jaw is locked, his bloodshot eyes are bugging at the advent of this impossible limbo. The engine races without purpose, the wheels spinning impotently.

From the moment the thing inside the nun had taken over control of the vehicle, it had been a roller coaster of an ordeal the likes of which Prast has never experienced. Not even the bad acid trip he had gone on years ago with Joe Lister on Tchoupitoulas Street—which had landed Prast in the parish prison for thirty-three days—could even remotely compare to the nightmarish carnival ride of the last fifty miles.

Now Prast's ass crack burns where he has shit himself. He wants so badly to escape this deathmobile. He wants to die. But most of all, he wants to get away from this horrible demonic entity inside this fat little nun. But that will have to wait. Prast can tell by the slimy laughter slithering out of the nun's mouth at the moment that the festivities have only just begun.

The nun's head tosses backward with each chortle, torquing the neck so severely the flesh starts to rip and run with tears of blood, which stream down the woman's neck and into the modest neckline of her embroidered denim shirt. Then, without warning, the grisly rendering of a once handsome, heavyset, dedicated member of the Cloister's nunnery mutates further.

A new pair of eyes like blisters popping open appear in the tangle of hair on the back of the nun's head. The eyes like burning embers glare angrily at the woman and baby in the rear seats.

A barrage of incomprehensible Latin explodes from the nun's

mouth, bombarding the dark-eyed goth lady in the shadows. Esmeralda Villainous has one arm around the jury-rigged cradle, which is nothing more than a large peach crate lined with a moldering blanket. But strangely, the baby is calm—one might even say pensive as it suckles its pacifier.

"In English, please," Esmeralda says in a terrified voice, unable to tear her gaze away from the second pair of vestigial eyes glowering at her through strands of grey hair on the back of the old woman's head. "Please, O Great and Powerful One."

The voice of Wormwood replies in its metallic rasp, "Hold on tightly to the child."

CHAPTER TWENTY-ONE
Inversion

1.

Spur reduces the Escalade's speed to a crawl as they slowly make their way southward down Highway 61, the vehicle's perforated hood now spouting tiny geysers of steam. The SUV's days are numbered, which only adds to the creeping diminution of confidence, of resolve, of hope that has slowed them down. Mirroring this hopelessness, the landscape has begun to thicken with overgrowth and deserted gas stations and boat docks, the rotten pilings and rusted signs strewn across the marsh like the ruins of ancient burial sites. This is the bootheel of Missouri, the true and gritty gateway to the South, the haunted place of lynchings, Civil War skirmishes, and riverboat politics. Just beyond this desolate forest lies Arkansas, and the deeper South.

Spur and his ragtag team have traversed twenty miles of this fecund darkness without speaking, each of them, in their own way, stewing in their anger, their doubt, their hatred of the Devil's minions.

"Wait! Wait—hold on—wait." Hack's disembodied voice sputters out of the speaker system, sounding alarmed. "Finally getting something on their GPS."

Everybody straightens up in their seats and focuses on the navigation screen. The luminous arrow skates along a serpentine symbol for Highway 61, going just over the speed limit. Their location is just north of the I-55 overpass a couple of miles south of Blytheville, Arkansas, about fifteen minutes away.

Spur puts the pedal down, and the Escalade roars, pressing everybody into their seats. "Can't lose them this time," Spur mutters as he fixes his gaze on the dark horizon beyond the reach of the halogen beams of the headlights. "Let's talk about the extraction."

"There's no analogy here," Boo says. "No precedent, no equivalency." She glances out the window. "And there's something else you should know."

Spur looks up at the rearview mirror, grabbing a glimpse of Boo's sculpted face draped in moving shadows, her dark eyes glinting with emotion. Spur sighs. "That's maybe my least favorite preface."

"It's something Lister told me," Boo says. "The ritual, the Satanic christening of the child, the way the Devil plants the seeds of the Antichrist that foment inside the baby, it takes a certain amount of time. It's a black mass that must be completed at the stroke of twelve midnight."

Hack pipes up from the speakers. "Is that daylight saving time?"

Nobody laughs. Spur shakes his head. "Do me favor, Hack, give the shtick a rest for a while."

"Just trying to lighten the mood," says the voice from the hive.

"What is the actual ritual, Boo?" Pin-Up wants to know. "Did Lister spell it out?"

"It's basically an inversion of the Christian baptism."

"What does that mean exactly?"

Boo shrugs. "You know the drill. You have the father and mother renouncing their sins. You have the child being held by the practitioner, and the font of holy water ready to go. The priest sprinkles the holy water in the name of the Father, the Son, and the Holy Spirit. That kind of thing, only turned on its head."

"How so?"

"You sure you're up to hearing this?"

"Boo, stop it. Just tell us."

"Well, for one, instead of holy water blessed by a priest it's the blood of a sacrificial animal, killed at sunset on the day of. You want me to go on?"

"Go on."

"The child is bathed in the blood, and instead of the parents renouncing Satan, a pair of witnesses kill themselves and are damned for eternity. I'm told it's a huge honor."

"And . . . ?"

"I guess the final step is the kiss."

Glancing over her shoulder, Pin-Up gives Boo a look. "The kiss?"

"Yeah, so, this part Lister wasn't real clear about. At first, he said it must be a demonic source, open mouth, a kiss from a person possessed. But then he said, no, maybe it's supposed to be from the Devil himself. He wasn't a hundred percent on that."

Spur has been shaking his head all through this, his rage smoldering, his knuckles white as he grips the wheel. "Fucking goddamn shit is crazier than an outhouse rat!"

Hack's voice: "Speaking of crazy, we're right on top of them—they're less than a mile away—take a look." The multifunction screen splits into two GPS landscapes, side by side, showing Highway 61 snaking through the wilds of Arkansas.

The Escalade's blue arrow is closing the distance, the two arrows almost perfectly lined up on the map.

2.

"Anybody got a visual yet?" Spur asks, and then under his breath: "C'mon, c'mon, c'mon, you goddamn peckerwood motherfuckers, show yourselves."

"There they are!"

Boo sees the rear taillights of the Ford Taurus in the distance, maybe a couple of hundred yards away. The sedan passes under the glow of a sodium-vapor lamp and shimmers as though in a mirage. She reaches for the M82, but before she has a chance to look through the scope the Ford Taurus literally pops out of existence, leaving behind a swirling cloud of carbon monoxide like a ghost, which vanishes on a gust of river wind.

"The fuck?" Boo mutters.

"Wait a minute, hold on," Hack says from the depths of his virtual world. "They've jumped over to I-55, fives miles west of here. You see them?" On the split screen the kidnappers' GPS shows the blue arrow now gliding along the interstate toward the Tennessee state line. "There's an entrance ramp up ahead, it's coming up in a half a mile, see it?"

A few seconds later, Spur takes the cloverleaf ramp at seventy miles an hour.

"Spur, slow the fuck down!" Pin-Up calls out, but Spur's anger has gotten the better of him now.

The Escalade climbs the curve at a little over 80 mph, shoving Pin-Up and Boo into their respective doors, the SUV sliding into a guardrail, throwing a wake of sparks twenty-five feet up into the night sky. Spur slams the accelerator down.

The SUV fishtails onto the interstate, throwing a fountain of dust and debris through the air. Spur gets a quick glimpse at the split screen in front of him, and sees the kidnappers' blue arrow suddenly vanish, and then reappear on the other side of the Mississippi, a few miles south of Memphis, once again gliding down Highway 61. "Impossible," Spur mumbles to himself. "Goddamn fucking impossible."

"Spur . . . Spur!" Hack's face has reappeared on the multiscreen. "Not to be critical but you're losing it. You've gotta calm down. We can pick them up down south when they get to wherever they're going."

"Where are they now?" Spur's voice has gone ice cold. "Give me the fucking coordinates." Spur's voice sounds like a fuse that's been lit, a soft hiss that's about to blow sky-high.

It's a sound with which Boo, Pin-Up, and Hack are all too familiar.

Over the years, they've heard this voice coming out of their unit commander only two other times. One of them was when they got pinned down outside an insurgents' encampment in the Sudan, and the terrorists decided to use a local boy as a human shield. The only other one was in the subterranean dungeon of the warlord Abu Osamir's compound in Karakistan. Two of Osamir's goons had decided to lop off Pin-Up's head and videotape the festivities.

In both instances, the voice preceded a wave of ultraviolence. It was not a promise of good times ahead.

Hack's voice buzzes: "They're south of Memphis on Highway 61 about a mile north of the junction of 175 . . . but Spur, you've gotta—"

"Save it, Hack. I don't have time for it right now." Spur gooses the foot-feed and pushes the Escalade up to 90 mph. The battered engine screams and vibrates, the undercarriage groaning, the pinions complaining noisily. The vehicle sounds as though it's about to fall apart as it roars past a few cars in the slow lane. Spur takes a shortcut around the city via Interstate 240 pushing 100 mph. At this hour the traffic is minimal, and the well-lighted bypass is bracing, like a series of slaps in the face as the cones of sodium vapor flash rhythmically over the cracked windshield like a mesmerist's strobe.

"Spur—" Pin-Up is starting to say something when she is interrupted.

"Nobody talk," Spur says in that deathly cold monotone.

Five minutes later, Spur reaches the point where the Ford Taurus had been one second earlier . . . and now, once again, without warning, the kidnappers' vehicle has ceased to exist.

3.

Spur slams down on the brakes, the SUV skidding to a halt on the shoulder. He bangs his fists on the side window, the luminous glow of a distant streetlamp reflecting off the glass.

"C'mon, cowboy," Pin-Up says softly, putting a hand on his shoulder. "Stop it, c'mon, you're gonna kill the car. C'mon."

Spur keeps slamming his fists into the window, his gauntlets clanging, cracks forming in the safety glass. Smudges of blood appear in the hairline fractures. He keeps pummeling. The blood runs down the inner surface of the window, seeping into the seams of the door.

"Spur!"

Pin-Up yanks him away from the window. Spur, breathing hard, looks straight at her, his eyes glazed with white-hot anger, as though he's looking through her, his bloody fists still clenched.

Unbeknownst to Pin-Up, however, something inside Spur is changing, metamorphosing, transforming. His ill-begotten superpower—something he has come to think of as a useful affliction, a sort of beneficial mutation—has always been the ability to reflect an enemy's power back at them, use it against them. Now this dark gift begins to turn inside out within him.

Fueled by his rage, galvanized by his innate need to save his only child, he feels a wave of pure, unadulterated, feral bloodlust, the kind of killing-hunger that he has not felt on any chaotic battlefield or during the bloodiest confrontations. It is a reflection of the superior demon, hell's denizen of the highest order, the innate need to destroy, to murder, to exterminate, to devour. Now this instinct grows and metastasizes inside Spur like a lightning-quick cancer. He has to kill. He has to. He feels this ugly, unclean, evil emotion smoldering way down in his marrow.

"What is that?" Boo says from the shadows of the rear seats.

"What is what?" Pin-Up asks.

"That sound." Boo cocks her head. The whistling noise rises and intensifies. At first it sounds like it's coming from an idling engine, a loose hose or a rusty flywheel complaining. But then it becomes clear it's coming from somewhere outside the car, like wind blowing through a pipe. "Hear it?"

The noise reaches Pin-Up's ears, and she looks out her window. She looks up into the dark, cloud-scudded night sky. The whistling has grown to a piercing level. "Is that a plane?" She takes a deep breath. "Man, I hope that's not the feds. Silver promised he wouldn't unleash the dog pound just yet."

Spur looks at Pin-Up, and then glances around the periphery of the car for the source of the earsplitting noise.

He looks up.

He peers through the sunroof.

His howl of rage drowns the sound of the massive object falling out of the sky.

4.

In the split second before impact, what Spur sees is the greasy, blackened undercarriage of a 2018 Kodiak Brown Ford Taurus plunging straight toward the roof of the Escalade as though dropped from the black heavens by an invisible giant. Something inside Spur snaps—a chemical reaction firing the moment the four thousand pounds of Detroit steel land on the roof of the Escalade with a thunderous crash.

In one heaving, enraged, involuntary gasp Spur slams his open palms against the SUV's collapsing roof. Every window, every square inch of glass encasing the interior, implodes as the roof caves. Diamonds of broken glass gust in every direction. Boo and Pin-Up instinctively hunch forward, covering the backs of their heads. The Escalade's titanium-reinforced endoskeleton threatens to collapse as the wheels of the Taurus grind and dig into the roof, spinning so wildly the Escalade's interior fills with smoke.

Spur, now in his fury and transformation, reflects the thousands of pounds of pressure being exerted upon the SUV with his own sudden and preternatural reserve of counterpressure. He lets out an ear-piercing howl as he holds the roof up, as steadfast as a human bridge trestle, his burly arms locked, his big, callused hands—rough from all the landscaping work he's been doing around the Cloister—preventing the Escalade's body from flattening and squashing the team inside it like bugs.

At last, the wheels of the Taurus gain purchase, and the

sedan suddenly launches itself off the Escalade's front hood. Spur, still staving off the cave-in with his bare hands, sees through the narrow opening of the ruined windshield the Taurus roaring away down Highway 61, vanishing in the darkness, bound for the border of Mississippi.

"Get out of the car!"

Spur can feel the endoskeleton about to collapse on top of him.

"Climb out!—Now!—That's a goddamn order!—Do it now!"

Out of the corner of his eye, Spur sees Boo forcing the bent rear door open with her legs, the hinges creaking loudly. She appears to be wounded, her regalia already soaked in her blood as she crawls out of the vehicle and rolls down the embankment.

Pin-Up has already made her exit from the SUV and now kneels in the darkness on the other side of the gravel shoulder, looking in with a worried expression. "Careful, cowboy!" She rises to her feet and hurriedly limps around to the driver's side. "Let me get your door open, and then get the fuck out of there!"

Spur can hear her struggling with the driver's-side door, misshapen and crumpled to the point of being lodged tightly under the caved-in roof. She pulls and pulls on it, groaning with effort, until the door budges just an inch.

Spur kicks it the rest of the way open, and then lurches out through the gap as quickly as possible as the roof caves in behind him, collapsing the rest of the way into the interior, the tires blowing out one by one like depth charges going off.

Lying in the weeds, Spur sees a hubcap spinning a few inches away from his head like a giant coin that's been tossed in a game of chance. Catching his breath, he watches the hubcap spin and spin and spin . . . until it finally tips over and goes still.

The stillness that follows is broken only by the drone of

crickets and the faint echoes of the Ford speeding off into the night.

The crackle of Hack's voice emanates from within the flattened ruins of the Escalade, a phantom speaking from beyond the grave: "Not to be critical but you people better find us another ride with a good navigation system, preferably On-Star if that's an option."

5.

Boo rolls over and checks her midsection in the gloomy light.

"Fuck—fuck-fuck-fuck," she mutters, feeling the wetness of blood inside her Shaolin robe, a sizable shard of glass sticking out of her tummy just below the rib cage. Above her, the brooding dark clouds have rolled eastward across the river, and now a full moon shines down on her, illuminating the wound.

She pulls the triangular sliver of window glass from her midriff and tosses it . . . and Pin-Up appears on the embankment above her, hurrying down the slope with wide-eyed concern. "Boo, you good? You okay? Talk to me. What's the damage?"

"It's nothing." Boo waves her off. "It's just, you know, cleanup on aisle two."

Pin-Up has already switched into field-nurse mode, and is kneeling next to Boo, gently opening Boo's robe, palpating the bloody wound.

"Pin-Up, I'm good."

"Sit still for a second." Pin-Up frowns, puzzled by the injury. "What the fuck . . . a gash that deep. Glass must have missed any major organs but that deep it would have nipped an artery."

"Pin—"

"Sit still. Breathe in and breathe out for me. C'mon."

"Pin-Up—"

"Hush! Breathe," Pin-Up says, putting pressure on the wound with Boo's sash, vexed by the lack of blood flow. Boo's

wound appears to have already started to thicken and coag-
ulate. Pin-Up presses her fingertips on Boo's neck in order to
check her pulse.

"Pin-Up," Boo says very flatly, her tone of voice that of a
mother about to chastise a child for forgetting to take off her
muddy galoshes. "Have you forgotten?"

"Huh?"

"You're not going to get a pulse because I have no pulse.
Remember?"

"Oh."

"Does the whole endowment-of-powers-by-the-Devil thing
ring a bell? The whole blessing-and-curse situation? Conduit
to the dead?"

"Oh . . . oh right," Pin-Up says, wiping her blood-sticky fingers on her Kevlar corset. "My bad. You're like . . . undead or
whatever."

"C'mon. Help me up."

6.

By the time they climb the embankment and rejoin Spur by the
flattened Escalade, Spur is on the phone with Silverback.

"No, no sir, negative, we need to keep moving," Spur is saying into his cell. Boo can see that the faceplate of the phone is
shattered. "Silver, we made a deal, you said twenty-four hours.
It's bad enough we gotta deal with local gendarmes been infected by the hellhounds, we don't need the goddamn *Federales*
stumbling into this thing, mucking everything up!"

Spur listens, and Boo hears the faint crackle of Silverback's
nervous retort.

"Okay, first of all, you're sure this is a secure line?"

Spur listens.

"Okay, number one. Hack is not dead . . . not exactly." Spur
listens and shakes his head. "I know, I know what Cthulhu
saw—" More crackling from the earpiece. "I'll explain it all in
the debriefing, after we get our kid back."

More crackling sounds.

"Listen to me," Spur says, visually about to explode, but somehow keeping it reined in for the sake of the mission, for his baby's sake. In the darkness, in his medieval regalia, he looks like he stepped out of the fifth century, like he's a time-traveling paladin of the Holy Land. "Number two, we have un-til midnight tomorrow." He glances at his shattered watch face. "That's a little less than twenty hours."

Silverback says something then on the other end of the line.

"Okay. We know this because . . . Okay. Again. I'll explain it all in the debriefing. But suffice to say, they need our baby for a ritual that the Devil has planned for him. Has to be com-pleted at exactly twelve midnight tomorrow."

Spur pauses, his eyes shiny with emotion. Boo notices that his jaw is set, his teeth are clenched. She has seen him con-trol his emotions before but not like this. He is in a terrible place now. But maybe, just maybe, that'll be helpful in the final stages of the extraction. They need the same controlled fury that only moments ago saved them from being squashed like ants under a bootheel.

"Three. We need to get the removals group involved right now." Spur tightens his grip on the cracked cell phone. "Pref-erably Pokorny and his people from the DIA, they're the fastest and the most discreet. We need—"

Silverback interrupts and starts to explain something to Spur.

"I don't give a sewer rat's asshole what clearance you need!"

Spur's booming voice echoes over the treetops along the marshland. The sudden explosive sound makes Boo and Pin-Up jerk back with a start, while a flock of mallards erupts from an adjacent phalanx of deadfalls.

"Okay. I apologize for raising my voice." Spur clamps down on his rage. "We're all just doing our jobs. Silver, the thing is, we need the wreck removed—you can copy the coordinates on this cell—and we need a new vehicle delivered within walking distance ten minutes ago. And make sure you throw in a box of crucifixes . . . for privacy. You got that?"

Spur waits to hear that it will be done . . . and the pause stretches.

7.

Silverback paces the shadows of an apple grove along the Cloister's eastern fence line, his secure mobile phone pressed to his sweaty ear. Jumpy, hyperaware of his surroundings, his ulcer burning a hole in his guts, he lets out a sigh and says, "All right, I'll get you the Cleaning Crew and the—"

A third voice interrupts, crackling in Silverback's ear like a ghostly transmission from outer space: "And at the risk of being a diva, it would be terrific if you could possibly make the new vehicle a Lincoln Navigator, Black Label, with Active-Glide. That model's got the best electronics."

Silverback freezes in the darkness, his hand clutching the phone tighter, his mind racing as he realizes no one else in the world sounds like that.

CHAPTER TWENTY-TWO

Fade to Black

1.

Being in hell is no picnic. Wandering aimlessly, crossing mile after mile of scorched, desolate wasteland, Ticker has lost all sense of time. He's been trudging across the endless landscape of hell now for what seems like an eternity. But then, it could be only hours, or minutes, or a scintilla of a second. It's impossible for him to tell. He's not supposed to be able to tell. Time is no longer his friend. Time is no longer part of the fabric of his life. He's one of the damned now, and time will no longer have any meaning whatsoever.

Eventually he finds himself outside a ruined, decaying, putrid city, and he decides the answers to his questions might be found here, in this awful, fetid corner of hell. He approaches the massive iron gates that stand at the city's threshold like the drawbridge of some immense derelict castle, the flames of great pyres blazing along each side of the entrance. He pounds on a gantry, and the great wrought-iron gates suddenly part like bat wings, allowing him to pass through.

Just inside the entrance he pauses, scanning the place, staring in awe as the city pulses and seethes in the radiance of gaslights. A miasma of smoke and steam blankets the narrow stone streets, which weave between uneven piles of retrofitted buildings, each edifice a distortion of different architectural styles and eras. He trudges down the squalid street, searching for answers that will never come, seeking logic and reason and sanity that will always elude the denizens of hell.

Something at the end of a crumbling alley catches Ticker's eye.

He turns down the passageway, and approaches a tragic little figure sitting rigidly on a ladder-back chair beside an old secondhand spinet piano. An empty stool sits next to her in front of the keyboard. She is familiar to Ticker, but why? At first, he can't figure out where he has seen this scrawny little old lady in the shawl, with the cat's-eye glasses and the spidery grey hair pulled back tight against her skull.

She looks up at him. "You are late once again," she says in her thick Italian accent, like a cat hissing at him. "Take your place at once, and commence playing your scales."

Ticker obeys Miss Sabitini immediately. He sits, and attempts—as he had so many times as a child—to play the C-major scale. He's a little rusty, and the piano sounds like it's in bad need of a tuning, but he gets through the scale.

"Not exactly Rachmaninoff but it will have to do," grouses the piano teacher. "Now I want you to show me something else."

"Yes, Miss Sabitini."

"From the Bach piece, it is called *Jesu, Joy of Man's Desiring,* I want you to play this line." She opens the sheet music and points her crooked, gnarled finger with its long nail painted blood red at the last line on the page. It ends with the symbol known among most piano students as the railroad tracks, its formal name being, of course, the caesura . . . or the pause.

Very carefully, Ticker rubs his hands together and then plays the last line in Bach's *Jesu, Joy of Man's Desiring.*

And when he comes to the caesura, he lifts up on both the keys as well as the sustain pedal, abruptly halting the music.

The atomic blast of silence forms a shock wave that unfurls across the hellscape, obliterating everything in its path.

2.

Ticker rolls over and slips off the edge of the gurney, pulling the IV stand as well as the bedside tray with him as he falls to the floor.

The plastic glucose pouch breaks open and spills clear liquid across the parquet tiles, soaking Ticker's gown, and waking him up. He gasps and blinks fitfully, looking around the Cloister's treatment room, trying to remember why he's here, and what the hell is going on. Was he dreaming?

He rises to his hands and knees, and that's when he notices he's not alone.

Darby Channing is a few feet away, as still as a statue in a wax museum, frozen in a pose of alarm, reaching out toward the bed as she rises from her armchair, her paperback tented open on the floor where it has fallen. Ticker stares at her, trying to get his bearings and understand what he's seeing.

His brain, still foggy, swims with fear and confusion as it starts coming back to him. He made this happen once before— recently—but when? Tonight? Earlier today? What day is it? He rises to his feet and nearly falls back to the floor on his wobbly legs. How long has he been here? He looks at the huge regulator clock on the wall, and he sees it's 5:11. Is that in the morning? A.M.? He notices that the venetian blinds are drawn, but there's no light coming through the seams.

He goes over to the frozen form of Darby Channing, and he tenderly strokes her hair. He misses her. The texture of her beautiful raven-black Louise Brooks bob is like sealskin in the Caesura. A surge of emotion travels through Ticker, a mixture of sadness and affection for this intelligent, stylish woman of substance.

It all starts coming back to Ticker. The curse of his superpower, the fellowship of the Quintet, the evening of Father Manny's seminar, the hellish banquet, the demonic takeover, all of it streams through his consciousness like a poisonous tide. He remembers lifting the Pause and then everything fades to black. Is that why he's here? His knees threaten to buckle again, and he has to grab hold of the armchair to steady himself.

He limps out into the corridor. The overhead fluorescent

lights have dimmed slightly in the Pause but are still so bright they make his eyes ache. He sees a nun he has never met at the end of the hallway. Thin, dour, middle-aged, sporting a scarf and grey housedress, the woman sits behind a laptop, her spindly fingers poised above the keyboard in mid-peck. He sees a second person slumped in a chair near the double doors, frozen in mid-doze, a newspaper draped over his fat belly. He recognizes the man as Father Dean, an elderly Franciscan who runs the team of security guards at the Cloister.

Ticker shuffles toward the exit. The faint predawn light has just begun to bruise the darkness outside the narrow windows. A wave of dizziness washes through Ticker as he pushes open the doors, walks outside, and runs directly into a huge black crow frozen in midflight across the threshold, its wings spread, its delicate form hanging in midair like an exhibit in a museum. Batting away the brittle sensation of feathers in his face, Ticker staggers backward, reeling out of control, and hitting his head on the doorjamb.

Sudden darkness pulls its shade down over his field of vision. The ground rises up and slams into the side of his head as he collapses.

And unconsciousness once again takes him down into its watery depths.

3.

"What the fuck just happened?"

Spur blurts out this rhetorical question behind the wheel of the brand-new replacement vehicle procured for them by Silverback, recoiling at the strange, inexplicable slippage in the passage of time that just gripped the brand-new Lincoln Navigator. The enormous SUV has all the bells and whistles in a color the manual calls Infinite Black, an irony not lost on the four members of the Quintet now pushing the vehicle at its top speed down Highway 61 just north of Jackson, Mississippi.

Pin-Up sits rigidly in the shotgun seat, clutching the armrests as though she has just ridden a frightening thrill ride at a carnival.

Behind her, Boo sits stone-still, processing the strange last few moments of the journey south. "I think . . . I think maybe . . . Ticker's going to be okay after all, thank God."

Pin-Up twists around and gives Boo a look. "What do you mean?"

Boo tries to figure out how to put it into words, how to articulate the inexplicable. "What just happened to us . . . it almost felt like Ticker had launched another time pause but . . . I don't know . . . it faltered? Crumbled under its own weight?"

A few minutes ago they were closing in on Jackson at eighty miles an hour, and the sun was just coming up over the Gulf, the predawn glow turning the shadows of the piney woods along the highway a deep purple, painting the treetops and clouds in luminous shades of magenta, when the world seemed to . . . just stop.

But not exactly.

Unlike other missions during which Ticker put things on pause—the results feeling to the other members of the Quintet like a jump cut in a film—this time they were fully conscious throughout the duration of the Caesura. One moment they were buzzing down the highway, planning the logistics of their imminent extraction, and the next moment, all movement suddenly decelerated to a crawl so slow it was akin to watching an hour hand on a clock. The vehicle had instantly slowed to a snail's pace. The passing landscape suddenly seemed to ooze by the car with the slowness of sap leaking. Even their bodily movements were caught in this bizarre wrinkle in the passage of time, moving at the speed of paint drying despite the fact that they were all completely awake, alert, aware of the change as though they were experiencing a mass hallucination.

"I'm just guessing now," Boo finally adds. "I'm not sure,

but you know how Ticker's been trying to calculate the outer limits of his power?"

"Yeah."

"Well maybe this is what happens when you're getting close to the edge of the Pause."

Spur speaks up. "I hope you're right about that because for a minute there I thought I was having a goddamn stroke."

Hack's face appears on the new navigation screen, his boyish visage rendered in shimmering pixels. "Should have felt what it was like in here. Be that as it may, I've got some breaking news for you."

Spur turns up the volume on the twenty-speaker sound system. "Go ahead, Hack."

"At the risk of being hyperbolic, it looks like they're taking Junior to the asshole of the universe. I've monitored two separate calls to the owner of the place, and from the looks of their GPS, they've already cut over to I-55, and they're on a straight shot toward the worst place in the free world."

"You got our attention, Hack," Pin-Up says. "What's the worst place in the free world?"

Hack measures his words, pausing for a long moment of silence, which, for Hack, is extremely off brand.

4.

The Herod Plantation sits on a remote wooded hill that rises out of the Cane Bayou marsh like an immense tumor about five miles northeast of Lake Pontchartrain. The main house and several of the outbuildings overlook a vast, overgrown, and treacherous wildlife area that's part primordial swamp and part impenetrable pine forest. The cornerstone was laid in 1828, and construction was completed two years later.

Herod Plantation's original owner was a notorious slaveholder named Charles Beekham, who came to be known as the most infamous "Negro breaker" in the antebellum South. The phrase refers to an individual to whom other slave owners sent their slaves to be "broken" in order to make them submissive and compliant. Beekham was a huge, burly, sadistic Englishman who many historians believe was also severely mentally ill. According to local legends, Beekham was possessed by demons.

One thing is certain. The man took great pleasure in his work, inventing new and diabolical ways to torture human beings.

To this day, many of the original buildings still exist, the upkeep and maintenance of which are mysteries to most Louisianans. The chain of ownership down through the years has been hotly debated. For a while, in the early twentieth century, the plantation sat boarded up and deserted. It later became a frequent hideaway of homeless squatters, felons, and junkies.

In fact, it wasn't until the 1980s that ownership was transferred to a shadowy consortium of rich businessmen thought to be part of the New Orleans syndicate. But their pedigree was far, far darker and more sinister than anyone would have imagined.

"Lemme guess," Spur says from behind the wheel, now tooling along Interstate 55, southbound, keeping the speed just under seventy-five miles an hour in order to avoid unwanted attention from state troopers. The morning sun now cants down through the windshield, flickering as it filters through the trees. For the last ten minutes Spur and the others have been watching and listening to Hack's impromptu TED Talk on the Herod Plantation, complete with archival images and news clippings. "It was a bunch of sick yahoos with hard-ons for Satan?"

"Give the man a stuffed poodle." Hack's voice hums through the matrix of speakers and subwoofers, the voice of a phantom god. "They were unofficially known as the Shining Order of the Black Lodge, and they were true party animals. Blood orgies, black masses, Satanic rituals, bake sales—"

"Cut the comedy, Hack, c'mon."

"Okay, admittedly that last one was a joke but they definitely sold stuff—drugs on the black market; paramilitary weapons to the mob and white supremacists; even underage girls into sexual slavery, yadda yadda. They had no ideology other than Hail Satan, and party like it's 1989, and slowly and incrementally— drip-drip-drip—they planned on one day destroying humanity so that the Antichrist could rise to power, blah blah blah."

On the navigation screen flickers a series of static, grainy, black-and-white surveillance-cam shots of the property.

Hack's narration continues buzzing out of the speakers: "Over the years they renovated the interiors, updated the security measures, installed cameras all over the place. Not to be pedantic or prescriptive in any way, but I'm going to pause here for a second, and we're going to zoom in on the main road."

Spur keeps his eyes on the interstate, intermittently glancing at the screen. They've just zoomed past the last exit to Jackson, Mississippi, and now the Lincoln barrels straight southward toward the Louisiana state line, still a good three hours away. The brutal Deep Southern sun hammers down on them, the day already as sultry and humid as a day on a tropical island. "What's the big deal with the main road?" Spur wants to know, shooting a glance at the multifunction screen.

The image now pushes into a grainy close-up of a dirt road winding through the thick foliage of a marshy pine grove. A checkpoint stands at the end of the road, amounting to an automated steel gate flanked on either side by tall fencing, crowned in nasty-looking concertina wire. Visible through the boughs and limbs are security cameras on iron stanchions.

"So . . . as you can see," Hack's voice narrates, "this is the only way up the berm to the main buildings. They've torn out all the other roads and points of egress."

Pin-Up leans in and studies the image. "No back doors? You sure? Looks like all they got is a fence and a bunch of swampy woods surrounding it. Hell, that extraction in Colombia, with that fucking moat we had to cross, that was a lot tougher than this."

"Sorry to burst your balloon, Pin, but there is a moat here. At least it serves as a moat." The image clicks to another angle on the forested area surrounding the grounds. "There's a massive fucking sinkhole surrounding the north and east sides of the property."

Spur glances at the image. "What do you mean, like quicksand?"

"It's a fucking bog is what it is. You take a wrong step out there, and you're gonna end up in China . . . or maybe down in hell with Lister." He clicks the image back to the checkpoint. "You see what I mean? This is the only way in, and that's the way they like it. They keep a close watch on that gate with all those security cams."

Spur lets out an irritated sigh. "Ideas, thoughts, anybody."

"Yeah," Hack's voice replies. "I have an idea and I even have a thought. Take another look at that checkpoint. The answer's staring you in the face."

"I'm looking at it, pardner, and I don't see shit. What are you talking about?"

The on-screen image slowly zooms in to one of the cameras mounted on a stanchion. "What do I have to do, Spur, draw you a picture?"

5.

"Looks like our illustrious guests have arrived."

The chubby man in the seersucker suit stands beside the surveillance desk in a room decorated in garish maroons and fuchsias, the walls adorned with lithographs of naked, nubile African women, slave auctions, and Satanic bric-a-brac. The man points at the lower right-hand corner of the big screen.

The Ford Taurus has pulled up to the checkpoint, and sits there now, waiting to be let in. The chubby man says very softly, very slowly, almost lovingly, as though speaking to a child, "Gerald, if you would be so kind as to let them in."

The man named Gerald, the head of security at Herod Plantation, moves a joystick, and then watches the gate slide open.

A lanky, sinewy man in his late fifties with massive porkchop sideburns that have gone almost all grey, Gerald Haben is a former member of the Louisiana National Guard and a sharpshooter, and at one time was Inmate Number 345113 at the state prison known as Angola, serving a thirty-three-to-thirty-six-year sentence for assorted sex crimes and morals charges. Released a year and a half ago on a technicality involving his arrest, Haben has raped a half dozen women that the state knows about, and another dozen that they don't. His father, Artemis Haben, was a founding member of the Shining Order of the Black Lodge.

Haben now watches on a sequential series of panels the myriad camera angles of the Ford Taurus as it wends its way up the serpentine dirt road to the front facade of the main house, which is a French Colonial mansion of incredible proportions. The front portico alone would make the White House in D.C. look like a shotgun shack.

Behind Haben, the chubby man lets out a beatific sigh. "Isn't it grand, Gerald, to host such an important guest here at Herod? To aid and assist in the performance of such historic, epochal rites?!"

"Yes indeedy," Gerald Haben purrs as he flips from camera to camera.

"Hail . . . Hail to the Prince," exclaims the well-dressed man. "Hail to the Great Dark One."

In his powder-blue seersucker jacket and slacks, his velveteen slippers embossed with gilded pentagram symbols, and his plump pink cheeks rosy with excitement, Lawrence Alvin Cripp cuts an impressive figure for a man only four feet, eleven inches tall. The ostensible leader of the Shining Order for nearly a decade now, Cripp sees his role as more of a diplomat than a director. He fancies himself as connective tissue between this world and the netherworld beneath it, an important cog in the coming of the New Dark Age.

His former doctor would most likely disagree, however, pointing out Cripp's many psychiatric misadventures, from countless electroconvulsive treatments to a host of antipsychotic drugs.

Now, buzzing with anticipation, he digs in his pocket and pulls out a small amyl nitrite inhaler about the size of a matchbook. He takes a big, hearty whiff, and flutters his eyelids in ecstasy, looking as though he's hearing the music of the spheres. "I shall go and give them a proper welcome," he announces. "Have the boys guard the perimeter throughout the duration, Gerald. I'm counting on you to protect the sanctity of this evening."

Haben assures him the home will remain undisturbed throughout the night . . . unaware that Herod's precious security system has already been breached.

CHAPTER TWENTY-THREE
The Labyrinth

1.

By late afternoon, the bayou sun switches on its broiler and pushes the temperature past ninety degrees. The sweltering, sticky heat turns the wetlands around Herod into a festering gumbo of fish rot, deadfall, and methane. The angry beams of sunlight filter through the trees and dapple the greasy surface of the swamp just west of the main road with radiant pools of light. Hectic with mosquitoes and shot through with heat fog, the sunbeams illuminate an ancient footbridge of rotting wood and baling wire protruding from the forest.

Three individuals appear out of the jungle of kudzu and Spanish moss at one end of the footbridge, and then trudge single file across the swaying span. Heavily armed, with cane knives on their hips, bandoliers of ammunition crisscrossing their bare chests, and machine pistols strapped over their shoulders, the men are sun-browned, heavily adorned with jailhouse tattoos, and muscle-bound from pumping iron in the prison yard.

One of the men is enormous and completely bald. Nicknamed "Curly" by Haben, this behemoth has lost his eyebrows due to some undiagnosed skin disease, and has filed his front teeth to a razor's edge for dramatic purposes. The ugliest of the threesome, Curly leads the group across the bridge to where Gerald stands waiting on the other side in the shadows of a gnarled cypress.

"Hail Satan," the gigantic man sings out in a surprisingly high and delicate voice, beads of sweat stippling his hairless pate, his blood-rimmed eyes twinkling as he reaches the end of the bridge and sees Gerald Haben step out of the shadows.

"Big night, gentlemen," Haben says with a grin, giving Curly a one-armed man hug. Haben has a satchel slung over his shoulder.

Following close on Curly's heels are two other men with impressive rap sheets and long and venerable histories of violence. The smallest of the three, a spindly heroin addict with a wild bouffant of fluorescent-red hair, is, of course, "Larry." His oily, leathery, half-naked body glistening with perspiration, he offers Haben a hand and a firm soul-shake. "Can't believe it's really happening."

"Believe it, brother."

"Is he here?"

"As we speak, Larry, as we speak."

"The baby, too?"

"Yessir."

The third member of the team—nicknamed "Moe," naturally—brings up the rear. Moe is the quiet one, a wiry little polecat of a man currently listed as an escapee from Angola while doing life-without-possibility-of-parole for three separate torture-murders. His sleeveless denim shirt is soaked through with sweat. "Hello," he says in a weird monotone by way of a greeting as he reaches the end of the bridge.

"Okay, you're all here, everybody follow me." Haben turns and leads the men down a winding trail. He pauses near the electrified fence. He glances up at the top of a stanchion and stares at the surveillance camera for a moment. "I won't lie to you, though," he murmurs, not taking his eyes off the camera, "security has got to be as tight as a nun's pussy tonight. You understand what I'm saying?"

They each tell him they understand.

"Good," Haben says, looking back at them. "Now pay attention. There's going to be three separate vehicles bringing VIPs to the event at seven o'clock sharp. They're coming in a convoy, all at once. Curly, I want you on the main road near the entrance. Wear your Kevlar."

The behemoth nods eagerly.

"You'll all get the guest list. Moe, I want you on the east roof. There's a Browning long-range rifle waiting for you up there, extra ammo, too, just in case. You see anything not on the guest list—man, animal, vegetable, or mineral—you shoot first and ask questions never. You got that?"

Moe tells him he's got that.

"Larry, you're going to be roving."

"Roving?"

Haben sighs. "Moving randomly, circling, covering the perimeter of the main house. You follow me?"

"Gotcha."

Curly speaks up. "Is that where the ritual's going down?"

Haben looks up at him. "What do you mean?"

"The main house, is that where the magic is happening?"

"First of all, that's none of your fucking business. Second of all, you think they tell me that kinda shit? I'm the last one to know that kinda shit. Any other stupid questions?"

The men are silent.

Haben opens the satchel and hands them each a walkie-talkie. "The guest list appears on your walkie's display screen at six o'clock, and then erased by eight. I'll be at the main desk in the house monitoring everything. Stay alert, and stay sober."

Nods from everybody.

Gerald Haben turns and heads back to his four-wheel ATV, but not before taking once last glance at the camera mounted on the pole.

2.

That evening, the guests arrive in their procession of sleek, black limousines, met at the checkpoint by a bald ogre with a TEC-9 automatic and no eyebrows. Curly checks each of the five VIPs—avid Satanists all—against the digital manifest on his two-way: a renowned club owner from the Quarter and his wife, a flamboyant NOLA city council member from the Ninth Ward, and a rich couple from Baton Rouge with shady connections to Donald Trump.

The party of five are led up to the main house by Larry, while Curly pays off the limo drivers and sends them on their way.

Esmeralda is put in charge of preparing the child and the two goats for the ritual. She is given her marching orders in the foyer from Wormwood himself—his words pouring out of the plump little nun at almost inaudible speeds—so fast that Esmeralda has to stop the demon several times in order to get it all written down in her notes.

Then the thing inside Sister Lucy June vanishes into the warren of rooms in the rear of the house.

3.

The Herod Plantation's floor plan is laid out in the fashion of most early-nineteenth-century residences—very compartmentalized, the rooms smaller than those to which a modern inhabitant would be accustomed. Vestibules, nooks, parlors, and all manner of sitting rooms form a mind-boggling labyrinth of chambers that make up the three floors of the massive edifice. Generations of lowbrow art collecting, decadent spending, and gaudy concepts of interior decor have turned Herod into a dollhouse for the insane.

After dinner, around eight thirty, Esmeralda and the baby are shown to the master bathroom on the third floor, a monstrosity of parquet tile, ruffles, exposed copper plumbing, fake bouquets, and countless framed folk paintings of children with inordinately large eyes. The room is the size of most living rooms, and is thick with the cloying odors of artificial pine and wintergreen.

After laying the baby in a bassinet near the window, Esmeralda notices the car deodorizers hanging from the ceiling, hundreds of them, like miniature green bats dangling upside down.

"I had them put in to counteract the smell of the goats," a voice says from the doorway.

Esmeralda whirls around and sees Lawrence Alvin Cripp decked out in his maroon sharkskin tuxedo, velvet lapels, bow tie, patent leather shoes, and ivory cane with a baby's skull as a handle. "The animals are in the tub," he says to her, "behind the shower curtain, in case you were wondering. I miss our dear Mr. Joseph Lister. Do you miss him?"

"Um . . . yes . . . I surely do, I miss him." Distracted by the prospects of dead goats in the bathtub, Esmeralda pulls the curtain back. Two enormous adult females lie nestled in opposite directions as though packaged for shipment. Their tongues loll out from between their jaws, their black and white fur mottled with blood. "Awright, good enough," Esmeralda mutters under her breath. She looks at Cripp, pulling the curtain shut. "It's all so exciting, like a dream."

"True, so true . . . to be part of something this grand and historical," Cripp says, shuffling across the room to the little bassinet.

Set high on a pedestal, trimmed in black bunting, the bassinet gives off an air of royalty. Moonlight shines through the ruffled curtains and illuminates the porcelain skin of the baby nestled inside it, now dozing quietly in his little cotton bodysuit, suckling at his thumb. The jumper features a graphic insignia on its chest of an infant with horns and a tail, the words LIL' DEVIL underneath it.

"The picture on the jumper, my compliments," the man in sharkskin says.

"Thank you kindly, Mr. Cripp."

The man looks down at the child. "Hard to believe this fragile little thing will become the Bringer of the Great Dark Days." He gazes down at the baby for another long moment. "It's odd, though."

"What is, sir?"

"He's unnaturally quiet for a baby of his age, is he not?"

"He is, yes."

The man narrows his eyes. "Seems like he knows something we don't."

"Hmm."

Cripp lets out a wistful sigh. He pulls a gold turnip watch from his pocket and looks at it. "Anyway . . . won't be long now. Have him ready by eleven."

Cripp walks out.

Esmeralda returns to her seat next to the bassinet, rocking the slumbering child, and sipping from her flask of absinthe.

4.

The time comes for Esmeralda to wake the child and prepare him according to her instructions. That's when the crafty and cunning Esmeralda Villainous—former dancer at the French Quarter's infamous Follies Brassiere on Dumaine Street, former madam of the Bayou St. John Massage Emporium and Waffle House—takes one last look at the child sleeping peacefully in his nest of blankets, and is suddenly stricken by an unexpected wave of emotion.

It floods Esmeralda with a sadness that she could have neither predicted nor understood in a million years. She turns away, digs in her purse, and pulls out a little miniature glassine ziplock with one tiny rock of methamphetamine left. She finds her pipe, loads it, fishes for her torch lighter, grabs it, walks over to the window, raises the sash, lets the warm night air toss her purple locks, and lights the ice. She takes a huge drag and lets it burn her throat and nasal passages.

The baby wakes up. Esmeralda can hear the whimpering and cooing coming from behind her. The bassinet creaks, and the baby snivels and clucks, and finally Esmeralda surrenders to her duties and goes over to the crib. The baby instantly goes still when Esmeralda comes into view. The two of them lock gazes.

A trickle of fear creeps down Esmeralda's solar plexus. She

drops the pipe and it shatters on the tiles, spilling the warm stardust of laboratory-grade stimulant across the floor. Babies this young are not supposed to stare like this. Or become this still. Or begin to change their expression. Or cause their little cherubic face to transform suddenly as though reconstituting inside a vacuum-form mold of a different baby.

Esmeralda jerks back as though scalded by the sight of the baby's new face—a girl with big blue eyes and a little dollop of downy-soft hair at the crown of the fontanel. "No, no, no, no, no, no, no."

An old black-and-white photo of this baby used to sit on the dining room sideboard owned by Esmeralda's foster mother. "That's you, silly," the woman used to tell the six-year-old Esmeralda. Those were the days when she went by the name of Sandy Muntz, when the Muntz family of Slidell, Louisiana, kept a roof over her head and cared for her, before the dark times of the father's insanity, and the secret fondlings in the back of the garage, and the abandonment that followed.

Esmeralda Villainous backs away from this alien thing in the crib that will not stop glaring at her and changing. What she doesn't know is that baby Paul Candell, aka "Junior," has inherited a perfect amalgam of each parent's superpower—Spur's reflective power of turning an enemy's strength back at them, and Pin-Up's shape-shifting power of reading an enemy's deepest fear and transforming into that very thing. And now the face of the child morphs in time-lapse motion, a photograph dunked into chemicals, a visual timeline, a relentless slide show of Esmeralda's tragic and pathetic life, one face melding into the next, the problem child with her trademark glower, the lines on the face deepening, the dark eyes caving in, collapsing to age and crow's-feet, the teeth darkening and falling out one by one as a result of hard living and profound addiction, the hair stiffening and greying, the jowls sagging, the years of drug abuse and crime and degradation dragging the face down, ever downward, down like candle wax melting into the earth.

5.

The scream reaches the ears of the guests in the third floor front parlor at precisely 10:47 P.M., but it takes a long moment to register.

For the last few minutes, Cripp has been holding court, rhapsodizing about the gravity of the evening, and serving from a sterling-silver trolley cart an array of after-dinner drinks, including Armagnac, Calvados brandy, and crème de cassis. But the pièce de résistance of the digestif course this night is a cocktail of forty-year-old French port mixed with the arterial blood harvested from the corpse of Johnny Prast.

The junkie's remains now sit propped up at one end of a Louis XIV settee, the cadaver wrapped in blood-soaked gauze and perched on a drop cloth, its punctured carotid tastefully veiled by a Hermès scarf, all of it a sort of avant-garde joke, a party favor, a prop to celebrate the unprecedented evening of sacred rites.

The presence of the corpse delights the guests, who, by now, are intoxicated by all the drugs and drink and drama unfolding around them. All of which explains why it takes Cripp and his companions so long to even be cognizant of the fact that someone has just let out a piercing shriek in another part of the third floor.

Cripp cocks his head, and licks the bloody port from his lips, and hears a splash echoing out across the night sky.

He whirls toward the door and quickly trundles out of the room, followed closely by the five delirious guests—the two couples and the crooked councilman—each in a different stage of undress.

CHAPTER TWENTY-FOUR

The Source of Dream Motion

1.

Hastening across the upper landing toward the master bedroom suite, Cripp is terrified that something has gone awry with the special child.

The chubby little man hurtles through the door of the enormous baroque bedroom, and then plunges into the master bathroom. The humid night breeze blows through the open window, the screen torn apart. Esmeralda is missing. Cripp lunges over to the bassinet. Thankfully, mercifully, the baby still lies in his blankets, unharmed, awake, staring innocently up at the ceiling, as mute and still as a doll.

The others pour into the bathroom, the MAGA couple so inebriated they collide with Councilman Hendry, who wears a fur loincloth now and bizarre headgear resembling an antelope's antlers. The three of them trip over their own feet and sprawl to the tile floor. At the same time, the owner of the famous Bourbon Street club known as the Lickety Split lurches across the room to the window. Joined by his wife, he gazes three stories down at the enormous kidney-shaped swimming pool.

In the luminous blue glow of submerged, recessed lighting, the body of Esmeralda Villainous floats facedown in the water.

2.

"It appears she offed herself," the scarecrow of a man with the flaming-red pompadour drawls into his walkie-talkie as he stands at the edge of the pool, gazing down at the body.

The leathery junkie nicknamed Larry has seen floaters before, some of them the result of overdoses, some at his own hands when he was a freelance hit man for the NOLA mob. "Either that or the baby pushed her out." He lets out a little stoner's giggle.

"Just shut your trap and fish her out," the voice of Gerald Haben crackles at him through the speaker. "I need your eyes and ears elsewhere."

"Ten-four, good buddy," Larry says, thumbing off the walkie and heading over to the cabana shack for the long-handled skimmer.

3.

The sensation is not unlike a roller-coaster ride through a snowstorm, except this snow is of the electronic variety, and this roller-coaster track is the Herod Plantation's surveillance system.

Hack wills his consciousness around the tight turns of the outer coaxial wiring, smashing through the nodes of the splitter boxes, and then up into the narrow chambers of the camera circuitry. He floats there for a moment, an astronaut without a body, a sentient entity spacewalking without a tether, a weightless spectral being about to dock with the opening of the Vidicon tube.

He finds the circular mouth and plunges into its maw, riding the electron beam down into the focusing coils. He sees the target—the cathode-ray source—and he dives inside it. Now the imagery of the plantation's front entrance looms before him, reflected on the back of the lens.

Upon closer scrutiny he can see the shadows of Spur, Pin-Up, and Boo hunkered in the darkness on the edge of the dirt road outside the gate: three silhouettes in mystical regalia, impossible for the naked eye to find unless it knows exactly where to look, now waiting patiently for Hack to perform his magic act.

The great illusionist will run his machinery in full view of the audience. Hack reaches out and rotates the memory card. He dials back the footage to one hour earlier, the same night-time scene in perfect registration. The only difference will be the absence of those three silhouettes lurking outside the gate.

"Almost there," Hack whispers into the ether, the adjacent airwave tuned to the Bluetooth communication system. "Just have to link the other cameras to the mother tube."

Spur's voice hums inside the hive. "Copy that, standing by."

Hack's astral body does a one-eighty flip and exits the focusing tube. He rides the sparkling coaxial railroad from one splitter to the next, flipping to the new fake footage.

Within seconds, the illusion is complete. "It's done, Skipper. You're welcome."

4.

Spur inserts a small digital prod into the gate's lockbox. The display spins and lands on the correct PIN. The gate softly clicks, and slides open. Barely making a sound, Spur, Pin-Up, and Boo slip onto the property.

The shadow of a massive, bald psychopath leaps out at them.

A few minutes earlier, Curly had decided to change his position from his original post a few hundred yards up the main road to a hollow log just inside the gate, where he'd been sitting, playing a video game on his phone, when the sound of the gate squeaking open roused him. Now he explodes out of the shadows, dropping his TEC-9, and barreling directly at Pin-Up. He tackles her to the ground, trying to get his cane knife against her throat.

Pin-Up grabs the man's testicles and squeezes with over two hundred pounds of pressure per square inch. But before the behemoth can even cry out, a flash of steel flickers across his neck. Boo steps back, retracting the blade of her katana, as Curly instantly slumps and drenches Pin-Up with his blood.

She barely reacts, shoving the massive body off her and rising to her feet.

"You good?" Spur asks, his voice barely a whisper in her earpiece.

"Totally."

"That was my bad, Pin, I had him positioned up the road a piece."

"Don't worry about it," she says in her cold, flat battlefield voice. "One down, two to go."

5.

Up in the command center, Gerald Haben has barely noticed the slight bump in the images caused by Hack's sabotage a few minutes ago. Now the screens in front of Haben continue to show multiple angles of the entrance and the main road without change, without incident, the same darkness and stillness that had draped the grounds one hour earlier.

Outside, in the dark, Spur pauses under a massive bald cypress, and without a word he and the others attach noise suppressors to their Berettas. Spur gives hand signals, first to Pin-Up, then to Boo, assigning each her own direction and human target.

In preparation for the extraction, Spur had ordered the other two to use only edged weapons if possible in order to keep the noise of the approach to a minimum, and the pistols only when absolutely necessary. But he has a feeling the firepower might eventually come into play, which is fine with him.

Up in the command center, Gerald Haben stretches and yawns, practically bored out of his wits by the prospect of staring at the same unchanging nightscape staring back at him. He would much rather be watching the ceremony of a lifetime about to transpire in one of the back rooms of the main house.

6.

Boo sees the man pacing the roof of the eastern wing of the main house long before he sees her. A small, compact, ugly little son of a bitch, the gunman has a sniper rifle over his shoulder like a toy soldier. Boo silently moves around behind the house, and then scales a trellis thick with ivy and kudzu.

She climbs onto the roof and pauses in the moonlight behind an ancient brick chimney, weighing her options. She decides to go with the firearm. She carefully draws the Beretta, the silencer tight against the muzzle, but when she lifts her thumb to de-cock the safety button, something goes wrong.

She stares at her hand. It's clenched around the grip as though it belongs to somebody else. Her thumb feels as though it's stuck in wet cement—moving very, very, very slowly—no matter how hard she tries to torque it down. She tries to move her body, tries to lift her gaze to the target, tries to prod her index finger into the guard and press it against the trigger . . . but no part of her will move more than a hair's width every passing second.

It's as though she has suddenly stumbled into a dream, and everything is moving like it's bound up in cold molasses, inching forward in that excruciating nightmare slow motion, and then it hits her. The realization. It strikes her with the impact of a sledgehammer: the source of the dream motion.

7.

The chiming of an alarm from one of the rooms shatters the late-night stillness of the Cloister's makeshift ICU ward, the crepe soles of two novitiate nuns squeaking loudly and frenetically as they rush toward the last door on the left. They bang into the room and see the man whose birth name was Samuel Elijah Johnson on the floor, curled in a fetal position, vomit dried on his chin, his eyes fluttering convulsively in semiconsciousness. His IV stand has fallen over again.

They gently lift the man off the floor and return him to his gurney, securing his glucose and nutrient sticks, wiping his face, re-taping the port punctured under his wrist. They monitor his vitals. They thumb his eyes open and see that his pupils have not fully dilated as they dance back and forth, scanning the chaos of some hallucinatory dream state.

Inside the mind of this man—this person code-named Ticker, deemed by the government as killed in action—a flickering shadow play sputters and flashes and sparks like firecrackers while enormous keyboards loom out of the darkness, the cruel voice of the Italian lady haranguing the boyhood Ticker, the woman's ruler lashing the boy's hands for playing the wrong notes, his pitiful reflection shimmering off Miss Sabitini's giant bifocal lenses, the sound of her taunts echoing, ringing, reverberating in his ears: The caesura!—ON!—The caesura!— OFF!—caesura!—ON!—caesura!—OFF!—ON!—OFF!— ON!-OFF!-ON!-OFF!-ON!—

—OFF!!!

8.

In the darkness of that windswept roof, crouched behind the chimney, Boo jerks with a start as the normal flow of time abruptly returns, and her thumb snaps the release on the Beretta M9 and she rises up and she lines up the little tin soldier across the roof in her sights and she squeezes off a single blast—

—which exits the pistol's muzzle just as another distant Caesura arrives.

In syrupy slow motion the 115-grain, full-metal-jacketed, 9mm round, which normally travels at 185 feet per second, now hangs in midair like a tiny pearl in the moonlight. It moves on a clear trajectory toward the wiry little serial killer known as Moe with the same glacial sort of slowness one might observe as a celestial body creeps across the night sky.

Boo can do nothing to speed the projectile on its path toward its intended target. Her movements have retarded into a snail's pace as well as the bullet's. Nor can the intended target— now slowly, slowly, slowly rotating toward the blast, prodded by the noise, lifting his weapon to his eye—do anything to return fire any faster than a shadow moving across a sundial.

In the far distance, Boo can see the tops of old live oaks in the dull moonlight moving in jerky spasms as the wind stops and starts, the phenomenon moving closer and closer to her. She's turning her gaze back to the one nicknamed Moe—it seems to take forever just to get her eyes to scan from the trees back to the target—when all at once, without warning, the Pause lifts just as Moe is raising his sniper rifle's scope to his eye and aiming the weapon at Boo, which is the precise same moment her single round strikes the scope's lens, travels through the housing, and penetrates the man's skull through his pupil, blowing half his brain out the back of his head on a gout of pink matter that atomizes in the wind.

Down on the front lawn, about a hundred yards to the west, the one called Larry has leapt out of the shadows and surprised Spur with a cane knife. Spur gets his beefy forearm up in a blocking position just as another wave hits the timeline.

The Pause catches the collision of the machete-sized blade and the gauntlet on Spur's left arm just as the sharpened edge of stainless steel meets the titanium metal of the gauntlet. Normal motion seizes up in a brilliant floret of sparks freezing in the air as though blossoming out of the contact point.

In that momentary retardation of time, Spur can clearly see over the attacker's shoulder Pin-Up frozen in the Weaver stance in the shadows about twenty yards away. In her matte-black wasp-waisted corset, chain-mail fishnet stockings, and obsidian combat boots, she looks like a figure in a wax museum that might be labeled DANGER DAME or POISON PENNY. She has her feet firmly planted at shoulder width, one hand bracing the bottom of her Beretta's grip, the other with its index finger on the trigger, her left eye aligned with the front and back sights.

The trigger has clearly been pulled, and the high-velocity round has already exited the muzzle in a still-life strobe of a flash, and now Spur can plainly see in the diminished moonlight the bullet halfway on its journey toward the back of Larry's head. Spur prepares for the imminent arrival of the slug by letting gravity do the work. He lets go—literally and figuratively—allowing his body to ever so gradually fall backward away from his attacker.

At first it's one of the strangest sensations he's ever felt, his body practically weightless, sinking backward through space as though he's made of helium . . . until the next time wave hits.

The Pause lifts and the bullet slams through Larry's skull, sending blood mist and fragments of bone and brain matter through the air as Spur lands hard on his back, his tailbone sending a stabbing pain up his spine.

9.

"That oughtta take the edge off the nightmares for a while," one of the nurses says to her colleague as she pulls the syringe clear of the IV port.

She has just administered five milligrams of Haldol, ten milligrams of Ambien, and a milligram of Xanax to Ticker.

He has now—almost instantly—fallen into a deep and dreamless sleep.

10.

On the grounds of the Herod Plantation, sprawled on the damp grass, Spur coughs and spits and rolls over onto his side, trying to recover his bearings after being covered with brain matter from the head shot that, just a moment ago, took the life of the one known as Larry.

As she approaches, Pin-Up's shadow slides across the dead body, which now has collapsed into a bloody heap a few inches from Spur. She stands over the dead man for a moment, a deadly siren in corset and push-up bra, a fishnet Valkyrie from some operatic pulp novel ejecting the Beretta's magazine and checking the remaining rounds. She slams the clip back into the receiver, jacks the slide, and goes over to where Spur lies wiping human matter from his face.

She helps him to his feet.

"Appreciate that, darlin'," Spur says, and glances over his shoulder at the deep woods. The wind looks constant now, the moonlight normal, crystalline bright. Spur glances up at the east roof.

Boo is giving them a thumbs-up.

Pin-Up looks at Spur. "You think those time wrinkles are over?"

Spur has to admit he has no idea.

Pin-Up looks up at the house, and then checks her watch. "C'mon. Less than twenty minutes left until zero hour. Let's go get our baby."

CHAPTER TWENTY-FIVE
The Unholy Hour

1.

At 11:43 P.M. eastern standard time, Cripp directs his group of revelers into a large parlor at the terminus of a narrow hallway in the rear wing of the third floor. All the drugs and drink and rich food and sacrificial blood and excitement have leveled off and commingled inside the two couples and the man in the antlers. Even those earlier glitches of super slow motion—conjured by Ticker's long-distance Caesuras—were written off as an effect of the psilocybin mushrooms served with the sweetbreads in basil-cream sauce.

The result of all these preambles is an almost zombie-like reverence toward what is about to happen as they take their seats on antique folding chairs that Cripp has draped with black doilies in a neat little row at one end of the room. At the other end of the room, under a sweeping backdrop of black velvet curtains cinched on each flank with purple vestments stolen from pedophile priests currently serving time at Angola, sits the little bassinet on its royal pedestal with its sepulchral bunting and black gauze veiling the top as though in respect for some pint-sized political leader lying in state.

The possessed nun, born Lucille June Fortnoy, now sits beside the bassinet, her cardigan sweater buttoned up to her neck wattle, her head lolling as ancient words pour out of her in an unbroken stream of Latin. It sounds almost like a pressure cooker letting out bursts of steam as shiny new black candles—hundreds of them, selected by Cripp, positioned around the room—spontaneously ignite, their tiny flames sputtering and sizzling ominously now in the sacred silence.

Cripp and Councilman Hendry move to the front of the room, standing proudly and deferentially behind the bassinet.

Sister Lucy June stands, and tosses her head back, and blurts, *"Quod nomen puero huic dabis."*

Cripp bows his head and paraphrases: "He has asked us what name do we give to this child."

Councilman Hendry says then, in his most pious, devout tone of voice, "Antichrist."

Lucy June's head is now wrenched backward so far her neck looks as though it's about to rip open as she snarls in Latin, *"Quid petis a diablo pro puero isto?"*

Cripp murmurs, "He wants to know what we ask of the Devil for this child."

Hendry says, "Baptism."

Across the room, there is a small, ornate, hundred-year-old Hepplewhite clock. Next to it sits the Devil in the form of an enormous, oily black sewer rat calmly watching the proceedings with its beady little ball-bearing eyes.

The clock says the time is 11:46.

2.

Spur and Pin-Up meet up with Boo in the darkness of the rear deck, exchanging not a word. The pool lights have been turned off, and Esmeralda Villainous's remains lie wrapped in a soaking-wet sheet beside the pool's rim. In the shadows they weave single file between the dead body and the gleaming stainless-steel outdoor kitchen, and pause in front of the locked sliding glass door. Spur pulls a bump key from inside his gauntlet. He silently shoves it into the lock bolt, then gives a quick punch, and the lock gives.

"Hack, we're in the rec room now, first floor," Spur whispers into his neck mike once inside the enormous back room. The lights are off but the silhouettes of pool tables, arcade games, and wet bars are plainly visible. Pin-Up and Boo draw their pistols, put in fresh magazines, and thumb the safeties off.

"I see you," Hack's voice buzzes in their ears. "Try not to bump into the furniture."

"Very funny. Where are they, Hack? We got like five minutes to shut this down."

"Third floor. Back parlor. Move straight ahead about ten feet. You'll see a flight of back stairs on your right."

"Copy that."

"Be mindful of the fact that there are blind spots, not covered by surveillance cameras."

"Copy."

They move cautiously and yet hastily through the darkness. The staircase looms. They ascend the steps single file, not making a sound.

When they reach the second floor, a figure is standing in the hallway waiting for them with a silenced .45 semiauto gripped in both hands. The muzzle flash in the dark blinds Pin-Up, and the blast hits Spur in the chest. Spur reels backward, trips, and sprawls to the floor, nearly knocking Boo over.

Gerald Haben takes aim at Pin-Up but pauses one beat too long when he sees that the little Asian woman behind Pin-Up has vanished. Like magic. Gone. Pin-Up—still flash-blind—gets off a single shot that grazes Haben's cheek and sends blood mist spraying across the adjacent wall, splattering a half dozen antique oil portraits of former slaveholders.

Haben staggers and then looks up just as Boo wall-walks to the ceiling above him. Then, with the grace of an Olympic gymnast, she flips onto his shoulders, and scissors her legs around his neck. He lurches backward, and the silencer pops three wild blasts into the ceiling before he runs out of air and folds.

Boo lands on top of Haben, and puts a bullet into his skull for good measure.

By this point, Pin-Up has regained her eyesight, and she hovers over Spur. "C'mon, cowboy, don't be a baby," she says to him.

With her fingernail she digs the flattened slug from his Kevlar vest.

"Jesus," Spur says with a gasp, wheezing for a moment as he tries to sit up. "You get the license number of that truck that just hit me in the chest?"

Hack's voice in their earpieces: "Not to be callous or insensitive, but you need to get your respective asses in gear and get up to the back parlor, one floor above you, like A-SAP."

Spur's chronograph says it's exactly 11:48 P.M. eastern standard time.

3.

In the candlelit parlor, the muffled thuds of silencer-muted gunfire from another floor are mistaken for Gerald Haben's regular opening and closing of doors as he patrols the property, and nobody takes much notice. They are too mesmerized by the possessed nun as she moves her lips with the twitchy tics of a puppet operated by a mad puppeteer. *"Rogasti ut antichristus factus sit hic puer."*

Cripp softly interprets: "He is confirming that we have asked that this child be baptized the Antichrist."

Councilman Hendry responds, "We have."

From the nun's mouth spews the incantatory question: *"Quod cum facis, suscipis responsibilitatem praeparandi as Novam Aetatem Obscuram?"*

Cripp says, "He asks us if we accept the responsibility of preparing the child to be bringer of the New Dark Age."

Hendry bows his head. "We do."

Wormwood's guttural growl: *"Perge ritibus tenebrisssssss!"*

At this point in the ceremony, only the huge, foul sewer rat on the far side of the room by the clock notices that the nun has suddenly flopped back down to her chair. She looks as though all the life has run out of her like water down a drain. Her head lolls forward as she slumps in her seat.

Cripp is too busy pulling his satin hood over his head to notice the nun's transformation. He had the hood specially made by a Savile Row tailor for the occasion, then shipped over from England. It has been embroidered with Satanic symbols across a field of purest black. With great drama Cripp now secures his hood.

At the same time, Councilman Hendry has put on rubber gloves, and has reached down into a galvanized tub next to the crib. Now he pulls a severed goat's head from the tub and holds it up for all to see. Blood and tissue dangle and drip back into the tub. The blood is the color of onyx, and as viscous as machine oil.

"My dear brothers and sisters," Cripp proclaims, his joyous expression draped in the shadows of the hood. "Let us ask our Lord Satan in all his wisdom to look lovingly upon this child."

The pair of couples seated in the back of the room cry out in unison: "HAIL SATAN!"

"We reject God in all His forms!"

"HAIL!"

The blood drips. The minute hand approaches twelve midnight.

"In Satan's name we baptize this child the Antichrist!"

"Hail!"

"The mark of the Dark Lord now shall be drawn with the sacrificial blood."

Cripp moves his hand under the dripping goat's head. The blood coats his index finger. He's leaning down to the bassinet, opening the veil—

—when the door across the parlor bangs open so hard the knob slams into the adjacent wall and sticks there, embedded in the plaster.

4.

Spur roars into the room first, followed closely by Pin-Up, each two-handing a noise-suppressed Beretta, each of their gazes instantly latching on to the bassinet at the front of the room.

Boo brings up the rear, and as she comes through the door in battle posture, her katana clutched in both hands, her robe flagging behind her, she's the first one to see the double-shot derringer in Councilman Hendry's right hand as it comes out of the back of his ridiculous fur thong as though he just defecated it into existence.

With neither premeditation nor hesitation Boo resorts to an old lesson given to her by her Shaolin master many years ago as part of her education as a young girl entering adulthood. It was an esoteric, little-known maneuver from the oldest martial art of Chan Buddhism, known as Shaolin wushu, or Shaolin quan. The move is known by the monks as *"shé de meìlì."*

In English, it translates as "the snake charm."

Boo cartwheels suddenly with alarming speed and precision directly toward Councilman Hendry. In the candlelight, the edge of the katana shimmers up across the councilman's face as he raises the tiny gun. At first it appears as if a candle flame has reflected off the deadly mirrored surface of the katana, illuminating the councilman's deep-set bloodshot eyes.

But when Boo spins away, pulling back, the derringer pistol drops from the councilman's hand. Followed by his head dropping from a neck so cleanly severed one might draw the conclusion from the shocked expression on his face that the detachment was as much a surprise to him as it was to everyone else in the room—

—including Cripp, who now lets out a strangely feminine shriek and staggers backward into the bassinet. It falls over, spilling its contents across the floor, including the linens and its two-month-old occupant, all of which now is bathed in the geyser of blood spuming out of Councilman Hendry's hemorrhaging neck.

His body finally gets the message that it's time to collapse.

By this point, Pin-Up has bounded across the room to where the baby lies, as Spur deals with the other guests, who are just now rising out of their seats, snarling profanities, looking almost rabid, a few of them actually drooling, each of them under the influence of myriad stimulants of both pharmaceutical and supernatural varieties.

The club owner makes the fatal mistake of pulling an old-fashioned straight razor from a pocket as if he's just stepped out of some summer-stock production of *Sweeney Todd*. He flicks it open and goes for Spur's face.

Reacting almost instinctively, his power of mirroring an enemy bolstered now by his righteous rage, Spur lashes out with a single motion as quick, powerful, and deadly as a thunderclap. He clasps his hand around the club owner's hand and turns the razor around and shoves it so deep into the man's eye socket that it lodges in his corpus callosum.

The club owner's wife—who probably secretly expected her mobbed-up husband to one day lose his life to a faceless, nameless contract killer—now kneels by the man with the razor sticking out of his skull, and all she can do is shake her head. "You stupid fucking arrogant idiots," she mutters, and then looks up at Spur. "You think you've saved the day here?"

The MAGA couple press in side by side, a little wobbly, but girded by their collective anger, boosted by the accelerant of drugs and Satanic reverie. "Look at you," the husband taunts. He lets out a barrage of laughter. "Big-time vigilante superheroes—you crashed the wrong party, you fucking morons."

Now Cripp joins in, laughing uproariously at the front of the room, laughing so hard he can hardly get the words out. "Oh dear . . . oh . . . you should . . . you should see yourselves . . . your faces . . . it's adorrrrrrable!"

Spur looks around the room, suddenly confused, hesitant.

At first he doesn't see Pin-Up standing near the fallen bassinet, holding the baby in her arms, staring at the child with shock and dismay. He sees something far more bizarre and worrying across the room.

Next to the antique pedestal clock, the enormous, greasy

black sewer rat is standing on its hind legs as though performing in a miniature circus. It tosses its furry head back with hysterical laughter along with the others.

That's when Spur sees Pin-Up holding a life-sized rubber doll.

"It's a stunt baby, you idiots!" the MAGA husband chortles. "A stunt baby!"

Spur stares at the realistic-looking doll in Pin-Up's arms, the painted face, the little molded ears, as the guests and Cripp chant, "Stunt baby! Stunt baby! Stunt baby! Stunt baby!"

Spur erupts with rage: "SHUT YOUR GODDAMN FUCKING PIEHOLES!!"

He shoots each of them in the kneecaps, sending blood mist and fragments of matter in all directions. They gasp and stagger and fall like drunken ballerinas. It doesn't make him feel any better. He has a black hole in his chest now from both the flattened slug hitting the Kevlar and the unabated tide of dread gripping his heart, and all matter is being drawn into the hole.

Across the room, in a puff of noxious smoke, the sewer rat transforms into an enormous black crow, and takes flight, knocking figurines off tables and pictures off the walls, soaring across the room, and flying out an open window at the precise moment the clock begins striking the chimes of twelve midnight.

CHAPTER TWENTY-SIX
Baptism

1.

The long, narrow room sits bound in shadows, the darkness so palpable it's almost soupy, thick with an invisible particulate of pain drifting for eternity through the musty, fetid air. The walls are draped in sinister souvenirs of a lost time when men owned human beings, and broke them here in this secret chamber.

At one end of the room is the old treadwheel, also known as the "everlasting staircase," its nail-spiked steps still stained with the blood of slaves who endlessly marched on the terrible treads, turning the grindstone that pulverized the bones of their brethren. Back then, the dust of the dead and the blood of eviscerated feet would sluice down a long gutter and into the hellish coal furnace down in the guts of the plantation house . . . where the runoff went up in smoke like the vanishing memories of the caretaker's victims.

On the opposite wall hang the timbers of old pillory devices, whips, branding irons, flogging sticks, and various tools for administering agony. Shoved into the shadows of one corner sits the old "rack," a bedlike frame of worm-eaten pine on which the slaves were tied and stretched to the point their joints and hips and spines dislocated. The screams are still smeared like stains on the fusty air of this room, scars that will never heal, mementos of misery and madness.

A low, metallic rasp fills the malignant silence: *"Tempus advenit ut novum antichristum baptizet."*

The ancient floorboards in this room talk, and some even

moan when pressure is applied, as it is now from the darkness near the doorway. The bassinet containing the special child rolls slowly, seemingly under its own power, across the cursed room to its place of honor under the severed head of the second goat, now hanging from a petrified ceiling beam.

"Cum virtute mea a Diablo investienda," snarls the demon Wormwood in his baritone growl, now floating inches above the floor in his natural state near the goat's head. In the darkness he resembles a living, breathing shadow, as if someone has anthropomorphized a column of smoke. Upon closer scrutiny, however, one would notice the creature's oily, black, bat-winged body, and his oblong, simian face with its insect eyes and lupine ears.

The entity makes a magical gesture with his enormous hand, his fingers as long and crooked as the dead boughs of a diseased tree. *"Ego hunc puerum Christi filium Satanae,"* the demon rasps.

The bassinet's cover abruptly and violently jerks back, opening and revealing the baby nestled inside, the same child born with the name Paul Candell, Jr., the offspring of two very special adults.

2.

"Hack! Hack! Talk to me!" Spur says, tapping his earpiece.

Hack has apparently gone off the air, and now every breath Spur takes pangs with a stabbing pain in his chest as he leads Pin-Up and Boo down a narrow back hallway, guns drawn, gazes shifting back and forth. The house's maze of nooks and side rooms and elegant corridors lined with original oils of the Old South seems to be growing before their very eyes, as though the hallways are literally telescoping away from them as they creep through the building.

They believe the baby is still on the property somewhere, but anything's possible. Spur has decided they should keep searching the premises until they're sure the child has been taken elsewhere.

At last, Hack's voice crackles in their earpieces. "Spur, you copy this?"

"Finally, Jesus, I thought for a minute there you went on the lam again."

Spur pauses at the end of the hallway, which opens up to a grand, sweeping staircase leading down to the central living room, which is now deserted, all the lights off. Spur gives the hand signal for everybody to halt for a moment.

"For your information, Skipper, I've been a little tied up checking every fucking surveillance cam in this fucking battleship of a house."

Spur lets out a weary sigh. "Okay, all right, I got it, so I'm assuming you didn't find anything."

"Nothing, nada, zilch-a-palooza. And believe me, these Satanists are not only evil motherfuckers, they're paranoid as hell. Either that or they're voyeurs. There's a camera in practically every room. I mean—"

"Hold your horses a second," Spur interrupts. "You said practically every room?"

"There's no camera inside the garage but I managed to jack into an SUV parked inside it and saw nothing out of the ordinary."

"Son of a *bitch!*"

After a brief pause, Hack's voice buzzes in their ears: "I still have to say, I don't think Elvis has left the building."

"What do you mean?"

"I think Junior is still somewhere in the house. I checked the last few hours of every camera outside on the main road. No vehicle, or anything else, for that matter, has budged an inch since the limo brigade got here earlier today."

"What about the swamp in back? You see any action back there?"

"Negative. Maybe a demon could float above it and make itself invisible to the camera but, you know, c'mon, I can't see them sneaking a baby in a bassinet through that shit."

Pin-Up chimes in: "What about the process of elimination?"

Hack's voice: "Meaning . . . what?"

"Meaning . . . I don't know. I'm not saying you missed anything. I'm just saying, what about rooms inside the house that are without a surveillance camera? There have to be a few."

For a long moment, the earpieces softly hiss as Hack checks something.

When his voice returns, the smart-ass has gone out of it, and it sounds spooked. "Hold on." Another brief pause ensues. "Wait a second . . . wait."

3.

In the darkness of the haunted attic, in the motes of misery floating through its moldering atmosphere, Wormwood reaches up to the ragged neck of the goat, and coats his gnarled, crooked fingers with sacrificial blood.

"*Hoc sanguine baptizo te,*" snarls the demon, and then he reaches down to the baby and carefully paints the sign of the inverted cross on the child's tiny forehead.

For the first time since the kidnapping, the baby and the demon lock gazes. Wormwood stares at the child with morbid fascination. The baby is awake, alert, unafraid, and very still as it stares back at the monster hovering over its bassinet.

What fascinates Wormwood most is the fact that His Lord and Master had planned this all along. Over the decades the Devil had been watching the father and the mother, had been following their progress as warriors, had orchestrated their capture in Karakistan, and had imbued them with unprecedented powers to pass down to their descendant . . . all in service of giving birth to the future bringer of the New Dark Age.

All at once, Wormwood blinks his compound eyes, and

their myriad visual receptors take in the contents of the bassinet—a million bassinets in a shimmering mosaic—and warning alarms spread throughout his being. The baby has begun
to change. The child's tiny face shape-shifts into that of a different child, an infant from thousands of years ago, a baby
whose mother, a prostitute in a small village outside Rome,
had died during childbirth. This new face calls out to Wormwood with the power of a tsunami.

Wormwood reels back from the bassinet, his insect eyes
widening. But he cannot look away. He is helplessly mesmerized. This new face is darker than Junior Candell's face, olive-
skinned, with a tiny aquiline nose and a profusion of dark
hair. This face is the face of an innocent child raised by a band
of thieves, given the name Agrippa Maledetto. This is the face
that Wormwood remembers seeing reflected back at him from
the surface of a pond when he was old enough to wander the
Roman countryside.

The demon gapes at the baby's shape-shifting features. The
face morphs into that of a young man. Feral, mean, hardened
by life, all the innocence drained out of it. The demon cannot
comprehend what this means. Wormwood feels the center of
his being unraveling. The boyish face has turned savage, bar-
baric, bloodthirsty, the eyes narrowing with madness and war,
the lines deepening, the lips curling away from the teeth. This
is the face of a soldier in the Imperial Roman army who went
berserk, who raped and killed his own men, who was executed
at the stake for abominations.

Like a faltering automaton, the superior demon Wormwood
absorbs the shock of his true nature as though he were being
engulfed in a tidal wave. This has to be someone else. This
cannot be him. He is the Devil's right hand, hell's field marshal. What is happening to him? What has this mutant child
done?

But before Wormwood can fully react or even utter a word,

the portal window across the attic—boarded and painted over for generations—implodes inward on an explosion of wood shards and glass.

The shadow of massive wings fills the room. Wormwood turns toward the source of the commotion and sees the Devil himself standing before him in the form of a gigantic black crow.

4.

At first, in the darkness of the attic, the Father of Lies is caught in mid-transformation, the gargantuan black bird so tall it has to stoop in order to fit its feathery crown within the bounds of the ceiling. Then the change comes, rippling down across its form from nape to claws, the massive black wings becoming translucent and insectoid, folding back against spiky, reptilian scapulars—the grotesque corruption of wings that once belonged to an angel. The enormous, hooked beak shrinks into itself, the eight-ball eyes narrowing and becoming luminous yellow pilot lights, and the bird's cranium transforming into the elongated wolflike visage of pure malevolence.

"Master," mutters Wormwood, as he falls to his knees and bows his simian head in supplication.

"*CONSUMMATUS ES!!*" the Prince of Darkness roars at the demon, telling him in Latin that he's finished, he's out, he has lost the battle, the voice a death rattle echoing up from the canyons of hell.

The transformation is now complete, Satan's horrifying and regal bearing reflected in his onyx breastplate and epaulets of petrified human fingers. His narrow features are the color of ox blood, an ancient ram horn now spiraling outward from each canine ear—an air of what Lister once described as simultaneously monstrous and elegant—as he slowly, dramatically, threateningly ambles toward the demon.

"*Mille paenitemus,*" Wormwood murmurs, staring at the floor, shamed, disgraced, humiliated. The words translate into English as "a thousand apologies," but they are insufficient in any language, all of which is perhaps why the Devil changes over to English, the language of pathetic, feckless mortals—a taunting, cruel, mortifying gesture.

"YOUR APOLOGY IS WORTHLESS!!" Satan booms as he takes a menacing step closer. "STAND UP, WORMWOOD, AND FACE ME!!"

The demon Wormwood has already begun to cower and physically shrink. It takes tremendous energy for him to simply rise to his feet, his limbs trembling convulsively as though he has aged centuries in the last few moments. He raises his head as if it weighs a million pounds and gazes up at Satan. "Sire . . . I . . . I . . ."

"You . . ."

The Devil utters the word as though it were shit on his tongue as he takes another step until he is looming over the demon.

"You . . ."

The Devil has the eyes of a dragon, with slits for pupils, which now smolder from inside, illuminated by the roiling madness of his brain.

"You . . ."

The Devil points a twisted, knotted, blackened, accusatory fingertip at the demon, and the words pour out in an unbroken stream of venom. "You fail to complete such a simple task?—Fail to turn this disgusting human child, this fleshy little thing that's barely able to see, that's powerless, that's unable to even speak?—And you . . . you . . . the king of all demons, the superior one, the field marshal, you hesitate, you lose the rest of your team, you lead those mongrel soldiers to this very place, this place of the sacred rites?—You're no field marshal!—You couldn't marshal a turd escaping a rectum!—You're not even worth destroying!—You should spend the rest of eternity in a sea of boiling feces!—You're not worthy of the smegma in the foreskin of a donkey's cock!—You're not worthy of the pus in a hag's blister!—You're less than nothing!—You're the afterbirth of an abortion!—You're a puddle of spent semen!—You're the lowest form of energy, lower than the gas from a monkey's anus, lower than a hog's fart!—You will never be given another mission because you no longer exist in my hierarchy!—You are finished, done, purged, gone, excised, eliminated, removed, eradicated, abolished from all the future campaigns of hell!—I will take over this piteous attempt at transforming the special child!—I will finish what you so ineptly bungled!—I will create the Antichrist in earnest, no thanks to you!—And you . . . you shall return to the festering sea of bile where you belong!—You shall be cursed for endless eons of agony and infamy!—The demon class shall laugh hysterically at the mention of your name!—You shall become the worst thing a demon can ever become . . .

". . . a joke."

With this last word flung like a dagger at the demon, a flash of blue light sears the darkness of the attic like heat lightning . . .

. . . and the withering monster hewn from smoke and cruelty, the thing that has terrified legions over millennia, the former orphan who became the most feared centurion in the Roman Empire, the human pain machine who tortured and raped and pillaged . . . this same entity lets out a piercing, otherworldly shriek as it disintegrates, its outer layers peeling away like a candle melting, the rest of it sinking into the seams of the attic floor, down through all the floors beneath it, down through the very ground on which the Herod bog has seethed and oozed for centuries, and finally down through the earth's crust and sediments . . . down . . . down . . . down to the lowest circle of hell, where the legend of Wormwood will fade away as though it had never existed.

5.

The attic returns to its deathly silence.

The Devil sighs and strolls over to the bassinet. He looks down into the nest of blankets. The eyes of pure innocence look back up at him.

If it's possible for Evil Incarnate to smile, that's what happens next. The lupine features stretch into a rictus of a grin.

CHAPTER TWENTY-SEVEN
Nevermore

1.

Outside the attic's portal window comes the sound of boots climbing the rungs of a metal ladder. The noise ruptures the stillness of the haunted room as the dull clanging thuds approach.

A figure appears, a familiar face leaning in through the gap. "Is it done?" Spur asks.

Across the room, standing over the bassinet, gazing down at its downy-soft contents, the insectoid creature with the face of a wolf and the eyes of a snake begins to shape-shift one last time.

The face changes and softens, the eyes transforming into the dark and lovely eyes of a former actress. The translucent wings and onyx breastplate morph back into the original wasp-waisted corset, chain-mail fishnet stockings, and combat boots of the baby's mother—a denizen of battlefields and the mean streets of East L.A.

"It's done, it's over," Pin-Up says without taking her eyes off her child. "C'mon, Junior, let's blow this Popsicle stand."

If it's possible for a two-month-old to smile knowingly as he's being lifted from his bassinet, that's just what the baby does.

In fact, all three family members are smiling now as Pin-Up carries Junior across the haunted darkness to the humid and fragrant air blowing in the open window.

2.

Silverback scrambles the rapid-response team exactly when he promised he would, twenty-four hours after the baby had been snatched.

At 1100 hours central standard time that night, three Black-hawks take off from Whiteman Air Force Base just south of Knob Noster, Missouri, and by dawn that next morning, a special unit of the Defense Intelligence Agency's Logistical Division—commonly known as the Cleaning Crew—has cordoned off the entire area around Herod Plantation.

Heavily armed specialists in hazmat suits move in and begin the process of wiping the property of all evidence of what had happened there.

On the third floor, in the rear parlor, the team finds the aftermath of a bloody skirmish that would make the assault on Bin Laden's compound look like a mild argument. The expensive Persian carpet and walls of the genteel little parlor are drenched in blood. One victim has been decapitated. Four others are barely alive, in hypovolemic shock from pinpoint blasts shattering their kneecaps and handicapping them for life. The sixth individual appears to have suffered a psychotic break.

Later identified as Lawrence Alvin Cripp, he sits in the corner of the room on a velvet-padded stool, seminude, dressed only in a Depends adult diaper, the word "Nevermore" scrawled in blood across his sagging pectorals. His gaze never leaves the open window as they administer the requisite dosages of midazolam and thiopental to induce permanent amnesia.

In subsequent debriefing sessions, one member of the Cleaning Crew swears he heard the man muttering "Nevermore" as he stared at a crow perched on the window ledge outside . . .

. . . a bird that seemed to take one last look at the carnage, nod its little feathery head, and then take off into the rising sun.

EPILOGUE

REUNION OF SOULS

And what I say to you I say to all: Stay awake.

—Mark 13:37

"I don't like the idea of you three being out in the open like this," Silverback mutters, almost to himself, as he pulls the SUV into a parking lot overlooking the verdant, fecund banks of the Mississippi. Cattails sway in the breeze, and the marsh roils with insects. Silverback scopes the place out and sees myriad exposure points, high trees in which a sniper could position himself, dirt roads in all directions, no fences, easy access. "Let me at least sweep the area first."

"You worry too much, Sean," Spur says with a gruff little laugh from the front passenger seat. "Look at this place. It's just river and sky. We'll be fine as a hair on a hog out here."

"Give the man a break, Spur, he's just doing his job," Pin-Up says from the rear as she unbuckles Junior from his car seat. The baby is bundled up in his little Texas A&M sweatshirt and stocking cap. It's a blustery day along the river for mid-September, and earlier in the week Pin-Up noticed that the child had developed a little bit of a sniffle.

Spur climbs out, goes around to the rear hatch, and grabs the picnic basket, while Pin-Up lifts Junior out of his seat and straps him into a tactical camo-patterned BabyBjörn against her chest. She climbs out of the car, and joins Spur on the long trek down the embankment to the lone picnic table by the water.

Silverback watches from inside the SUV. He sees them sitting down at the table, opening up the basket, pulling out sandwiches, giving the baby his bottle, and chatting idly in the sun and the wind. Little Junior Candell is going on six months old now and sometimes seems so high-functioning that Silverback suspects he's probably capable not only of holding his own bottle, but of calling up the store and ordering more formula for himself.

For a moment, the threesome resemble a normal little starter family to Silverback. What casual observer would ever dream in a million years that they are now at the center of a government program the size and scope of the Manhattan Project?

* * *

In the aftermath of the assault on the Cloister—which still seems to Silverback as though it were yesterday, but was almost three months ago—word leaked out that these five neo-humans were secretly shacked up at this strange military monastery outside St. Louis, and the blowback had been horrendous. The media got ahold of it, and Silverback's section became embroiled in the controversy.

Darby pleaded innocence, assuring everybody that the writing of an authorized book one day when it was safe to do so was all that she ever wanted from her deal with Ticker. But Silverback's intel officers traced the original leak back to Alec Soames at the tabloid-news site Transom.com, who had Darby shadowed by a private investigator. Much to Silverback's dismay, however, the ultimate result of the leak was not what he expected.

Last month, he was called into a big hush-hush cloak-and-dagger-style meeting at the Pentagon. He walks in and, lo and behold, the gang's all there—Joint Chiefs of Staff, three top section chiefs from the CIA, the head of the NSA, and even the goddamn secretary of defense. "Full disclosure, Sean," the secretary says after locking the door of the conference room, "we know all about these freaks of yours, we have for a while; but it looks like we need them on the payroll now."

They went on to explain that the situation had become dire around the world, authoritarian governments becoming more and more malevolent, bellicose, and just plain evil. They claimed that some dark force had altered the balance of power. They used phrases like "the age of the unprecedented" and "the ancient battle that started before Christ" and "weaponizing the neo-humans."

It all made Silverback's head spin. In fact, he has yet to break this bizarre news to Spur and his people. He isn't sure how it will impact their lives or their futures. It seems like a trap. But maybe it's simply another fait accompli. He has managed to buy some time by assuring the military complex that the Devil's Quintet will need a few months of R&R before they can get involved with such an epochal project.

Meanwhile, Ticker has fully recovered from his Caesura-induced collapse and subsequent syncope but has dedicated himself to studying the biological effects and geographical limitations of the time pause. He managed to get a security clearance for a former colleague at MIT to help him with the project.

Hack now lives in the grid and claims that he prefers it to his former corporeal existence. In his words: "It's a little slice of heaven not having to worry about my expanding waistline or my bald spot ever again." Boo, on the other hand—still deeply in love with the man—has not gotten over the loss of his physical body. She now carries an extra-large Google Pixel with an eight-inch screen and a dedicated channel to wherever Hack decides to travel in the digital hive.

On this day, however, in the genial sunshine along the river, Silverback tries to push it all out of his mind, lowering his seat back, and gazing up at the clouds through the open sunroof.

He thinks back to the lovely, poignant, healing memorial service held in Chicago at the majestic Holy Name Cathedral for those who perished in what had come to be known as the Great Demonic Fire. The music of the choir, the comforting words of the Catholic dignitaries offering their eulogies, the sense of a reunion of souls in heaven all served as a balm on the pain and loss of that terrible night. The names of the dead—

constantly running in a heartbreaking loop against a montage of lives well lived—continue to haunt Silverback:

STEVEDORE THEO COOGAN

CHAPLAIN ALEX JORGENSON

STAFF SERGEANT BRIAN WORKMAN

FATHER RAFAEL GASPERI

FATHER GORDON SHAMUS

CARLOS LAMBORDINI

TACTICAL OFFICER DALE SIMMS

MONSIGNOR CHARLES MCALLISTER

* * *

Among the survivors of the assault on the Cloister, the one with the deepest emotional scars is probably Father Emmanuel "Manny" Lawson.

For years the little unassuming priest has counseled families who have dealt with demonic attacks and the madness of exorcism, but Father Manny has never really known what lingers inside a person who has been hijacked by an evil spirit. Now he knows. And it is devastating. The guilt of bringing the parasites into the fold of the Cloister is only one facet of the post-traumatic stress eating away at the man. Nightmares, visions, panic attacks, and spontaneous bouts of amnesia all have plagued the priest in the aftermath. He has tried writing about it, and has given up. He has tried medication but has found little relief.

In a last-ditch attempt to break through his pain, he has gone overseas with Catholic Relief Services to Central Africa.

He writes a long, detailed letter about his struggles every week, and airmails it to Spur.

* * *

Now, in the parking lot next to the riverside picnic area, a loud thump awakens Silverback from a deep sleep.

He stirs in the warmth of the late-afternoon sun canting

down through the opening in the vehicle's roof, and then jerks forward with a start. Blinking at the bright light in his eyes, still groggy and dazed, he turns and sees the source of the thumping noise: Pin-Up, her horrified face stippled with blood, pressing against the driver's-side window, the terrifying squeak of her mottled flesh on the glass as it slides downward, leaving a deep scarlet leech trail.

Silverback lets out a scream of horror but no sound comes out of him.

* * *

"Silver!—Wake up!—Sean, you're dreaming, c'mon, wake up!"

Pin-Up shakes Silver awake. He sits up with a start, looking around the interior of the SUV, confused, his heart racing, beads of sweat on his face. He blinks and blinks. "What happened? Pin, are you—?"

"Am I what?"

She stands just inside the open driver's-side door, Spur behind her, holding the baby, looking on with a worried expression. A gust of wind suddenly blows his cowboy hat off his head.

"I'm sorry I—I guess I—wow." Silverback rubs his eyes. "That was a doozy. Vivid. Very real. Sorry I scared you."

"Looks like you were the one got scared," she says with a crooked smile.

Silverback takes a few deep breaths, adjusts the seat to its original position, and is starting to say something else when a passing bird drops a load of disgusting white guano on the windshield.

They all stare at it. Even the baby stares at it. Silverback starts to laugh, and the laughter is contagious. Soon they're all chortling at the oddly random commentary on the day.

* * *

The black crow that shat upon the SUV now ascends into the sky, skirting the clouds, soaring across the river, banking southward, following the serpentine trail of the muddy Mississippi.

Through the cottony wisps drifting across the firmament, the patchwork farm fields come into view, crisscrossed by endless highways and access roads like the lines on the face of a dying old man, a dying human race, a dying world.

Deeply amused by recent events, the malignant thing inside the crow now swoops down and brushes the treetops, spreading Dutch elm disease and pine needle blight and leaf rust. But as the diabolical bird vanishes on the horizon, the thing inside it recalls with pleasure watching Pin-Up imitate him in the haunted attic, playacting, pretending to be the Devil himself, banishing Wormwood to the nether regions of hell.

How surprised she will be when she learns that it was all an elaborate test, a sort of dry run to see if the baby and his parents have the raw materials to fulfill the glorious plans the Devil harbors for them in hell.

And with that, the crow vanishes into the heat waves emanating beyond the horizon.

ACKNOWLEDGMENTS

The author would like to once again pay tribute to the late, great Stan Lee. His legacy is woven through every word of this book. His invention of the flawed, ambivalent superhero, his simplicity in storytelling (which turned out to be quite complex in its own way), and his humanity continue to inspire this writer. Additional thanks to my brilliant editor, Greg Cox; the good folks at POW! Entertainment®, including Gill Champion and Kim Luperi; the staff at Tor Books, including Laura Etzkorn, Robert Davis, and Emily Mlynek; our men in Hollywood, Craig Titley and Andy Cohen; super agents Susan Crawford and Natalia Aponte; and last but definitely not least, my partner in life, my better half, my advisor, my publicist, my best friend, and cohost of *This Should Be a Podcast,* Jill Norton.